MW01027664

A WHIFF
OF REVENGE

Enjoy —

Neal Sanders

Neal Sanders

The Hardington Press

A Whiff of Revenge is a work of fiction. While certain locales, references to historical events, and organizations are rooted in fact, the characters and events described are entirely the product of the author's imagination.

Also by Neal Sanders

Murder Imperfect
The Garden Club Gang
The Accidental Spy
A Murder in the Garden Club
Murder for a Worthy Cause
Deal Killer
Deadly Deeds
A Murder at the Flower Show
Murder in Negative Space
How to Murder Your Contractor

A brief description of each of these books can be found beginning on page 299.

For Brandy (1971-1987),
Alfie (Alfred Lord Tennisanyone) (ca. 1988 – 2002),
and T.R. (Tabby la Rasa) (ca. 1995 – date).
Like the fog, inspiration can come in on
little cats' feet

A WHIFF OF REVENGE

Penny Walden never wanted to be famous. Though only in her late twenties, what she mostly wanted to do was to escape her past. She certainly had no intention of becoming three women's go-to guide for getting even with a bastard of an ex-husband, an emotionally deadbeat dad, or a paramour with fraudulent credentials on his résumé and large-scale embezzlement in his heart. Especially if the target of the three women's wrath happened to be the same man.

All she ever wanted was to be a scientist. Even if it meant the epitaph on her tombstone read, 'She invented the stuff that made your cat stop scratching your sofa'.

The past from which Penny Walden was attempting to escape was of her own making. It began with a book. Seven years earlier, she had been a publishing sensation due to *The Professor with the Wandering Hands*. The book itself started as an exercise in boredom. Penny attended UCLA, an exceptionally competitive school filled with extremely bright minds. Penny was outstandingly smart (her IQ placed her in the top three percent of the population) but, in a college that was a magnet for hyper-attractive students of both sexes, Penny's merely conventional 'pretty' looks meant her social life was rather bleak.

One date-less Saturday evening early in her senior year, Penny began thinking about something her roommate had recently confided in her. In less than a month, Penny had cobbled together a story about getting revenge and put it up anonymously as a giveaway on Kindle. To her astonishment, more than ten thousand people downloaded her story and gave it rave reviews. So she expanded the tale, began charging, and used her initials and last name as its author. At 100,000 downloads at 99 cents, a resourceful agent called, asking if the 'P.D. Walden' listed as the book's author was, by any chance, the same person with whom she was speaking.

With an editor's guidance, three months later, a re-written *Wandering Hands* went up at $7.99 on Kindle and in softcover at $15.99 and half a million people ponied up. Three months after that, Penny had a hardcover deal and a film sale. She took off a semester to promote her book.

That was when her publisher discovered that P.D. Walden was an ordinary duckling in a media world that expected their literary swans to be glamorous and sexy. Her smile was dazzling but her face was just a bit too square, her hair a common brown, her chin a tad prominent, and her eyes too far apart. Penny could be transformed into an acceptable cygnet only with the lengthy and excruciating intervention of a stylist, and then only long enough to take a dust jacket photo.

Unwilling to spend ninety minutes a day to look like her publicity photo, Penny began wearing a wig and sunglasses to book signings. Moreover, Penny discovered that she hated saying the identical thing over the course of a week to a hundred nodding, interchangeable reporters. She also hated travel and loathed hotel food.

More than two million people bought her book in sixteen languages, making Penny moderately wealthy. Sale of the book's film rights added substantially to her bank account but, in the process, she gave up creative control over the subsequent screenplay and film casting. Two years later, the film adaptation of *Wandering Hands* appeared to mixed reviews. Most critics wondered aloud and in print, how Patrick Dempsey got cast as Professor Dalrymple when the part had Jeremy Irons written all over it. Critics were somewhat kinder to Emily Blunt, even though Ashley, the character she portrayed, was described in the book as plump and plain-looking.

Wandering Hands sold exceptionally well in paperback, especially as a movie tie-in. However, by the time the film debuted, 'P.D. Walden' gave only phone interviews. To the inevitable question of the when her next book would be published, her answer was invariably, "Probably never." Asked if she was still in college and, if so, where, Penny equivocated. She wanted nothing more than to put the maximum distance – physical and psychological – between herself and her two-initial alter ego.

Also, by the time of the film's release, Penelope 'Penny' Walden had long since received her undergraduate degree in Biology from UCLA and had been accepted at Duke's graduate program in the same area of study. All of this was information she studiously avoided revealing in interviews. Long before *Wandering Hands* was viewable on Netflix, Penny had earned her Master's, and was formulating research topics for a doctoral thesis.

In addition to its academic reputation, Duke had the additional benefit of being three thousand miles from Los Angeles. No one in Durham had any idea that she was 'P.D. Walden' and she certainly didn't mention it in her graduate school application. She had achieved the impossible: she had successfully vanished from public view.

It was at Duke that she became interested in pheromones. For the uninitiated, a pheromone is a chemical that serves as a signaling agent to either alert or change the behavior of members of the animal kingdom. The signal is generally given via smell. Humans have such poor senses of smell that we mostly ignore them, but pheromones are like the Internet for insects and most mammals.

Penny's interest, though, was more in the specialized area of plant-to-plant communications over long distances. She ultimately earned her PhD in Pheromone Biochemistry by documenting the ability of oak trees to 'warn' oaks miles away that an infestation of gypsy moth caterpillars was denuding its leaves. The alerted trees began producing chemicals that made their leaves non-nutritious to caterpillars, halting the advance of the caterpillars.

Her newly minted doctorate brought Penny to the attention of recruiters from multiple universities and biotechnology companies. One of them was a venture-capital-backed enterprise in Cambridge, Massachusetts called Pheromonix.

She liked the idea of Boston. It was about as far away from Los Angeles as you could get and still be in the United States. This was not a whimsical consideration. Penny was all too aware that, in seeking obscurity, she had heightened her celebrity status among a sizeable group of hard-core devotees. 'P.D. Walden' had fangirl websites, chat rooms, and social media pages. All of them sought to resolve the question of how someone who had written a book so satisfying as *Wandering Hands* could disappear so completely and have left almost no biographical details.

The Pheromonix recruiter had taken the time to skim Penny's thesis and asked intelligent questions during the interview. Not one of them was about whether Penny was acquainted with a famous woman writer with the same surname as hers back in her undergraduate days in Southern California. Penny was delighted by the interview and resolved to accept an offer if one was made.

She of course did not need to work for a living. She suppressed a smile when the recruiter said, if Pheromonix successfully brought its first product to market and completed an initial public offering, her stock options could be worth 'a couple of million dollars.' The smile was because the smartest thing Penny had ever done, after signing her book contract, was to interview a dozen money managers and hire the one who didn't ask her what color Mercedes she had picked out. Penny had a mid-seven-figure nest egg that, except for her graduate school expenses, remained untouched after six years.

An offer was made and Penny accepted. Not wanting to look conspicuous, in mid-June, Penny emulated her fellow, newly-hired doctoral recipients and rented a trailer hitch and a U-Haul, and drove a two-year-old Honda Civic from North Carolina to

Massachusetts. She carried with her all her worldly belongings together with the promise of a life doing what she loved most. Her lone concession to her financial independence was to lease a one-bedroom apartment in an upscale block of relatively new buildings out at the Alewife terminus of the Red Line. As to purchasing clothes, jewelry, accessories, or the other trappings of the material world, Penny demurred. She had spent the past six years in jeans and was content to have her worldly belongings fit into half a dozen moving boxes.

Penny Walden could not have been happier. She was twenty-eight years old and ready for her real life to begin.

* * * * *

Pheromonix occupied part of one floor of a grey, six-story, one-hundred-year-old building on Binney Street, six blocks from the MIT campus. With its eleven-foot ceilings, it might have once been a factory producing machinery or farming implements. Two decades earlier, it had been gutted to its outer walls and rebuilt as a new kind of factory: one that produced ideas.

The building was a way station of sorts. Four companies with now-multi-billion-dollar capitalizations had gotten their start here. Those companies now had their own signature buildings designed by 'starchitects'. The founders of Pheromonix had successfully 'flipped' two other biotechs, selling them off to pharmaceutical giants who paid hundreds of millions of dollars for R&D which they could have done themselves if they could have attracted the right people and given them a free rein.

Starting a company in the building was no guarantee of success. Pheromonix, had sublet its space from a failed web startup that, in its two-year existence, lived off of venture capital. When it failed to build an app that teenagers and twenty-somethings couldn't live without, the company disappeared one weekend into the dustbin of failed enterprises and dashed financial riches.

Penny was issued a badge saying she was Employee Number

58. She quickly noticed that visitors to the company glanced at her badge number before they introduced themselves. Single-digit people, regardless of their position, got automatic deference. Low-numbered two-digit badges received almost as much respect. Those with a badge higher than 30 had to earn their way into people's hearts.

The largest single group of Pheromonix employees – roughly twenty - were in R&D. Five had PhD's, the rest were lab rats or administrators. Her boss was Helga Johanssen. She was in her late 40s, had her degree from Uppsala University, and was the kind of person who would have chain-smoked two packs of cigarettes a day had she not been in a non-smoking building in a city that would gladly prosecute for crimes against humanity any tobacco executive who dared show his or her face on Mass Ave.

Instead of indulging in known carcinogens, Helga consumed causal ones, carrying in a Starbucks drink cup every morning, and refilling it hourly until she departed, sometimes fifteen hours later. She wore Badge #11. The low badge number was unusual in one regard: she had not worked at one of the earlier corporate incarnations. Most low badges belonged to an inner circle that had followed the company's founders through two previous ventures. Those employees already had stashed away their own nest eggs. They were working as much for the adventure as for the next shot at potential wealth.

Helga had come to Pheromonix from the Massachusetts Institute of Technology where, in eighteen years, she had published a dozen major papers on pheromones but lived from grant to grant. While she was attracted by the challenge, Helga was at Pheromonix primarily for that potential seven-figure payoff. Helga was a big woman and, being a Swede, blonde. It was she who gave Penny an unexpected dose of reality on her first day.

"We're under intense pressure to get a product out the door," she said, eyeing her nearly empty coffee cup. She may have been born in Sweden, but her English carried only a hint of an accent, and that whisper was from the U.K. Anyone expecting sitcom-style 'Svee-dish' sentence construction or cadence was bound to be sorely disappointed.

"You're not in a research lab anymore," Helga said. "This is product development. And the product segment we've identified is huge."

Everything about this conversation was news to Penny. The truth was that she had absorbed just two things from the recruiter. The first was that, Google-style, she could do anything she wanted to with a quarter of her time. In the most glowing of terms, the recruiter had promised that Penny could follow her private research dream using the best tools in the world and, if it resulted in a breakthrough product, reap the financial results. The other thing she heard (and, if pressed, she would admit she wasn't listening all that carefully after that first bit) was that Pheromonix was pursuing 'blue sky' R&D. Penny was promised she was going to be chasing and helping catch unicorns. Pheromone-based unicorns.

"Have you ever had a cat?" Helga asked.

Penny thought about it. Her family was dog people. Mutts, mostly, with la-la-land names like Marilyn and Scooby Doo.

"No," she replied.

"Do you know why you never had a cat?" she asked.

Penny tried to think of an acceptable answer. The real answer was that there are 'cat people' and there are 'dog people' and she had been raised by 'dog people'.

"I really don't know the answer," she said, hoping neutrality would win the day.

Instead, Helga got excited. "Thirty-five percent of American homes have cats," she said. "That's ten points less than the percentage of dog households. The biggest impediment to having cats? They scratch. A four-kilo cat can reduce a two-thousand-dollar sofa to fabric shreds in an afternoon."

"What does that have to do with us?" Penny asked.

Helga sighed. "Why do you think a cat scratches? You're a scientist. Think it through."

Penny thought it through. "A cat scratches to sharpen its claws. Fabric offers the right amount of resistance, plus it probably provides a sense of accomplishment."

Helga was smiling. "And so.....?

"We find the right pheromone that tells the cat this is not scratching territory."

"A billion dollars," Helga said.

"Pardon?" Penny asked.

"A billion in sales in the first five years," Helga said. "Cats are the perfect pet. You don't have to walk them. They're small. They're happy in an apartment. They keep themselves amused. Their lone downside is that they'll destroy humans' precious artifacts in the name of sharpening their claws or perhaps boredom. De-clawing is considered inhumane, so sixty-five percent of people in America and Europe will not have anything to do with that otherwise perfect pet."

"And we're going to identify and market the pheromone that tells cats to stay away from the curtains," Penny said with dawning understanding.

Helga smiled as she nodded. "Cats are our ticket to wealth and fame."

"Are we close?" Penny asked.

Helga's smile turned to a neutral look. "We've had successes. And failures."

"Do you want to tell me about them, or just give me the lab results to read?"

Helga sighed. "It isn't a single chemical or marker. It seems to vary from breed to breed, male to female. Even cat to cat. Last week we sprayed a test piece of furniture with a promising molecule; an epideictic. Five female cats gave it a wide berth. Five male cats sprayed on it. A necromonic molecule kept Siamese cats of both sexes on the other side of the room. Where they defecated to the exclusion of their litter boxes."

"It sounds hopeless," Penny said.

Helga shook her head. "No. Not hopeless. Just harder than we thought. Cats have secretion glands on their mouth, chin, forehead, cheeks, lower back, tail and paws. We still don't know if it is one molecule or a combination that will do the trick. That's why you're here. A fresh perspective and a more recent degree."

With that, she excused herself to refill her coffee cup. That was the extent of Penny's company indoctrination.

* * * * *

At least Penny's office was everything she had been promised. Extraordinarily powerful computers, the newest in lab equipment. And room to stretch. Two weeks before departing Durham, Penny received a call from the company's facilities manager asking if she had anything specific in mind for office furniture or décor.

Penny said she liked to pace when she was working on a problem.

"How many paces do you need before you turn around?" the man asked. Penny apparently wasn't the first person to inquire about pacing room. She told him ten or twelve.

"Is a cot OK or do you want something more comfortable?" he asked.

A cot for my office, Penny thought. *This was paradise. At Duke we used sleeping bags.*

"Let's start with a cot and see where it goes," she responded.

Penny arrived to find a remarkably comfortable looking cot in her personal office. Long and narrow, she could easily take twelve moody paces without encountering an obstruction.

* * * * *

Penny spent her first days on the job going through three months of trial results. Each molecule tested was catalogued for its effects on different felines, no matter how undesirable the outcome. She also quickly discovered why there were so many assistants on the payroll. They were cat wranglers.

In Cambridge, a corporation does not keep a supply of cats on hand for experimentation, even if the extent of their participation is to have their body swabbed in a dozen places and, on occasion, be placed in a room with an unsuspecting and invariably doomed piece of furniture. If word got out that a company was imprisoning cats, the PETA folks would simultaneously picket the company, launch a midnight rescue mission, and file suit in the name of the suffering animals.

Instead, Pheromonix advertised for 'subjects' with a payment of fifty dollars for every successful 'enrollee'. Every Wednesday and Thursday morning, there would be thirty or more women (yes, women, pandering to the worst stereotype about 'cat ladies') with their felines in carriers. One by one, a lab tech would take tabby's history in considerable detail. Then, with the cat still in the woman's arms, the lab tech would start swabbing, stopping to place each sample in a sterile container. If the cat objected, the process paused until the animal was again pacified.

On the days potentially effective pheromones were tested, lab techs encouraged the cat ladies to watch their companions from behind a one-way mirror. Pheromonix wanted no rumors of cat abuse. Instead, the company earned a reputation as the easiest fifty bucks to be had in the Greater Boston area.

Pheromonix's techs were uniformly good-natured about their work. Many had college degrees, though mostly not in the life sciences. But they were smart enough to realize how large a task was in front of the company.

Penny learned that Helga briefed the 'Executive Committee' at least twice a week. She never returned from those meetings with a smile, and she frequently immediately consumed two or even three cups of coffee afterwards. On her third day at work, when Penny asked Helga how things had gone at such a briefing the previous day, Helga waved Penny off and said, "Just keep working."

And Penny never lost sight of that promised 'personal investigation' time. She had brought with her a folder filled with clippings and printouts about bees and hive collapse. The generally accepted scientific thesis is that it is not one specific chemical that is the reason for the dramatic drop in the bee population Rather, it is an accumulation of multiple man-made events, many of them having to do with the introduction of a new generation of plants treated with insecticides and, in some cases, with those insecticides made part of the plant's genetic structure.

The spare-time investigation Penny wanted to pursue was to figure out if there was a way to tell bees to stay away from the pollen of plants laced with neonicotinoids. She had no idea if such a feat was possible, but that is what research is for. (Of course, banning neonicotinoids is the preferable alternative, but that's another story.)

FRIDAY

Chapter Two

On her fifth day on the job, Penny looked up from a trial journal to see a slender woman leaning on her doorway. Actually, 'slender' and 'woman' were only marginally accurate descriptions of the person, and she was slouching rather than leaning. She was maybe seventeen or eighteen – too young to be one of the company's lab assistants – and though at least five-foot-ten, she couldn't have weighed a hundred and ten pounds. Not quite anorexic, but also not quite *not* anorexic either. She had waist-length jet-black hair with an unfortunate interruption of magenta half way down. The hair was arranged around her face to hide more than half of her visage. Penny could see dark eyes, a small nose, and a mouth with what looked like a perpetual pout. She was dressed in short-shorts (it was late June, after all) and a tank top advertising what Penny suspected was a band she had never heard of and would likely not enjoy listening to.

"Can I help you?" Penny asked.

The girl nodded and said in a high voice, "You're Penny Walden." Given that Penny had arrived on Monday to find a metal nameplate already affixed to her door, the woman's opening statement seemed rather obvious and more than a bit redundant. "I wanted to see what you looked like," she added.

"Does that mean I've already helped you?" Penny said, allowing a trace of annoyance to creep into her voice.

It must have had some effect because the girl said, "Uh, sorry." She placed the fingers of one hand on her chest. "I'm Helga's daughter. Allie."

"And your responsibility is to assess the personal appearance of all incoming scientists?" Penny asked.

Allie rolled her eyes. "I read your résumé. Helga brings home the good ones and asks me my opinion. I don't know if she follows all of my advice but I said you looked like a good one. Candidate, I mean."

"Then I thank you for that vote of confidence," Penny said, relaxing somewhat. "Would you care to take a seat?"

Allie had been waiting for the invitation. She plopped into the office's second swivel chair and began swinging in half circles.

"You call your mother 'Helga'," Penny said. "Is that for my convenience or is that a Swedish thing?"

Allie stopped swinging. "It started when I was fourteen. That's also when my father chose to dump his family."

"Do you also call him by his first name?" Penny asked.

"I have other names for him," Allie said in a lower voice. "And I don't care if he hears them."

Helga had made no mention to Penny of her marital status. Penny assumed if Helga wanted to say something on the subject, she would have done so.

Allie pulled a phone out of her pants pocket. "Do you mind if I take your picture?"

"I have a strong sense that, if I said 'no', you'd lay in wait for me by the building entrance and take it anyway," Penny said. "I am trying to work, though, so how about just one?"

"That's all I need," Allie said. "How about turning your head just a little to the left?"

Penny complied. Allie was her boss's daughter and she assumed there was some affection between the two if Helga shared interesting résumés over dinner.

Penny heard a clicking sound and assumed she had fulfilled her duty. She turned back to her desk and the reports on lab trials. Allie, however, stayed in her chair, fiddling with her phone.

"God, this is one amazing app," she said, tapping her screen.

"Is there a Pokémon in this office?" Penny asked.

"Something infinitely rarer. Just another sec," Allie said.

"There."

Allie turned the screen toward Penny. "Here's the shot I took." Allie had zoomed into a 'head and shoulders' shot. It was a competently arranged photo. Penny nodded her assent that it was, in fact a likeness of her. *Me and my pointed chin, pooh-bear nose, and pale skin*, she thought.

"The neat thing about this app is that it can show what you'll look like in ten years, twenty years – you just plug in the current age and the app does the rest with algorithms," Allie said.

"May I say I'm not interested?" Penny said, being both honest and trying to inject that Allie was getting on her nerves.

"It also works the other way," Allie said casually. "It can take a pretty good guess at what you looked like ten or twenty years ago."

Penny felt a chill run down her spine. Allie was smiling. She tapped the phone one more time.

"Voila," she said. "Penny Walden seven years ago; age twenty or twenty-one." She tapped the screen a second time and another, particularly familiar photo appeared alongside the one she had just taken.

"And P.D. Walden, from seven years ago," Allie said, showing the dust jacket photo that had adorned the hardcover and trade paperback editions of *Wandering Hands*.. "I could add the wig to your photo or subtract it from P.D.'s, but I think that's unnecessary. What do you think?"

* * * * *

Penny didn't know what to think.

Until that moment, she had lived with the satisfaction that there were only three people who knew where 'P.D. Walden' was spending her literary retirement. Her parents knew. And her financial advisor knew. As far as most of the rest of the world was concerned, 'P.D. Walden' had vanished into some literary Neverland: a one-book wonder.

And, at least in theory, P.D. Walden should certainly not have been missed. *Wandering Hands* had not been at the forefront of the genre called Empowered Woman Getting Revenge on the Lecherous Professor. Other books had already explored the theme and, within a few years, shelves would bulge with similar-sounding titles.

Moreover, all of those books were increasingly an anachronism; subjects made historical curiosities by the march of progress. By the middle of the second decade of the new century, the act of leering at students – male or female – was something that would quickly imperil the careers of faculty members who engaged in such behavior. Penny had written *Wandering Hands* before the era of trigger warnings and microaggressions. In theory, novels about women taking retribution against lecherous professors should be quaint artifacts,

But that was theory. The facts were considerably more troubling.

Nevertheless, Penny decided to play it cool. "How did you guess it was me?"

Allie grinned and tapped the side of her head. "Well, right initials and last name. And you did your undergraduate work in Southern California at the time the book was written and the betting money has always been that the school in the book is UCLA. But the rest of it was intuition. When P.D. Walden stopped giving interviews, it was a pretty good indication that she had moved to someplace where people wouldn't suspect who she was. Durham, North Carolina fit the bill. But then you got your degree and moved again, even though there are plenty of biotech jobs in the Triangle and the weather is a lot nicer. It seemed to me you were covering your tracks." Allie shrugged. "It was worth taking a photograph."

"O.K.," she said, and managed a slight smile. "You have me dead to rights. So what?"

"I read your book," Allie said. "I loved it." Then she added, "I hated the movie."

"So did everyone else," Penny said, and this time, the smile wasn't forced. There were several months when all she heard around her friends at Duke was that a really good book had been turned into hash by a Hollywood studio.

Then Penny asked, "What were you doing reading my book? Shouldn't you have been devouring Harry Potter?"

Allie again rolled her eyes; an eighteen-year-old's non-verbal equivalent of 'spare me'. "I read those when I was, like, nine and ten. Then I grew up. I wanted something a little juicier. You were perfect." Allie paused. "But then you stopped writing. Why?"

"The writing was fun," Penny replied. "The marketing wasn't." She pointed around the room at the lab equipment. "*This* is fun. Otherwise I wouldn't have spent all those years getting a PhD."

"But your ideas were sheer genius…" Allie started.

Penny waved her hand dismissively. "It's fiction. A number of reviewers pointed out that the whole plot depended on Dalrymple deciding to leave his office for a private call just as Ashley was trying to figure out how to break in. The phrase one reviewer used was, 'just a little too convenient'."

"But you…" Allie started to say.

"Allie," Penny interrupted. "A long time ago, a roommate told me about an enormously suave professor who put the moves on all the pretty girls. We spent one evening fantasizing about how to get even with the guy. My roommate got up the next morning and went to class. I didn't have a class that morning, and so I started writing. Beginning, middle, and end of story."

Allie was silent for a moment.

"So, you know who I was," Penny said. "I consider that a closed part of my life. It's why I go by my given name instead of the initials my publisher insisted on. I'm never going to write another book. The one I wrote was a fluke. I knew I wanted to be a scientist before I wrote the book. I became a scientist after I wrote it. If I don't talk about it, it's because I don't want to be P.D. Walden any more, and I wasn't exactly overjoyed for that year when I *was* her. On the other hand, I'm ecstatically happy being who I am today. Are we good?"

Penny looked to Allie's face to see if she had gotten through.

"Yeah, I guess we're good," Allie said. "I see your point and I totally respect it. And I'm not going to send this photo off to Entertainment Tonight, TMZ, or The Smoking Gun. I'm not going to send it to any of the freaky sites that love to do those "look where they are now" exposés. And I especially won't send it to the 'WhereIsPDWalden' website which is where the real freaks reside, because those guys would start pitching their sleeping bags here and at your apartment building just for the chance to get a glimpse of you. A lot of them want to marry you. Both the men and the women."

Penny felt she was about to retch. She knew exactly where this was going. It was the thing she thought she had put behind her. Except here it was in front of her; dressed in a tank top and short shorts.

The mistake Penny had made was not allowing P.D. Walden to become boring. Instead, she became the writer who stopped giving interviews and doing signings while the book was still a best seller. When the film came out, the handful of interviews she gave were over the telephone and, in each one, Penny pointedly declined to say where she was and what she was doing.

She became a cult figure; a twenty-first-century J.D. Salinger. Which made her background and present whereabouts the subject of intense scrutiny. Her dust jacket bio said only that she was "enrolled at a large, Southern California college", and her fictional 'Topanga College' mixed elements of half a dozen institutions.

"However, to ensure that I don't do any of those things, I want you to help me," Allie said, snapping Penny back to the present.

"How much?" Penny said, resigned to either watching her career evaporate after five days or writing an exceedingly large check. Probably the first of many large checks.

"I know it's ten million," Allie said. "And twice that when you throw in dividends and interest and that other stuff."

Penny gasped. Just the ten million was several million dollars more than what she had in her investment account from her book earnings. Allie intended to bleed her dry. "You can't be serious."

"That's what he stole," Allie said. "That's what I can document…"

"You said 'he'. Who is 'he'?"

Allie blinked. "My father. He embezzled about five million bucks before he walked out on us. Since then, he's stepped up the pace. He has stolen another five and it has all been invested so it's more than twenty million. He hasn't spent any of it. I know that much. He's living off of *her*. But I think I know how to get it back. And, when we do, there won't be a thing he can do about it, unless he wants to spend the rest of his sorry-ass life in jail. It would be a great story, though. Every news site would have it as a banner for weeks. 'World Famous Horticulturalist Caught Green-Handed.'"

"Why me?" Penny pleaded.

Allie stared at Penny for a long second. "Because I read your book," she said. "You may not know it, but you have one of the most devious minds I have ever come across, and you are not afraid to put that mind to work on behalf of righting a wrong, even if it means causing considerable discomfort for the bad guy. You have a gift, and I want you to use your gift one last time before you make the world safe from cat-clawed curtains."

Penny slumped back in her chair. "Allie, maybe you want to start at the beginning."

Chapter Three

"You have no idea of who my father is?"

Penny shook her head. "Remember, I'm new to Boston."

Allie nodded. "Then you've never heard of New England Green?"

Penny racked her brain. Nothing. She again shook her head.

"For about two hundred years, there was an oh-so-proper Brahmin institution called SEAICE - The Society for the Encouragement of Agricultural Improvement and Cultivation of Ethical Reasoning," Allie said. "Emerson and Thoreau were among the founders. The Lowells and Cabots were heavily involved. If you lived in Boston and had a summer home in the country – meaning five hundred acres in Waltham or Dedham – you were a member. The Leveretts and the Saltonstalls made it even bigger and more important. SEAICE financed all manner of agricultural innovation. McCormick got seed money from them, as did Deere."

"OK," Penny said. "Rich people giving back."

"No," Allie corrected. "Rich people getting richer. In exchange for that seed money, they got shares. SEAICE was like a venture capital firm for nineteenth-century America. They had their hand in everything. Got a better canning system? SEAICE would help get your factory up and running – for ten percent of the business. If you had a new peach to bring to market, you first got the SEAICE seal of approval, which meant you gave them a piece of the action. It might be tiny – a penny a bushel – but it added up."

"Then the big agricultural action moved to California and, all of a sudden, SEAICE was in a farming backwater. They couldn't find projects to sponsor. Meanwhile, they were spending down their capital building parks and promoting agricultural fairs. By the 1930s, they were a shell of what they had been just thirty years earlier."

"What changed?" Penny asked.

"Elliot Anderson White. 'E.A.' to his friends, of whom he apparently had thousands," Allie said. "White was a lawyer. He understood wills and estates and, especially, the estate tax. If you died and left your five hundred acres in Scituate or your historic house in Winchester to your four sons and daughters, the state and federal government wanted something like sixty percent of the assessed value. If you left it to SEAICE, the transaction wasn't taxed and the overall estate size was smaller. So, SEAICE started getting donations of houses and land all over New England. Towns especially loved it because, even though the land went off the tax rolls, it meant a perpetual conservation easement. One less tract housing development for your town. One fewer school to build and maintain. White changed the name of the organization to New England Green in the 1940s; a play on the 'town green' idea."

"Where does your father come into it?" Penny asked.

"White ran the organization for nearly sixty years," Allie said. "He died at his desk. The Trustees, who had essentially slept through the preceding half century, were forced to go looking for his replacement. My father had been named a Trustee a year earlier. He was their Horticultural Advisor, assessing each parcel of land and telling the Society which trees were rare and which plants were invasive. He has a PhD from a university in England. He was a really good horticulturalist. He told New England Green it ought to start leasing out land for farms – what would come to be called Community Supported Agriculture. They loved it. They put him in charge and went back to sleep."

"I don't hear anything bad so far," Penny said.

"My father says he found that the books were a mess. Families gave New England Green houses and land, but no money to maintain them. So, starting when he became Executive Director, everything had to be endowed. People understood. He also said there was property that ought never to have been accepted. It was too small, too remote, too something. The money from those land sales went to maintain other properties, and to start the agricultural program."

"I'm still waiting for a shoe to drop," Penny said. "Your father sounds like a paragon of virtue and a decent businessman."

"Then zip ahead a year or two," Allie said. "He and Helga got married, I was born, and the family needed something larger than the gardener's cottage on the estate being used as New England Green's headquarters. My father offered to buy one of their 'surplus' properties. To his astonishment, the Trustees one-upped him: as a token of their gratitude they offered to lease him one of their most historic houses: a thousand dollars a year for fifty years. They would pay for all of the maintenance and upkeep; we got to live in it for practically nothing."

"So I got to grow up in the Josiah Willard House in Coolidge Hill," Allie continued. "That act of unexpected generosity apparently gave my father ideas. I remember playing in his home office and looking through his desk. I would see these brokerage statements in places they shouldn't be. So I showed them to Helga. She just shrugged and she said they were part of New England Green's paperwork except that, even to my ten-year-old eyes, it didn't make sense that they were in my father's name and they weren't kept in the same place as his work papers." Allie paused. "So, I started taking pictures of them with my phone."

Allie got up from the chair and began picking up and examining small items around Penny's office. She no longer made eye contact with Penny. What she was about to say was extremely difficult for her.

"Then, four years ago, my sleazebag of a father took up with another woman. And not just any woman: a genuine heiress. Miss Emily Taylor Rice, age thirty-one at the time, and the sole descendant of the Taylors and the Rices. He ostensibly moved into her 'little house' on Beacon Hill while she nominally was living in the 'big house' in Hingham. They're both in Hingham, cozy as can be in the family waterfront mansion."

Now, Allie looked directly at Penny. "Before he had the opportunity to clear everything out, I photographed it all," Allie said. "Every scrap of paper I could lay my hands on. I've been organizing it ever since."

"Your father still runs New England Green?" Penny asked.

"Of course," Allie said, scoffing. "You've never heard of 'the' Brian LaPointe? That's my father. He's there because you can't keep stealing if you don't have a place to steal from."

"Is there a reason you can't just take all of this to the state Attorney General?" Penny asked. "That's probably the office that would know what to do with all your paperwork. The one down in North Carolina…"

Allie shook her head violently. "My father is the slickest talker in the world. He would spin a story that would sound so convincing that the investigators would pull out their own checkbooks and start writing. Believe me, I've already thought about half a dozen law enforcement and oversight organizations that *ought* to have caught onto this long before now. The only way to get that money out of his hands is to steal it back from him."

"Why is it important?" Penny asked.

Allie looked at Penny oddly, perhaps trying to see if what she had said had made any impression. "My father is a man completely without a moral compass," she said. "He has stolen from a non-profit. He walked out on his family without caring what harm he was doing to us. He is living the high life and genuinely believes he deserves every good thing that is happening in that rarefied existence of his."

Allie paused, considering her next words. "The only thing that will get through to him is waking up one morning and finding he has lost everything. I want to see the look on his face when he realizes what has happened to him."

"And you want me to help you?" Penny asked.

"Yes," Allie said. "In the words of Princess Leia, 'Help me, Obi-wan Kenobi. You're my only hope.'." After a pause, she added, "And if you don't help me, that little psychotic corner of the world that wakes up every morning thinking about P.D. Walden is going to have their most precious wish come true."

Chapter Four

Brian LaPointe listened earnestly as the two elderly women across from him made their case. As he understood it, Marisa Holder and Celeste Tomlinson had both been lifelong members of New England Green. They believed fervently in the mission of the organization. They wanted to help. One was widowed, the other never married. The one that had been married had children that had long since left New England and had no intention of returning. The sisters had, sometime in the 1970s, jointly inherited from their parents a modest parcel of land. Now both in their eighties, they wanted to ensure that this parcel remained, as they put it, 'forever wild'.

The interesting part of the story, as summarized in the sheet in front of him, was that the 'modest parcel of land' was ten acres on East Bay in Osterville, a Cape Cod community oozing with cachet. The market price of those ten acres, assuming they were buildable, was at least five million dollars.

Marisa or Celeste – he wasn't certain which one was which – had been told that her heart was not strong. They wanted to get their affairs in order, and finding a safe, permanent guardian for their 'modest parcel' was at the top of their list. They had considered the Nature Conservancy and Trustees of Reservations, but their heart was with New England Green. Decades earlier they used to come to hear E.A. White's horticultural lectures, and he was just the most charming man…

"There is more involved to this than just deeding over your land," Brian said when there seemed to be a break in the conversation. He spoke in earnest but cautious tones, and the two women leaned in closely to better hear him.

"There was a time when New England Green took in

properties by the dozens. E.A. was famous for it." He paused, allowing them to savor the image of their fondly remembered hero collecting parchment deeds dripping with authentication ribbons from outstretched hands. He then lowered his voice to a conspiratorial whisper. "He almost put the organization out of business, you know."

The two women gasped in unison.

Brian held up his hands in front of his chest. "He wasn't trying to undermine the organization, mind you. His intentions were noble. He just didn't realize that there was more to land management than having title to it. Every parcel seems to have its own, special nagging problem. A town wants to put a road through it. A developer thinks he can invalidate the easement and put up a hundred apartments on it. Beavers decide to build a dam on it. Somebody walking through the land falls, breaks a leg, and decides to sue for millions in pain and suffering. The list goes on and on."

"Our job is to protect the land in perpetuity," Brian said. "But protecting it… costs money. The worst thing that could happen is that something totally unexpected makes it impossible for us or any other organization – to keep your land. And then for it to fall into the hands of a developer. That's why we ask for an endowment."

The two women looked at one another. One of the sisters – it may have been Celeste – said, "How much will you need?"

An hour later, Brian walked across his richly appointed office and opened a cabinet – actually, a cleverly disguised refrigerator door – above a filing cabinet. He took out a bottle of well-chilled Grey Goose Magnum and poured two fingers into a glass. He took the glass back to his desk and swirled it in his hand before taking a drink.

Not bad for a morning's work, he thought. The old ladies had not flinched at the idea of laying out a quarter million for an endowment. He now had the contact name in a trust department where he would get the ball rolling. It would take a few months, of course, and he would bury them in paperwork. But in the end, two wire transfers would be made as per the somewhat odd but customary and entirely legal protocol established years ago for New England Green.

One of those wire transfers would, in fact, form the endowment for the land. The second one would find itself placed into an administrative account where it would be parceled out to lawyers and surveyors and other professionals. Miraculously, after bouncing around for weeks as a series of ones and zeroes, the checks written on that administrative fund would finally settle comfortably into yet another account, this one belonging to Brian LaPointe.

And, when the old ladies bought the farm, he would re-visit the terms of the transfer and, if the land was indeed developable and there were even a hint of a loophole, he would tug on the thread of that loophole until the whole skein unraveled. If it did, he would find a way – as he already had done with eight New England Green holdings – to dispose of it to the highest bidder with a double-digit percentage of the sale price going into his personal account.

God, he thought, *I love this job.*

A year into his employment at New England Green, Brian became convinced of an immutable truth about venerable institutions: that they attract Trustees who, other than padding their obituaries, have no idea what they are doing. These Trustees came to meetings having read none of the reports sent out ahead of time. They spent the half hour before the meeting drinking decent wine and catching up with friends they had not seen since their boats were tied up alongside one another in Boothbay Harbor or they were in first class on the same flight back from Paris. Their faith in the management of the institution was both explicit and implicit.

It was that inattention to detail that had captivated Brian almost two decades earlier when he found himself the token competent Trustee for New England Green. Brian had been hired a year earlier as the organization's Chief Horticulturalist (though, naturally and in keeping the organization's Yankee thrift, without a staff), and several Trustees had wondered aloud if it might be a good idea to have this particularly pleasant fellow close by where they could easily seek his advice about their gardens and the right way to deal with their lawn services and whatnot.

Brian also found himself the lone Trustee without a trust fund and, for a year, he freely dispensed accurate and pointed advice in addition to the duties enumerated on his job description. He was especially explicit in noting whenever he felt contractors were taking advantage of Trustees by performing unnecessary maintenance. This further endeared Brian to the Board.

When the legendary Elliot Anderson White failed to come out of his office for a luncheon appointment one summer day, the Trustees knew exactly who should take his place. Dr. Brian LaPointe not only was a known quantity (thus sparing the Board the time, effort, and expense of a formal search), he was also an indispensable part of their personal gardening management decision process. Were he to be passed over, Brian might feel compelled to leave, placing Trustees at the mercy of avaricious landscapers and arborists.

Brian accepted the job with two provisos. The first was that New England Green begin a formal policy of devoting arable parcels within its system to growing high-quality produce. Part of the output would go to food pantries in towns adjacent to those gardens. The bulk, however, would be devoted to a new kind of farming: Community Supported Agriculture. Trustees readily agreed. It was the kind of 'feel good' project that allowed them to tell their friends and families that New England Green was on the cutting edge of something, even if they only vaguely understood what it was or how it worked.

The second of Brian's preconditions was initially cause for concern. He insisted that unless New England Green immediately begin requiring an endowment when gifts of land were made, the organization would be bankrupt within a decade. The Trustees protested that periodic cash gifts and a hefty endowment had sustained operations for half a century. Brian countered that the endowment was dangerously depleted and no match for inflation, and that gifts were primarily from the Trustees themselves. It took a 'Special Commission' of Trustees just three hours to comprehend that the only flaw in Brian's prediction was that insolvency might be less than five years away rather than ten.

Brian did not set out to steal from his employer. Installed as the new Executive Director, he rapidly implemented the Community Supported Agriculture plan at a dozen sites. Of the first dozen individuals who approached New England Green to take ownership of land, only one balked at the idea of an endowment. Within a year, the organization was on a stable financial footing.

But there was no oversight by the Board. The staff was almost exclusively volunteers with little or no financial experience and the Audit Committee consisted of three octogenarians who were more than two decades removed from their accounting firm partnerships. They now stared at the financial reports and balance sheets, saw that printouts were neat and beautifully bound, and accepted their accuracy without question.

And so Brian began to skim. Special buckets of funds titled, 'Administrative Discretionary Accounts' were created along with endowments. The amounts – roughly ten percent of the value of the endowment – were small enough (and the 'real' auditors sufficiently relieved that New England Green was no longer in financial peril) that they were not questioned closely. Every new endowment created a fresh need for a small cadre of professionals to scrutinize different aspects of the property, and every penny of those funds became Brian's.

After ten years, more than five million dollars had been

diverted and was in the hands of an investment advisory firm that made a point of never questioning the source of Brian's deposits, and prided itself on its ability to keep its clients' funds out of view of the Internal Revenue Service. Now, in his eighteenth year as the head of the revered institution, and with New England Green sitting on a $250 million-plus endowment, the sky was the limit. This new contribution would push his deposits into his investment account across the ten million dollar threshold. Including investment gains, his latest statement showed a total balance of just over $21 million.

From his richly appointed office at the Beckwith Estate, the 'jewel in the crown' of New England Green, Brian could look out his windows to manicured lawns, meticulously maintained gardens and, in the distance, a working farm.

On the wall of his office was a wonderful parchment certificate topped with a polychrome crest attesting to his achieving a Doctorate of Sciences in Plant Science and Technology from Leeds Polytechnic. Alongside it was a much more humble certificate attesting to his Bachelor's Degree in Horticulture from the University of Massachusetts' Stockbridge School of Agriculture.

Those two diplomas had been his tickets out of the circumscribed life into which he had been born and would otherwise have been consigned: the fifth generation to eke a meager living out of a fifty-acre dairy and truck farm near Athol, Massachusetts. He had been immersed in practical horticulture from the age of four. His UMass education was the product of a scholarship from the local Rotary Club and a willingness to forego the pleasures of campus living and commute each day via pickup truck from his family's farm.

The Doctorate from Leeds Polytechnic, as Brian had explained to the Trustee charged with interviewing candidates for the New England Green horticultural position, was the lucky product of his being in the right place at the right time when, at the last minute, another Stockbridge graduate backed out of a funded fellowship to the Yorkshire institution.

He knew when he applied that the PhD would have great weight in the decision of whom to hire for the position. New England Green valued advanced degrees, although the extent of the questioning at the time of the interview was to ask whether Leeds was as wet as its reputation. Brian agreed the climate was damp, but that the educational environment was warm and invigorating.

Elsewhere on the wall was a gallery of photos, nearly twenty in all. Brian LaPointe was a photogenic man. At age 42 he still possessed a thick head of tousled black hair and a rugged, square-jawed face. He was tall and lean, and a more than competent tennis player and golfer. The photos on the wall showed Brian golfing with governors and congressmen. In the center of the display was Brian at the Vineyard Golf Club in Edgartown sinking a fourteen-foot putt as an admiring Barack Obama looked on. Currently next to it, sadly without a sports context, was a photo of Brian sharing a confidence with Hillary Clinton. In a nearby cabinet was an identically sized photo of Brian teeing off alongside Donald Trump. The two photos were routinely swapped out depending upon the political leanings of the office visitor.

On his desk was a single photograph. Emily Taylor Rice smiled radiantly from the front of a sailboat. Her shoulder-length blonde hair blew out behind her in a stiff wind, and a one-piece bathing suit displayed a slim, attractive body. Her face showed only freedom and happiness; there was no hint of care or concern around her perfect, unlined face and intelligent eyes.

Brian could look at that photo all day. He had taken it the previous summer on their Fourth-of-July stay on Block Island. Emily was perfection. A graduate of Dartmouth's Amos Tuck School, she effortlessly juggled her duties on four corporate Boards of Directors with the oversight of the endowment of the exclusive girl's school she had attended just twenty years earlier. She was an endearing hostess who could not only select the perfect menu but also sense when something was amiss in the kitchen even though no one gave her warning.

They had lived together now for four glorious years. They had known of one another for more than a decade, but it was at a private dinner in a home on Marblehead Neck where, seated next to one another for two hours, their mutual attraction became apparent. She was 31 at the time and he was 38. He was also married. She said she could not respect a man who cheated on his wife.

Two days later, he asked his wife of sixteen years for a divorce.

He seldom if ever thought of Helga or Allie. It was not as though he had closed one chapter of a book and started another. Rather, it was that he had closed a book altogether and placed it on a shelf, never to be re-opened.

Because she was five years older than he, Brian knew Helga would now be 47. Allie was born in June, so she would have just turned eighteen and would be starting college in a few months. Helga was likely still doing research at MIT. Laboratories were her thing. She would still be stalking $200,000 grants from government agencies that would keep her team of graduate students occupied for six months. Peanuts, really. It was pitiable.

There had been nothing wrong with Helga. Well, except for her weight. He had married a stunning Nordic blonde at the peak of her beauty and with a knockout figure. When Helga got pregnant with Allie two years later, she put on something like thirty pounds. OK, that was normal. But, after Allie was born the weight... stayed. She was still attractive, but no longer the woman who turned every man's head as she walked by. He had enjoyed the thrill of seeing other men lust after what was his. When those men stopped staring, Brian lost interest.

Helga also had that Swedish depression thing. She would bury herself in her work, not coming out of the lab for days at a time. In the last few years of their marriage, she became a caffeine freak, downing ten cups of coffee each day. Put at its simplest, Helga had changed. She was not the woman he had married. That's what he told her when he said he was leaving. He stressed that she and Allie would continue to live in the Coolidge Hill house at its ridiculously low lease rate. He thought it best to leave out the part about his romantic conversation the prior evening with one of the wealthiest women in New England.

Helga's response had been just to stare at him, nod her head, and say she had a lab experiment to monitor.

As for Allie, all he could do was shrug. Allie was bright. Hell, not just bright; her IQ was measured at something like 145. She was probably headed to MIT or CalTech. She would do fine. A year after the divorce, he tried to get in touch with her. He told her he wanted to stay in her life; send her emails asking how she was doing, that sort of thing. Allie's response was to send back her own emails with horrific viruses as attachments disguised as innocuous photos. He got the message. It had been three years since they last communicated. If she hated him, it was her fault.

Which brought him back to Emily. He had thought by now they would be married. Four years was a long time and he knew Emily wanted children. It was her wealth that was preventing her from committing. He had made clear he would sign any prenuptial agreement placed in front of him. It was her he wanted to be with; not her money. He would deal with dissolving the pre-nup after they were married.

Still, she held back. And that troubled him.

Chapter Five

In a cubicle on the fourteenth floor of a nondescript, 1920s-era office building in the Garment District, Zoe Matthews stared at a binder that, she believed, held her future.

Zoe was twenty-two. She had graduated thirteen months earlier from the School of Journalism of the University of Missouri in Rolla with a specialization in Print and Digital News. Working through the prestigious school's placement office, she had envisioned a fast-track career with Google or another online news aggregator.

Instead, after four dispiriting months of submitting hundreds of résumés that went unacknowledged, she had been invited to apply for an unpaid internship at *'Entertainment Now'*, a syndicated television show and website that was a second-rate imitation of its glossy brethren. Zoe spent her days trolling other celebrity sites, looking for tidbits she could re-write for the EN crawl. She read Twitter feeds for the outrageous nuggets that she knew full well had been written by publicists.

Her compensation for all of this was the opportunity to raid meeting rooms for the leftover sandwiches after executive lunches had been held, and to be handed the occasional swag bag when too few people had shown up. There was no salary or benefits attached to what she did. Instead, she was told, she was 'learning the ropes' and 'getting the real inside knowledge on the industry' that would give her 'a tremendous leg up in her career'. She would, of course, 'be at the top of the list' when a paying position came open.

She was an attractive woman. She wore her strawberry blond hair long, the better to accentuate her perfect oval face. With green eyes, fair skin and expressive brows, she had a perfect face for television. She stood five-eight in her flats and possessed a figure that seemed just right for the camera. Of course, the only time Zoe had ever been allowed near EN's broadcast studio was to deliver coffee.

After nine months at EN, she knew it was all a hoax. Three other interns worked elsewhere on the floor. All had been promised the same thing. Like the other interns, she was still there because the only 'industry' openings were other unpaid positions.

In turn, Zoe was able to stay at EN because her parents deposited a thousand dollars each month into her bank account, and because she had an aunt and uncle in Paramus. There, she lived in their spare bedroom and rode a New Jersey Transit bus each day to Port Authority.

The binder in front of her had the power to change the life she had come to hate. It held the 'wish list' exclusives after which every celebrity news program, magazine, and web site lusted. For the most part, the list was out of Zoe's – or anyone's – reach. Johnny Depp or Beyoncé were not going to open their door to Zoe Matthews if they had already turned down every other writer in the business.

But there were a few, 'where are they now?' listings. Number one on the page was 'P.D. Walden'.

Zoe had been just thirteen when *The Professor with the Wandering Hands* was released and the book meant nothing to her. It was not until she got to college and discovered *Wandering Hands* was on everyone's Kindle that she read it and fell in love with the story. Ashley was every woman who had ever caught the eye of a lecherous male professor, and Ashley's tale of revenge was so satisfying that Zoe would re-read the last hundred pages three or four times each year.

Zoe knew P.D. Walden had not written another book, but learning that she had deliberately dropped out of public sight was new and fascinating information. A Google search and a perusal of the half-dozen blog and websites devoted to the writer explained why EN wanted to be the organization that found the woman who, presumably, was the 'real' Ashley and tell her story to the world.

Via posts, multiple visitors to internet sites detailed their own, unsuccessful searches. Some were as uninspired as simply trolling on-line white pages, but a few had tried a more intelligent methodology. The first hurdle was determining which school Walden had attended when she wrote the book. Her publisher's squib said Walden attended a 'large, Southern California college' which could be any of a dozen schools. The fictional 'Topanga College' seemed to indicate Los Angeles. But one enterprising researcher with a copy of the first independently published Kindle noted that the earlier draft's setting was 'Westside University'. To that reader, only the University of California at Los Angeles fit the geographical context. The reader further buttressed his conclusion by pointing out that the earlier version referenced several existing restaurants on Westwood Blvd. that were changed to fictional ones when the book was picked up by Simon and Schuster.

Zoe went through the clues each blogger or blog contributor posted. Walden was assumed to be a major in English or creative writing, but there was nothing written by a UCLA student in any university-affiliated publication. Moreover, UCLA itself, citing privacy laws, pointedly declined to assist in identifying any student or graduate named 'Walden'. It might even be a pseudonym.

Zoe wondered if there might be other clues in that earlier version of the story. It had long since been withdrawn by Amazon, but bootleg copies must be out there. A few clicks proved that they indeed were. Zoe downloaded one.

For the rest of the day, Zoe Matthews ignored texts and news alerts. She immersed herself in a nine-year-old story that still read as raw as one completed last week.

* * * * *

Allie returned to Penny's office at 7 p.m. The lab rats had decamped for dinner or home, giving the two women a quiet office.

Allie carried a large white paper bag. "Mainely Burgers," she said. "I took a guess you'd like yours medium."

Penny had not thought about dinner. Rather, she had spent much of the afternoon wondering if her best course of action was to pack a suitcase and look for the first flight out of Boston to a country where the populace spoke a language into which *Wandering Hands* had never been translated.

It was disturbing that someone just eighteen years old had deduced her identity using such simple logic. But then Allie was obviously not an average teenager. She appeared to have inherited her mother's intelligence. She was inordinately bright and inquisitive; far more adult than child.

But the need to seek revenge against her father seemed more of an adolescent fantasy. She had spent an hour researching Brian LaPointe. The man seemed to be universally admired for 'saving' New England Green as well as for his advocacy of community agriculture. *The Boston Globe* had just run a glowing profile of the organization's fifteen gardens in inner-city locations in Boston, Brockton, Chelsea, Chicopee, and Lawrence; growing produce on vacant lots and teaching adults and children the basics of good gardening. Brian was photographed at the Brockton site, showing a seven-year-old Syrian refugee girl how to harvest spinach.

Was it possible that a man who seemed so selfless could also be the monster Allie painted him as being?

"Along with the hamburgers, I hope you brought some evidence," Penny said.

"More than enough to get us started," replied Allie. From her purse she extracted an iPad and opened a file. She began pulling up photos of brokerage statements and memoranda of purchases and sales.

"I'm still trying to get the hang of this finance stuff," Allie said, "but what's going on here is reasonably evident. Every time someone gives New England Green a piece of land and establishes an endowment for it, ten percent of the funds get set aside into a special fund. Brian, in his wisdom as Executive Director, allocates that money for engineering, environmental and legal work supposedly related to the piece of land. The cute part is that he manages to make a series of deposits into his account at a place called 'Pilgrim State Investments' that total the exact amount of that special fund. The Pilgrim State account doesn't belong to New England Green – it's in Brian's name. He's skimming ten percent, right off the top."

Penny stared at the screens, trying to make sense of them. Finance had never been her forte. She could read a mass spectrometer's output as easily as a newspaper and follow a complex chemical reaction as it unfolded. But numbers in columns either held no interest or seemed to swim around on the screen.

"Help me out," Penny said. "This is a foreign language to me."

Allie swiped at her iPad, looking for a particular screen shot. "This is from seven years ago," she said. "The Brewster family gave $400,000 as an endowment on land in Ayer." She pointed to a legend at the bottom of a bank check. "$40,000 deposited separately for Discretionary Administrative Account." She flipped to the next screen. "Here are New England Green checks totaling $40,000 written to lawyers and surveyors, all signed by my father. Two weeks later, Pilgrim State Investments records five deposits totaling $40,000 with the annotation, 'Brewster'. This is repeated thirty or forty times. Only the amount varies. The biggest was for $150,000. I totaled up nearly five million dollars up to the time he moved out."

"Don't auditors catch these kind of things?" Penny asked.

Allie shook her head. "I'd need to do a lot more research on that before I could answer you. My guess is that if you move it around to enough accounts, it gets lost. Or, supposedly spent, except that it hasn't been spent. All I know is, it ends up in his account."

"And what is Pilgrim State Investments?" Penny asked.

Allie tapped a web browser tab and typed the name. "It's a 'boutique wealth management services firm' located on Boylston Street. It is currently closed to new clients."

"How do you know you father is still stealing?" Penny asked.

"Because I read his private email," Allie said, allowing a faint trace of a smile on her face.

"You have access to his email?" Penny said, incredulously.

"Actually, I have access to his computer," Allie said. "I hacked it a year after he left." This time she smiled. "He emailed me trying to be all buddy-buddy; 'I may not live in the house, but I still want to be your father'. He dumps us, then sends me emails telling me it wasn't my fault; blah, blah, blah. So I sent him a Trojan horse. I captured all of his passwords and set up a data logger. Once it was working, I sent him a couple of really obvious malware files embedded in photos. That put an end to his trying to be an absentee parent. But I still get a notification every time he changes a password."

"You did this when you were fifteen?" Penny asked.

"I could have done it when I was twelve," Allie replied with a shrug. "I just didn't have a reason to do it back then."

"So you know how much your father has skimmed?"

"Just about ten million now," Allie said, then added, "Your hamburger is getting cold."

Penny obediently unwrapped the hamburger.

After a bite, Penny said, "You're convinced, though, that your father could talk his way out of this if he was confronted with the evidence. Even by the state's Attorney General."

"I know my father," Allie replied. "He can be the most charming man you will ever meet. He has an answer for every question and he's a master at changing the subject. And, when all else fails, he says he'll 'get back to you tomorrow with all the paperwork'. I've heard him use that one a couple of times."

"Then prove it to me," Penny said. "Show me everything you have."

For the next three hours, Allie and Penny reviewed Brian LaPointe's financial statements until they both understood the extent of the skimming and how it was hidden.

At ten o'clock, Penny said, "So, do you want all that money to go back to New England Green or are you angling to keep some of it as a finder's fee?" The hamburgers had long since been eaten and they were now scrounging chips and candy bars from the Pheromonix cafeteria.

Allie did not answer immediately. "I don't need it," she said after perhaps thirty seconds. "MIT is giving me the full ride, and it's not because of Helga. And this place is doing OK by her." Allie swept her hand to indicate she meant Pheromonix. "Finder's fee? I don't know. Maybe. The problem is that no one at New England Green can see my father for who he is. No one questions him. That doesn't say a lot about the organization."

It was Penny's turn to take her time responding. She deliberately took another bite of a Snickers bar. "Did your mother ever see your father for what he really was?"

Allie looked up, startled by the question. "My father left his family. Just came in one day and said he 'needed to be free'. Did Helga know it was coming? No. It hit her hard. She cried a lot those first few months. But then she stopped crying and started telling me things: signs, she called them. He was around rich people all day and he wanted to be one of them, not just like them. She said he was a poor farm boy who was smart and got lucky, but who never got over having started off as that kid in dirty overalls."

"But you said she looked at the brokerage statements and said they were just part of New England Green," Penny said.

"She said he didn't have it in him to steal," Allie replied. "Obviously she was wrong."

"Should Helga know what you're planning to do?" Penny

asked. She took another bite of the hamburger.

Allie was silent. "What do you think?" she asked after almost a minute.

"I think you don't want to blindside her," Penny said. "This is going to affect her, too. I think you want her as your ally. I'll bet she knows things about your father that you don't."

"You have something in mind, don't you?" Allie asked, her voice rising with excitement.

"Just a general outline," Penny said.

"Tell me."

Penny collected her thoughts. "If you have his passwords, you could empty out those accounts tonight. The problem is that, tomorrow morning, that firm you mentioned – Pilgrim State Investments – will see the transaction. They'll call your father and ask if that's what he intended to do. When he says, 'no', they'll cancel the transfers and then start looking for the person who initiated them." Penny added, "Believe me, this is something I know about."

"So, what we have to do is figure out a way to have him hand over the money back to New England Green. And then he has to confess publicly that he stole the money."

"He'd never do any of that," Allie said.

"You'd be surprised at what people who think they're above the law will do," Penny said. "Let's plan to talk to Helga Monday morning."

Chapter Six

Emily Taylor Rice had closed the door to her office more than half an hour earlier, telling Darlene she wanted no calls and no disturbances. Her hands were still shaking and she had yet to ponder any conclusions, let alone courses of action.

Two names ricocheted through her mind: Christian Karl Gerhartsreiter and Sandra Boss. Those two names had been imprinted on her mind for almost a decade. They were the characters in a cautionary, all-too-real-life tale of a woman in love, duped by a man, and having her life nearly destroyed because of that love.

Am I to be the next Sandra Boss, she thought, her heart thumping against her chest wall.

It had started innocently, just two days ago. She was looking for a surprise gift for Brian. Something he wouldn't see coming. She settled on the idea of a getaway trip to an unusual destination. It should be to a place that had meaning to Brian, rather than to her. All the places they had gone over the past four years were to the haunts of *her* circle of friends. This one would be all about Brian.

The destination had come to her in a bolt of inspiration. It was there every time she was in Brian's office. The diploma from Leeds. The issue date was twenty years ago this summer.

There must be a reunion planned by the University. Alumni giving was the lifeblood of American universities and the same must be true of those in Great Britain. A quick web search showed that, indeed, the Leeds College Alumnae gathered each August for a long weekend of reunion activities. And, like their American brethren, five year increments marked the big push for securing attendance. There, in the shadow of the institution that had nurtured their minds, well-trained university staff planted the seed that a gift to one's school was not an act of charity but, rather, recognition of and appreciation for the role played by that college.

As part of its reunion activities, Leeds Beckett University, as Brian's alma mater was now known, was hosting a colloquium on crop genetics and sustainable agriculture. It was perfect, she thought. An American alumnus coming for his twentieth reunion – and who was head of one of the most distinguished U.S. land trusts – might be a worthy addition to a panel on one of those subjects.

Her aide, Darlene, had tracked down the Chair of the colloquium and Emily had made the call herself. That was two days earlier. She explained to Sir Charles Pickney that she was whisking her fiancée – she had reluctantly fudged the nature of their relationship but wanted to convey their closeness – to Leeds as a surprise for his twentieth doctoral reunion, and that he would be a distinguished addition to their roster. She had followed the conversation with an emailed copy of Brian's c.v. and several glowing profiles from magazines. Sir Charles promised to respond within two days.

She had spent those two days in a state of heightened satisfaction with her ingenuity. She had also researched several suitable hotels and restaurants. This would be a trip to remember. August was just a few months away, and she tingled with excitement.

The return call had come forty minutes earlier. Sir Charles had been extraordinarily courteous; even apologetic. Brian LaPointe's credentials were indeed superlative; just the kind of across-the-pond figure to enhance the stature of the event.

This was where he faltered. "However, we have done an exhaustive search of our records," he said. "Exceedingly diligent. Even spoken to some of the older faculty. The truth of the matter is that we did not grant a doctoral degree to anyone by that name twenty years ago, nor in any other year."

And no one by the name of Brian LaPointe has ever been enrolled at Leeds Polytechnic either as a graduate or undergraduate, Sir Charles told her. The only Brian LaPointe ever to have enrolled at Leeds College did so in the 1950s, and did not earn a degree.

Sir Charles offered the names of two or three homophonic academic institutions with horticultural programs and suggested she might contact those schools if she still wanted it to be a surprise. "Otherwise," he counseled, "just ask him for the proper name."

He added one nugget of information. "The chaps in alumni relations knew your fiancé's name as soon as I mentioned it because they cull the web for prospective donors. They assumed it was a misprint or some other transcription error. Actual misrepresentation at that level is almost unheard of."

Emily, of course, had seen the diploma. The crest of the college was unmistakable and the name on the certificate was his. There was only one conclusion to draw.

She thanked Sir Charles for his efforts and for the inadvertent confusion she had caused. That was when she told Darlene to stop all calls.

The conversation explained certain things. UMass continually peppered Brian with 'alumni only' offers, so his degree from that college was genuine. But now she knew why there had never been comparable overtures from Leeds. Barely a week went by that she did not receive a communication from Dartmouth inviting her to become more deeply involved in the alumni association, including regular Boston-area dinners and even nights at the BSO.

It also explained how a twenty-two-year-old American could obtain an advanced degree from a British university in so brief a period of time. The one time she had asked, Brian had said there was nothing to do in West Yorkshire but study. And, his fellowship stipend had a time limit on it, so he worked twice as hard. After all, he said, he had graduated from UMass at twenty, completing four year's education in three. Also, it explained why Brian never mentioned his degree to anyone unless specifically asked. Any effort to append "Doctor" to his name as an honorific was met with a rebuff. He explained his reticence by saying that only medical professionals should use the honorific; for anyone else, it was unwarranted boasting.

But all this left one indisputable fact: the man with whom she was living had a fraudulent degree hanging on his wall. He had obtained employment from New England Green using that degree, and she was relatively certain it was a factor in the decision to make him Executive Director eighteen years earlier.

The indisputable fact opened the door to a frightening but unanswerable question: what else about him might be fraudulent?

This was where the name Sandra Boss weighed on her mind. Boss was a graduate of Stanford with an MBA from Harvard. She was a rainmaker at McKinsey; not just pulling down a huge compensation, but reigning as one of the world's most sought-after experts in risk management. In 1995, Boss married a man who said his name was Clark Rockefeller and that he was a member of that distinguished family. They were married for nine years until her husband's erratic behavior and emotional abusiveness caused her to file for divorce. In 2008, during a supervised visitation, 'Clark Rockefeller' kidnapped their seven-year-old daughter. The resulting week-long national manhunt raised the question of who 'Clark Rockefeller' really was. His true identity - Christian Karl Gerhartsreiter – was ascertained two weeks later. That notoriety, in turn, led to Gerhartsreiter being identified as a long-missing suspect in a California murder investigation. Gerhartsreiter was convicted of that murder in 2013.

Through all of these events was the continuing – and in Emily's view morbid – fascination with the question of how Sandra Boss could have been deceived for so many years and how a successful, intelligent woman could have not only married an imposter, but a man who turned out to be a murderer. In court, Boss said there was a difference between intellectual intelligence and emotional intelligence.

Emily had been just two years out of Amos Tuck when the search for 'Clark Rockefeller' first brought unwanted attention to Boss. Emily read everything she could find on the McKinsey executive, even calling some of the sources interviewed in a Vanity Fair article, *The Man in the Rockefeller Suit*. She stopped seeing a former business school classmate because she caught him in a series of small lies. They were ridiculous things but, to Emily, telling. He boasted of having played tennis with Matt Damon. He claimed to have learned to skydive. Her beau confessed he had simply embellished his life story to make himself more interesting to her. She refused to ever see him again.

Am I the next Sandra Boss? Emily asked herself. Is claiming a bogus degree a signal that something is seriously corrupt inside a person, or is it a one-time aberration? Brian had made no secret of his humble origins. Heading for Williamstown one weekend, he had made the detour off of Route 2 to show her the derelict remains of the farm that had once been his home. And his stellar work at New England Green was a matter of public record; he had turned a flailing, directionless organization into a model of not-for-profit stewardship. His compensation as Executive Director - $625,000 a year – should certainly place him beyond the need to steal.

But there was also the matter of Brian's divorce. Few divorced couples remain on friendly terms with their former spouses, but children were another matter. Once a father always a father. However, his estrangement from his family was complete. Brian had told her that his daughter – Alexandra? – blamed the divorce entirely on him and would have nothing to do with him. He once even showed her emails that were as caustic as they were profane.

That was one seriously angry adolescent.

Emily was left with a dilemma. The man she loved – and had privately concluded she would marry – had at least one stain on his record that could not be eradicated. Moreover, it was the kind of transgression that could not be overlooked. She had dealt with credentials misrepresentation on three of the Boards of Directors on which she served. In every case, the executive who padded his résumé was quietly let go. Stellar performance and position in the organization were not mitigating factors.

Emily had no formal association with New England Green. Though she personally knew several of that organization's Trustees, she had no responsibility to call anyone's attention to Brian's misrepresentation. Legally, she was innocent of any wrongdoing.

But ethically…

The biggest minefield was her own reputation. Everyone knew Brian lived with her in the house on Crow Point. There was no longer even the pretense that he rented her townhouse on Beacon Hill. They had been inseparable for four years and it was assumed that he was 'the one'. Her friends told her Brian was 'a great catch' and 'the perfect guy' and if Emily was to have a family, 'she needed to get a move on'.

She began making notes on a yellow legal pad. She outlined 'Scenario A': *I explain to Brian what I know and how I came to know it. I tell him he has to step down from NEG for health or other reasons and bluntly explain to him the consequences of not doing so…*

Do I also tell him I'm leaving him? She thought this but did not commit it to paper. *Do I tell him he has to move out and give him a deadline? Do I be honest and explain that I can't be caught in a scandal if he was forced to step down when his forged credentials became public?*

Emily sighed and wrote 'Scenario B' on a new page. *I tell him that I'm breaking up with him. No explanation.* She looked at the last sentence and crossed it out. *I tell him simply that he's not the one. I'm going somewhere out of the country for three months and I expect him to have moved out before I return.*

Emily thought to herself, *And then, a few months or a year later, do I quietly let it be known that his academic credentials are suspect, or do I wait for someone else to discover it at some point in the future?*

She wrote below those lines, *Do I need to find out what else he may have done?*

And then she wondered if she was already in some jeopardy. The news about Brian breaks, the college is contacted and Sir Charles Pickney says to a reporter, *"Yes, an American woman called some time ago. Said she was his fiancée…"*

She turned the page and started writing again. *Scenario C. I go public with what I know and to hell with the consequences. I did what I knew was ethically demanded. People think whatever they're predisposed to think.*

To that she added, *At least they won't think I'm Sandra Boss.*

MONDAY

Chapter Seven

Penny Walden had devoted much of her weekend to reading everything she could find that mentioned Brian LaPointe and New England Green. He was part of, for lack of a better description, Boston royalty and the organization he headed was revered around the region for its environmental good deeds. Every issue of *Boston* magazine bore at least one photo of him, usually on the arm of Emily Taylor Rice.

There were several profiles of him, including some in national and international periodicals. He espoused a philosophy that, while creating 'forever wild' parcels of land was a noble undertaking, acreage near cities should serve recreational and agricultural purposes as well. His words as well as his ideas seemed thoughtful; hardly those of a man who was engaged in theft on such a grand scale.

Older articles mentioned that he was married and lived in an historic house in Cambridge. No newspaper or magazine in the past four years spoke of his divorce, and more recent publications excluded any reference to marital status.

Penny concluded Brian LaPointe reveled in the glow of public admiration. He loved being in the camera's field of view. In video clips, he was the one who stopped to chat with reporters and offer the succinct, carefully crafted sound bites that made the 11 o'clock news.

Penny found Emily Taylor Rice an intriguing figure. She looked to be in her mid-thirties and was more than just attractive; she was beautiful. She was the heiress to two fortunes and seemed intent upon giving it away; always to noble causes. She also worked for a living. She headed the foundation that bore her family's name yet found time to be an activist director for four S&P500

corporations. The MBA from the Tuck School proved she was smart.

So, why hadn't she figured out her boyfriend was a crook?

There were no long profile pieces on Emily. Apart from those charity dinner photos of her, she maintained a polite screen of privacy from the rest of the world. Penny concluded that Emily Taylor Rice simply had no use for celebrity or its trappings.

Which made the woman a kindred spirit to Penny. And, when her boyfriend was exposed as a world-class embezzler, it would make her look, at best, foolish and, at worst, complicit. The woman in those clippings didn't deserve to be held up to ridicule. Any plan Penny dreamed up needed to take into account the reputation of Emily Taylor Rice.

When she had exhausted the subject of Brian LaPointe, Penny turned her attention to the stack of printouts and reports from Pheromonix's R&D efforts during the past year.

It was, she quickly saw, a comedy of errors. Every chemical marker that seemed to hold even the slightest promise was replicated in the laboratory and tested on cats, almost always with unintended results. Researchers had identified substances that would attract cats of every breed, that would cause male cats to act as though an impregnable female was nearby, and that would invoke a command to certain breeds of cats to yowl incessantly. Each of these molecules – more than a hundred thus far – was charted and accompanied with notes on production options.

Pheromonix, at least as far as these reports were concerned, was no closer to a universal cat repellant than it had been on the day the company was organized. Yet there was a staff of exceptionally bright people who kept toiling away, seemingly unaware of their failure.

Penny could glimpse a reason why she had been recruited to this Manhattan-Project-style research project. She knew the science and hers were the only set of eyes that had not been dulled by repetition.

She called a pizza delivery service and began going through the analyses of experiments, page by page.

* * * * *

Helga Johanssen was more than a little surprised to see her daughter and her newest researcher in her doorway on Monday morning. Allie's face showed excitement and anticipation. Penny's showed lack of sleep and wariness.

Helga took a long drink of coffee from her second container of the day and beckoned them to come in.

"Are you together or is this serendipity?" she asked.

Allie answered first. "We need to talk to you about something really important."

Helga looked at Penny for confirmation.

Penny nodded and said, "We do need a block of your time."

Helga looked at her schedule. There was nothing pressing until early afternoon. She had a vague sense of unease. Her daughter had shown more than the usual interest in Penny Walden's résumé, and it was not uncommon for Allie to introduce herself to new employees. But there was a different relationship at work here. One she did not readily understand.

"Tell me what this is all about," Helga said.

"Your ex-husband," Penny said. "Brian LaPointe. Do you ever hear from him?"

It was the last question Helga expected to hear from someone who had started work just a week earlier.

"We had a final settlement conference in a lawyer's office. That was three-and-a-half years ago," Helga said. "Any further discussions were between the lawyers. I have neither seen nor heard from Brian since that day."

"Allie says she showed you financial statements for about two years before the separation," Penny said. "Did you ever…"

"Stop," Helga said. "Whatever this conversation is about, it doesn't involve you. You are here as a research scientist, not a marriage counselor."

"She's a lot more than a research scientist, Helga," Allie said.

Helga looked at her daughter and then back at Penny. "What's going on here?"

"You hired a ringer," Allie said. "Oh, she's a real scientist. And an uncommonly good one from what I can tell. But you also hired P.D. Walden."

The name meant nothing to Helga.

"*The Professor with the Wandering Hands*," Allie prompted. "Penny wrote that."

"Is that fiction or non-fiction?" Helga asked, still not comprehending.

Exasperated, Allie said, "You watched me read that book fifteen or twenty times when I was twelve or thirteen. I dragged you to see the movie."

"I genuinely don't remember," Helga said. "I'm sorry."

Allie walked over to her mother and took her hands. "What you need to know is that, in addition to hiring someone who is a top-notch researcher on pheromones, you also got someone who is a world-class authority on smart revenge."

"Why do we need an authority on revenge?" Helga asked.

"Because Brian walked out on us," Allie replied. "Because he upended our lives; dumped us for a better deal. Took up with a rich bitch…"

"Stop," Helga said for the second time. Penny noted that, whatever dynamic was at work between mother and daughter, Allie never ignored her mother's command. She had stopped in mid-sentence.

"Penny," Helga said, turning her attention to her new researcher. "How did you come to be involved with this 'revenge' thing my daughter is talking about?"

"Allie came to see me last Friday," Penny said. "She had

correctly deduced my 'alter-ego' identity. She asked me…"

Helga interrupted. "This 'P.D. Walden' identity. Is it one you would rather people not know about?"

Penny nodded. "I wrote the book when I was much younger. It gave me a certain notoriety that I'd rather not relive. It turned me into an exceedingly private person that way."

Helga nodded. "Then you did not offer your help," she said. "My daughter approached you…" She paused. "Allie threatened you." She said the words as a statement of fact.

Helga turned her gaze to her daughter. "You threatened her with – what? – exposure? You knew she is private person and so you threatened to tell the world where to find her?"

After a moment's hesitation, Allie said, "Yes."

Helga stared at Allie for several seconds, a look of repressed anger on her face. Then she looked at Penny. "You have my word that my daughter will never disclose your identity to anyone. I will make clear to her the repercussions of doing so. And, if you believe that your being recruited to work here was in any way influenced by Allie suspecting your other identity, you may feel free to leave at any time. I will do my utmost to ensure that being here for so brief a period of time does not leave a stain on your résumé…"

"I want to help," Penny interrupted.

"Pardon?" Helga said.

"After I heard Allie's evidence, I did my own research. I made up my mind I was going to help her. Hear what Allie has to say," Penny replied. "Please, just do that."

Helga turned to Allie. "Tell me."

"In addition to his other faults, Brian is an embezzler," Allie said. "He has stolen something like ten million dollars from New England Green."

"How do you know this?" Helga asked.

Allie shrugged. "I keep tabs on his computer."

"Is that legal?" Helga asked, and then answered her own

question. "Of course, it's not legal. Why would you do that?"

Allie replied, "I knew something was wrong seven or eight years ago. I tried to tell you about it but you said it was just bank records from his work. I started taking photos of them. It took me a while to figure out what he was doing. After he tried to get back in touch with me…"

"He tried to get in touch with you?" Helga asked.

"He emailed me a year after he left," Allie said. "Said he would be there if I needed something. Total bull. So, I sent him a Trojan horse. It got me into his accounts. He had already stolen five million by the time he left. He's just about doubled that in the past four years."

"So, take what you know to the police," Helga said. "They'll arrest him."

"You know and I know that won't happen," Allie said sharply. "Mister Smooth will talk his way out of it. It's the thing he does best."

"Then tell me what you know," Helga said. And, for the next hour, Allie produced what were now printouts of the screen shots and documents she had photographed over the years.

Penny marveled at the degree of organization Allie had brought to the project in just a weekend. What had been a jumbled compendium of images stored on a phone was now a coherent narrative with highlighted words and numbers. Allie was more than just a bright young woman. She was someone with a mind that functioned at a level far higher than any eighteen year old she knew. Her analyses were sharp and her arguments crisp. *How will she use those talents?* Penny wondered.

"I completely missed it," Helga said when Allie had finished her presentation. Her look seemed far away. "I was completely focused on my own work. Brian lived in one world, I lived in another and those two worlds never met. He had big ambitions. And, apparently, a need for money. He grew up poor. But becoming Executive Director gave him a big salary and us quite a nice house. I would think that would have been enough."

Helga snapped out of her reverie. "What do you want from me?"

"Nothing," Penny said. "I told Allie I wouldn't help her unless you had full knowledge of what we were planning."

"And just what are you planning?" Helga asked.

"A way to get back the money he stole and to get him to confess what he did," Penny replied. "And, before you ask, I'm still working out a plan."

Helga asked, "How can I help?"

It was Allie who responded. "This is my war, not yours."

"Maybe it's mine, too," Helga said quietly.

Allie and Penny were quiet.

"I still think about Brian," Helga said. "Probably more than is healthy. We were two people who had only science in common; that plus a physical attraction. I was five years older than Brian and, in hindsight, marrying someone with so little to talk about was an enormous mistake. I thought that in five years or ten years, the age difference would not matter. Instead, it was always there. I was always more mature. But he was ambitious; almost the antithesis of the men I had known in Sweden."

"He cherished Allie when she was born, but I'm reasonably certain he stopped loving me. I don't know that there was anyone else; he just stopped being interested in me as a woman. I took it hard and began to focus on my lab work and on raising Allie. By then, of course, he was established at New England Green and was making a name for himself. And he shut me out of that. It was almost as though I did not exist."

"When he left it was not so much that he rejected me, but that he also rejected Allie. And he did all of this in order to be with another woman – one who, interestingly, with more of an age difference than there was between the two of us. Of course, she is younger, and I suppose that is something important to a man. And she is wealthy – an heiress…"

Helga must have realized she was rambling. She looked at Allie and Penny. "I'm sorry. I keep that part of my life in a box. But what Allie has found…" Helga indicated her daughter's computer with her chin. "Allie has demonstrated fairly conclusively that Brian is a thief. And, apparently, we are the only people who know about it."

She paused for a moment, choosing her words. "For most of the past four years I have deluded myself into thinking that his leaving was my fault; that I was not a good enough wife and mother to keep him.   I have slowly come to realize that he left simply because he was tired of me – and had been so for quite some time – and he met someone younger, prettier, a lot of money, and the right social cachet.   And so one night he came home and announced he was leaving. He did not give a thought to me or to Allie and how it would affect us – change our lives. In short, he was and is a bastard. Finding out that he is stealing from the same organization that entrusts its future to him is all I need to know that going after him is not only justified, but the right thing to do." She looked first at Penny and then at Allie. "Count me in. I will do whatever I can to bring him to justice."

It was Penny that broke the silence that followed. "Give me until later on today. Then, I'll tell you what I've been thinking."

Chapter Eight

Zoe Matthews had printed six articles that might hold the key to locating P.D. Walden. The printout on top profiled Michelle Ketchum, P.D. Walden's one-time literary agent. It had been written about six months after the hardcover publication of *Wandering Hands* and Ketchum's career was in high gear. In interviewing Ketchum, the author of the article had asked two penetrating questions, the answers to which Zoe has circled: how Ketchum had tracked down the student author, and why P.D. Walden sought anonymity when millions of fans wanted another book and, especially, another book about revenge.

The author quoted Ketchum as saying, "Finding P.D. took more than a month because no one knew who she was, everyone I spoke with had a different theory, and each theory pointed in a different direction. None of the logical or straightforward assumptions panned out, so I decided to follow the money. I called in favors and I didn't take 'that's impossible' for an answer. When I finally had her number, calling her was the bravest thing I had ever done."

'Follow the money.' So, Zoe thought, *Ketchum probably had a source inside Amazon who looked up the author's contact information, or perhaps Walden's bank information. Nice trick if you have the contacts.*

On the privacy question, Ketchum said, "P.D. had no expectations for the book and so was completely overwhelmed by its success. She was and is a shy and private person. She even asked me about hiring a stand-in to do personal appearances. My assistant spent half her time coaxing P.D. to do interviews…"

So there was an assistant, Zoe thought. Her research showed that Ketchum and Walden had parted company just a month or two after the magazine article appeared, and no agent took Ketchum's place. Probably because of a contractual agreement, Ketchum had never revealed P.D.'s real name or her whereabouts, but a former assistant might be more forthcoming, especially in return for some media exposure. Of course, assistants came and went from literary agencies with frightening speed. The chance that one might still be at the firm seven years later was near zero.

Michelle Ketchum's literary agency website showed photos of two youngish women. They would have been in high school when P.D. Warren was a client, so contacting them had no value. But Zoe had a wonderful tool at her disposal: the 'Wayback Machine'. A website called 'archive.org' indexed billions of web pages going back more than a decade. She typed in the website's name and, almost magically, was rewarded with a list of dates on which a screen shot of the page had been taken. She selected one from seven years earlier, hit 'enter' and watched as the same photo of Ketchum that appeared on the current site greeted would-be writers.

Vanity, thought Zoe.

But the rest of the website reflected a time nearly a decade earlier, including just one earnest, young face. It belonged, according to the caption, to Elaine Yamamoto.

A Google search turned up more than a million results for the name and hundreds of Facebook entries. A LinkedIn search coupled with a refinement for 'literary' or 'writer' trimmed the list to 32 names.

My fallback position, Zoe concluded, scrolling through names, then thought to try one more refinement: 'Ketchum'.

A lone entry remained on the screen. Zoe tapped her screen to see details. Elaine Yamamoto, now an associate producer at Marble Arch Productions in Studio City, California, listed Michelle Ketchum Literary Agency among her 'prior employment'.

Zoe tapped the 'Contact' button and wrote an upbeat note saying she was a senior editor at *Entertainment Now*, needed background for a story, and could they talk by phone? She re-read her note, briefly considering downgrading her position to something more believable, but left the title unchanged. She pushed 'Send'.

Three other articles intrigued Zoe. All were local news stories from five years earlier and coincided with the release of the film version of *Wandering Hands*. The articles were about women who claimed to be the model for, or who knew the 'real' Ashley. Zoe noted that there was no indication of anyone stepping forward when the book first came out. It took transforming the slightly dumpy character in the book to the ravishing Emily Blunt to bring would-be Ashleys out of hiding.

The first was Farrah Buettner of Las Vegas, who told the *Las Vegas Sun* that, as a USC sophomore, she had penned an essay for her Creative Writing class that recounted many of the events of the book, including the pseudonym 'Dalrymple' for the libidinous professor. Buettner had read several pages of it aloud in a writer's circle and said a woman in the group, another sophomore, had asked for a copy. The woman was P.D. Walden.

It was a nice story, Zoe concluded, but she was confident that Walden wrote that first giveaway edition while attending UCLA and that Walden would have been an upperclassman.

The second contender was Lizette Robles, who said Penelope Walden was one of her suitemates at UCLA early in her senior year. Walden seldom had dates but loved hearing about Robles' encounters. One night, Robles confessed her two-month fling with an English professor who had an unerring radar for seducible coeds. The professor had just ended the relationship, and Robles and Walden spent the night concocting outrageous revenge scenarios. Robles thought no more about the evening, even after she heard about an e-book circulating on campus. The next month, Robles left Los Angeles to spend a semester in Spain. She returned to find Walden had left school and that a mysterious e-book had morphed into a publishing sensation, with everyone on campus trying to figure out who was the doomed 'Professor Dalrymple'.

Robles' story had appeared in the *Houston Chronicle* under the headline, 'Cypress Station Woman Says She Is Model for Film's Amanda'. Robles was now – or was five years ago – in the Public Relations office of ExxonMobil.

The story had a ring of truth to it, Zoe thought. It was the right school and the timing was accurate. Moreover, Robles was in PR. P.D. Walden would likely also be in advertising, PR, or some spinoff of journalism that required good storytelling skills.

The third news story was *The Oregonian* and told of a Portland woman named Beth Kingsbury who said she did not realize she was the model for Ashley until she saw the film. "I'm not much of a reader and Patsy never told me she was going to write about the things I told her," Kingsbury told the newspaper. "After seeing the film, I went back and read the book and discovered that I was the woman in the story. I was Ashley."

Zoe crumpled the sheet of paper and threw it into a wastebasket.

The final item was a response to a review of *Wandering Hands* on the Internet Movie Database. The reviewer – not a professional – had savaged the film for not being true to the book and for 'sexing up' Ashley.

The response read, *I knew the real Ashley as well as the person who wrote as P.D. Walden. In fact, she was my lab partner and we got to know one another quite well. She couldn't have written about her own experiences because I doubt she had five dates in the time I knew her. The real Ashley – her roommate – was a looker, but I suspect P.D. made her less sexy in the book because it was more true to P.D.'s perception of herself. So, don't go hard on Hollywood for casting Blunt. Professors – at least at UCLA – don't make passes at girls who wear lab smocks and smell of formaldehyde.*

Zoe pondered this last item. It was unsigned, though a viewer could leave a comment that would, in theory, trigger a notification to the writer. It was an intriguing claim with a wealth of clues in a single paragraph. It mentioned UCLA but it also spoke of Walden as a 'lab partner' and mentioned 'formaldehyde', implying Walden was taking science courses. Also, there was no boasting; just a recitation of a few facts.

Zoe found the IMBD site and the review. She typed, *Do you still keep in touch with Ms. Walden? Drop me a line.* Zoe included her personal email address. She then went to work on Facebook and LinkedIn looking for Lizette Robles.

* * * * *

Brian LaPointe prided himself on possessing a keen instinct for spotting nearly imperceptible changes in other people's behavior. He sensed one in Emily's attitude toward him. Last Tuesday she had been almost giddy with pleasure about something. And, from four years of knowing her, he knew that she most often displayed that behavior when she was pleased with herself for coming up with what she believed to be an original or clever idea. In time she would tell him about it, reinforcing his assurance that he knew Emily better than she knew herself.

The giddiness had lasted three days. Then, as quickly as it had arrived, it was replaced with an unspoken sense of something like melancholy. Emily's Big Idea apparently not only had not panned out; it had backfired. That, too, had happened before. Once, she thought she had uncovered a nonprofit grant recipient with a truly innovative business plan. Closer inspection showed a glaring gap between execution experience and ambition. Usually, by now, Emily would have come to him with her tale of disappointment and he would have consoled her. He would then have praised her for not throwing additional resources into a dead-end idea.

But not this time. On Friday afternoon, Emily called him to say she had to go to New York for the weekend on what she called 'Foundation business'. She was both friendly and apologetic about the short notice but, after the phone call, there was only silence.

There were no calls, texts, or emails. Usually, when she was away on business, he would receive two or three 'thinking about you' messages.

With no formal social obligations, he had spent most of the weekend in his office, reviewing budgets and a new fundraising appeal. New England Green did not need to raise money, of course; its endowment generated more than enough income to cover the organization's expenses. But Brian had learned two decades ago that, unless a nonprofit organization periodically rattled its tin cup, would-be patrons forgot about the importance of the group's mission. And so New England Green was about to raise $50 million to preserve the imperiled Little Androscoggin River watershed.

Brian had chosen the project himself by more or less opening the *Maine Atlas* to a random page and finding out which river was represented by the meandering blue line. The fundraising project was, in his view, secondary (and maybe even tertiary). He had no idea if the Little Androscoggin River's watershed was threatened. The goal was simply to mobilize donors and give members a reason to check the box for an additional donation. 'Save the Little Androscoggin' would be New England Green's battle cry for the next twelve months.

The lone downside to the appeal, in his view, was that there was no way to skim money from the project. It was a discrete undertaking, and tapping it for personal gain might arouse the curiosity of otherwise somnambulant auditors and trustees. Of course, he could always invent a consultant or two...

He brought his attention back to the real subject at hand: Emily Taylor Rice. She had returned Sunday evening, said she had a pounding headache, and said she needed rest because she had a full Monday schedule. This morning she had offered no insight to the 'Foundation business' that had taken her to New York nor a summary of what lay ahead of her today. Her car had appeared twenty minutes earlier than usual and she left without explanation.

In his office he gave a mental shrug. Things were still moving swiftly along toward a wedding. Emily wanted children. Time was running short. He was, in his view, the ideal father.

When he saw her this evening, he would poke Emily about what had happened in New York. Get things fully back on course.

He went back to his paperwork but found he was bored. So he instead placed a call from a phone he kept in his top desk drawer. The ever-eager Amber Oakes in Development answered immediately. She, of course, was not working on anything special. She would leave her office immediately and have drinks ready upon his arrival and, from there, they could 'chill and Netflix'. He had never heard that term until he met Amber six weeks earlier. 'Chill and Netflix' was the Millennial Generation's all-purpose solution for how two people could amuse themselves on a muggy summer morning. It was a synonym for energetic, commitment-free sex.

God, he thought. *I love interns.*

Chapter Nine

Emily Taylor Rice wanted only to sleep. Since Friday afternoon when she learned that the man with whom she was living had invented a doctoral degree, she had closed her eyes for less than six hours. She had spent the balance of her days and nights in a state of nervous exhaustion.

She had called the one friend in whom she had total confidence. Elaine Farr had been her roommate at Dana Hall. While they had not attended the same colleges or graduate schools, they had both followed professional careers and had remained close friends for more than two decades. Moreover, Elaine had received her law degree from the University of Chicago as did her husband, and a lawyer or two who were both discreet and unquestionably on your side sounded just right to Emily. When she phoned from the Acela to say she needed a shoulder to cry on and a place to stay, Elaine told Emily she would clear her schedule for as much time as was needed.

That first conversation in the Boerum Hill brownstone lasted until three o'clock on Saturday morning. Elaine interrupted only to elicit additional background information. They reached no conclusion; none was expected in that opening round.

For Emily, it was the catharsis that allowed her to hear, for the first time, her thoughts spoken aloud. She knew Elaine would not judge her and she held nothing back.

Over breakfast a few hours later, Elaine asked if it would help if Alan, her husband, joined the conversation. "Not yet," Emily said.

Elaine was tall, svelte, and athletic. Her fair complexion exuded health, her face, intelligence. Over croissants and coffee in the small garden behind the brownstone, Elaine took control of the conversation.

"Your instincts are exactly right," Elaine said. "Brian has too important and visible a position for this to be overlooked. The non-profit world may look at him as 'Saint Brian' but it isn't going to matter when this comes out: he got his job under false pretenses. His Board of Trustees will have no choice but to act."

Elaine took a sip of coffee, looking for a reaction in Emily's face. "And telling him to resign for 'health reasons' isn't going to fly. Unless they have six months to live, 42-year-old men don't step down from positions like that. It's the kind of action that starts people wondering and, once they start asking questions, the answers begin to dribble out. When some enterprising reporter starts checking academic credentials, the dribble will become a flood. The *Times* will put it on page one."

"That's when the blowback hits you," Elaine said, taking Emily's hand. "It won't have been your fault, but neither will it make any difference. When Brian is unmasked, it will make you a public joke and hurt everything you've worked to build."

Emily felt herself choke up. "That was pretty much my conclusion," she said.

"We need a plan and a 'to-do' list," Elaine replied. "And I think Alan needs to be part of the conversation."

* * * * *

It did not require hours of explanation to bring Alan up to speed. Elaine sketched the problem in broad strokes. His area of expertise was patents, where misrepresentation of any kind was the quickest way to call a filing into question.

"On the one hand," he said, "if either Elaine or I had the right kind of clients, we could make Brian disappear." Looking at the two women, he saw that his attempt at humor had failed miserably. "I'm sorry. There's nothing funny about this. It's obvious to me that Brian is completely oblivious to the time bomb he's sitting on, and he has never thought through the damage he'll cause. I suspect the reason that's the case is because he has gotten away with it for twenty years, Brian has assumed he will never get caught. Otherwise, he would never put out the diploma for everyone to see and admire."

Alan turned to Emily. "The way you salvage your reputation is to be the one who blows the whistle. You don't tell him what you're going to do. You don't even hint at it. You don't give him the opportunity to try to talk you out of it or to threaten you. This has to be a thunderbolt."

"A thunderbolt," Emily repeated. "But we live together…"

"I didn't say you did it tomorrow," Alan replied. "I think you'll have time enough to create and follow a plan. I worry that, having contacted Leeds Beckett, you may have started them thinking that they ought to reach out to Brian. But universities move at a glacial pace and it is summer. The timeline I'm thinking about is measured in weeks."

"Then I think we ought to get started," Emily said. Then, a thought came to her. "Brian has an ex-wife and a daughter living in a house owned by New England Green. If Brian is fired for lying about his doctorate, what happens to the two of them?"

Elaine winced. "The Trustees would argue it was a case of fraudulent conveyance based on factual misrepresentation. They'd want their house back, I'm afraid."

Emily nodded slowly. "They share no part of his guilt. I would be surprised if his ex-wife even knew of the deception."

"Do you want to find a way to warn them?" Alan asked.

Emily nodded. "It's the decent thing to do."

"It will be tricky," Alan replied. "But we'll find a way to give them fair warning."

It was Elaine, silent through much of the discussion after Alan entered the conversation, who offered the most cautionary note.

"I've met Brian only a few times," Elaine said. "But what impresses me most about him is his ability to turn adversity to his own advantage. He's exceptionally quick on his feet and he can be extremely persuasive."

"What are you trying to tell me?" Emily asked.

"I'm saying that, instead of denying everything or folding, Brian may say, 'I screwed up twenty years ago, but judge me by what I've accomplished.' You and I live in a world where academic fraud is grounds for automatic dismissal. From what you've told me over the years, Brian has assembled a group of complacent Trustees that just might give him a pass."

"If that happens," Elaine continued, "and he's still standing after the dust settles, then he's going to use every tool at his disposal to get back at you."

Until that moment the idea had not occurred to Emily.

And Elaine's words were the most frightening she had ever heard.

* * * * *

In the course of an afternoon, Penny Walden had discovered an immutable truth: that it was infinitely easier to create a satisfactory act of revenge when you could rearrange facts and events to suit a story line, than it was to stage-manage a plan based on actual people and the moving pieces that constitute real life.

For two hours she had tried to diagram a workable plan. The raw material was certainly there: Brian LaPointe was an embezzler who had walked out on his family to take up with an heiress. He was a man who needed to fall hard. Helping to bring him down to earth would be a pleasure.

But the reality of how to accomplish such a feat was daunting. She knew from her own experience that any attempt to tap Brian's account – other than through his own request – would be met with suspicion and a barrage of phone calls to ensure that everything was legitimate. It could work if Brian's account was at some on-line brokerage firm with hundreds of thousands of accounts, but not one in which an account manager was charged with overseeing

$21 million of assets. Good 'personal bankers' didn't accept instructions from strangers or blindly process emailed withdrawals.

In truth, the right way to deal with Brian LaPointe was to take the information they had gathered, find the right legal authority, and let justice take its course. There would be no clap of thunder when the man was brought down. Instead there would be years of claims and counterclaims and the possibility, if Brian was a smooth a talker as Allie claimed him to be, that he might be cleared of any wrongdoing.

It was now Monday evening. Penny, Helga and Allie were in Helga's office at Pheromonix, a tote bag filled with Chinese takeout occupied one end of Helga's work table; a small whiteboard, taken down from a wall and laid flat, took up the balance of the table. Penny was trying to explain the hopelessness of it all.

"The FBI and the state Attorney General," Penny pleaded. "That's how you bring him down."

"The FBI doesn't care that Brian walked out on us," Allie said sullenly. "Does he get a walk on that?"

"Allie!" Helga said sharply.

Allie shook her head defiantly. "We already have access to most of what we need. We have full access to his financial accounts. We have the passwords for his Facebook and LinkedIn accounts. We also have his Twitter account if we need it, but the first two ought to do it."

"The only way it works is if we magically get Brian to confess and willingly turn over all his assets," Penny said. "That isn't going to happen."

"You can find a way," Allie replied.

"That was fiction," Penny pleaded. "In fiction you create a perfect world and everyone behaves the way you want them to. This is reality. The minute we started liquidating his accounts, any competent banker would call Brian and ask what was going on. And, when Brian says, 'What transfers?', the banker cancels the trades. This Pilgrim State Investments outfit sounds like they specialize in holding the hands of wealthy people. They won't liquidate an account without authenticating the request."

"So we dictate a set of instructions for that money manager, and run them through Auto-Tune until we get a voice that sounds like Brian's," Allie suggested.

Penny sighed and shook her head. "I have my book earnings with a money management firm. They're not dumb. They also want to talk. They schmooze for a living. They wouldn't buy a machine-altered voice for an instant."

"So, we take this to the authorities," Helga concluded.

"No!" Allie shouted. "He goes down. And so does his girlfriend."

"I don't think she's part of his scheme," Penny said. "I read as much as I could find about her this weekend. She is a good person and an innocent party in all of this…"

Allie cut Penny off. "She can't be that innocent. I don't think it's a coincidence that Brian came home and asked Helga for a divorce and, two days later, he's stashed his stuff at this woman's Beacon Hill townhouse. I'd say they had it all planned. In fact, I'd say…"

"Enough," Helga said sharply to Allie.

"I think she's in it up to her neck," Allie snapped back.

"Give me any piece of evidence," Penny replied. She nodded at Allie's computer. "You have every financial record for the past four years. Show me where she is connected to them."

Allie was silent, a sullen look on her face.

"Allie," Helga said, "you have to separate your feelings. If Penny says we can't do this, then accept it."

"I didn't say we can't do it," Penny said softly. "I just said I don't have the answer yet. I need to keep thinking. To actually put together a plan and a timetable, I have to get to know this Pilgrim State Investments and find out how sharp they are. Their website is really generic; I mean, anyone can be a 'boutique money management firm'. That's meaningless."

"Why don't we just try transferring some money out and see what happens?" Allie asked. "A few thousand dollars."

"We can't do that because it could make everything else unravel if they notice," Penny said. "But here's what you can do: poke around. See if you can find other clients. Pull together a dossier on anyone you can find who is associated with the firm. That will be immensely helpful. Obviously, I need to work a lot more on this plan before we can even think about executing it."

Allie nodded her understanding. It didn't mean she agreed with everything her mother or Penny said. What it meant was that the idea that had burned in her mind ever since she saw Penelope Walden's résumé now was going to come to fruition. She would finally get revenge against her father. And if Penny couldn't come up with a plan, Allie would do it herself.

* * * * *

Zoe Matthews was walking to the Port Authority bus terminal when her phone buzzed. She glanced at the screen and saw an unfamiliar email address. It was probably spam, but Zoe found a space against an office building wall out of the flow of pedestrian traffic and tapped the screen.

Haven't heard from Penny since she left LA for NC, a message said.

Zoe thought back to the post she had seen on – what? – the Internet Movie Database. The author claimed she knew both 'Ashley' and P.D. Walden, and that they had been lab partners. If the writer of the email was being truthful, 'P.D. Walden' was 'Penny' and she had moved to North Carolina. But why? To live? To get married? To write her next book?

Zoe texted back, *Where in NC?* She was tempted to add, *Can we talk?* but thought it might scare off her source.

She waited against the building wall, mumbling, '*come on, come on…*'

Her phone buzzed again. *Duke. PhD program. Probably grad by now.*

Zoe felt her heart beat faster. She was looking for Penny Walden with a doctorate from Duke. Based on the 'formaldehyde' reference, it would be in some area of science. Her degree would likely have been issued in the past two years.

She reversed course and headed back for the offices of *Entertainment Now!* Zoe felt she was closing in on her scoop – her ticket to a real job.

But three frustrating hours later, she was no closer than when she began plugging search terms into Google. Duke offered PhD programs in dozens of areas and there was no list of names in graduating classes. The alumni association offered no useful information and the university's placement office provided only bland statistics.

Frustrated, and aware that the last bus for Paramus left at 10:45 p.m., Zoe went back to the search for Lizette Robles, who had claimed to have been a suitemate of P.D. Walden and was now (or had been five years ago) with ExxonMobil.

Zoe found a Lizette Robles McCullough in The Woodlands on LinkedIn. A further search provided a home phone number. It was 9:45 p.m. in New York; an hour earlier in Houston. Assuming the 'McCullough' meant she had married, Zoe had an idea. She placed the call and crossed her fingers.

"Hi, my name is Zoe Matthews and I'm trying to reach Lizette Robles who went to UCLA. Have I finally found the right person?" Zoe made her voice as friendly as possible.

"May I ask what the call is in reference to?" replied a cautious voice on the other end of the line.

"Well, if this the right Lizette, we lived across the hall from one another. Penny Walden was one of your suitemates. I was Penny's lab partner; the one she said was always screwing up the experiments." Zoe crossed her fingers even more tightly.

"You were one of Debbie Cicirelli's roommates?" the voice said with a note of cautious relief.

"Yeah, that was me. Zoe Matthews. The short brunette, though I wasn't there a lot on account of being in the library or the lab…"

"OK," a relieved voice said. "Zoe Matthews. It's been a long time. How can I help you?"

"Well," Zoe said, "I'm getting married next June…"

"Congratulations!"

"Yeah," Zoe said. "It took him long enough to propose. Anyway, I wanted to send a 'save the date' card to Penny. The last address I had for her was at Duke. It came back today marked as undeliverable, and the email address I have for her is also a 'duke.edu'. I know how Penny values her privacy, but do you have any idea of how I could get an invitation to her?"

"You tried her agent?" Lizette asked.

"I don't think they're on speaking terms." Zoe replied. "Can you think of anyone? The last time I heard from her, she was almost finished with her PhD. I haven't heard anything since…"

"Yes," Lizette said, laughing. "Pheromones for trees. Isn't that a riot?"

The statement electrified Zoe. *'Pheromones for trees…'*

"I certainly didn't see it coming," Zoe said, writing furiously.

"I wish I could help you," Lizette said. "With Penny, though, we have to wait for her to start the conversation. I'm sure she'll get back in touch." Zoe heard the wail of an infant in the background. "Hey, I've got to go. If you talk to Deb, please tell her 'hi' for me. OK?"

The phone went silent and Zoe replaced the receiver, her hand trembling.

'Pheromones for trees…'

Penny Walden received her PhD from Duke. Her subject was pheromones for trees. A quick Google search brought her to a site called 'DukeSpace', which included an electronic repository of masters and doctoral dissertations from students at the university. There was a tab for a keyword search. She typed in 'pheromones'…

Walden, Penelope. Pheromonic Transmission System as a Chemosignal Alert for Lymantria Dispar Invasion Within Quercis Populations'

Zoe looked at her phone. She could just make that last bus. As she left the building, she thought, *'Tomorrow is going to be my lucky day…'*

* * * * *

As requested by Penny, Allie had done further research on Pilgrim State Investments. Now, she leafed through the thin sheaf of printouts that told the cursory tale of the firm. It was, indeed, a registered investment advisory service located in the wealthy Chestnut Hill neighborhood a few miles west of the financial district, but attempts to delve below the surface were frustrating. The firm had been in business for 23 years, had $1.2 billion under management in 131 accounts, and the overwhelming majority of its customers were listed as 'high net worth individuals'. Pilgrim State listed three managers, but the information on them went no further than their education and a listing of the professional exams they had passed.

What was missing were the glowing articles and news of new clients. The firm did not advertise and its website seemed filled entirely with stock photos and generic copy about providing 'superior, individualized service to a discerning clientele'.

Yet, eighteen years ago, her father had entrusted this firm – then five years old – with the money he began skimming from New England Green. How did Brian find the firm and why did he choose it? Did anyone inside Pilgrim State have suspicions about the source of the funds?

Allie pulled up the websites and ratings for three other comparably-sized Boston-area investment advisors. The difference was stark: the other firms openly and aggressively sought new clients; the graphics were bright, and the charts reassuring. The firms each had a dozen or more principals and dozens of employees. A wide range of services were provided with easy-to-understand descriptions. One site even offered to open an on-line dialogue with a representative.

Those similarly sized firms also sought recognition in the media. There were blogs and 'ask an expert' social media forums. One firm highlighted the fact that one of its principals was a consumer financial advisor on a Boston radio station.

Compared to these other sites, Pilgrim State didn't seem to want anyone's new business. The firm was perfectly content with those 131 accounts.

Allie next tried researching the names of the three principals. That search yielded results as threadbare as those of the website. Their names turned up in no membership rosters of civic organizations or professional groups. They were not affiliated with any charitable organizations and they did not give to political candidates. A search for a home address also yielded no satisfactory answer.

A perusal of the 'consumer information' section of the website of the Securities and Exchange Commission reassured investors that pseudonyms and aliases were not allowed in the industry. So, the 'David Hale' who was listed as the Chairman on Pilgrim State had to have been born with that name.

What's up with this organization? Allie kept thinking as each query reached the same dead end.

There was a way to short-circuit these questions, she knew: hack into Pilgrim State's computer system. She had the passwords to view Brian's accounts. She could use that access to try other systems inside Pilgrim State and see if anything was unprotected. She had both the tools and the expertise.

But a nagging sensation inside her head said that caution should be exercised. And so she tried the simplest route: a worm. The website had a 'contact us' form. She filled out the form with plausible names and information, and created a fresh Gmail account for their response. Assuming someone at the firm opened the email, even if it was to generate an autoreply that Pilgrim State was not currently accepting new accounts, the act of opening the email would launch a worm inside whatever server the firm's email system was located.

Tomorrow, she could check to see the worm's progress. It might still be inside the lone server or it might have migrated to other computers. It all depended on the extent of the interconnection of the firm's computers. The odds were in her favor: because of the resources required, few organizations went to the extraordinary measures needed to provide state-of-the-art protection against malware.

Allie sent the email and went to the kitchen to find something to eat.

TUESDAY

Chapter Ten

The office of the Gerald and Abigail Rice Foundation occupied
a full floor of a modern office building overlooking Post Office
Square in Boston's Financial District and, from Emily's office she
could look out over the picturesque triangle. The park below her
window was more than just a beautiful bib of greenery in a bustling
commercial zone.   It was also an object lesson in combining
business acumen with philanthropy. The park – its full name was
the Norman B. Leventhal Park at Post Office Square – represented
the vision of a man who had been equal parts real estate developer
and humanitarian.   Beneath the serenity of the park was seven
floors of underground parking that funded the public space above.
Emily considered the park her visual 'point of inspiration'.

Emily's parents had created the foundation she now headed as
a way to cope with the wealth that had accumulated and passed
down through six generations of Taylors and Rices. That wealth
was anchored in Captain Archibald Taylor's shipping ventures in
the eighteenth and early nineteenth centuries; a business that
included the transportation of slaves across the Middle Passage and
of opium into and out of China. Later, there were lucrative oil
ventures with the Rockefeller family, and South American mining
operations that were wildly profitable while also ecologically
catastrophic.

It had taken until the middle of the twentieth century for the
families to generate wealth respectably.   The minicomputer
industry in Massachusetts owed its growth and financial stability to
investments from Emily's venture capitalist grandfather, Stephen
Rice, and a half dozen medical device manufacturers had been
funded by members of the Taylor family.

The marriage of Gerald Rice and Abigail Taylor had created a family fortune worth, according to *Forbes* magazine, more than five billion dollars. Their foundation was required by law to disburse five percent of its assets annually, but the rising stock market of the 1990s meant that the foundation's assets rose rather than fell.

That Emily Taylor Rice would be somehow involved in the foundation had always been a given. She had pursued an MBA specifically because she intended to know as much as the advisors who managed the day-to-day activities of her family's investment office. The plan was that she would ease into the work, taking multiple jobs to best understand how the organization worked. She needed look no further than another Boston family, the Johnsons, where another daughter was being carefully groomed to take her father's place as head of Fidelity Investments.

Three events interrupted that orderly plan. The first was being told by her mother that the surgery that was supposed to have contained the ovarian cancer had, in reality, only slowed the cancer's advance and only momentarily. Abby Taylor Rice died within a year. Her death at 48 devastated her husband, Gerry, who had just turned 50. Within two years he, too, would die. The official cause was a massive cerebrovascular incident – an embolic stroke that moved from his leg to his brain in a matter of minutes. The more accurate cause, Emily suspected, was the loss of Abby. At 27, Emily found herself the sole beneficiary of a massive fortune and a family foundation.

The third event came in June 2010 in the form of an invitation to have dinner with a man Emily had never met: Warren Buffett. At that dinner, Buffett outlined his plan for a 'Giving Pledge'. Those who signed it promised to give away to philanthropy most of their net worth either during their lifetime or upon their death. Bill and Melinda Gates were already on board. Was she interested?

Emily seized on the idea as the perfect solution to the uneasiness that had plagued her most of her life. Her family's wealth was tainted by its exploitative source. The Gerald and

Abigail Rice Foundation did good works, but was also a self-perpetuating entity. *Give it all away.* She signed the pledge.

Grief over the loss of her parents resulted in large grants into the search for cures of and treatment for cancer and stroke. Medical research, at least, was capable of absorbing large inflows of money, and efficiently deploying funding with a minimum of waste. Many of her other areas of interest were both hindered and frustrated by either too many organizations doing the same thing, or else finding that an organization with an original idea lacked the management depth to scale itself to a meaningful size and still operate efficiently.

But on this Tuesday morning, neither the park nor the operation of a multibillion-dollar foundation were on her mind. Instead, it was on a handwritten list she had composed with guidance from Elaine and Alan.

She had come into work early to prepare for this day – as well as to avoid Brian. Ten minutes after her arrival she heard activity in the areas outside her office. She walked to her door and found Darlene Harris, her admin, settling into her desk with a cup of coffee.

"Can we spend a few minutes together?" Emily asked.

The logical personal assistant to someone in Emily's position would have been a fresh-faced liberal arts graduate eager to gain entry to the glamorous, non-profit world. The first dozen candidates she interviewed three years earlier had been just such individuals. They were excited at the opportunity to trade their $250,000 education for a job that paid $32,500 because it meant grabbing onto the bottom rung of a dream job: spending other people's money on noble causes.

By contrast, Darlene was an African-American woman in her mid-30s. Only an inch or two over five feet and with a slender build, she could be mistaken at first glance for someone in her late teens. But Darlene had borne two children and the welfare and education of her son and daughter directed her every action. Emily had looked past Darlene's Mission Hill upbringing and community college certificate and seen someone intelligent and highly motivated to succeed. And, in offering Darlene the job, Emily gained someone with unquestioned loyalty.

That loyalty was now key to the execution of the plan that had been put together over the weekend.

"Is your passport still current?" Emily asked.

The question caught Darlene by surprise. "My passport?"

"You went to the Bahamas last year," Emily said.

Darlene nodded. "Yes. I just got it two years ago."

"Can your mother watch the kids for two or maybe three days?"

Darlene's mother had Lupus and had retired on disability from the MBTA. "She can watch them." Darlene swallowed involuntarily.

"Do you remember Sir Charles Pickney?" Emily asked.

"The man from the college in England," Darlene replied.

"If you are willing and able, you're going to go see him. You are going as my personal representative. This has nothing to do with the Foundation. And, if you do this, you cannot tell anyone where you are going, why you are going, or where you were until I tell you otherwise."

Darlene swallowed again.

"Will you do this for me?" Emily asked. Her voice was firm, her eyes were locked on Darlene's.

"Yes," Darlene said.

"And, as soon as you get back, I'll have another assignment for you; just as important and just as secret."

"I understand," Darlene said.

"Then we had better get started," Emily said.

* * * * *

Helga Johanssen pondered why she was feeling so… different.

One week earlier, things were looking, if not bright, then less dark than they had been for quite a long time. She finally had a researcher with a first-class mind. She had someone who could offer the fresh perspective on a problem that she had begun to sense was unsolvable. She had someone who could get the Management Committee to give her additional time.

Then, after just five days on the job, Helga's researcher had been commandeered by her daughter to carry out some long-simmering act of revenge against her father. And there was no way to assess or even postulate what reaction that act of revenge might precipitate. Allie was a brilliant young woman. But the necessary emphasis was on *young*. She was impetuous. Last evening Allie had shown she was still given to tempests of emotions over which she seemed to have no control.

Allie's ability to solve visual, spatial, and mathematical problems drew the attention of even the most jaded educators and psychologists. Hers was an intellect to be cherished and nurtured. Her horizons were unlimited… but only if she could rid herself or grow out of that dark side of her personality.

And, of course, that depressive corner of Allie's mind came from the maternal genes. Helga recognized she had seldom known happiness. School and college, yes. Receiving her degrees, certainly. Seeing Allie for the first time, of course. But much of the rest of her life was a muddled blur; a carousel of sepia-toned slides that could be assigned a season or year only with difficulty. Coming to America. Meeting and being wooed by Brian. Getting married. Her early years in research at MIT.

She knew when she was young she was considered beautiful. Her parents and her friends told her so, and it was her appearance and not her mind that had attracted Brian and the men who came before him. But beauty had never been the focus of her sense of self. Allie's birth and the growing success in her research were the turning points that defined her inner identity. Those two events freed her from an illogical game of expectations. After Allie's birth and her first major grant – events separated by just a few weeks – she no longer felt the urgency to meet expectations about her appearance. She was, once and for all, liberated.

But the meetings Monday morning and Monday evening with Allie and Penny – ones that might have filled her with renewed dread – instead made her commute into work this morning one of eager anticipation.

Helga carefully analyzed her altered mood and recounted the previous day's events. The change, she concluded, came when Allie told her, *This is my war, not yours,* and she had replied, *Maybe it's mine, too.*

It is *my war,* Helga thought. For four years she had considered herself a non-combatant in some undeclared conflict with only a vague beginning and cessation of hostilities. She still lived in the same house, so she could not be a displaced person. She had suffered no physical wound or even financial deprivation. Brian's devotion to his work made him both an absentee father and husband, so there was little loss of companionship. He was still alive and so she could not be a widow.

But there was a psychic scar inside her and, if she allowed herself to think about it, that wound was as deep as it was painful. Celebratory times – especially Thanksgiving, Christmas and birthdays – were holidays Helga struggled to make special for Allie because they were inextricably tied to the idea of family. But for Helga, Brian's abrupt departure had destroyed the joy that those holidays brought others.

Brian had walked out on his family when he found a better situation. He abandoned an impressionable daughter and deserted a wife to begin over with someone younger. Someone more in keeping with his view of himself and his place in the world.

But it turned out that for much of their life together, Brian was also a criminal. He stole from an organization that placed its trust in him. And, his taking up with a woman of wealth and beauty had not assuaged his greed. His stealing had only increased in the intervening years.

And she, Helga, along with her daughter and a woman she barely knew, now had the power to bring Brian to his knees.

It was, she thought, delicious.

* * * * *

By 10:30 a.m., Emily had sent Darlene home to pack and make arrangements for her children. A round-trip business-class ticket to Heathrow with a connecting flight to Leeds Bradford Airport had been purchased and paid for on Emily's personal credit card. A suitable hotel had been booked for the night. Darlene had full instructions on what she was to do and Emily had full confidence in both Darlene's ability to accomplish her task and in her discretion to never speak of her role.

Emily had made the first of her two difficult calls. The first had been to Sir Charles Pickney, whose formal title was Chancellor of Leeds Beckett's Horticultural Sciences school.

She told Sir Charles she was sending a personal representative to meet with him, and she hoped he could clear an hour to hear what was requested. Sir Charles had replied that her call and the request was not unexpected, and that being mid-summer, his schedule was relatively light.

Emily ended that call knowing that her request would be handled with both respect and with a privacy suitable to the delicacy of the matter. She smiled and thought that, ironically, if all went well she would be the one to write a check to Leeds Beckett's alumni fund.

The second call was much harder. She had to call Brian and invite him to lunch. Moreover, she had to act contrite and both explain her absence and apologize for her silence during that absence. It had to be a bravura acting performance on her part.

She reached for her phone.

* * * * *

At 12:30, Brian arrived at her table. They were at Café Fleuri, a sun-filled restaurant in the hotel adjacent to her office building, and they were seated at a window table that, like her office, overlooked the park.

Emily took his hands warmly, smiled, and kissed him. "I didn't want to wait until tonight to apologize in person," she said. "What I did was inexcusable, but I owe you an explanation."

What followed was a story that had been worked out between Emily and Alan, with Elaine critiquing Emily's performance.

"I had some devastating news Friday afternoon," Emily began. "I don't know if you remember but, last year, Sloan Kettering invited us in on funding for an investigational drug for an ovarian cancer treatment. You know how I feel about anything that had even a glimmer of a chance for progress in that area…"

She waited for Brian to nod before continuing.

"The science was sound and the group – it's in western Pennsylvania – has a good track record. Sloan Kettering was asking us to put in five million and I signed off on it personally. I handed the folder off to one of my junior people. I didn't give her any specific instructions, but I've trained everyone that, even for something where we didn't originate the project and it isn't a lot of dollars, we keep in touch with the investigators just to make certain they know we're looking over their shoulder."

"Sloan Kettering also invited in a second sponsor – a small foundation down in Maryland. That foundation also handed off review to a junior administrator. Her name is Julianne Robinson and I met her this weekend. Julianne read the full proposal and was delighted because her boyfriend is from Little Rock and one of the investigational sites is UAMS; the medical school at the University of Arkansas." Emily paused to see if Brian was paying attention. The look on his face said he was.

"Two weeks ago, Julianne and her boyfriend flew down to

Arkansas for a three-day weekend, and Julianne used one of those days to drop in at UAMS. She had the name of the head of the group that would be seeing patients locally. Julianne handed him her card and explained the purpose of her visit. All the researcher did was, in her words, give her a blank stare. He had no idea he was part of an ovarian cancer treatment program and, while he knew of the group in Pittsburgh, he knew no one there and had never been asked to be part of an investigation."

"Julianne was back on a plane to Baltimore that afternoon. She and the head of the foundation in Maryland were on a train to New York the next morning. Sloan Kettering handled it from there. They started making lots of calls. And, what they found was that, three years ago, this same group in Pittsburgh had funding for another study. Six remote sites. Five of the sites went smoothly. The sixth one, ostensibly a university-related hospital in Mississippi, screwed up the record-keeping and their results had to be thrown out."

Emily saw that Brian was hanging on every word. His face was contorted and pale, and his hands were clenched into fists.

"There was a full record of payments to the hospital in Mississippi, but when Sloan Kettering called them, the group had no idea they had ever been a clinical site and had never received any payments, which were supposed to have totaled half a million dollars," Emily continued. "And, of course, there was a paper trail of funding going to UAMS with checks written as recently as two weeks before the audit. The total budgeted amount was about $600,000."

"I got the call Friday afternoon that Sloan Kettering needed to see me, in person. This, of course, was the first time I heard anything about any of this. The people at Sloan Kettering were, as you might imagine, full of apologies. They said it was their fault and that they ought to have done better due diligence."

"And, of course, on the other side of the table sat Julianne

Robinson, looking like the cat who ate the canary. She did – for the three or four million that her foundation put into the project – what no one else had done. She actually checked the veracity of the details. The fact that she did it because she happened to be somewhere for pleasure makes it all the more telling. Sloan Kettering has let go the administrator that processed the grant application. That almost never happens."

Emily reached across the table and took Brian's clenched fists. His hands were cold. "Brian, I signed off on our participation in that project. I took the word of a friend that it was sound science and good people. Then I passed it onto a young woman who, after this lunch, is going to be told, by me, that someone was using that grant to pocket more than half a million dollars. And, worse, it was someone in a position just like hers that uncovered the issue and blew the whistle. I have spent the past 72 hours kicking myself, and wondering what and how I'm going to tell my staff."

Emily looked pleadingly into Brian's eyes, her own eyes moistening. "I'm sorry I didn't call or email you. I hope you can understand why. But what should I do? I could really use your advice."

Emily carefully studied Brian's face during the long moments before he spoke. She and Alan had worked to get the details of the story right, for it had two purposes. The first was to tell of an event so personally and professionally devastating to Emily that she would remain incommunicado for several days. The second was to telegraph how Emily felt about betrayal.

Emily could see that Brian's mind was working; parsing the story and her emotions as she told it. But there seemed to be something deeper going on behind his eyes. How often (if ever) did Brian even think about his non-existent degree? Did he even consider such misrepresentation as worthy of being upset about?

"Here is what I think," Brian said at long last, his voice silkily smooth. "You are being far too hard on yourself and not nearly hard enough – in fact, not hard at all – on Sloan Kettering. They leveraged their reputation to ask you to give your money to a project, knowing that because it was ovarian cancer you couldn't turn them down. *They* hadn't done sufficient due diligence."

"But I've known Sandy for years," Emily said. "She…"

Brian held up a hand; a request for her to stop speaking. "Let me ask you a question," he said. "In the philanthropic world, if there is just a single funding source, what happens when a grant blows up like this – the foundation or whatever learns something crooked was going on? I mean, assuming the foundation doesn't learn about it by reading in on the front page of the *New York Times*? Do they ask for their money back? Do they go public? Do they warn other philanthropic groups?"

"You almost never hear about such things," Emily replied.

"You almost never hear about them because they're so rare or because foundations never talk about them?" Brian shot back.

"The word goes out," Emily said. "Privately. There were 'disbursement irregularities' or 'procedural problems' at a recipient. The word goes out that they're not a good investment."

"But apart from being blackballed, there's no penalty," Brian said.

"I didn't say that," Emily replied. "Sloan Kettering will make certain the right people at Duquesne know what happened."

"But no one is asked to make restitution," Brian pressed. "You're out five million."

"A little less than two million, actually," Emily said. "The funding was in four tranches."

A smile seemed to come over Brian's face, Emily noted.

"Here's what I suggest," he said. "First, you call up your friend – Sandy? – at Sloan Kettering and you read Sandy the riot act. You tell Sandy that the next time he or she plays on your emotions to spread out a bet, that the due diligence had better be ticked and tied from the title page to the last footnote."

"She would never speak to me again," Emily said.

"Emily," Brian said, leaning across the table and speaking in a low voice. "What your good friend Sandy should do is to offer to reimburse the Gerald and Abigail Rice Foundation for every penny it put into the project. And she should offer to do the same for the outfit in Maryland and pay their analyst a whopping bonus."

"And here's what else I think," Brian said. "This afternoon you call in the person to whom you handed responsibility back a couple of months ago, and you say only that the project has been cancelled. Nothing else – just cancelled. But then, in a month or six weeks, you call an all-hands meeting where everyone gets the same training in Due Diligence 101. You bring in an outside facilitator, and all you tell that trainer is that someone in your office missed a low-level red flag, and you don't want it to happen again."

"And, one more thing," Brian said, now taking Emily's hands in his own. "You don't ever kick yourself over something like this again. You did nothing wrong except to take a friend's word that you were putting your family's money into something that might have a huge benefit for science and medicine."

"Repeat after me: I did nothing wrong," Brian said. When Emily did not say anything, Brian slightly tightened his hold on her hands. "Repeat after me: I did nothing wrong."

"I did nothing wrong," Emily whispered.

"I did nothing wrong," Brian said more forcefully.

"I did nothing wrong," Emily said with conviction.

Brian smiled. "You did nothing wrong. Remember that. And you owe me no apology for anything."

When the lunch was over, Emily thanked Brian for his advice and kissed him goodbye.

When she returned to her office, she went to the deserted women's room and retched. In a stall, shaking, she attempted to regain her composure. She felt Brian's hands tightening on hers. She heard him saying as he restrained her, *"I have done nothing wrong."*

She felt she had been threatened.

You've just made this easy, Emily thought to herself. *It is going to be a pleasure giving you what you deserve.*

* * * * *

Brian resisted the urge to skip as he made his way across the fifth underground level of the garage across the restaurant. It would be, he concluded, unseemly.

But skipping was certainly how he felt. That luncheon had been an unqualified victory. Emily was his. He had come into the restaurant to find a woman on the verge of tears. He had left one with a smile and tears of gratitude. He had been responsible for that change.

There had been a few moments – terrifying at the time, a simple misjudgment in hindsight – when he thought the conversation was going in a completely different direction. Emily was talking about someone discovering misappropriation of funds in such a way that it might have been him. Then, listening more carefully to the timbre of her voice, he knew that this was about someone else.

The takeaway had been that she was a woman who could not bear to be betrayed. OK, he got that. Don't get caught betraying her. Well, there was no way she or anyone else could learn about 'the fund'. In eighteen years, no one had even suspected.

But she was a woman who could be controlled. That soft, oh-so-subtle squeeze of her hands at the end of her story. She hadn't wanted to say she did nothing wrong. That gentle squeeze got her to say the words. He would employ them again in the not too distant future. When he asked her to say 'yes' to marrying him.

He was feeling euphoric. It was a beautiful summer day. Far too beautiful a day to go back to the office.

He was supposed to use only the throwaway cell phone to call Amber, and she to use only the one he bought her to respond. But that phone was locked in his desk drawer and he had no idea of the number assigned to her cell. So, using his own cell phone he called

Beckwith Estate and asked to be put through to Amber.

"Ms. Oakes," Brian said, allowing his giddiness to show through his voice. "It is far too glorious an afternoon to waste in a stuffy office poring over donation reports. I am giving you the rest of the day off. Would you care to join me on a quick jaunt to inspect one of New England Green's properties?"

He smiled at her answer.

* * * * *

Allie was puzzled, an uncommon state for her. The web form she had filled out and returned to Pilgrim State Investments had sat in a server, unopened, for nearly eighteen hours. In her experience, such routine items typically would be swept up three or even four times every day. The email would be opened and, even if turned over to an autoreader for a standard reply, the worm she implanted in the form would have been inside the target's system, ready to spread and do its work.

But this form had gone into a cache at a Verizon server farm in Culpepper, Virginia. No one seemed interested in opening it and there was no forwarding instruction. Until someone logged into that account, her worm was going nowhere.

Allie was by nature impatient. She had been told since the age of three that she should take into account that the world around her did not possess her mental agility. Other people, even gifted people, took longer than she to comprehend the gist of a page of information or to analyze and solve a complex equation.

Through Helga's contacts within the MIT community, she had ensured that Allie was exposed to every aspect of science and math so that she would not be herded into a field she might later come to hate. The allied fields of computer science and math were where she was happiest. And, while she was nominally entering MIT as a freshman in September, Allie had already completed large swaths of the university's first and second year math and computer science curriculum.

In Allie's estimation, Helga had been a good mother. She taught Allie all of the fundamentals of life, neither flinching nor dodging even the most direct and blunt of her daughter's questions. Allie was brought up to be self-sufficient. She could cook relatively simple meals, take care of her personal needs, and manage money.

What had been neglected in her upbringing was any integration into the social fabric of people her own age. In theory, Allie had been educated at the Shady Hill School and, later, Buckingham Browne & Nichols; both highly regarded private schools a few blocks from her Coolidge Hill home. In reality, Allie was on campus for no more than two or three hours a day. Her true academic education had been conducted mostly by adult tutors at MIT in Kendall Square, and her sense was that most of those tutors had no more social graces than did their prize student. The male tutors were generally and inexplicably afraid of her. The women tutors were of another generation and could not help Allie navigate the minefields that comprised the teenage years.

She considered television and popular music beneath contempt because that media assumed anyone under the age of twenty (or older) was either an imbecile or obsessed with sex. Instead, she gravitated to classical music for its mathematical underpinnings. A voracious reader, she consumed both fiction and non-fiction in equal parts which is how, at the age of twelve, she had come to read *The Professor with the Wandering Hands*.

Allie had never been on a date. She was not even certain if she was gay, straight, or bisexual. She interacted with male and female peers identically; the gender of that person played no role in what Allie said or how she acted. In her reading, she had come across the concept of an 'asexual' orientation and, to give herself an anchor until such time as she felt a need to commit one way or another, she kept that orientation in reserve. She had, however, never been asked, which was just as well.

Even though Allie had met Penny Walden just a few days

earlier, Allie both liked and admired Penny. Penny was a fellow 'super-bright' who saw the world through a lens of science and reason. Ten years older than Allie, Penny appeared to have come through college none the worse for the experience. When the time came that she was comfortable around Penny, Allie had resolved to begin a conversation that might shed some light on how Penny had succeeded in avoiding becoming one of the cardboard characters portrayed in the media.

But now, Allie had a problem: that un-opened email. She also had an idea that Penny might be the solution to that problem. Allie took a chance that Penny would be willing to help. After all, it was Penny who had said, *I have to get to know this Pilgrim State Investments and find out how sharp they are...* Well, this would be her opportunity.

* * * * *

At 3 p.m. on Tuesday afternoon, Penny stood at the entrance of a modest, two-story office building on Boylston Street in the Chestnut Hill neighborhood that straddled Newton and Brookline, two exceedingly affluent towns just west of Boston. Across the street was a flashy 'lifestyle center' and, a block further up, a mall anchored at either end by Bloomingdales. This building, it seemed to Penny, exuded anonymity. Clad in red brick and concrete, it was simply 'there'. No anchor tenant's name was on the building or even on a pedestal sign at the entrance.

Beyond the aluminum-framed glass doors was a dimly-lit foyer, two wooden doors and a single elevator. To the right of the elevator was an inconspicuous directory listing four tenants. Pilgrim State Investments was on the second floor. Somewhat warily, Penny pressed the elevator button and heard the wheezing of machinery.

She had visited her own financial advisor in Pasadena only a handful of times, but everything about the facility in which it was housed was the antithesis of where she was now. The interior of the building was bright and welcoming, the signage was clear. Here, the message seemed to be, *'nothing to see here, move along…'*

The second floor consisted of a short – less than twenty feet in length – hallway. At the end of the hallway were two entrances. On the right was a pair of glass doors leading to an apartment rental service. On the left was a solid wooden door with a small sign reading, 'Pilgrim State Investments' and, underneath that, an index card with the handwritten message, 'No Solicitors'. The door was unlocked. Penny turned the doorknob.

Inside, there was no receptionist's desk nor a receptionist, only a warren of cubicles separated by a walkway. But she heard a chime that likely had been triggered by her opening the door.

A few moments later, a middle-aged man appeared. Attired in a green polo shirt and chinos, he wore frameless glasses and his hair was short-cropped and graying.

"Can I help you?" he asked. There was nothing in his voice that indicated friendliness or, indeed, an inclination to be of help.

"I'm looking for David Hale," Penny said. Hale was listed as the firm's Chairman on the Credio.com website that contained the most information she had found on the firm. Credio presumably aggregated information from regulatory filings.

"And you are…" the man said, still no hint of warmth in his voice.

Penny thought to herself, *show time.* "My name is Abby. I'm looking for an investment advisor. I've just moved here from North Carolina and my current…"

"We're not accepting new clients," the man said. "If you had called, we could have saved you a trip."

"If I had called," Penny replied, "I wouldn't have gotten any sense of what you spend on overhead. Right now, I like what I see."

The response seemed to take the man by surprise. In a somewhat more accommodating voice he said, "Look, we have all the clients we can handle and we don't…"

"You have $1.2 billion under management," Penny interjected. "That is the same size as my current advisor. I have $7.8 million to invest and a goal to grow that substantially. Being three time zones from my advisor is no way…"

"You said you had moved here from North Carolina," the man said. "The last time I checked, it's in the same time zone as Boston."

"I'm from California and came into the money when I lived there," Penny replied. "I've been in graduate school getting a PhD for the past six years. But if you don't even have the courtesy of introducing yourself, I don't care to answer any additional questions."

The man grimaced. "That was rude of me. Most people who come through that door are trying to sell something." His voice was now conciliatory. He put out his hand. "I am David Hale. I'm the Chairman and President of Pilgrim State. And I'm sorry, but I forgot your name,"

"Abby Fasanella," she said, shaking his hand.

"Ms. Fasanella," Hale said, "every client we have comes to us by referral. It's mostly people of considerable means with long investment horizons."

"So, no one can walk in the door and invite you to manage their portfolio?" Penny asked.

Hale again grimaced. "We've already done all the trading we're going to do for the day. Why don't you come back to my office? I'll explain as best I can. I owe you that much."

Penny followed Hale past twelve cubicles, none of which were occupied. At the end were three glass-walled offices, the exteriors of which overlooked Boylston Street. Hale entered the first one, pulled a bottle of water from a small refrigerator and offered one to Penny, who accepted it.

She looked around the office, which was small considering that it was the nerve center for the management of more than a billion dollars of assets. On Hale's desk was a standard two-screen Bloomberg terminal, a laptop, and a telephone. No papers were present.

A small round table filled one corner of the office and Hale took one chair, gesturing Penny to take the other. Hale smiled. "Hi, let me start over. I'm David Hale of Pilgrim State Management. Welcome to my office. How can I help you?"

The change of attitude brought a smile to Penny's face. "I want you to help me open a lab in less than ten years."

"A lab?" Hale tilted his head to emphasize the question.

"A research lab," Penny said. "I'm a research scientist. I currently work for a start-up in Cambridge. My goal, though is to have my own lab."

"How much will that cost?" Hale asked.

"To do it right, I'll need about $15 million," Penny replied.

"And I heard the number $7.8 million mentioned earlier," Hale said.

Penny nodded.

"So, you're looking to double your money in less than ten years," Hale said. "May I ask who is your current advisor?"

Penny again thought to herself, *show time*. She reached into the oversized purse she had selected for the trip and withdrew from it an iPad that she and Allie had spent an hour doctoring for just this moment. She tapped the screen half a dozen times and the front page of a PDF appeared on the screen. She handed it to Hale. "Cordova Street Management in Pasadena. Here is my latest statement. My apology that I've removed the account number, but we don't know one another."

It was Hale's turn to smile. "I don't know Cordova Street, but then that's a different world out the West Coast." He scrolled through the pages of the statement and shrugged. "They're doing all the right things. You own all the right stocks and all the best funds. You've got great diversification and enough downside risk protection that if the bottom falls out of the market, you won't get hurt as badly as most other people."

Hale handed the iPad back to Penny. "In any halfway decent market, these guys will get you your lab in ten years. My advice is to live with the time zone difference. When you're managing money, you're up early anyway."

Penny left the statement on the table. "What if my horizon is five or six years instead of ten?"

Hale squinted. "You're – what – in your late twenties? May I ask how you came to have this kind of portfolio at an age when most of your peers are struggling to pay off student loans?"

Penny paused. "The answer is that I'd rather not say. I will tell you I came by it over a period of about three years and I don't have any student loans. If you want to think of it as an inheritance, that's fine. But please respect my privacy."

She added, "And I repeat my question: what if my horizon is five or six years to open this lab?"

Hale picked up the iPad and again scrolled through it. He paused at a few pages. He again placed it on the table. "Not a chance in the world. You're waiting for the market to double and then some. You're hedging against the downside and, all the while, you're paying taxes on your gains. That's my honest assessment."

"Then how does your firm make money?" Penny asked. "Why won't you take new clients?"

Hale took a drink from his bottle of water. "We do unconventional investing and keep reportable gains to the bare minimum."

"Like private placements, pre-IPOs, and distressed bonds?" Penny asked. "My advisor says they're too risky."

Hale waved his hand in front of his face, as though getting rid of a bad smell. "What they are is a guaranteed way to lose money," he said. "Do you want to take a guess what percentage of start-up investors ever get a payout? Even the 'can't miss' ones. Especially the 'can't miss' ones. Remember Theranos? From a valuation of ten billion to functionally zero in a year."

"How do we make money?" Hale continued. "We make particularly large bets where other people fail to see the opportunity when it is still at its earliest stage. Last year, our principal bet was that Venezuela was going to slip into hyperinflation. The smart money said the IMF or China would bail them out. We looked at the political climate and concluded that the government would just start printing money, which is what they did."

"Did you worsen the situation?" Penny asked. "Did your bets cause the inflation to be even higher?"

"No," Hale said, shaking his head. "All that misery you see is the product of stupidity on the part of government. All we did was wait while tyrants destroyed a country. When the currency hedgers moved in big time, we sold our positions and solidified our gains."

"And what are you doing this year?" Penny asked.

Hale smiled and tapped the side of his head. "That's my secret. Come ask me next year and I'll tell you what it was." He took another drink from his water bottle. "Which brings up the other reasons we don't take fresh money. First, we don't know if we can invest it. Second, we self-custody, which makes a lot of people nervous."

Penny shook her head. "The first part I get. I don't know what 'self-custody' means."

Hale picked up the iPad and pointed to the front page of Penny's statement. "Right here in the upper right hand corner. It says 'Merrill Lynch'. They physically hold your funds – they're the custodian. You give Cordova Street Management the right to make trades in your account. When you're betting against the Bolivar, Merrill Lynch isn't set up to do that. We hold everyone's funds in-house and, when bets are of multi-month duration, there isn't the kind of liquidity that most people expect. Other times, we hold a large position in a single for a day or two when we think there is going to be a big move. When it moves, we sell. But the trading is all done offshore to limit tax exposure."

"But you issue statements, I assume," Penny said. "Your clients know where they stand."

"Of course," Hale replied. "But clients agree that they can only withdraw a certain percentage of their funds on demand. We use a wonderful little device called a Cook Island Trust. All your funds pass through the trust. The good news is that they become functionally untaxable. The bad news is that getting funds out of the trust without triggering taxes takes time. If you need small amounts – say, up to fifty thousand – we can tap our house account and have you money in a day. For a larger sum, it could take weeks or even months. But that has never happened. We deal with patient, well-heeled individuals who have long investment horizons."

Penny placed the iPad back in her purse. "I'm sorry you're not taking on new clients. I have a strong sense you could get me that lab." She began to rise from her chair.

"I like doing things for people who have noble purposes," Hale said. "Let me speak to the other partners. May I print out a copy of that statement? It would go a long way toward convincing them."

Penny smiled. "I'll do you one better." She reached into her purse and pulled out a thumb drive. "This has PDFs of both the current statement and year-end summaries going back two years showing what trades have been made. If your partners are interested in my account, put together an investment strategy and get back to me. My contact information is on the drive."

Hale laughed. "You came prepared."

Penny smiled broadly. "It's my experience that telling someone they can't have something is the one sure way to make certain they'll want it even more. But I want to see the investment plan, in detail. This is my entire nest egg we're dealing with. This is my future."

She held out the thumb drive and rose from the table.

Hale stood, smiled, and accepted it.

* * * * *

David Hale showed Penny to the door, shook her hand, and said he would be in touch within a few days. He then went back to his office and did two things. First, he emptied and bagged the water bottle from which 'Abby Fasanella' had just drunk. Second, from his personal computer, he downloaded into a separate file the security footage of Fasanella approaching the building and coming into the office. He found a frame with the clearest view of her face and preserved it as a separate file. He then viewed the security monitors from the north and south ends of the building. Ms. Fasanella had walked south. He followed her, hoping she hadn't taken a cab or an Uber to get to Chestnut Hill. A short distance from the building she paused, reached into her purse, and pulled out a set of keys. Brake lights flashed on what looked like a late model Honda Civic. She got into the car and pulled out of the space.

Hale slowed the security footage to a crawl. As the car cleared the space and pulled into the street, he got a clear view of the front license plate. He zoomed in and captured an image. He noted that it was a North Carolina plate; the first confirmation that Abby Fasanella might be who she said she was.

Walk-ins were a rarity and only twice had they ever become customers. There was, put simply, far too much risk. Pilgrim State screened its prospects carefully. But there was a continuing need for those new accounts. Referrals had been sufficient until now, but you never could tell.

Only when he had completed these tasks did he turn his attention to the thumb drive Ms. Fasanella had given him. He inserted it into his laptop and performed three separate virus scans. Five minutes later, he was satisfied that it contained no contaminated files. He opened the drive's single file, which he noted had been created and loaded today. The statements appeared genuine. There was no obvious cutting and pasting. She had whited out the account number on the current statement as well as on the year-end ones. The address on the earlier statements was McQueen Drive in Durham. He would check to make certain the address tied to the license plate.

The address on the current statement was 10 Glassworks Avenue, Apartment 12H in Cambridge. Google Maps showed him a new apartment building two blocks from the Lechmere MBTA Green Line station. OK, that, too made sense. She said she was working for a start-up in Cambridge, which most likely meant Kendall Square. The two were walking distance or a short drive from each other.

But it was also curious. Cambridge was teeming with financial advisors, many of them catering to affluent young people like her. Why choose one seven miles away through rotten traffic? She had said the size of the firm and its lack of ostentatious premises was the attraction. He decided to let that pass for now.

The contact information she provided was a phone number and an email address. The phone number was an 857 area code, which was the 'spill-over' for cell phones in the 617 service area. There were a few reasons why someone might have changed phones when moving from one state to another, though it was his experience that most people kept their cell numbers for as long as possible. But why would you change cell phone numbers and not change your license plate, which was a legal requirement?

He let that, too, pass. And began studying the 1099s to see how stupid financial advisors slaved away to earn a few bucks off their client's accounts.

* * * * *

Allie and Penny paged through screens of data, trying to make sense of the information in front of them. It was four hours since

Penny had returned from Pilgrim State Investments and, once again, the contents of a bag of takeout food – this time, Thai – filled Penny's work table.

In addition to food, Allie had brought an oversized laptop; five, two-terabyte solid-state drives; and a printer of the kind a business traveler might pack into a briefcase. Allie explained that her goal was to leave no easy trail of digital breadcrumbs for anyone to follow. Her laptop was connected not to Pheromonix's Wi-Fi network, but to that of a company in a building across the plaza (whose administrative password she had compromised two months earlier). That network, in turn, was buffered by two different internet service providers, and Allie had further rigged a one-time-use device number to her computer. She pronounced her system un-hackable.

When they had met earlier in the afternoon, Allie had been dressed in what Penny thought of as 'typical Allie clothes'. Cut-off blue jeans, a tank-top, and flip-flops. Now, she was attired all in black. Allie noticed Penny eyeing her change of clothes. "If we're going to be spies, we need to dress the part."

As Allie had suspected, David Hale had first initiated a series of virus scans in the thumb drive Penny had supplied. Each one promised to detect the latest viruses and malware. Each one failed in its task because, like the generals who lose because they prepare for the next war by re-fighting the last, a good hacker is always two steps ahead of those in the business of protecting computers.

In a matter of minutes, the worm that Allie had imbedded in the thumb drive along with the brokerage statements began gathering and transmitting files from Hale's laptop. When its contents were copied, the worm leaped effortlessly from Hale's laptop to Pilgrim State's in-house server and, from there, to other computers in the firm. In three hours, Allie's deck-of-cards-size hard drive contained all current data from Pilgrim State. She then copied the data to each of the other four drives.

Allie then carefully erased each network link she had painstakingly created except for one. The link she left in place went from Pilgrim State to a server in an internet café in Amsterdam. If or when Pilgrim State's network administrator suspected the firm's files had been hacked, the act of initiating diagnostic tools would send a message to that server in the Netherlands. Allie could anonymously log into that server and see if her 'trip wire' had been touched.

The two women had started organizing the files an hour earlier. One particularly useful folder contained employee information for the Pilgrim State staff. Being new to the area, the home addresses meant nothing to Penny. Allie said the principals of the firm were 'living large' in Newton, Brookline, and Weston. To demonstrate her point, Allie pulled up a photo of David Hale's three-acre, eighteen-room 'cottage' on Hidden Road in Weston. "Nice work if you can get it," Allie said.

A second folder held the names of other account holders.

"I think I recognize some of these names," Allie said. "I can Google them, but they sound like politicians whose names are always in the news." She pointed at one name. "I don't pay a lot of attention to local news, but this guy runs a union local. He was in some kind of trouble earlier this year."

They decided to focus on Brian LaPointe's account. Its current value was $21 million. With the tap of a few keys, the entire history of his deposits into the account were laid bare. Every deposit going back eighteen years was there and, with every deposit, a scan of both sides of the check deposited. In almost every case, the deposit consisted of a check from New England Green, signed by Brian LaPointe, made payable to a company, and then the same check was endorsed by the company and made payable to LaPointe.

The firms were environmental consultants, engineers, surveyors, and attorneys. They each got checks from New England

Green on the same dates, and promptly turned those checks back over to the personal account of the man who had signed the check.

"It's called skimming," Penny said. "Your father authorizes New England Green to pay out money to these companies. These may not even be real ones. It's all designed to look on the up-and-up, but it's all illegal. The thing is, financial firms – including Pilgrim State Investments – are required to monitor deposits for suspicious activity and report anything that raises a red flag. The people who run Pilgrim State obviously aren't doing that."

"So, you're saying this is a financial company that caters to crooks," Allie said.

"Yes," Penny said. "And the question is, what do we do?"

After a moment's pause, Allie said, "We eat this food before it gets cold. We figure out to whom we give these hard drives so the information can't be lost or stolen. Then we go see Helga."

* * * * *

Zoe Matthews finished reading Penelope Walden's doctoral dissertation shortly after 8 p.m. It had taken six hours, much of that time spent Googling the meaning of words contained in the document. Until noon, she had been aware of pheromones only as something added to high-end perfumes and lotions as a lure for the opposite sex; a proposition that sounded dubious at best. Now, she knew that pheromones were all through the plant and animal kingdom.

So, why would someone who probably made millions writing about revenge against a professor who regularly seduced his female students choose to devote her life to the study of trees communicating with one another?

It was a perplexing anomaly. P.D. Walden had written a book that made her famous, then *ran* away from that fame and buried herself in science. To get a PhD she had to first get a Masters. It was likely she had spent the past six years hiding in the anonymity of academia. Only a few close friends knew where she was and P.D. – or Penny or Penelope – strictly controlled the circumstances of whatever communications took place. As Lizette Robles had said, *With Penny, you have to wait for her to start the conversation…*

But here was P.D. Walden. Two hundred pages including footnotes. Years of research on an arcane subject. And, in all likelihood, not a single person at Duke had ever made the connection between the graduate student in the next seat and the woman who penned that deliciously satisfying story.

And, here at the end of the dissertation, was her next clue: *'I would especially like to thank my thesis advisor, Dr. Rafael Madan, for his support and encouragement. Without his guidance, this dissertation would have been abandoned a dozen times.'*

There was only one Rafael Madan listed in the Durham area. She could have called him at home, but she needed to be fresh and to have an inventive story. She had progressed so far so quickly, and she was now so close. She could wait a few more hours.

* * * * *

"How could he do something so stupid?" Helga asked for perhaps the fifth time. "Brian is many things. Stupid is not one of them."

Penny and Allie were at the Coolidge Hill house. Allie had printed out more than thirty sheets of paper showing check images and account deposits. Collectively, they told the damning story of Brian LaPointe's near-two-decade-long theft from his employer.

"This isn't stupidity," Penny said. "This is greed. I don't know him and I certainly don't pretend to know why he skimmed all that money from New England Green. But what he has done here is exceptionally smart. Somehow, eighteen years ago, he managed to hook up with a money manager who is more than willing to take in dirty money."

"And you're certain that's what Brian has gotten himself into?" Helga asked, looking tired.

Allie answered the question. "There's no other explanation. I Googled these companies that are supposedly doing work for New

England Green. I can't find any record of them. They exist just for the purpose of receiving checks and turning them back over to Brian."

"And no one at New England Green has figured this out?" Helga asked.

"Guess who hires the bookkeeping staff?" Allie replied. "They may not even be employees. New England Green prides itself on being staffed by volunteers. My guess is Brian looks for the dumbest people who cross his doorway."

Helga sighed and shook her head. "I had no idea."

"There is no other way to read these deposit slips," Penny said. "Your ex-husband invests his money with people who cater to criminals. I expect they take a hefty fee for looking the other way."

"*Må den jäveln få vad som kommer till honom*," Helga said.

Penny looked at Allie, hoping for a translation.

"May the bastard get what's coming to him," Allie whispered. "Truer words were never spoken."

WEDNESDAY

Chapter Eleven

Emily Taylor Rice's cell phone chirped at 8:42 a.m. She was on the Southeast Expressway's express lanes, which crept along only a few miles per hour faster than the non-express inbound lanes. The call's origin bore a '44' country code. It was coming from the United Kingdom.

There was no privacy panel between the front and back seat of her car, so Emily leaned as if to look out the back window as she answered.

"Ms. Rice, this is Darlene Harris. My phone won't work over here, but Sir Charles let me call from his office."

"How did it go?" Emily asked, feeling the pounding of her heart.

"I have everything you asked for. Sir Charles made it awfully easy."

"When are you coming home?" Emily asked.

"It's just before 2 p.m. here," Darlene said. "A University car is taking me to the Bradford Airport. "There's a 4:40 flight that gets in at 7:20, but I don't know if I can make that one. If not, I can be on a 6:55 flight that gets in at 9:30 tonight."

"Either flight is fine," Emily said, trying to contain her excitement. "Did he push back on the wording?"

"It's almost exactly what you asked for," Darlene said. "I don't even see the difference. There's no — what's the word? — equivocation. You can only read this one way."

Emily felt a flush of gratitude. "Thank you, Darlene," she said. "Will Sir Charles let you call home to let your mother know you're on your way, or would you like me to make that call for you?"

"We got along pretty well," Darlene said. "I think I can squeeze in one more call. The car should be here in about five minutes."

"Then I'll see you bright and early tomorrow morning," Emily said. "And, once again, I can't thank you enough."

Emily looked up to see her driver's eyes in the rear view mirror.

"I hope that was good news, Ms. Rice," he said, seeing the smile on her face.

"The best kind of news," Emily replied. "In fact, I'm going to lay my head back and try to get a little rest."

* * * * *

Zoe collected her thoughts, went through a deep-breathing exercise, and felt ready to make her call. Her research notes were in front of her, spread out across her cubicle. She pressed the buttons on her cell phone.

Two transfers later, she heard a ringing at the other end of the line. On the second ring, she heard, "Rafael Madan." It was a statement.

"Dr. Madan, my name is Zoe Matthews and I work with Clark Search in New York, and I'm having difficulty tracking down one of your doctoral candidates. I wonder if you can help me?"

"I'll try," Madan said. "Which one?"

"Penelope Walden…" Zoe replied, and promptly heard laughter on the other end of the line.

"She *is* a hard one to get hold of," Madan said. "I'm afraid you're about ten days too late. She just started a job."

"You're kidding," Zoe said. "I find the perfect candidate for a dream job, and she's been snatched up by someone else?"

"That's what I said," Madan replied.

"In plant-based pheromones?" Zoe said, skimming her crib sheet. "A university? I'll bet my client can offer double what she's getting."

There was more laughter. "No, this is corporate R&D. A start-up. Scads of options, first-rate funding. I've never seen her more excited."

"In plant-based pheromones?" Zoe said. "I read her dissertation. She has some brilliant insights."

"Not plant based, but she gets a quarter of her time to pursue independent inquiry with world-class equipment. I'm sorry, but you know I can't say who her employer is."

Zoe was writing as fast as she could.

"I understand that you can't tell me the company," Zoe said. "But do you think she might consider something in the Northeast?"

"I can tell you her job is… in the Northeast," Madan said. "This is really plant pheromones your client is doing? I know Monsanto R&D is in St. Louis and…"

"Ms. Walden has a unique skill set," Zoe said. "If I give you my number, will you ask her to get in touch with me?"

"I can do that," Madan said. "But why weren't you down here in the spring?"

"If it had been my assignment back then, I would have had her on a plane in a heartbeat," Zoe replied. "I've only been looking since last Wednesday. May I at least ask what city she's in?"

More laughter. "Give me the phone number. We'll let her tell you the city if she's interested."

Zoe concluded the call and went immediately to Google. *Start up, high funding, pheromones…* She plugged in search terms from her notes. Satisfied, she tapped the little magnifying glass icon.

From the *Boston Business Journal*: *Pheromonix Comes Out of Stealth Mode, Leases Kendall Square Offices.*

Zoe read the article. This had to be the company Madan had been referring to. 'Product-ize' pheromone research and a start up with blue-chip funding. A further Google search on Pheromonix turned up recruitment ads for researchers with the inducement of offering 'ample time for independent inquiry using state-of-the-art lab tools'.

She found the telephone number for the company in

Cambridge and, as she suspected, she found herself in a telephone tree.

"For our dial-by-name directory, you may say or type in the last name of the person you are trying to reach…"

"Walden," Zoe said, and held her breath.

A woman's voice said, *"Hi, this is Penny. I'm out right now…"*

Zoe hung up. *I finally found you.*

* * * * *

Brian felt on top of the world. Outside his window, he could see a docent-led tour of the Rose Gallery. Dozens of other visitors wandered the gardens with maps and cameras in hand. In those gardens, volunteers on their hands and knees happily worked at weeding; a ten-dollar pizza was ample reward for four or five hours of labor that would otherwise cost the organization hundreds of dollars.

New England Green was a money machine. Fewer than two dozen paid staffers – most of them site managers – oversaw more than two hundred volunteers and interns. Even critical positions in finance and accounting were staffed by retirees giving of their time for a noble cause.

In the meantime, everyone who walked through the gate at the Beckwith Estate, Grey Harbor Beach, or any of New England Green's 72 properties paid either ten dollars admission or showed a membership card for which they had paid between $85 and $250.

Yes, there was upkeep. Old buildings needed new roofs and fifteen-year-old trucks broke down. New England Green's monthly newsletter, *The Greensward*, chronicled each and every capital expenditure. When Brian could cajole a roofing company into doing an installation for free, he was more than happy to appear in a photograph with the company's owners at the installation site, and to feature the act of generosity in *The Greensward*.

Staring at a stack of invoices for vehicle maintenance, he had an idea: why not allow members to 'adopt a truck'? For a hundred dollars a year (on top of membership dues), someone could have their name on a piece of New England Green's rolling stock. He wrote the idea on a pad of paper. Later, he would flesh it out into a memo to go to the organization's Communications Director.

He also thought of yesterday and this morning. Emily had greeted him so warmly when he arrived at Crow Point last evening, blissfully unaware that he was fresh from a romp in the hay – literally – with the nubile and always-willing Amber Oakes. Emily had made dinner and paired it with an exquisite Burgundy. She maintained a lively conversation through the evening and even snuggled next to him when they retired to bed. This morning, she was still all smiles.

Life is good, he thought. His little display of dominance in the restaurant had paid huge dividends.

This weekend they were supposed to be at Popham Beach in Maine. Their hosts would be a lovely couple in their sixties from New York who shared several of Emily's causes. There would be ample time alone. Perhaps this was the weekend to finally have that serious conversation about marriage.

Brian signed the auto repair bills and took them to the headquarters accounts payable clerk, a 72-year-old woman whom Brian knew doted on him. He took care to cultivate his relationship with Priscilla Wilson. Half a dozen times a year she unquestioningly processed a sheaf of professional services invoices for non-existent firms providing illusory services.

"Good morning, Priscilla," Brian said and smiled warmly. Priscilla beamed. "These good people have kept our motor fleet in tip-top shape. I think we ought to pay them. Would you take care of this?"

Priscilla had a look of gratitude on her face. "Of course, Mr. LaPointe."

"I see what looks like a garden club group down in the rose

garden," Brian said. "I think I'm going to go down and say 'hello'."

Life isn't just good, he thought as he left the building. *It's downright spectacular.*

* * * * *

Penny saw the light go on briefly on her office phone, but the caller didn't leave a message, which was good. She was in no mood to speak to anyone.

She had slept poorly, her mind trying to come to grips with what she and Allie had learned about Pilgrim State Investments.

In the middle of the night, unable to sleep, she had opened her computer, plugged in one of the portable drives containing a copy of the Pilgrim State server contents and began Googling the names of other account holders. The other individuals that had entrusted their nest eggs to the firm included a Boston city councilman, two mayors of faded Massachusetts cities, eight state representatives including two from Rhode Island, several judges, multiple presidents and business managers of union locals, and an assortment of wealthy individuals. All had multi-million-dollar accounts, many in eight figures.

While they all could be honest people with legitimate investments, Penny suspected otherwise. She picked a half dozen names and looked at their history of deposits. The Boston city councilman tended to bring in $50,000 and more in cash. One Rhode Island state senator deposited $300,000. A union president dropped off $10,000 each month, always in cash.

Pilgrim State Investments catered to dishonest people who worked in sectors of the economy where rivers of cash flowed by them every day. These people had elected to periodically scoop buckets full of that money from that river. Pilgrim State did not ask why someone brought in a briefcase full of hundred-dollar bills to deposit. They just accepted the contents and gave the thief a receipt.

It was entirely possible that David Hale had assumed her funds were also the product of crime; perhaps drugs or embezzlement. Why else would a woman in her late twenties have so much money and be so vague about its origin?

Trying to fall asleep, Penny asked herself another question: why had Hale initially rebuffed her? If her money was tainted, then it was joining a billion-dollar pool of similarly ill-gotten gains. He should have tried to sign her up on the spot. But he had instead played a cat-and-mouse game of telling her to stay with her current firm before relenting and telling her he would try to accommodate her account. Even crooked investment advisors should be willing to take the occasional honestly-earned nest egg.

Just as she was finally back to sleep, she awoke with a start. Two words had formed in her mind: *'tainted fruit'*.

Her initial advice to Allie had been to take evidence of Brian LaPointe's theft from New England Green to a law enforcement agency; either the FBI or the Massachusetts Attorney General.

Before last night, Allie might have been able to make a case that, for years, her father had left account statements lying around his desk. Now, she had hacked into a money management firm's computer system without a warrant. Pilgrim State's attorneys would argue – successfully – that any law enforcement action was based on that illegal search and therefore inadmissible as evidence.

David Hale and everyone else at the firm could walk away free, while she and Allie went to jail.

She needed an expert on such things, or someone who had access to experts. But how do you tell someone that, in the process of trying to ruin the reputation of a thief, you've stumbled upon evidence that there's a financial advisory firm in Chestnut Hill that specializes in investing dirty money?

There was one possible person to ask: Emily Taylor Rice.

Helga said she planned to tell her what they were planning to do. Allie had been more ambivalent. To the best of Penny's knowledge, neither had yet made the effort to reach out to Rice.

And, this being Wednesday, Helga would be in a staff meeting much of the day.

Penny felt the plan had passed a point of no return. Until last evening, there was a chance that Allie might reconsider. Now, that was no longer possible.

And so, at 6:30 a.m. with perhaps two hours of sleep for the night, Penny had again turned on her computer and pulled up the website for The Gerald and Abigail Rice Foundation. Oddly, Emily Taylor Rice's photo was nowhere to be found. But there was an address: One Post Office Square.

How do you approach the head of a multi-billion-dollar foundation who has no idea of who you are?

Penny ran through the possibilities, each more likely to be a dead end than the last. In the end, she kept coming back to the first option: a full, frontal assault.

She did not own a wardrobe that would radiate an aura of seriousness. Her small closet was filled with jeans, tees, and sandals. She had briefly owned what she called 'interview' clothes for her book tour, but she had long since given those clothes away. Her job search had been largely conducted online, including Skype interviews that required no special clothes. Absent a time-consuming trip to a department store, what she was wearing would have to suffice.

Penny gathered her purse, into which she slipped her iPad and two of the small drives containing one of the copies of Pilgrim State's records, and set off for the Red Line and work. She would give Emily Taylor Rice an hour or so to have a normal day, then head back across the Charles River and make her pitch.

* * * * *

Emily settled into her office and unfolded a list she had written the previous day. There was nothing on this list that she could set into motion until Darlene's return tomorrow morning, but she could at least relish the plan.

1)   Identify and rent effective immediately an appropriate furnished apartment for Brian. Two months should be adequate.

2)   Engage a moving service that can be ready to go to work on an hour's notice. One mid-size truck should be adequate.

3)   Engage a round-the-clock security presence for Crow Point starting on one day's notice. Off-duty police as backup?

4)   Prepare announcement. Vet with attorney as needed.

5)   Prepare personal statement. Vet with attorney as needed.

6)   On the day of the announcement and after he has left for work, tag everything at Crow Point that belongs to Brian.

7)   Change all locks at Crow Point.

8)   Make and distribute announcement to media and NEG trustees.

It was an eminently satisfying list, all in all. In one glorious day, Brian would be out of her life. She could state in complete truth that Brian no longer resided at Crow Point and that she was no longer in contact with him. It would be clear, though, that she was the person who called attention to the Trustees and the world that Brian LaPointe was a fraud.

No one could ever link her name to Sandra Boss.

Re-reading the list, though, Emily realized that she had failed to include notification of Brian's ex-wife. She had promised herself and told Elaine and Alan she would do so. There was every possibility that, when the Trustees fired Brian, they would also terminate the lease on the Coolidge Hill home that was, at least nominally, Brian's of-record place of residence.

How much advance notice should they get? It should be no later than the time the announcement was approved, but that might be less than a day before the whole matter went public. Surely, as innocent parties, they deserved more than a day's notice…

The phone on her desk beeped, indicating a call from the reception desk. Ordinarily, Darlene would have answered, but she was on her way to an airport in Yorkshire and Emily did not want a temp at such a crucial time.

Emily picked up the phone. "What's the problem?" she asked.

The receptionist spoke in a somewhat hesitant voice. "There's a woman here who insists on seeing you. She doesn't have an appointment but she says it's an emergency. She says it regards Helga Johanssen and Allie's father."

"What's the woman's name?" Emily asked.

There was a muffled conversation and then the receptionist came back on. "She says her name is Penny Walden but that you and she have never met. She said she is working with Helga and Allie on a critical matter that involves Allie's father." The receptionist added softly, "Do you want me to call building security?"

'Helga Johanssen and Allie' could only mean Brian's ex-wife and daughter. Emily was seized with panic. *What if they've already somehow found out about Darlene being in Leeds? What if word is already leaking out?*

Emily said, "Ask Ms.... I forgot her name... if she is an attorney."

Another muffled conversation. "No," the receptionist said. "She says she is not an attorney. Her name is Penny Walden and she is just someone who is working with 'Helga and Allie'."

Emily felt sick to her stomach.

"Shall I call building security?" the receptionist repeated.

"No." Emily said. "I'll be right out."

Emily's first impression of the woman in the reception area was that she might be a lost, out-of-town tourist who had wandered in from the park and was looking for directions. Late twenties, moderately tall, straight brown hair that fell below her shoulders. An intelligent face, but a woman dressed in jeans and a white tee. Either this was a spur-of-the-moment decision to come here or else something was wrong.

She held out her hand but offered no smile. "I'm Emily Taylor Rice."

The woman took her hand in a firm handshake. "Penny Walden."

"Can you tell me what this is about?" Emily asked.

Penny shook her head and indicated the receptionist with a tilt of her head. "Not here. This has to do with Allie's father. *It affects you.*" She said those last words in a low but forceful voice.

There was an earnestness in the woman's voice. This was no ploy to sneak in to plead a cause or seek employment.

"I know of whom you're speaking," Emily said. "Let's go back to my office."

* * * * *

Penny's first impression was how young Emily looked. Gorgeous, with blonde hair in a salon cut and a fresh blow-out. Impeccably dressed in a green skirted suit, discreet gold earrings, and with perfect makeup. She had heard from Helga that Emily was in her mid-thirties, but this woman could be five years younger. There was not a blemish on her face and not an extra pound on her body. This was Woman as Perfection.

Emily led her through two corridors of offices. The walls were a muted blue-grey and adorned with artwork. A few doors were open and, in them, youngish men and women worked at computers, spoke on phones, or read reports in spacious, well-lit offices.

Emily's office had an unattended secretarial station outside of it. She beckoned Penny in, then closed the door behind her. Emily went to a small round table and took a seat. She made a gesture that invited Penny to join her. Beyond the round table was a rectangular desk and a bookshelf that stretched the length of one wall. The focus of the room, though, was a floor-to-ceiling window that spanned twenty feet. Beyond the window were the tops of trees in the park across the street.

"Why don't you start by telling me who you are and why you're here," Emily said. She used a business-like voice and there was more than a little wariness in it.

"My name is Penny Walden. I work at a start-up in Kendall Square called Pheromonix. Helga Johanssen is my boss and the…"

Emily shook her head and held up a hand. "I'm sorry, I believe Helga works at MIT."

"She did," Penny replied. "Helga is a recognized leader in pheromone research. She was hired last year to head R&D at Pheromonix. She recruited me from Duke, where I just got my PhD."

"And what does this have to do with Brian?" Emily asked. There was still no warmth.

"Last week, Helga's daughter, Allie – Alexandra – approached me to help her…"

"Allie is still in high school, I believe," Emily said.

"She just graduated and will be going to MIT in September," Penny replied. "She is an exceptionally bright lady. And I'll cut to the important part: Allie has conclusive proof that her father has been skimming millions of dollars from New England Green. It has been going on for more than a decade and it totals ten million dollars."

Emily could not breathe. She placed her hands on the table to steady herself.

"Do you have some kind of identification?" Emily asked after she recovered.

Penny took her Pheromonix lanyard out of her purse, and her North Carolina driver's license from her wallet. "I didn't ask for business cards," she said. "I didn't think I'd have much use for them."

Emily picked up the two laminated plastic cards. Both had photos of the woman in front of her. One could have been taken today; the other was two or three years old but unmistakably this woman. The lanyard had a telephone number on it.

Emily held up the lanyard. "Do you mind if I verify this?"

"My extension is 58," Penny said. "Helga's is 11. She's in a staff meeting, though."

Emily said nothing, but tapped keys at the phone on her desk and listened to the responses. Three minutes later, she hung up the phone and returned to the table. She returned the two tags to Penny.

"You are who you say you are," Emily said, taking a seat at the table. "Now, tell me about ten million dollars you say Brian has skimmed."

For half an hour, Penny spoke almost without interruption. A few minutes into the explanation, she pulled out the same iPad she had used at Pilgrim State, which now contained PDFs of Brian LaPointe's brokerage statements. Penny toggled between statements, showing New England Green checks written to attorneys, land surveyors, and other professionals; each of which had endorsed those checks over to LaPointe for deposit into the brokerage account.

Then, using Google, Penny demonstrated that the firms existed only on paper as conduits for just such transactions. After seeing the third non-existent firm, Emily said, "You've convinced me. But how do you know I'm not going to take all of this straight to Brian?"

"I don't," Penny replied. "It's possible you may care so much about him that you'll have that receptionist call building security to have me detained somewhere while you and Brian figure out how to hide this."

Penny paused. *Here it goes*, she thought. "But I can't imagine that someone who had made it her life's work to give away money to make the world a better place would knowingly condone someone stealing money from an organization like New England Green. I'm telling you because you need to know while you still have some control over how people see you after this comes out – which it will."

"But why are *you* here?" Emily asked. "I've never met Helga Johanssen and she certainly has nothing to fear from me. Why isn't *she* here? I don't see how you fit into this. For a start, you're brand new to the company."

Penny was silent, wondering how much to say about herself. She came down on the side of saying less.

"In a sense, this is all Allie's doing. Based on the papers she regularly found in Brian's desk, she suspected something even... before he left. It took her several years to gain enough understanding of banking and money to put the pieces together. When she did, she wanted to go public with it." Penny paused and spoke carefully. "Allie never forgave her father for leaving. It's something that has been festering for four years. Helga made it clear she planned to tell you before anything was said publicly. She doesn't want you to be caught off guard or taken down for something you knew nothing about. She believes – as do I – that you're an innocent party in all of this. You've done nothing wrong."

The words took Emily by surprise. *You've done nothing wrong.* They were the same words Brian had used at lunch. But that had been in response to her telling him a completely fabricated tale about a supposed theft of funds...

That's it! Emily thought. *Brian's abnormal physical reaction as she told him the story seemed so wrong – the clenched fists and pale face. He thought I was talking about him! He thought I knew.... And then he began squeezing my hands so hard that it hurt...*

Emily realized her eyes were closed as she recalled that tense moment. "I'm sorry," she said. "This is a lot to absorb."

"It was for me as well," Penny said. "But I need your advice." She took out the hard drive containing a copy of Pilgrim State's server contents and laid it on the desk. "We need your help in figuring out what to do with this. In the process of documenting one crime, we've uncovered a larger one: that Pilgrim State

Investments is a haven for people with dirty money. It isn't just Brian. I went through enough accounts this morning to convince myself that many, if not most, of their clients are using Pilgrim State to hide and invest money they can't take to a bank."

Penny paused to make certain her words had registered. "My problem is that Allie and I used illegal means to get this information. I don't pretend to understand the law, but I suspect that what we did can undo a criminal investigation if a law enforcement agency relied on it. I have no idea what to do next. But I'm hoping you know people who may be able to help."

"The 'exclusionary rule'," Emily said. "I know there are exceptions to it, but I don't know what they are. I do know some people…"

"Then you'll help?" Penny asked.

Emily looked into Penny's face. There was no question but that what this woman was saying was true. The anguish was genuine. Emily still did not know and could not guess why Penny Walden had gotten so deeply involved in this matter in such a brief period of time. But she had made an extraordinary effort to reach out…

She deserved to know the rest of the story.

"Penny, there's one more element to this that you need to know about," Emily said. "By comparison to what you've told me, what I have to tell you is so minor as to be… a parking ticket. But it has haunted me for the past week."

Emily saw that she had Penny's attention. "I'm sure you know by now that Brian and I have lived together for most of the past four years. Until last week it would have been fair to say that we were on the verge of making plans to be married. It was only my hesitation that stood in the way, and I had come around to the idea that marrying and starting a family with Brian was the right thing to do."

"I had been casting around for a surprise present and I hit on the idea of taking him to his alma mater – the university in Great Britain where he got his doctorate. This is the twentieth anniversary and I assumed there would be some kind of reunion this summer. Because Brian is such a respected figure in horticulture and conservation in this country, I thought Leeds Beckett – the school he attended there – might like to have him speak."

Emily paused, collecting her story. "I got in touch with the gentleman pulling together the reunion. He told me – gently but in no uncertain terms – that Brian does not hold a doctorate from there. He never attended the school. Yet, I've seen the diploma in his office a hundred times."

"Incredible," Penny said. "Academic fraud."

Emily nodded. "And the more important position someone holds, the more serious the repercussions. I sit on several corporate Boards of Directors. I've personally been part of the decision to fire senior vice presidents who claimed MBAs or other degrees they didn't have. You don't allow it. Now, imagine that the Executive Director of one of the most prominent horticultural organizations in the country is found not to have the PhD that got him the job."

"What were you planning to do?" Penny asked.

Emily rose from her chair and went to her desk. From it she extracted the sheet of paper she had written just yesterday. She gave it to Penny. "You can choose to believe me or not, but just a little while ago, I was trying to decide where 'notifying Helga' ought to go on this list."

"Why tell her ahead of time?" Penny asked.

"Because she – and Allie – live in a house owned by New England Green. It's leased to Brian. If I were New England Green, I'd want it back."

Penny read the list. Puzzled, she asked, "What 'announcement' are you referring to?"

Emily again sat down at the table. "Yesterday I sent my PA to Leeds. She is on her way back right now. She is carrying a letter – actually, multiple copies of a letter – stating what I told you just a minute ago; that Brian is claiming a PhD he never earned. I plan to make that public."

Penny glanced down at the list. "And you plan to have all his things removed from 'Crow Point' and sent to an apartment. And then post a security guard."

Emily nodded. "Yes. All of that. Crow Point is where we live in Hingham."

"You feel that strongly?" Penny asked.

"It isn't just that I feel that strongly," Emily replied. "It's the ripples of what happens after something like this becomes public. If I say, 'Clark Rockefeller', what does that mean to you?"

Penny immediately said, "The German guy. He kidnapped his daughter…"

"What about his ex-wife?" Emily asked.

"That poor woman…" Penny said.

"Exactly. '*That poor woman*'. She had a Harvard MBA and a rising career as an international consultant as a partner at McKinsey. When 'Clark Rockefeller' was found to be a fraud, someone who had a glorious future became 'that poor woman'. She had actually been divorced from him for several years when all this happened. I won't let that happen to me. But a fraudulent degree is fairly trivial compared to stealing millions from New England Green. More like a postscript… 'Oh, and by the way, he didn't have the degree he claimed, either'."

"What do we do?" Penny asked.

"I make one or two discreet phone calls," Emily said. "This list grew out of an all-night conversation I had this past weekend with some old and quite close friends, one of whom happens to be an exceptionally good attorney. He's not criminal law, but he may have some useful ideas." She paused and added, "The Foundation also has one of the biggest and best law firms in the country on retainer. They might know a few things… though the problem is discretion…"

Emily again paused. "One of things Alan – my lawyer friend – said is that a man like Brian may well try to charm his way out of his box. It might have worked if we were just talking about a degree. Millions in an account is something quite different."

Emily rose a final time and, sensing the meeting had come to an end, so did Penny. "Go back to your office," Emily said. "Tell Helga and Allie we spoke. I don't know if I can get you an answer today, but I will try."

She added, "Thank you for being brave enough to come. We've just met, but I have a sense we're going to get to know one another extremely well over the next few days. Maybe you'll even feel comfortable enough to tell me how you got involved in all of this, because it certainly doesn't seem to be your fight. Above all, though, thank you."

The two women walked back to the reception area of the Gerald and Abigail Rice Foundation. Emily took Penny's hand in both of hers and held it. "This can't and shouldn't wait. I or someone I trust will be back in touch very soon," she whispered.

Chapter Twelve

"I've got *Entertainment Now's* biggest exclusive of the year," said Zoe Matthews confidently. "This story is going to lead every celebrity magazine's next issue, and I'll bet it even makes it over to the mainstream guys. And it's all ours."

Zoe was standing in the office of Michele Silverman, Senior Producer for Entertainment Now! Enterprises. Her office was not especially large and it was cluttered with boxes and electronic paraphernalia. Moreover, while the office had a window to the outside world, it looked out not onto Madison Avenue or even 37th Street but, rather, into the brick wall of an office building twenty feet away.

Silverman was vaguely aware that Zoe Matthews was still at *EN* and that she, Silverman, was nominally this intern's manager and 'mentor'. And Silverman was also painfully aware that the syndicated television show that anchored *EN's* existence had just lost its 7 p.m. time slot in Dallas and Minneapolis.

Were those things not the case, Silverman would have ordered Zoe out of her office and berated her for having failed to feed the website crawl for three days. She might even have fired the girl, except that Zoe was an unpaid intern and Silverman had no idea if interns could be fired.

Silverman was also something less than an inspiration to anyone in search of either a mentor or someone to emulate. She was 38 and, like Zoe, had once upon a time received a degree in journalism, though from Queens College. But her path into the industry had been a product of being born in the right year. She graduated when the Web was new, celebrity magazines were hot, and syndicated television seemed to be the solution to fill the 500-channel cable systems of the new century. Because Michele

Silverman had a pulse, she had a job. She had, however, stalled at the 'Senior Producer' level (the lowest rung of that particular food chain) and was careful to make no demands on *EN* management that might bring her existence to the attention of anyone with budget-cutting as part of their purview.

In fact, her greatest contribution to *EN*'s still-positive cash flow was her recommendation that no offer of full-time employment need be made to Zoe or any of the other interns. 'They're hungry. They'll stick around,' had been her words of wisdom and, indeed, she had been proven correct.

That Zoe was living off of uneaten executive sandwiches and bags of chips nagged at Silverman's near-nonexistent conscience, and it was that thought that caused her to humor Zoe. "And what is this monumental exclusive?" Silverman asked.

"I need a camera crew and I want a guarantee of full-time employment starting immediately," Zoe said, dodging Silverman's question. "And I want to produce the segment."

Silverman gritted her teeth. "I can't agree to any of that if I don't know the story. If I don't get the courtesy of that information, my hands are tied and I can't do a thing."

Zoe pondered the counteroffer. "I've found P.D. Walden."

Suddenly, Silverman was interested. Many story conferences ended with the Senior Executive Producer joking, 'Don't call me unless you've got Johnny Depp or P.D. Walden in the Green Room.'

"And where is she?" Silverman said, feigning indifference by twirling a pen in her fingers.

"Just know that I've found her," Zoe countered. "I know where she's been for the past several years, and I know where she's working right now."

"And how can you be so certain of these things?" Still more feigned indifference.

"Research," Zoe said. "I'm a hundred percent solid on my

facts."

"You've spoken to her?" Silverman asked. "She has agreed to be interviewed?"

"I'm not stupid," Zoe said. "I know how this works. I've been paying attention for the last *nine months*." Zoe thumped the 'nine months' as an accusation.

Silverman's mind was working quickly. Her intern had indeed done the right thing. She had identified the subject and verified the information without actually confronting the subject until a trap could be set.

"I can't just turn loose a crew on your word, Zoe," Silverman said soothingly. "I need to take this up the chain of command. My boss is going to have to take it to her boss. I need a memo. Outline how you found P.D. Walden and what sources you used. Tell me how many people you'll need and what kind of travel allowance it will take. Tell me if you'll need overnight accommodations. If you have a preference of talent and crew based on who you've seen around here, tell me who *you* want to work with on this assignment. And give me a separate memo with a suggested salary."

The last two parts were intended to be the hook. Make this dumb intern think she's going to go out and produce the hottest story of the year, and get a producer's job on the strength of one interview.

"Oh," Silverman said. "Zoe, why do you think the MSM is going to find this newsworthy?"

Zoe grinned. "Because she's working in a research lab. P.D. Walden is a scientist."

Silverman's pulse raced. *Jesus Christ. This is a New York Times story. Lead story in the Arts section at minimum, even page one if we pitch it right.* What she said, in a modulated voice, was "Just get me the memo. Today."

Zoe retreated to her office, fuming. Going to Michele had been a calculated risk. The result she had hoped for was one of

Silverman reaching for her phone to tell her boss, Jillian Martin, that the two of them were on their way down with a scoop. The even better outcome would have been for the three of them, arm-in-arm, to march down the hall and bang on the door of Stephen Brooks, *EN*'s Senior Executive Producer. Instead, Zoe had been asked to "write a memo".

What kind of an idiot does she take me for? Oh, certainly, Ms. Silverman. I will write down all the details you need to take this into your boss – with my name omitted and yours inserted – and your boss will take it to the top level with her own name on it. I should have seen this coming. But guess what? I didn't give you the information you wanted, did I?

Zoe began carefully composing her memo, which was created as a Word document rather than an email. While her name on the proposal that ultimately went to the show's Executive Producer would bear no trace of her identity, she did not want any digital trail that led back to her. *Patricia (P.D.) Walden is currently working as a researcher at…*Zoe pulled up LinkedIn, typed in 'Patricia Walden', and began scrolling through entries. *…Bristol Meyers Squibb in Lawrenceville, NJ. She has been employed there for the past two years. She received her graduate degree (MS in Chemistry, PhD in Molecular Chemistry) from the University of Washington. I traced her…*

After thirty minutes, she had composed a completely plausible contact chronology for P.D. Walden. She appended a list of camera and audio people who ought to be involved (in her view, the ones with the biggest egos and least talent); and the glossiest, brassiest, and most empty-headed on-camera 'personality'. If all went well, next Monday or Tuesday, some unsuspecting woman was going to go out to her car after work and be ambushed by lights and cameras. If all went *really* well, the woman would have a viable multi-million-dollar lawsuit against Entertainment Now! Enterprises.

Zoe briefly considered what to write in a memo with a salary request. Go big or go reasonable? It made no difference, of course.

Until the interview blew up in someone's face and heads began to roll, her name would not be mentioned and her contribution would be strenuously denied. Only an autopsy of a scoop gone horribly wrong would resurrect the ghost of her existence at *EN*.

Of course, in a legitimate news operation, each of Zoe's facts would have been meticulously checked prior to the interview and, when that first 'contact' turned out to be an invention, the entire chain would become suspect. As more sources were called, questions would mount until it became clear that the entire story was a fabrication.

However, because *Entertainment Now!* was built on a foundation of ephemeral and ultimately pointless gossip, checking facts was an expensive and time-consuming abstraction. Zoe could be completely certain her two-page memorandum would be taken as gospel right up until the moment the Senior Executive Producer understood that the bewildered scientist in the parking lot was not the person he had been promised by his staff.

Zoe dashed off a note with a salary request that was eminently reasonable. She added a second paragraph to the note saying, apologetically, that she had a doctor's appointment in New Jersey and would be out for the balance of the day. The note went into an envelope and was placed in the interoffice mail box. She then collected the most personal of her cubicle artifacts, leaving behind just enough items to make it appear to the casual observer that she had every intention of returning.

From under her desk she took a modest-size pink shopping bag. In it were fifteen high-end Android phones she had accumulated from unattended swag bags during the preceding four months. She already had a cash buyer for these phones, which would finance her trip to Boston.

Instead of leaving through the lobby, Zoe slipped down the stairwell. As the door closed behind her, she silently said goodbye to nine months of her life that produced a series of 'teachable moments' she would never forget, and make certain she never repeated.

* * * * *

Two hours after returning to her lab, Penny's office phone rang. It was the receptionist and she was in a foul temper. "There's someone in reception asking for you. He won't give his name."

"I'll be right out," Penny said.

Two days a week, Pheromonix hosted what it called 'scent trials'. Cat owners were invited to bring in their pets with a promise of a fifty dollar payment for allowing their pets to react to pheromones culled from volunteer animals and reproduced in small samples in Pheromonix's lab. Although the company now had a database of more than seven hundred felines representing every age and breed, word continued to spread about the program. On this Wednesday afternoon, some thirty women, all with cats in carriers, waited hopefully to be added to the inventory. The fifteen-by-thirty-foot room was a cacophony of plaintive mewing, which accounted for the receptionist's mood.

There was only one person in the lobby who was not holding a cat carrier and Penny approached him. He was a tall man in his late twenties, dressed in neatly-pressed khaki pants and a checked shirt. His hair was blond, he wore glasses, and Penny had a vague sense that she knew him from somewhere.

"I'm Penny Walden," she said, offering her hand.

"Jason Curran," the man said, giving Penny a firm handshake. "I'm here at the request of Emily Taylor Rice…"

Penny's eyes widened. "That was fast."

Looking around the room, Curran said, "Can we find a place a little less noisy to talk?"

"Come with me," Penny said, smiling.

With the door closed in Penny's office, Curran said, "I'm with Steele & Hanley." Seeing the blank look on Penny's face, he added, "It's a large law firm over on Boylston Street."

"Maybe you ought to tell me why you think you're here," Penny said. It wasn't that she didn't trust this person who had showed up without calling first. She just wanted to know what information Emily had divulged in order to get a lawyer on two hours' notice.

Curran smiled. "I'll tell you if you let me sit down."

"That was rude," Penny replied. "How about water or something else? We're well stocked."

Curran took the chair Allie had sat in five days earlier; the meeting that had started all of this.

"I'm good for now," he said. "Actually, in the annals of stodgy, white-shoe law, this is the most cloak-and-dagger thing I've ever done. About 45 minutes ago, my boss showed up in my office, closed the door behind him, and asked, 'Do you have any personal or professional connection to New England Green?' I said 'no'. Then he asked, 'Do you know anyone who works at New England Green?' I racked my brain and couldn't come up with anyone. Then he asked, 'Do you still remember your criminal law courses?' I said it had been four years and I hadn't had occasion to put it to use, but that I remembered what I learned. He pondered that for a moment and then said, 'I'm sending you on a personal mission for one of our clients. If I say Emily Taylor Rice, do you know who I'm talking about?' On that one, I said that I knew the name and knew her foundation was a client. He told me to come here. He gave me your name and said I was to use Ms. Rice's name and to be of whatever help you needed. He said it in a voice that implied I was to drop everything."

"Wow," Penny said.

"Like I said, cloak and dagger," Curran replied. "Tell me how I can help. And then, if you have time, tell me about those cats out there." He tilted his head in the direction of the lobby.

"I'm trying to figure out how badly I've stepped into something," Penny said. She then told Curran the story of being approached by Allie, of Allie's and Helga's relationship to Brian

LaPointe, LaPointe's theft of funds from New England Green, and Allie's hacking of Pilgrim State's computers. She left out only Emily's telling her of Brian's fraudulent degree.

Then Penny said, "You're not taking notes. Are you recording this?"

"Notes and recordings are subject to discovery," Curran replied. "My memory isn't. Fortunately, I have a pretty good memory."

"So, how much trouble am I in?" Penny asked.

"Let me ask you a few questions," Curran replied. "First – although I think I know the answer to this one – are you or Ms. LaPointe part of any law enforcement agency?"

"I don't think so," Penny laughed. "No, definitely not."

"Did any law enforcement agency approach either of you and ask you to visit Pilgrim State or steal their files?"

Penny shook her head. "We cooked that up completely on our own."

"Were either of you in contact with any law enforcement agency just prior to the time you and Allie set up this plan?"

"No, but that reminds me I need to change my driver's license and plates," Penny replied.

Curran smiled. "Here's what I know: Ms. LaPointe broke multiple laws by breaking into Pilgrim State's computers. You are an accomplice to what is called 'intellectual property theft' by having handed over that thumb drive knowing that it had a virus implanted in it."

"So I go to prison and Pilgrim State walks away free," Penny said, glumly.

"No, that's where you're wrong," Curran said. "There are a couple of loopholes in the Exclusionary Rule. I think you fit neatly into one of those. If a law enforcement agency – say, the Computer Crime Unit of the FBI – did what you and Ms. LaPointe did without first obtaining a warrant, all the resulting evidence would be thrown out. That's the 'tainted fruit' that awakened you last night. Similarly, if another law enforcement agency – say, the Mass State Police – obtained that information and then handed it over to the FBI, it would still be inadmissible. That's called the 'silver platter' standard. But if a private citizen like you and Ms. LaPointe provide that information – even though it was obtained illegally – it's all admissible."

"So I may not be going to jail," Penny said.

"Well, two things," Curran said. "First, Pilgrim State's attorneys would come down on the two of you pretty hard trying to establish that the FBI or someone else put you up to it. But, if there's no link, there's no case. On the other hand, they could come back at you with a civil action and, in that kind of a case, the fact that they were knowingly handling accounts filled with dirty money wouldn't matter. You stole their property. Of course, they'd be up to their neck in legal trouble with the feds, but they might do it out of spite – take you down with them. Treasury's Financial Crimes Enforcement Network or whoever gets this information could offer you immunity from prosecution and a criminal charge, but civil court is another matter. I'd have to research that one."

"Should I feel better?" Penny asked.

"You should feel like you've dodged a bullet," Curran said, again smiling. "If I have your permission, I'll ask if we can be the intermediary to take this to the right law enforcement agency."

"I'll have to clear that with Allie," Penny said. "This is all her doing." The she paused and looked quizzically at Curran. "You never asked me how I got involved in all this. Is that a lawyer thing?"

Curran laughed. "May I ask you two questions?"

"You haven't asked me enough questions yet?"

Curran leaned toward Penny. "Did you grow up in Southern California? Somewhere in the San Gabriel Valley?"

Penny's brow furrowed. "Yes…"

"Did you go to Flintridge Prep?"

Penny laughed. "Yes."

"I was a year ahead of you. You graduated with my sister, Sarah Curran."

"I remember her," Penny said and laughed. "She was all about theater and art. You ran track and played basketball."

Curran nodded and smiled.

"How did you end up on the East Coast?" Penny asked.

"My parents moved west when my Mom went to work for JPL. They thought I ought to get a 'real' education, and so I got shipped to Colby College, where I was called 'surfer dude' and froze for four years. But several professors at Colby got me interested in the law and I applied to Harvard. That got me an offer from Steele & Hanley, where I'm a fourth year associate."

"But that doesn't answer how you knew about my getting sucked into this whole thing," Penny said.

Curran let out a sigh. "When I went back for Sarah's graduation – she went to USC – she told me she had seen you in a bookstore in Santa Monica a few weeks earlier. You wore sunglasses and even maybe a wig, but she was certain it was you. You had written a book..."

"Yeah," Penny said. "I wrote a book. Which I've been running away from for the past six or seven years. I can't wait until everyone says, 'P.D. who?'"

"I suspect guys weren't your primary audience, but I enjoyed it," Curran said. "You really had the revenge thing working. I was impressed."

"And so was Allie, who connected the dots," Penny added. "So, where do we go from here?"

"How do you feel about wine and pizza?" Curran asked.

"I'm sorry?" Penny replied. Then she understood the question and her face turned red. "I meant, what should I tell Helga and Allie?"

It was Curran's turn to be flustered. "My apology. That was out of bounds. You should tell Helga and Allie that we spoke and that my preliminary legal advice is that you aren't headed for Leavenworth anytime soon. You should put the evidence in a safe place and sit tight."

"There's another wrinkle," Penny said. "When I went to see Emily this morning, she told me about something else that is going on that relates to Brian LaPointe. I don't feel comfortable discussing it without her permission. I will tell you she has a timeline for a set of events and that it involves a public statement that has to be cleared with attorneys, according to the sheet I saw. There is some chance that Emily's issuing that statement might trigger Brian LaPointe to want to access that account."

Curran's surprise showed. "Would you say that announcement is close?"

"I would say that it may be closer than you can imagine. Emily told me she sent... someone she trusts to get verification of something, and that the person is due back this evening. But please don't ask me anything else."

"I won't," Curran said. I'll keep my ear to the ground. My boss and Ms. Rice are close. If there's an announcement to be vetted, he is the likely guy she would go to. I'm just trying to figure out what I can tell him when I get back."

"Everything I've told you just now I told Emily a few hours ago," Penny said. "Tell your boss as much of it as you think is useful." She then reached into her purse and pulled out the second of the hard drives Allie had given her the previous evening. "And, just so that you're an accomplice, too, here is a copy of what was on Pilgrim State's server. Allie made five copies. The more people who have it, the greater the chance it will get viewed by someone who can understand it."

Curran smiled. "Thank you. That helps a lot." He rose from the chair and accepted the drive. "I'll sort this out in my mind on the way back to the office, then I'll take a look at what's on this thing. There's also a major disclosure statement investment advisors are required to file with the SEC every year. I'm going to pull that and see what Pilgrim State has been telling the Feds. I suspect their filings haven't been a model of honesty."

Penny escorted him back to the reception area where the crowd of cat ladies had thinned appreciably. At the elevator, Penny said, "I adore pizza and I love wine. But I have to warn you that everyone in Durham is a wine and pizza connoisseur and that 'their' place has the only authentic recipe in the world and the best wine list; and I spent six years at Duke."

Curran's face brightened. "I'll be in touch."

* * * * *

David Hale made one more pass through Abby Fasanella's brokerage statement. He plugged a few numbers into the template that was the basis of his customized 'pitch' document.

She was a perfect candidate. According to the Form 1099s helpfully supplied on the thumb drive, during the past three years she had tapped the account only for tuition expenses. Cordova Street Management reinvested all dividends and interest, automatically deducting its fees from a small cash fund. Ms. Fasanella had at least a five year horizon during which she would be content to gaze at her statements and congratulate herself on having found such a wise investment advisor.

In the meantime, New York wanted another ten million and Ms. Fasanella's nest egg would make meeting that commitment much easier.

Thinking of New York, he realized he had not sent the photos of the woman and her license plate for a final verification. He also had the glass with her fingerprints in his desk.

He completed the proposal and emailed it off to the email address Fasanella supplied. In the cover note, he suggested a meeting on Friday, perhaps for lunch. If she accepted and signed the paperwork, he could initiate the transfers that afternoon and have funds as early as Monday.

It was getting toward five o'clock. Hale composed a note and attached the two photos. A click on the 'send' button and they were on their way to New York. Whatever sources the guys in New York used usually took about a day to respond.

Hale leaned back in his chair and stretched his arms and legs. There had been times when he thought he could never keep up this juggling act. Now, it actually seemed to be getting easier.

* * * * *

Allie, in her bedroom, continued to read and digest the columns of numbers downloaded from Pilgrim State's server. Accounting was a foreign language to her, and the whole idea of 'money management' was an alien concept.

She focused her attention first on the idea that people would pay roughly two percent of the value of their portfolio just to have someone hold their cash, stocks, and bonds. Why did people need 'advisors' in the first place? But it was a lucrative profession, at least for the top people. Pilgrim State's small staff was paid lavishly from these funds. The three principals each pulled down half-million-dollar salaries plus periodic bonuses. The rest of the staff appeared to be mostly hourly clerks, although their pay, too, was generous.

The part Allie was having trouble with was the periodic withdrawals of millions of dollars, which was transferred to a bank in Hempstead, New York. Why should someone else be getting all this money? But the transfers had been going on for years. Allie probed at the Hempstead bank's security system to see if she could gain more information about who controlled that account, but quickly determined that the bank had excellent defenses in place.

Allie pondered her options. The workaround for those defenses was to attach a small program to the next fund transfer. It would have been easy to do while she was downloading Pilgrim

State's data, but now would require re-creating the labyrinth of transfer points she had put in place for that hack.

There was an alternate plan, though one with risks. She had created a trip wire to warn her if someone at Pilgrim State became sufficiently suspicious to begin trying to trace her computer activity. The trip wire went to an internet café in Amsterdam. Once tripped, the server in Amsterdam would perform the innocuous task of opening a browser window for a dummy website on one of the computers in the café. No alarm bells, no email messages; just a notification of the window being opened. It was all the warning she needed.

That trip wire, though, remained as a 'back door' to Pilgrim State. She could upload the program. If no one was watching, it would find its way to the instruction set used to initiate transfers to the Long Island bank. She could, in theory, send that next wire transfer anywhere she wanted, once she figured out how it was done.

And, since it was all crooks' money in the first place, who was going to yell, 'foul!'? Why stop at one transfer? Why not just keep transferring money until someone caught on, or the money ran out? She could send a million to Greenpeace and another million to the Nature Conservancy. She could send back to New England Green the ten million Brian had stolen, though not until Brian was fired or under arrest.

Allie pondered what she could do using that 'back door'. It was one of those 'Robin Hood' opportunities. Steal from the crooks and give to the deserving.

Night fell, Helga returned home exhausted from a long day of meetings; the cheerfulness she had exhibited in the morning sapped by other departments grilling her on the lack of progress in isolating the correct pheromone; blaming her for adding to staff while everyone else's headcount was frozen.

Helga told Allie she was tired and, if Allie was hungry she

should order something to be delivered. Allie had wanted to discuss her idea of re-directing Pilgrim State's wire transfers, but her mother was too tired to listen. As a result, Allie went back to her room and began coding.

* * * * *

At 9:35 p.m., Emily's phone buzzed for an incoming email. It was from Darlene and contained the single, almost magical word, 'landed'.

Emily had listened through the evening as Brian discussed his Little Androscoggin River campaign. She nodded in all the right places and encouraged him to keep talking. The last thing she wanted was a conversation about what she had done today.

In truth, Penny Walden's visit had turned what was going to be a straightforward set of actions into something much more complex. It was, of course, more damning to Brian. Academic fraud would cost him his job. Embezzlement would send him to prison. She would, fortunately, be out in front on both stories.

Brian LaPointe did not know it, but he was in his final, few days as a man of respect and comfort. She had the pleasure of watching him squander that time feigning enthusiasm for a project she knew was nothing more than a publicity stunt. It gave her comfort – no, a warm glow – that this vain man was going to find himself abandoned.

THURSDAY

Chapter Thirteen

Emily could not wait to get into the office. Her car was in the driveway at Crow Point a full ninety minutes early. Brian, still in his robe, could only look at her quizzically and say, 'It must be important'.

If only you knew... Emily thought.

Darlene Harris, looking tired but smiling with anticipation, met Emily at the elevator. They would have the office to themselves for another hour.

In Emily's office, Darlene presented her ten copies of a single page letter on the stationery of Leeds Beckett University. Emily took the topmost copy and read:

To whom it concerns:

A formal request has been made of Leeds Beckett University (prior to 2005 known as Leeds Polytechnic College) to verify a Doctoral Degree in Horticulture granted to a United States citizen by the name of Brian James LaPointe.

The University has thoroughly researched its enrollment records for the period since 1990. During that time, we can attest that, of the Doctoral Degrees in Horticulture granted by the Institution, none were granted to a person with the surname of LaPointe or any homophonic variation on that name.

We can further attest that no student by that name was enrolled in any graduate program in any academic discipline, and no degree of any kind has been granted to a person of that name.

We have taken the further step of contacting current and retired Horticultural Sciences faculty members. None has any recollection of any student by the name of 'LaPointe'.

Finally, we have had delivered to us a copy of a photograph that includes an individual identified to us as Brian James LaPointe, and in the background of that photograph is a framed diploma purporting to be a Doctoral Degree in

Horticulture from Leeds Polytechnic and issued to Brian James LaPointe. While the diploma matches the style used by Leeds Polytechnic during the period that includes the clearly visible date on said diploma, we can state unequivocally that the diploma was not issued by this Institution.

Charles Pickney KBE, FRS

Chancellor, College of Horticultural Sciences

The letter was perfect. It was ironclad evidence of academic misrepresentation. As if additional damning evidence was needed, the photograph in question had been taken in Brian's office where he was being given an award by Massachusetts Governor Charlie Baker. The diploma was clearly visible between Governor Baker and Brian as he held the award.

"I'll find the right way to thank you when this is all over," Emily said, "but right now we have a lot to do." Emily then pulled the list from her drawer and assigned Darlene the tasks of finding and renting a short-term furnished apartment, engaging a moving company, and setting up a security service to be at Crow Point.

She added, "I'm expecting Ray Nittolo from Steele & Hanley in about half an hour. We'll work in my office and we'll need privacy and no interruptions."

* * * * *

Most law firms in Boston have long abandoned formal dress codes, but Raymond Nittolo, a Managing Partner at Steele & Hanley and the person responsible for some eight million dollars of annual billings from the Gerald and Abigail Rice Foundation, would no more have walked into Emily Taylor Rice's office in slacks and a polo shirt than he would ask to be buried in such attire. He had earned his law degree in the early 1970s, long before 'casual Fridays' took root. He was a portly man in his late sixties with thinning gray hair and a distinguished, neatly trimmed moustache.

He read the letter several times, and admired the added touch of embossed stationery and the gold foil seal of the University on the lower right hand side of the page. With ten copies of the letter, each Trustee on New England Green's Executive Committee could receive an original, with a copy left over for the *Globe* and for Emily's personal file.

"How do we do this?" Emily asked.

"Well, there's also the other matter," Nittolo replied. "I sent my best Associate to see Ms. Walden yesterday. That account is infinitely more powerful ammunition."

Emily shook her head. "But it was obtained by illegally hacking into computers. I know how this works: everything gets muddied when Brian starts talking legalities and due process instead of facts." She held up one of the letters. "This is conclusive. I get to announce it. There's no chance I was blindsided. Even the photo referenced was taken by a photographer working for New England Green and sent out as a press release. It doesn't get much more public domain than that."

"I agree with your analysis, Emily," Nittolo said, learning forward to drive home a point. "But if we did this on, say, Monday morning, and news broke on the embezzlement the next day, your story would be buried and forgotten in the space of twenty-four hours."

"I was thinking more like tomorrow afternoon," Emily said, still holding the letter. "And if it is all disclosed together, no one will even pay attention to this. Do you even have an idea of how you're going to verify the information from that firm's computers? All you have is an eighteen-year-old girl's word that it's genuine. You haven't even seen the data. All I've seen is a few dozen screen shots. How many people do you devote to putting it all in order, and are those people breaking the law?"

Nittolo paused before answering. "We can give it all to the *Globe's* Spotlight Team. John Henry and Brian McGrory will both take my call."

"And they'll be ready to publish in – what? – three months?" Emily shot back. "I can't wait three months."

Nittolo shifted uneasily in his chair. "It isn't my place to ask, but is just telling him you're breaking up with him an option?"

Emily looked at Nittolo coldly. "He lives under my roof. He sleeps in my bed. What do you think?"

After thirty seconds of reflection, Nittolo said, "I understand."

"Here's what I've put together," Emily said, extracting a sheet from a leather portfolio that had lay on the desk unmentioned until now.

Nittolo picked up the sheet and read:

For approximately four years, I was in a romantic relationship with Brian LaPointe, Chairman and Executive Director of New England Green. That relationship recently ended when I learned through my own due diligence that a doctoral degree claimed by Mr. LaPointe was never issued to him. I am making the findings of my investigation public because it goes to the truthfulness of Mr. LaPointe, and I have sent original documents to New England Green's Executive Committee.

"I would strongly advise you to let me work on this," Nittolo said. "Someone who doesn't know you as I do might draw a completely different conclusion than the one you want them to draw."

"Please do it quickly," Emily said. "This is tearing me apart emotionally. I don't have three months or even three weeks. I need to deal with this now."

"Could you go out of town for a week?" Nittolo suggested. "That would give me time…"

Emily cut him off. "I've already 'disappeared' for a weekend since learning this. I don't want Brian checking up on my cover stories or having him call every fifteen minutes. I don't want him to suspect what is happening. Every hour counts. And if you can't help me, I'll trust my instincts."

"Please give me a day," Nittolo said. Looking down at her list, he added, "I doubt you'll find an apartment or hire a mover in a day. I understand your need for speed. Let me put together the best strategy that gets this done with the greatest certainty of success."

* * * * *

Helga felt overwhelmed. First by her daughter, and now by Penny.

She had awakened at her usual hour of six o'clock. She had showered, dressed and began preparing breakfast. Usually, those actions roused Allie such that, by the time she was sitting down to eat, her daughter would appear.

Instead, at seven, Allie was still asleep in her bed. Concerned, Helga gently touched her daughter's arm, only to have Allie sit bolt-upright and begin crying.

"I can't stop thinking I did something wrong," Allie said. "I missed a step or got the coding wrong..."

"What are you talking about?" Helga asked, genuinely frightened.

"I hacked back into Pilgrim State..."

"What's 'Pilgrim State'?"

"Brian's investment advisor. Where he keeps all his stolen money."

"OK. I remember the name now," Helga said.

Allie looked at her mother, realizing she had been out of the loop since the meeting on Monday, two days and a flood of information ago. "I want to get back some of that money..."

"Are you in trouble?"

Allie shook her head. "I don't know. I don't think so. But it was late. I needed to do something..."

"Can I help?" Helga asked.

"I rigged it so I will get a warning if someone gets suspicious," Allie said, shaking her head. "But I have this feeling that I left out a step..."

"When did you get to sleep?"

Allie looked up blankly. "I'm not certain. Three o'clock,

maybe four…"

"Go back to sleep," Helga said. "Let your subconscious work on this."

Helga got to her office only to find Penny Walden standing by her door.

"We need to talk," Penny said. "I've been to see Emily Taylor Rice."

For the next hour the two women talked. Penny held back no details and Helga added what she knew about the second hack of Pilgrim State's computers.

"I am so sorry I've gotten you involved with all of this," Helga said. "You've done nothing to deserve to be dropped into the middle of this mess."

"It's only a mess if we don't keep control of it," Penny said. "My problem is that I can tell myself we've got that control, but I have no way of knowing if I'm kidding myself. There are so many moving parts."

"The important thing is that you and Emily Taylor Rice are on the same side," Penny concluded. "She has discovered he's a louse, and she wants to be rid of him."

"I wish I knew what to do," Helga said, shaking her head. "But more than that, I wish I knew what Allie has done and why she is so afraid that something she did went wrong."

* * * * *

Jason Curran flipped through screens on the laptop he had brought from home that morning. The external hard drive held 1,450 gigabytes of Pilgrim State data, all of it searchable but none of it organized.

He thought of Penny Walden. What an odd thing running into her after a decade. At Flintridge he had been the jock who studied just enough to keep up his grades. She was the studious academic who had neither the interest in nor the time for people like him. And so naturally, being unattainable, he had a secret crush on her.

Back then she was attractive, though hardly what anyone would have called 'beautiful' but, when she spoke, everyone could feel her intelligence, energy and vitality. Ten years later, she had achieved a natural grace borne of not having to conform to anyone's idea of how she should look or act. In the process, she had become, well, beautiful. Conversely, Curran, either because of his athletic built or his blond hair, continually felt the need to reinforce the fact that he had graduated from Harvard Law, had been admitted to the bar, and had been recruited by one of Boston's top law firms.

And Penny had accomplished one other magnificent feat: she had written a great book and then disappeared from public view, never to have to explain why she didn't want to write its sequel or become part of some literary scene. She had re-invented herself or, perhaps more accurately, gone on to complete the invention of the person she was in the process of becoming when she paused to write a best seller.

In short, Curran's secret crush was back in full force. And he had blown it by asking her out for a date when all she wanted to know was how he could help her.

The word you are searching for, he thought to himself, *is schmuck*.

Curran went back to the problem at hand. Steele & Hanley did not have an in-house forensic accounting group so he had no internal resources upon which to draw. His manager, Ray Nittolo, had given him no specific instructions on what to do with the hard drive. And so he used his own, rudimentary accounting knowledge to piece together what was going on at Pilgrim State.

It was the client list that captured Curran's attention. He recognized perhaps fifty of the names. They were 'names in the news' including several politicians whose published salaries gave no clue to why they would have seven- and eight-figure balances. A quick look at the nature of their deposits showed why they were doing business with Pilgrim: cash and more cash, and the wizards in Chestnut Hill even had the wisdom to capture serial numbers off the bills being deposited. He had never seen so many politicians on the take. Who said public service had to be about self-sacrifice? And then there were the union guys. My God, they were making deposits every week.

Brian LaPointe fell into a category of his own as far as Curran could tell: a highly lauded not-for-profit executive who had both hands in the cookie jar. In all, there were at least fifty people who were going to go to state or federal prison when this broke open.

So here, Curran thought, *is a genuine time bomb. It is so much greater than one man's graft. It is the kind of thing that, when disclosed, will take down careers and institutions. When Patriots and Red Sox players lose their fortunes to crooked advisors, people say, 'overpaid athletes getting lousy investment advice'. But when a Boston City Councilman making a hundred grand a year is found to have thirteen million dollars in an account, people will ask, 'where did it come from and why was he trying to hide it?'*

Curran re-read the names of account holders he did not initially recognize. He wondered how many of them were in that tier of businessmen and public servants whose names never made it into news stories? How many were attorneys?

He suddenly felt a queasiness in his stomach. *This is one of those things that turn Associates into Partners… or ends their careers.*

* * * * *

Raymond Nittolo wrote on a traditional yellow legal pad using a writing instrument that, while not a fountain pen, produced a result that satisfactorily emulated the look of such a classic tool. Before him was Emily's worrisome draft of an announcement; a paragraph that fairly screamed of personal betrayal. Reporters would have had a field day with it, sniggering among themselves about what could have caused such an emotional outburst from a woman whose calm professionalism was universally known and admired.

The right thing to do, Nittolo knew, was for a third party to privately confront LaPointe with the evidence of his academic record and present him with the stark choice of either resigning for personal reasons or finding his malfeasance on the front page of the *Globe*. Emily was wrong in believing that persuasive men of stature could talk their way out of the corner into which they had painted themselves. They might hang on for a few days or weeks but, inevitably, they found themselves on the short end of a Board vote of 'no confidence'. He had seen such scenarios play out dozens of times over the course of his long career.

The business with the stealing, if true, was much more problematic. Obviously, any funds misappropriated needed to be returned voluntarily and quietly. Legal repercussions could be left to the discretion of the state Attorney General's office. Going public with such allegations would be a legal nightmare.

The notion of an entire money management firm existing to cater to the needs of criminals was suspect on its face. It was the stuff of John Grisham thrillers. There were half a dozen regulatory units to ensure any nonsense was spotted quickly. Advisory firms had to file reports and their accounts had to be audited.

Could such a fund garner more than a billion dollars without being spotted? It was unlikely, but it ought to be looked into by the right authorities. Nittolo had acquaintances in the Securities and Commodities Fraud Unit of the FBI in Washington as well as at the Bureau's field office in Chelsea.

His Associate's back-of-the-envelope analysis had been on-point. Private citizens, or neutral third parties representing them, could take the fruits of their otherwise-illegal searches to the proper authorities. It was the logical exception to the Exclusionary Rule. Nittolo had never quite understood how hacking worked, although it certainly had frightening repercussions.

While it was no longer the stuff of myth that eighteen-year-olds could gain entry to sophisticated computer systems, it was definitely suspect that two people with no background in accounting could somehow deduce in a matter of hours that a money management firm was seeking out and catering to white-collar criminals. Give this hard drive to the FBI and to the state Attorney General, and let the law sort out the veracity of everyone's claims.

And, of course, if any of it turned out to be true, Steele & Hanley would be in line to earn considerable credit from the affair. It was an interesting idea that needed to be discussed with the Partners Committee.

For now, his goal was simple: talk Emily down from the emotional ledge on which she was standing. Get her to realize that it was in no one's interest to go public with all of this. Breaking up with her paramour was her business, but don't involve the media, for God's sake. Just tell the man to leave.

With his priorities set, Nittolo began to write.

New England Green's LaPointe Forced to Resign
After Revelation of Fraudulent Doctorate

New England Green's Executive Director of 18 years, Brian LaPointe, was ousted yesterday following the revelation that a PhD long claimed by LaPointe as a highlight of his résumé had never been issued by the prestigious British university he said he attended.

The discovery was made by LaPointe's former girlfriend, foundation executive Emily Taylor Rice, and brought to the attention of trustees last week.

The diploma from Leeds Polytechnic College (now Leeds Beckett), has hung on LaPointe's office wall for nearly two decades. An affidavit from Sir Charles Pickney, Chancellor, College of Horticultural Sciences, said, "While the diploma matches the style used by Leeds Polytechnic during the period that includes the clearly visible date on said diploma, we can state unequivocally that the diploma was not issued by this Institution."

In a prepared statement, the Trustees said, "There are offenses for which there is no mitigating explanation. We consider academic fraud as one of those. It goes to the heart of the trust among an institution, its employees, and the public we serve."

Nittolo considered adding additional paragraphs, but thought this would be sufficient to make his point. On a new page he wrote:

New England Green's LaPointe Will Step Down This Month

Brian LaPointe, the charismatic leader who rejuvenated a venerable but floundering institution and expanded its mission for a new century, said yesterday he will step down as Chairman and President of New England Green, effective at the end of the month.

New England Green's Executive Director of 18 years cited health issues and said the treatment of a recently diagnosed condition will make him unable to fulfill his responsibilities for the foreseeable future.

In a prepared statement, the trustees said, "We owe Brian LaPointe a profound debt of gratitude for his leadership, vision, and tireless advocacy. His legacy will endure for decades to come."

Nittolo looked with satisfaction at what he had written. These two visions of the future were all that was necessary to convince LaPointe he had to resign – and to talk Emily Taylor Rice off that ledge.

* * * * *

Zoe Matthews stood on Atlantic Avenue outside Boston's South Station. The four-and-a-half-hour, $21 MegaBus trip had not been her first transportation choice for the most important interview of her life, but she did not know how long she would be here or how long her funds would have to last. The sale of the phones had netted her $1,900; less than she hoped but it should be a sufficient stake to see her through her plan.

That she had received neither phone nor text messages from Michele Silverman in the twenty-two hours since she left the office was not at all unexpected. Michele would have, by now, taken Zoe's memorandum (now under Silverman's name) to Jillian Martin, her Executive Producer. Michele would have answered all of Jillian's questions, inventing details as needed. Then, believing her own future advancement was bright, Michele would have treated herself to lunch at a trendy East Side bistro. In the late afternoon, Michele would have had it gently explained to her by

Jillian that *EN*'s Senior Executive Producer, Stephen Brooks, would be handling all elements of this most crucial of stories, but that Michele's contributions were gratefully acknowledged. Michele would have promptly gone home and taken solace in a purloined bottle of Absolut Elyx.

In short, because of in-house treachery and backstabbing, it might be days before anyone noticed a lowly intern was missing.

Zoe's first order of business was to meet with a friend and fellow University of Missouri journalism graduate who had majored in Radio and Television Production. Like Zoe, Tyler Malone had lowered her sights to find that first, entry-level position but, unlike her friend, Tyler's job actually paid a salary. As DigBoston's Visual Media Coordinator, Tyler was a one-woman video production unit, handling camera, lights and sound for an arts-and-music oriented weekly newspaper with a lively website and social media feed.

Zoe tapped in DigBoston's address and found it was less than a mile away. The walk would take her through Chinatown, and she had worked up an appetite. She tapped in 'dim sum' and headed toward her future.

* * * * *

Penny flipped through the summaries of the previous day's lab trials. The results were labeled 'mixed'. In Penny's view, the better one-word description would be 'dismal'. Six 'promising' molecules had been exposed to a total of 72 cats. The pheromones had prompted reactions ranging from incessant yowling to spraying (euphemistically called 'territorial marking' in the summary).

None of the six molecules had triggered the 'avoidance' reaction sought. At some point during the morning and afternoon, at least one cat (and in one case, five of the six) had walked over and began to leisurely claw at the curtains and sofa on which the molecule had been sprayed.

What she was seeing implied one of two outcomes. Either there was no pheromone that would tell a cat to stay away from a treated site – which meant that an 'avoidance molecule' did not exist and the search for it was fruitless – or else that pheromone was a random molecule with a grouping of carbon, hydrogen, and oxygen atoms; plus the addition of some 'secret sauce' element. If the molecule did not exist, then Pheromonix needed to close its doors and stop burning through its investors' cash.

If finding the repellant was a matter of serendipity, they were doing the right thing. The problem was that, while dozens of major advances in chemistry and physics were the products of accidental discovery, none were the result of deliberately setting out to use random science to achieve a specific end result.

Penny pondered this reality as she continued reading the research commentary. Amused, she noted that at least the company had already isolated the one molecule that was the polar opposite of the goal of their research. In its first weeks of operation, Pheromonix had identified the one pheromone that was guaranteed to attract every breed of cat to which it had been exposed, and to send that cat into a frenzy of shredding and spraying.

Not exactly the stuff of great science, or of commercial applicability.

Penny began to wonder if her tenure at Pheromonix was destined to be a short one.

* * * * *

David Hale stared at his phone, on which was a Snapchat message unlike any he had ever received.

Critical you respond immediately with 'understood'. NC license plate BHA-2907 is tied to a Honda Civic, but owner is not 'Abby' or 'Abigail' Fasanella. There is no one by that name in the motor vehicle or voter registration database. Registration ties to 'Penelope Danforth Walden' of Durham NC. Driver's license photo appears to be same person as in security camera photo. Assume a law enforcement connection. A team is on its way. Have no contact with Walden under any circumstances.

Hale's face and hands felt cold.   In twenty-three years of running Pilgrim State, no 'team' had ever been dispatched because of something he had done, though he had heard of what happened when New York sent out a 'team'. It meant two things: first, that everything he had done over the past year would be placed under a microscope by unforgiving eyes.   And, second, the team would extract from him every detail of his interaction with 'Abby Fasanella' and they would use every resource to track her down and likely kill her.   They would learn, using whatever force was necessary, why she had come to his office carrying fabricated brokerage records and a false name.

And, depending on what they learned from her, he might well be dead within 72 hours.

His first thought was to get his wife and children out of town. They owned a condo in Florida, but that was within easy reach of the New York people. He could put them on a plane to Europe or Asia, but that would be seen as a sign of both fear and guilt.

I am guilty of nothing except talking to a walk-in customer. Of course, that was against protocol.   Potential customers were referred by 'feeders' and were pre-screened.   There was an established dance of rebuffing the prospect at least twice before agreeing that maybe something could be done. *If New York hadn't been looking for another ten million, I wouldn't have even let her in the door.* But that argument would go nowhere with New York.   It was his job to keep coming up with funds while playing by New York's rules.

I gave her no useful information. In fact, he had given a standard sales pitch.   There was nothing that the FBI or Treasury Department could use.   Of course, even a cursory review of the firm's annual report filed with the Securities and Exchange Commission would start with the fact that the Auditor's Opinion was a complete fabrication.   PWC had never examined Pilgrim State's books.   But the Opinion looked official and gave prospective customers comfort that one of the 'Big Three' was looking over their investment advisor's shoulder.

All I did was take her brokerage statements and use them to write a proposal letter. That, too was standard operating procedure. Hale always verified that the new account's assets were real and easily transferred. How was he to know that the brokerage statements had been altered to show a phony name? That explained why she gave them to him in PDF format on a thumb drive instead of paper copies...

The thumb drive. Oh, my God. The thumb drive.

His hands were now shaking. *What if the purpose of 'Abby Fasanella's' visit hadn't been the FBI's effort to plant an Agent's account with Pilgrim State but, rather, to gain access to the firm's entire financial records? But that would require a subpoena, wouldn't it?*

A magazine article he had read a few years earlier came to his mind. The Israeli government had created a virus specifically to attack Iran's secret and ultra-secure uranium enrichment facilities. The virus caused centrifuges to spin out of control and destroyed or damaged thousands of those machines. The Israelis had gotten around the Iranian government's extensive computer virus detection system by the simple expedient of leaving hundreds of seemingly unused thumb drives at internet cafés all over Iran. Engineers pocketed them, plugged them into their computers, and inadvertently let loose the virus.

In his desk was the agreement letter and instruction book for Pilgrim State's computers. He found the package and began reading. He learned his server was continuously monitored using the most sophisticated malware detection system available. Every possible threat was assessed. Each day, hundreds of new viruses were created by hackers, but as soon as they were discovered on any customer's system, a detection and confinement protocol was uploaded to every computer monitored by the company. The industry's best computer experts were working around the clock for his benefit. It was an extraordinarily comforting paragraph.

Besides, he had run multiple virus scans on the thumb drive before opening it.

There was a number to call if a customer had any reason to believe any of its systems might have been compromised. Should he call?

His thoughts were interrupted by the chime of his phone. It was another Snapchat message.

Expect crew by 6 p.m. Do not leave office. No 'Fasanella' or 'Walden' in residence at 10 Glassworks Avenue, Cambridge. Assume this is law enforcement action. Run computer scan immediately.

Hale punched in the phone number for the computer service firm. His hands were now shaking uncontrollably.

* * * * *

Brian re-read the email, frowning,

Forgot to tell you about Women's Leadership Forum this evening. It's an all-girl thing and won't break until late. Staying at the town house tonight. Leftovers in the fridge or take yourself out for a decent meal. Luv U, ETR.

Emily hadn't mentioned anything about it and he didn't remember seeing it on the master calendar they kept in the kitchen. That was odd.

But it also gave him a free evening. What he would do with it was a no-brainer. He reached into his desk drawer and retrieved the special phone. He clicked on the lone name in the contacts list.

"I just found out I'm free this evening," he said. "What do you say we get together?"

* * * * *

Allie heard a mechanical 'boing' and nearly jumped out of her chair. She was in her bedroom, reading her Kindle. One of her three laptops was on the other side of the room and she had to look at all three to identify the source of the unfamiliar noise. It came from the middle computer.

It was a notification that, at the Coffeeshop Crush on Marnixstraat in Amsterdam, laptop number 11 had just opened a browser tab for the Bolshoi Ballet. The instruction had come at 23:16 Central European Time.

It was now 5:18 p.m. in Cambridge. Two minutes ago, someone tripped the alarm.

Where did I screw up? Allie thought.

The trip wire was only what the name implied. Someone at Pilgrim State or whatever firm serviced Pilgrim State's computers had requested a detailed log of all activity on the server, something that would only be done if there was a suspected intrusion. It didn't tell Allie if the scan revealed what she had done or who was conducting the scan. It only said that someone had reason to believe Pilgrim State's computers had come under attack.

What could they learn? They would certainly know that twenty-three hours earlier, the entire contents of their server had been uploaded to a certain Internet Protocol, or IP, address. She had disguised the route the traffic took to make to appear it was going to a computer in Russia. A competent tech could, with time, see that the data moved back out of Russia to the United States and, if they were uncommonly good, they could even trace it to the router in Kendall Square she had tapped into.

At the same time, a diligent tech would start looking for the source of the virus, and it would be fairly easy to determine that it has been uploaded into a laptop belonging to David Hale at about 4 p.m. yesterday.

That fact would point them directly to Penny. Penny was protected only to the extent that she had given a false name, that she had been asked to produce no ID, and that she said she had parked half a block away from Pilgrim State's office. She was an anonymous woman who had come and gone in under an hour. The false name Penny had given offered no hidden clue to her identity, or so she had said. The California investment advisory firm was real but had been chosen after a cursory Google search, as had the apartment building listed as her current address.

With the benefit of hindsight, they shouldn't have chosen an advisory firm in the same city in which Penny had grown up, and they ought to have chosen an apartment building in some place other than Cambridge. But they didn't have time to construct a more complex back story. And, besides, it would almost certainly not be needed.

But Penny needed to be warned all the same.

Then the harder problem hit Allie. This morning, she had impetuously done something more dangerous. With the 'boing' sound still being issued every thirty seconds, it was an audible reminder of her lack of self-control. It couldn't come back to hurt Penny. It could definitely hurt her father, but he was the cause of all of this.

Allie reached for her phone to call Penny.

* * * * *

In Chestnut Hill, David Hale realized he was completely covered in sweat. His polo shirt was soaked and he continually wiped his brow with a now-sopping-wet paper towel. Two of the four men who had arrived at the office of Pilgrim State Investments at 5:45 p.m. elected to say nothing about the sweat. They were focused on his words as they had been for the two previous hours.

'Al' did most of the talking. He made no attempt to be anything other than what he was: an emissary sent to glean and verify every piece of information possible. It was clear from both his mannerisms and vocabulary that Al was an intelligent man. He bore no resemblance to the organized crime figures from popular culture. But his black eyes and pock-marked face betrayed no semblance of empathy or understanding for what had occurred in this office.

Describe what she was wearing. As accurately as possible, what did she say about starting a research lab? Did she have any regional accent? Would you guess her hair was dyed? What brand of purse was she carrying? What about her shoes? What exactly did she say about working for a start-up in

Cambridge? How did she visually react when you asked about student loans? How did she characterize how she had come into that money? Did you see anything else on her iPad?

To each question, Hale answered carefully and tried to make certain his answer was consistent with what he had said the last time he was asked. A second man said nothing, but carefully wrote down every answer Hale gave.

A third member of the group – 'Rocco' – had gone to work immediately on Hale's computer; running diagnostic tests and printing out documents. He would periodically interrupt Al and whisper something in his ear.

The fourth member of the group spent his time on the phone with BGZ Computer Services in Andover, Massachusetts. The tone of that conversation was not going well and, at one point, there had been a discussion of whether two men should break away to meet in person with the computer monitoring firm.

Of particular interest to Al was why no one else at Pilgrim State Investments had seen the woman and why they were not here now. Hale explained that only his two partners were full-time. One was on vacation with his family in Morocco and the other was, well, just taking a day off. The other staffers came in only at the end of the month when statements were being prepared.

At the end of the third hour, the four men met at the far end of the small warren of offices. Hale was told to stay in his office. He could not make out anything the men were saying; neither could he see their faces. After twenty minutes the four men returned, but only Al spoke.

"How would you propose finding Penelope Walden?" Al asked.

"If she's a Fed, it won't do us a lot of good," Hale replied. "Call the FBI field office."

Al did not smile at the response. "There are some odd things going on. She may be, in fact, recently arrived from North

Carolina. Her car's registration there is still current. But no one by that name works or has worked for a federal agency anywhere in that state. And, yes, our sources are good enough to be confident in that answer. It's possible she was recently recruited and this is her first assignment: a simple drop to entice you to make use of that thumb drive, but that's not the way federal agencies work."

Al continued. "That thumb drive contained a virus that evaded every standard scan, and it is incredibly clever. It downloaded everything from your server and sent it via a route that made it look like it was headed for Russia. Again, that kind of complexity is something the FBI or Treasury would be unlikely to know how to do. But the data came back to an office building in Cambridge where it was downloaded."

"So she isn't a Fed?" Hale asked.

"We're working with the theory that this is something like extortion," Al said. "Someone figured out what we're doing here and they're holding the data ransom; expecting a big payment. There are groups in Russia and Eastern Europe that make a killing doing exactly that. Sending in the woman was sloppy but necessary. Phishing won't work because you don't respond to outside emails. Someone had to physically hand you that thumb drive and give you a good reason to plug it into your computer."

Al continued. "Finding her is the key. She gave you a local phone number – which goes to a burner phone, by the way – but she hadn't changed her car registration. My guess is that she still has her North Carolina phone. We're working hard to get that number from our sources at the various carriers."

"You can ping her phone," Hale said.

Al nodded and, for the first time, gave a hint of a smile. "Stupidest technology idea ever. Allowing your carrier to know where you are, even when you aren't on your phone."

"Then you grab her," Hale said.

Al shook his head. "We cross that bridge when we come to it.

We want to know how they found out what we're doing, and who else might know. Pilgrim State has been a gold mine. We don't want to lose it. What we do when we find her isn't my decision."

"And what happens to me?" Hale asked.

Al didn't smile. "That isn't my decision, either."

* * * * *

Tyler Malone shared a two-bedroom apartment with three roommates, two of them male, in a fairly new building in Dorchester's Harbor Point neighborhood. Zoe was offered a sleeping bag in the 'girl's' bedroom. She gratefully accepted, as the least expensive Airbnb listing she had found was $165 a night.

Like Zoe, Tyler was twenty-two and an attractive woman. In other ways, the two were an odd couple. Born in the British Virgin Islands, Tyler spoke with a clipped Caribbean accent. Her cocoa skin was accented by dark brown eyes and she wore a near perpetual smile.

The two women spoke in low tones for more than two hours at the apartment's kitchenette table, hammering out a deal for Tyler's services. They agreed Zoe would pay Tyler $500 cash for a complete, high-quality video with a duration of up to twenty minutes, with Tyler getting full, on-screen production credits and twenty percent of any media sale over $2,500. Both women agreed that the right interview should fetch upwards of $50,000.

In her nine months at *Entertainment Now!* Zoe had observed at close range the 'right' and 'wrong' way to approach and gain access to a reluctant celebrity. She had spent much of the bus trip preparing and silently rehearsing her questions and her means of getting P.D. Walden to sit for the interview. She knew she could do this, and carry it off in a way that would do credit to her career.

Because of their work together in college, Zoe also knew that Tyler was critical to the success of the interview. She was quiet and unobtrusive. She changed camera angles without being noticed by the subject and had a sixth sense for knowing when to come in for the tight shot. In their biggest interview, Tyler's near-invisibility – despite having a camera and a directional mic in the hand – had kept a University of Missouri official talking long past the time when a sensible person would have walked away.

* * * * *

At the Josiah Willard House in the Coolidge Hill community of Cambridge, three women sat around an early 18th Century trestle table hand-hewn by John Townsend. The women stared at the screen of a 21st Century MacBook Air Pro created by Steve Jobs.

"I have no idea who or what triggered the decision to audit the server," Allie said. "It was done by a computer service firm about twenty miles north of here. Maybe it's something they do every Thursday afternoon, but I don't like the timing."

"It even looks routine," Allie added. "It's a general system scan, starting with root folders and then going by file groups." She pointed to the screen, where blobs of color – meaningless to the two other women – slowly spread. "They weren't looking for anything specific; otherwise they would have jumped directly to David Hale's computer. It was almost half an hour before they realized the server had been hacked."

"But they know now," Helga said.

"Definitely," Allie said. "And by now, they certainly know that the source of the worm was the thumb drive."

Penny inhaled involuntarily. Helga and Allie turned to look at their companion.

"What do they know about you?" Helga asked.

It took Penny more than ten minutes to recount what she had said to Hale at their meeting.

"They know you've recently moved here from North Carolina," Allie summarized. "They know you work at a start-up in Cambridge. If they've got really good tracer technology, they'll even know what building the data went to."

Allie added, "Do you remember seeing a security camera?"

Penny shook her head. "I wasn't looking for one."

"You should assume there was at least one," Helga said. "We have them all over the floor at Pheromonix and MIT was filthy with them."

"So they also have your photo," Allie said glumly.

Penny stared at the screen and pointed at blobs of color. "How can you have this information? Isn't it dangerous?"

Allie shrugged. "This is just a back-door thing. Computer services firms aren't expecting hackers to mess with their own systems; just their customers' computers. This was my trip wire."

"Unless you can think of an awfully good reason to keep that connection open, please close it down," Helga said.

Allie shrugged, tapped at the screen in several places, and the image disappeared.

"Tell me again why you took every scrap of data from that server," Helga asked Allie.

"It was easier than looking for just Brian's files," Allie replied. "I figured I could look through them at night, figure out what I wanted, and ditch the rest." She looked at Penny. "I really screwed up on this one. I'm sorry."

"I guess you're not going home tonight," Helga said to Penny. "Fortunately, we have a spare room."

FRIDAY

Chapter Fourteen

Emily met with Ray Nittolo over breakfast at her Beacon Hill town house. She read the two versions of the hypothetical news article Nittolo had brought with him.

"I don't understand," she said, handing him back the two sheets of paper.

"We give him the choice of how he wants to go out," Nittolo said. "He can gracefully resign and keep his reputation intact, or the world can know he was an academic fraud who was fired."

"What about the money he stole?" Emily asked.

"He gives it back, with interest," Nittolo said confidently. "He does it quietly. We can force him to do that."

"I rather prefer that second option," Emily said, sipping her coffee. She tore apart a piece of croissant. "Let the world know he was a fraud and a crook."

"Emily, he'll be gone," Nittolo said. "I don't think this is about revenge on your part. It's about untangling a relationship with a man who disappointed you."

Emily set down her cup. "I don't think you have the right to assume, much less tell me what this is about. I know this man. He's a snake and he'll slither out of it unless you cut off his head." She paused to consider her words. "Metaphorically speaking," she added.

"He's also a realist," Nittolo countered. "You have him dead to rights."

Emily breathed a sigh that conveyed her impatience. "Last year, at one of my companies, we had a comparable misrepresentation. A senior vice president with fifteen years of service was being considered for a 'C'-suite position. I handled the routine vetting of his résumé. Everything was fine except for his

MBA from the University of Chicago. He listed it as having been awarded in 1980. The University confirmed the date, but said they were confused because the Laurence White they knew had died of pancreatic cancer two years earlier and the school had received a bequest from his estate. I sent someone out to confirm the details face-to-face. 'Our' Laurence White had been using 'their' Laurence White's résumé for more than two decades. We compared photos and even University medical records. 'Our' Laurence White was a fraud with an MBA from some cow college in Texas."

"When we confronted him and told him he was being terminated, his reaction was to threaten what he called 'the nuclear option'. He had been collecting memos and reports going back to when he was hired. He showed us two examples and said it was the 'tip of the iceberg'. They were genuine and horrifying. He told us his first stop on the way out the door was going to be to pick up two boxes of material from a self-storage unit. His second stop was going to be the local bureau of the *Wall Street Journal* where he had been cultivating a reporter for just such an eventuality."

"What did you do?" Nittolo asked.

"My recommendation was to have him arrested and sue the bastard for fraudulent representation and ask for fifteen years of wages and benefits," Emily shot back. "What the rest of the Board did was agree to give him a $15 million severance package in return for those two boxes of material."

"Who got the better deal?"

"He was showing us the meat," Emily replied. "The rest of it was routine corporate swill. The last I heard he was sailing the Caribbean in a fifty-foot boat and offering 'consulting services'. Probably to other résumé cheats. You tell me who got the better deal."

Nittolo nodded. "So what do you propose we do?"

"Just what I said yesterday," Emily replied, refilling her coffee cup. "We have the college's affidavits. We deliver them to the

Trustees. We give a copy to the *Globe* and run off some Xeroxes for the television station. We issue a statement from me saying I discovered the fraud. We also suggest that the Trustees look carefully at expense disbursements related to establishing endowments for New England Green properties and provide a few avenues to pursue. They'll figure out the rest."

Nittolo shook his head. "I think this is exactly the wrong way to proceed. It will come off as an exposé by a jilted lover and people will wonder how long you knew before you blew the whistle."

Emily stared at Nittolo. After a few moments she said, "Raymond, I'm leaving from here to go to Crow Point, where I'm going to tag every one of Brian's belongings. Everything will be out of the house by this afternoon, the locks will be changed, a guard will be at my house, and there will be a key to an apartment delivered to Brian. At 4:30 this afternoon I'm going to make a statement. I can write it or you can write it. I thank you for your input but my mind is made up. If you choose to resign the Foundation account over this, that will be your prerogative and I will not hold it against you personally."

With that, Emily rose from the breakfast table and collected her purse.

"You're welcome to stay if you need to make calls," she said. "Please let yourself out when you're ready to leave."

* * * * *

Brian stopped for coffee and a pastry at a Starbucks on Route 3A on his way to Beckwith Estate. It was a day that promised nothing particularly interesting. He had no meetings planned and little to keep him occupied. It was high season for New England Green; entry fees would be nearing their high point for the year.

Of course there was always Amber Oakes. Last evening had been spectacular. Emily really ought to stay in Boston more often. He could not remember better or more uninhibited sex. He felt like he was twenty again.

But you couldn't do that every day. Someone might notice or, worse, the girl might start getting ideas that there was more going on than just casual screwing. Last night had been – what? – their ninth or tenth time together in five weeks. Ten times with an intern was probably a record since he moved in with Emily. Usually he was bored after three or four trysts.

But Amber… she knew things no twenty-year-old should have in their bag of tricks. She would likely be returning to college toward the end of August. *Where exactly does she go to school?* he thought. *I need to get hold of her internship application. It would be embarrassing if the subject came up and I didn't know.*

He was miffed that Emily had not called him. She hadn't even texted him. Just the lone email saying she was at that leadership thing. *God, the idea that women feel a need to have their own leadership groups*, he thought. *What a crock.*

It was also odd that Emily hadn't said anything about going to Maine this weekend. How were they getting there? Well, she always took care of those things or had her assistant do so. Maybe he should call the assistant – Darlene? Darla? – and ask. No, it was still morning. He'd call this afternoon and say something directly to Emily. Make it casual.

The closer he got to Beckwith Estate, the more Brian realized he really didn't want to be in the office today. The clowns from Development would want to bend his ear about Little Androscoggin because face time with the boss was what they craved. He didn't give a damn about what the campaign would look like. Just get the stupid thing underway so New England Green could start collecting pledges.

I'm driving a Porsche 911 S Turbo convertible, the hottest car on the planet, he thought. *I'm wealthy and I'm respected. It's too gorgeous a day to waste it in an office.*

Where could he take Amber Oakes that he wouldn't be

recognized? Not the Cape. Too many people recognized him there. The Berkshires were almost three hours away and there was always a chance he'd run into one of one of Emily's cronies. Newport? Castle Hill or the Chanler would impress the hell out of Amber; but he had stayed there before with Emily and, while they were discreet, they might look askance at a forty-something guy checking in at noon with someone half his age, and then leaving at five. On the other hand, the Hyatt Regency was both impersonal and luxurious. They didn't care when you left as long as you paid.

Brian reached for his phone and called the main number for Beckwith Estate. He ought to use the special phone in his desk, but this was an emergency. He got the dial-by-name directory and waited patiently for her name. He tapped the screen.

"Hi, this is Amber. I'll be out of the office today…"

He closed the call, frustrated. *Why the hell isn't she at work? Why didn't she say something last night? Is she just taking the day off because she's screwing the boss? Has something happened to her?*

He turned his car into the main gate for Beckwith Estate and waved at the elderly ticket seller. God, he loved volunteers. He pulled his car into his reserved space and tried to paste a smile on his face.

He felt like his day had just been ruined.

* * * * *

"There's no way you're going to the office today," Allie said. "They'll be looking at everyone going into the buildings within signal range of that router."

"What makes you think it's 'they'?" Penny said. "It's one guy as far as we know."

Allie cocked her head. "For someone who was such a hotshot writer, you don't know much. Put yourself in this guy Hale's place: yesterday afternoon you learned someone downloaded every scrap of information in your computers. By now, even an eighth-grader would have traced the data path to Kendall Square. You're not the least bit curious about who this woman is who handed you a worm on a thumb drive?"

"And these people are up to no good," she added. "They handle dirty money. You don't send out 'a guy' to try to intercept you. You send out an army. As many guys as you can find; all of them armed with your photo. So, no, you aren't going anywhere near that building. You can stay here and use my computers."

"What about you and Helga?" Penny asked.

"We're going in," Allie said. "Nobody knows we're involved. I'm going to be looking to see if anyone is lurking around the building entrance. I'll call you and let you know. I'll take pictures so you can see if any of them is that Hale guy."

"I do have work to do," Penny said. "Not that I've gotten a lot done this week because of you."

"You'll have the place to yourself," Allie said. "I'm going to go see if Helga is ready."

Penny sat down, exasperated by being left out.

* * * * *

"What the hell do we pay these people for?" It was Al – his last name was Luchetti, though few ever used his surname when referring to him – and he was speaking with a heightened voice into his phone. To anyone who knew Al, his 'heightened voice' was the equivalent of a scream, and an explicit threat.

"There are all kinds of new laws," the nervous voice on the other end of the phone said. "These phone companies have been hit with thousands of lawsuits for providing personal information."

"So a damned telemarketer in Delhi can call my unlisted cell phone with impunity, but I can't get the cell number of one phone company customer?" Al's voice was especially heightened. "What do you need to persuade them?"

"Just time, Al," the nervous voice. "Give me a couple more hours. I'll talk sense into them."

Al put his phone down on the table, clearly angry.

"Pending getting the information we need, we go to plan 'B'," he said.

David Hale's laptop displayed a Google Maps view of Kendall Square. Luchetti pointed to a series of low buildings, a mix of new construction and one-time factories, one of them a full block long. "This is One Kendall Square." He then tapped the screen to zoom in on a modern building near the southern end of the complex. "The router that broadcast the data was on the third floor of this building. A router has a range of maybe two hundred feet. We assume Walden and her associates weren't dumb enough to use their own router, but were close enough to tap into it. Once we pinpoint the router, we look at every space the signal could have reached: above and below the space and in adjacent buildings. We're likely going to be looking at upwards of two dozen possible companies because this space is full of tech employers. We have to assume that Walden works for one of them. We call, we walk in, we ask. We are polite."

He zoomed out of the image to show the complex and surrounding areas. "There are three or four parking garages within walking distance, but this one – he tapped the screen – is huge and closest to the router. We look for her car. North Carolina plate BHA-2907, a tan Honda Civic. If we see it, we're golden. If we find out which company she works for, we're golden. It's eight o'clock. There are six of us. We ought to have her by two this afternoon and, if we get her phone, we'll have her by noon. We take two cars so we have room to stash Walden when we find her. Let's get going."

* * * * *

Zoe got off the Red Line train in Kendall Square and oriented her phone to show the best way to make the half-mile walk to One Kendall Square. It was just 8:30 a.m. but the heat of the day was already settling in.

At One Kendall Square, she discovered that her destination

was not one building but, rather, a cluster of roughly a dozen structures, each one home to multiple companies. From Pheromonix's website, she found the additional information that she was looking for 1400 West, which turned out to be a block-long, six-story building. A tenant directory guided Zoe to the third floor and Pheromonix's reception desk.

In her nine months at *Entertainment Now!*, Zoe had listened to both sides of the argument for 'ambushing' unwilling or recalcitrant subjects. One school of thought was that a celebrity with a secret wasn't going to agree to an interview without a press aide or attorney present, and the questions would be shut down as soon as the questioning veered into anything uncomfortable.

As such, the only way to get a celebrity on the record was to catch them off guard: the 'ambush' strategy. Also, an ambush always made for better visuals. In a scheduled interview, the celebrity was always attired, coiffed, and made up to perfection. The ambushed celeb might be in a sweatshirt and Lululemons without even lipstick.

The counter to that argument was that the typical ambush interview lasted twenty seconds, much of it laced with profanity. Whatever the charge, the target denied the allegation, gave the camera the finger, and then walked away. The lone way to get a serious discussion was to tell the celebrity that the show was going with a 'verified report' (which might or might not be the case) and the show wanted to hear the other side of the story. What followed might be a tissue of lies, but those prevarications could be countered with facts presented on-camera or added in post-production.

Zoe had thought through both avenues and had come to the conclusion that the lone, salable option was to let P.D. Walden tell her story, her way, on camera. Zoe was prepared to go as far as to omit mention of the city in which the interview was being filmed and the name of the company for which Penny now worked. What would be interesting to viewers was that the mythic author had abandoned revenge for science. It would be a compelling story; head and shoulders above the usual *EN* swill.

She was sitting in Pheromonix's lobby, working up her courage, when a young, gaunt woman in her late teens and an older, heavy-set blonde woman walked through the door together and went immediately to the receptionist.

The older woman spoke with authority. "Elena, if anyone comes in here with a photo of Penny Walden and asks if she works here, you're to tell them she doesn't. If anyone calls and describes her, then asks you if someone by that description has come to work for the company in the past month, you're to say that no one who looks like that has started here this year. As soon as they've left, call me immediately."

"Is Penny in trouble?" the receptionist asked, a worried look on her face.

"She may be," the older woman said, though clearly the urgency of the request said that she believed the danger was imminent. "In fact, can we take her out of the phone system until I give you the 'all-clear'?"

The receptionist thought for a moment. "I can sequester her voice mailbox. Is she going to be in today?"

At this point, the younger woman turned to survey the room. Zoe was the lone person in the lobby, and she did not seem to be of interest.

The older woman, who spoke with a slight British inflection, said, "Penny is going to be out at least for today. We'll see about the weekend. We'll know more later on today. I don't mean to sound mysterious, but it's important."

"If someone on staff needs to get in touch with her, what should I do?" the receptionist asked.

"Send them to me. I'll put a note to that effect on her door," the older woman said. She turned to the younger woman, and Zoe noted for the first time that there was a family resemblance. This might well be a mother and daughter. The older woman said, "Allie, do you think email is safe? What about her phone?"

"I told her to feel free to use the computers in my room," the younger woman said. "They're a lot more powerful and faster than her phone. I don't know about having anyone call her. That might be dangerous and I don't want to take the chance."

"Are you going straight back home?" the older woman asked, confirming the mother-daughter relationship.

"I'm going to stick around for a little while," the daughter said. "If I start crowding Penny too much, it might..." The daughter's eyes went to the receptionist, who was hanging on every word. "I'll be around the office for a while."

The two women disappeared down a corridor, talking to one another.

Zoe took out her phone and went to the Pheromonix web site. The older woman was someone of importance. She had the authority to tell the receptionist to make Penny Walden invisible to the outside world.

The web site contained no identified photos of anyone except the company's Chief Executive Officer. But there was a listing of headquarters staff. Of six names, three had women's first names.

Penny Walden was a scientist. Pherominix's Chief Research and Development Officer was Helga Johanssen. The Chief Marketing Officer was Trish Yarbrough and the Chief Financial Officer was...

"May I help you?" the receptionist asked, her question directed at Zoe.

"Was that Helga Johanssen?" Zoe asked excitedly. "I'm looking for job as a lab assistant..."

"Yes," the receptionist said coolly, "and you're welcome to put in an application through our web site, but there aren't any vacancies at present. There's a hiring freeze right now."

"Oh," Zoe said, her face full of disappointment. "Then I won't waste any more of your time." She rose to leave, a dejected job seeker looking elsewhere for her big break.

Outside the building, Zoe found a bench and began parsing the conversation she had overheard. Her initial thought had been that some other news organization was hot on P.D. Walden's trail and Helga and her daughter, whom she had called 'Allie', were trying to protect her.

But the urgency of the request said something more was at stake. Someone who knew what P.D. Walden looked like but who did not know her name was looking for her and had reason to believe she worked at Pheromonix. Or, perhaps, at another company in the building. Whatever was going on, Penny was hiding from someone. But who?

There was one tantalizing bit of information alluded to: that Penny Walden was currently at Helga and Allie's home, wherever that was. *"I told her to feel free to use the computers in my room,"* Allie had said. Not 'my apartment'. Helga and Allie lived together, or at least were doing so this summer.

Find Helga and Allie Johanssen's home, and you find P.D. 'Penny' Walden.

Zoe plugged 'Helga Johanssen' and 'home address' into Google and got plenty of results for 'Helga Johanssen' but none that included a home address, though several references said 'of Cambridge'.

Zoe logged into Instagram, YikYak, Tumblr and Snapchat, the four sites that Allie Johanssen would be most likely to use. She found no account user by that name in Cambridge. Adding Facebook and LinkedIn, she tried 'Helga Johanssen'. She found Helga on Facebook and Instagram. The Facebook posts were stale, the most recent three years old. The Instagram posts were more recent, including one of Helga and Allie at a seashore. Tapping Allie's face brought a surprise result: *'Allie LaPointe'*.

OK, different surname, Zoe thought. She plugged the new name into the social media sites and was rewarded with accounts on Instagram and Tumblr. Scrolling through photos and captions, Zoe was rewarded with references to 'BB&N', 'Coolidge Hill' and 'Josiah Willard House'.

She plugged 'Helga Johanssen' and 'Josiah Willard House' into Google.

'*New England Green's Brian LaPointe and his wife, Helga Johanssen, entertained Japan's Boston Consul General Rokuichiro Michii at their home, the historic Josiah Willard House in Coolidge Hill...*" The *Boston* magazine entry was six years old but had everything she needed save for a specific street address.

Five additional entries linked Helga Johanssen to the Josiah Willard House, including one from earlier in the year.

Finally, Zoe typed in 'Josiah Willard House' and 'address'. The Cambridge Historical Society obliged with '*288 Coolidge Hill Road*' and '*A New England Green Historic Property. Not open for tours.*'

Zoe tapped her Uber icon.

* * * * *

Penny was uncertain whether she should answer the house phone. It was only after four rings and Allie's plaintive voice on the answering machine asking her to pick up the receiver that Penny did so.

"Anyone who comes to Pheromonix looking for you is going to go away empty-handed," Allie said. "As far as the company is concerned, no one answering your description works here. I'm going down to the plaza to see if anyone suspicious is hanging around. There's no question in my mind but that they're going to be here today – and my bet is that they're here this morning."

"You think these people are that smart?" Penny asked. "I can't stay here forever."

"Just until they lose interest," Allie replied.

"I've been thinking about how to make them lose interest a lot more quickly," Penny said. "This may take Helga's intervention."

* * * * *

Jason Curran knew his boss was angry, though he didn't know why. Nittolo had stormed into the office, gone into his office and slammed the door. After an hour, Curran had tapped on Nittolo's door and heard a gruff "Come," from the other side.

"How can I help?" Curran asked.

"You can't," Nittolo replied. "Regardless of how you try to help them, some clients are intent on shooting themselves in the foot."

"Emily Taylor Rice?"

Nittolo nodded. "She wants to make a statement this afternoon. By now, she's down in Hingham cutting her paramour's clothes into shreds. Of course, when it all hits the fan, it blows back on us."

Nittolo looked up at Curran. "I'll work this out. Just go back to your office and be productive. While you're at it, take a closer look at those financial files."

* * * * *

Helga narrowed her eyes. The idea sounded... frightening.

"We can do it," she told Allie cautiously. "We may even have more than enough on hand to get started. I'll have the lab generate some more, just to be certain."

"I'll go check what we have in storage," Allie said. "Penny mentioned one sample specifically. There is another one she may not know about. Personally, I think it sounds kind of cool."

* * * * *

It took an hour just to pile all of Brian's clothes onto the blue sailcloth in the foyer. Emily had no idea the man owned twenty-three pairs of athletic shoes. Eight of them were in their original boxes, still with wads of packing tissue. There were seventeen suits in his closet, more than fifty dress shirts, and at least a hundred ties. As he never wore a suit to his office, why did he need so many?

Yes, Brian was well compensated for his work at New England Green, and so had every right to buy fine things for himself, but here was evidence of a man who devoted an inordinate amount of time to his appearance. As she cleaned out the bathroom drawers that held his toiletries, she counted four shavers (one just for nose hair). She had never noticed that he used three distinct line-hiding skin creams 'formulated for men', but then she generally left for her office well before him. Those, along with multiple colognes, went unceremoniously into a cardboard box.

She next tackled Brian's 'home office', a second-floor jewel of a room with a wrap-around view of Hingham Harbor, Slate and Grape Islands and, off to one side, World's End. It had been her mother's private sanctuary and, in her final illness, a hospital room. Brian had found a grand mahogany desk in the basement – it had likely been her grandfather's – and had installed it where he could survey both this large, impressive room and the world beyond the windows.

Brian had resisted Emily's efforts to decorate it for him. He said this room was his 'personal space', though there was little of a personal nature in it. A framed, signed Tom Brady jersey hung on one wall; though Brian had never evinced any interest in football. The shelves held perhaps a dozen books, primarily mysteries and suspense. The surface of the desk was clear of any papers. Brian used just a single computer that traveled with him between Crow Point and his office.

The upper desk drawers held only pads of paper, an assortment of pens, and the usual detritus of stationery items such as tape and paper clips. On the bottom left drawer were four years of financial statements from Pilgrim State Investments. Emily smiled as she placed these in a box. *You got some 'splainin' to do, Lucy*, she thought.

The top right-hand drawer contained some bills and letters. They had never merged their finances. Brian had offered to help cover property taxes and maintenance, arguing that he should help to bear some of the cost of the house. She had declined. The family office took care of those expenses. The small stack of envelopes went into the cardboard box.

The bottom right-hand drawer held a beautiful rosewood box roughly a foot long and eight inches wide and high. Emily had never seen it before and it was certainly not something she had given him. The box was locked but, beneath it in the drawer, was a key.

She had declined to look through anything that appeared to be personal and, at first, simply taped the key to the top of the rosewood box and placed it into the cardboard container. The weight of the box and its contents, though, seemed quite light; almost as though it was empty.

Emily detached the key and inserted it into the box's locking mechanism. It turned easily. She opened the box. And gasped.

The box was full of panties and thongs. Each bore a pinned piece of paper in Brian's handwriting with a name and a year. *'Sarah Tutweiler 2008', 'Chloe Dupuy 2016', 'Ellen Cameron 2013'.* The topmost one bore the name *'Amber Oakes'* and the current year.

All of the panties appeared to be expensive and all were of a style that would catch the eye of a younger woman, likely a college student.

Emily felt sick to her stomach as she dropped the panties back into the box. When she and Brian had first become serious about each other, she had taken his hands and told him that she did not want to be 'the other woman' or ever learn that there was 'another woman'. If Brian tired of her, he should be honest and end the relationship. It would be hard, she said, though not nearly as hard as learning that someone else shared his heart or his bed.

Brian had responded by looking deeply into her eyes, taking her face in his hands, and telling her that he was a 'one-woman man' and that he was, by temperament and character, not capable of cheating.

Well, here is a trophy case full of other women's underwear to prove you were lying, Emily thought.

It was odd that, while every year since 2003 was represented, that no year appeared on more than one pair of panties.

I wonder, she thought. She went downstairs and, from her purse, retrieved her phone. She Googled the main number for New England Green. When the receptionist answered, Emily said, "Amber Oakes' office, please."

A few seconds later, she heard, *"Hi, this is Amber. I'll be out of the office today. Leave your name and number and I'll get back to you as soon as I can."* Emily hung up.

It was a young, still-high-pitched and carefree voice. Someone in her late teens or perhaps twenty. Probably exceedingly pretty. Likely a summer intern who worked in the Development Office at Beckwith Estate from the time her semester ended in mid-May until Labor Day. She would be the kind of free-spirited woman who saw no harm in having a summer affair with the top man in the organization, provided he wasn't *too* old and was cute. At the very least she would get some good dinners out of the experience and some tales to tell her friends in the fall. She could also count on a glowing letter of recommendation and, just maybe, a job referral that would bypass all those stupid Human Resources people.

Amber Oakes would have at best a vague idea that unequal power relationships were inherently coercive and had been banned by corporations and non-profits for two decades. Her various corporate board Ethics Committees dealt with a string of such events. The higher the executive and the lower the second employee, the higher the eventual payout.

She knew New England Green had such a policy because she had read and commented on it to Brian, telling him it was especially broad and gender-neutral. Yet, each May, New England Green's Executive Director had eyed the new crop of interns and chosen the most attractive to be his plaything.

She still felt the nausea. But she also knew that this rosewood box was her ultimate weapon. She retrieved it from the cardboard box and set it aside.

Emily tapped her phone to call Darlene Harris.

"I'm almost done here," she said. "You can send the truck."

* * * * *

Zoe Matthews looked up at the imposing house. From its front lawn emerged a sign measuring three feet by five feet. *Josiah Willard House 1743*. Below that was a logotype and the name, *New England Green*. At the bottom of the sign in capital letters was the admonition, *PRIVATE PROPERTY. PLEASE STAY OFF THE GROUNDS. NO ADMISSION EXCEPT BY WRITTEN PERMISSION*.

During the fifteen minute ride from Kendall Square, Zoe had pondered the implications of the conversation among Helga Johanssen, Allie LaPointe, and the Pheromonix receptionist.

"Is Penny in trouble?" "She might be." "If I start crowding Penny too much, it might…"

The urgent tone of the whole conversation was what troubled Zoe. She could rule out a competing news organization. This was way beyond having a 'secret identity' discovered. This sounded like a threat on her life. But, in the real world, who made such menacing statements? But if Penny Walden feared for her safety, why would she let a stranger in the door?

Her first words were going to have to be a lie.

She walked to the front door and rang the doorbell. When, after a minute there was no response, she rang the doorbell again. Penny was likely inside trying to get a look at the person outside.

Zoe stepped back five paces on the sidewalk so she could be seen by any window in the front of the house. She waved and smiled, then went back to the front door and rang the bell for the third time. This time, the door opened a crack.

"Please go away," a firm voice, presumably Penny Walden's, said.

"I'm Zoe Matthews, Penny. Helga and Allie sent me to see if I can help. Please let me in."

There was a hesitation. Zoe had identified herself, dropped three names, and intimated that there was trouble.

"Come in, quickly."

Zoe squeezed through the door which was promptly closed and locked. The woman standing in front of her was P.D. Walden. The hair was different, of course, but the face was the one on the dust jacket, but nine years older and more experienced.

"You don't look like anyone from the lab," Penny said warily. It was a statement.

"Hear me out," Zoe said. "My name is Zoe Matthews and I'm not from Pheromonix. In fact, as of yesterday, I don't work anywhere. I was a flunky with aspirations of being a journalist until I went to work for an *E.T.* wannabe. My path to success was to track down and interview P.D. Walden…"

Penny's face was contorted with rage. "Get the hell out of here. Now. Or I will call the police and have your ass in jail…"

"Maybe you need to call the police," Zoe said. "Not because of me, but because you're in trouble."

"What makes you think I'm in trouble?" Penny's voice had a slightly lesser edge.

"Because I overheard Helga and Allie talking. They're worried about you. Afraid for you is more like it."

"You don't really know anything about this, do you?"

Zoe shook her head. "What I know is that I want to help. And you sound like you could use an extra set of hands."

Penny considered the woman in front of her. Early twenties. Midwestern accent. But something about her looked tough. "Show me some identification," Penny said. "Lots of identification."

Zoe reached into her purse – a purple Michael Kors clutch that had been appropriated from a swag bag – and handed Penny her wallet.

Penny looked at a Missouri driver's license with a photo that was definitely the woman standing in front of her. The lone other photo ID was an elevator card identifying her as working at 232 Madison Avenue. There was also a New Jersey Transit interstate bus pass and two credit cards.

"No business card?" Penny asked.

"Interns don't need business cards." Zoe replied. "We're highly expendable and, besides, business cards cost money."

"Why aren't you still interning there? Wherever 'there' is."

"Because my alcoholic boss-*cum*-mentor promptly stole my idea…"

"Somebody else is coming?" Penny asked, her eyes widening.

Zoe shook her head. "No. I sent them to New Jersey. Some time, probably Monday, a molecular chemist named Patricia Walden is going to step out of her laboratory in Lawrenceville and get the full 'walk of shame' treatment. With luck, by early next year, she'll be a couple of million dollars richer for her trouble, courtesy of an invasion of privacy lawsuit."

"You don't look the least bit prepared for an interview," Penny said sarcastically. "Where's your camera?"

"If you had agreed to an interview, a talented classmate of mine would have done the audio and video work. But you didn't tell me why you don't have this place surrounded by police cars."

Penny gave a rueful smile. "Because it would start a chain of dominoes that would end in a posse of people like that alcoholic mentor of yours showing up to be the first to interview 'the' P.D. Walden. And, besides, about half an hour ago, I put in motion a plan that just might solve that particular problem."

"If I ask politely, will you tell me what it's all about?"

Penny shook her head. "It's too convoluted to…" And then

she paused. She looked Zoe over carefully. "Just how good an interviewer are you?"

"I was a finalist for…"

"No, I mean, could you do a *'60 Minutes'*-quality job of buttering someone up and then moving in for the kill?"

"If you had let me finish, I would have said that I nailed a Dean at the University of Missouri for selling ten thousand dollars of student sports tickets on Craigslist," Zoe said, then added, "The Dean was unemployed two days later."

"What kind of video crew did you need?" Penny asked.

"I have a one-woman army named Tyler Malone on speed dial," Zoe said. "And before you ask, that person is here in Boston and agreed to do the video with you."

Penny was silent for a moment, composing her idea.

"If you really want to help, I have an idea that just might solve the other half of my problem," Penny said. "If it comes off, you may finally get your career off the ground. Are you willing to do it?"

"Yes, but with a condition," Zoe replied. "If it does everything you want it to do, then when it's all over, you give me that interview with P.D. Walden."

* * * * *

Spotting the first two men was easy. One had come into Pheromonix's office at a few minutes after ten. The lone surprise was that, in addition to a photograph, the man used the name 'Penelope Walden'.

The spray tank used by the techs to coat fabric and curtains for testing was far too large to be easily concealed. Scrounging in the lab turned up a pressurized atomizer capable of holding ten milliliters of fluid, and a length of ultra-thin transparent tubing. By the time the man left Pheromonix's reception area (having been told in no uncertain terms that no employee by that name or description worked at the company), Allie was already positioned by the elevator with the 'down' button pushed. Attired in pink shorts and a white tee and with a small backpack, and with her face buried in parsing an urgent message on her phone, Allie was functionally invisible to an adult. The two rode the elevator to the ground floor without exchanging a word.

The man, wearing a coat and tie, quickly buttonholed a similarly dressed man. As the two of them spoke in anxious tones, Allie casually walked behind them, her face still intent on her phone, and depressed a button that sprayed a fine, un-noticeable mist on their pants. When they continued speaking without noticing her, Allie made a second foray.

The second man pulled a phone from his shirt pocket and made a brief call. The two set out across the brick plaza where they met a second pair of men in suits though without ties. On a lazy, early summer Friday morning with hundreds of people looking for an excuse to go outside and wander, spraying all four while attracting no attention took less than two minutes.

The original two went back to the west entrance of Building 1400, with one stationed at either end of the passageway that linked the brick plaza with Binney Street and the parking garage beyond. Allie decided they were sufficiently saturated and so stayed with the second pair.

Another phone call was made. One man stayed at the entrance to Building 600. The other set off on a brisk walk that took him to a parking garage. There, a fifth man was just coming down from the upper levels, shaking his head in disappointment.

There was too little traffic to approach the pair anonymously but, fortunately, they walked across Binney Street where they paused when one of their phones emitted a ring. Allie took a quick walk by them to give the fifth man his first dose, and the other one his second.

Were there more than five? Allie sat on a bench and observed for fifteen minutes.

A sixth man stopped to speak with the first two. His demeanor, coupled with the deference shown to him by the other two, led Allie to suspect he was managing this operation. He spoke with his hands as much as with words, and his motions seemed ominous. He wore a black, expensive-looking suit, and his face appeared to have pock marks on it, as from a long-ago scourge of acne.

As he crossed the plaza, scowling, Allie rose from the bench and walked at an angle to his path. As they converged Allie let go an especially dense spray. The man showed no notice.

For the next hour, Allie shifted benches. Five men had staked out the three logical building entrances that were within the roughly 200-foot range of the router. The sixth man made a continuous circuit of the area and also paid periodic attention to the garage. The men did not appear to be frustrated; rather, they were patiently waiting for Penny to walk into their trap. Whenever there was a crowd around any of the men, she used that opportunity to freshen the already potent cocktail on one or more of the men, being careful not to spray bystanders.

At noon, Allie's phone chimed. It was Helga.

"It's a good thing the techs like you," Helga said. "They've cooked up another ten milliliters of the stuff you're using now. They also found the other one you wanted, but just fifteen milliliters."

"You take the fresh stuff and save the other one for me in case we need it," Allie said. "Then I guess you're going to take a drive."

"I have the addresses." Helga replied. "This will take most of the afternoon. You stay in touch and don't let them see you."

Thirty seconds later, Allie's phone chimed again. This time, it was Penny.

"You know that revenge plan I was working on?" Penny asked. "I think I know how to make it work. Get ready to take some notes."

* * * * *

Emily looked at Zoe. She had expected – no, hoped – for someone more mature. But she spoke well and Emily could quickly tell whether the person with whom she was speaking understood the magnitude of a problem or an opportunity. Clearly, Zoe did.

It had taken ten minutes for Penny to convince Darlene Harris that she urgently needed to speak to Emily. Darlene was steadfast in protecting her employer's privacy. Only when Penny realized that the person she was speaking to was the same one whom Emily had sent to England and Leeds did Penny have the opening she needed. "If I tell you that Emily and I discussed the purpose of your trip to Leeds, is that enough to put me in touch with her?"

It was. Emily returned Penny's call in under five minutes. She immediately seized on Penny's idea. "It's brilliant. And I think I know how to make it happen today."

In the hour it took for Emily to drive from Hingham to Cambridge, Penny educated Zoe on the multiple transgressions of one Brian LaPointe and his role at New England Green. Penny printed off key pages from Brian's financial statements including check images showing checks nominally made payable to law and engineering firms, simply being signed over, in an illegible scrawl, to Brian's account at Pilgrim State.

Emily's arrival coincided with that of Tyler Malone, who quickly adjusted to the idea that the project was no longer an interview with P.D. Walden – even though the writer was there in the room with her – but to nail a smooth-talking non-profit executive.

"You're playing to his ego," Emily told Zoe and Tyler. "He *saved* this organization from its imminent demise. In the public's mind he is inextricably linked to its success because every press release New England Green has issued in the past fifteen years explicitly calls out his role in 'bringing a revered organization into the new millennium'. He is a monumental egoist and that's your ticket."

"Have him take you on a quick tour of the garden at Beckwith Estate," Emily said. "It's his pride and joy. Let him tell you how he personally brought the garden back to its 1920s glory. But don't linger too long. Tell him what you really need is a sit-down interview in his office."

Emily continued. "I would start the 'office' part of the interview by asking him to speak about how requiring an endowment for properties made such good sense. If he doesn't bring up the subject of the hard work of surveying and qualifying a property before it is accepted, then you should. Just get him to agree that the money spent on engineering and legal work pays big dividends down the line."

"Next, you get him on the record on all of the 'motherhood and apple pie' issues. We need to hear him saying that New England Green adheres to the highest ethical standards; that neither he nor anyone in the organization would ever condone illegal behavior." Emily paused and added, "It would be nice if you can work in non-tolerance for workplace sexual harassment."

Emily produced the affidavit from Leeds Beckett University. "When you do your 'reveal', I'd start with this. It will take him by surprise, of course, but I'm certain he will try to handle it smoothly. He'll say there must have been a missed communication somewhere because he certainly remembers being there and receiving his diploma. Let it pass. In the great scheme of things it's the least of his transgressions, even though it is grounds for dismissal all by itself."

"That's when I'd start mentioning names of some of the professional services firms New England Green has used. He'll probably say he doesn't keep track of that sort of thing. So, show him some bills. By now, he'll be getting suspicious. You know how long you can keep the conversation going before he says he has no more time…"

Zoe nodded. "That's when I throw everything at him. And then have Tyler run for the exits before he decides to grab the camera."

"Not quite," Emily said, smiling. "On your way out, you hand him this envelope." From her purse she produced a standard business envelope. "This contains the address of the apartment I've rented for him and the keys to that apartment. He'll find all of his belongings there. There's also a sheet of paper listing names and years. I'm reasonably certain he'll be able to figure out their significance."

"How do I know he'll see me?"

Emily again smiled. "It's all arranged. He's expecting you at three. You're the granddaughter of one of my dearest friends. You're in graduate school and you're working to build your portfolio. Make up the rest as you go along."

Chapter Fifteen

The American Society for the Prevention of Cruelty to Animals estimates there are 70 million feral cats in the United States. In addition, there are somewhere between 74 and 96 million cats residing as pets in homes in the country, a sizeable percentage of which are not confined to indoors.

America's feral cat population is concentrated in cities where there is ample food available from dumpsters and garbage cans. Cambridge, with more than 600 restaurants within its city limits, is an especially fertile gathering place for strays.

It was less than half an hour after Allie began spraying that the first cats took notice. They were members of a colony of some fifty felines living behind a small apartment building on Bristol Street, downwind from the spraying. Within two minutes, a second group of cats that had been scavenging the dumpster behind a restaurant called Flat Top Johnnie's also caught the scent.

One group of cats lingered at the western edge of the plaza in an area used as a loading dock for the complex. Another group assembled on its eastern end in an area of tall weeds along a seldom-used rail spur. Generations of living independent of humans had taught them to be wary of interactions with people. But there was an intense, overpowering scent in the air. It was alluring; overwhelming. It beckoned in an all-consuming, uncontrollable way.

Molecule #17 had been extracted from the forehead gland of a three-year-old tom named Casey A. The swab had been done in the first month of Pheromonix's existence when clinical procedures were still being established and large-scale tests —meaning upwards of thirty volunteer cats were exposed to a large sample of the pheromone – were run on every sample.

The result had been legendary. The pheromone had proven to be both a powerful attractant and one that induced aggressive behavior, especially scratching. In the lone laboratory test, thirty cats – male and female alike – had reduced a sofa and two pair of curtains to ribbons in minutes. It had been immediately dubbed 'the Demon Spawn' by the lab staff.

Penny had read the 'autopsy' report on that lone clinical trial. At the time, her reaction was one of wonder: Pheromonix had managed to produce in one of its first experiments, a chemical that was the perfect antithesis of the product the company sought to create. The report had given her hope that a pheromone having the opposite effect: repelling and docile behavior, might be achieved by isolating the components of Molecule #17.

The memory of that report, still fresh in her mind, became an improvisational part of her plan when she learned that men from Pilgrim State Investments were at her place of employment.

Ten milliliters of Molecule #17 had been replicated and preserved for future study. Three milliliters of that stock was now on the clothing of the six men who were, for all intents and purposes, staking out the entrances to two buildings within the One Kendall Square complex.

The feral cats strained to adhere to the common-sense behavior patterns ingrained into them. Here was a plaza filled with dangerous humans. But their feline brains were also hard-wired to respond to the power of pheromones. Each group – which grew by the minute – edged closer to the brick area that marked the beginning of the human zone. They began to yowl.

To the cats' consternation, but also delight, their keen noses determined there were six, identical sources for the alluring pheromone. Unable to resist, they crossed onto to the brick.

The first two cats reached the legs of David Hale, sniffed once, confirmed that this was one of the targets they sought, opened their claws, and began scratching.

"What the hell?" Hale exclaimed. Two cats, purring loudly, had already put a long gash in his chinos. He shook his leg to make them go away, but it only seemed to make them more determined.

He swatted at one of the cats, which snarled and snapped at his hand.

Twenty feet away, Sam Ashton, his second-in-command at Pilgrim State Investments, had three cats trying to climb his leg. He, too, swatted at one of the cats, which promptly bit his belt.

Hale saw a dozen more cats trotting toward him.

"Sam, let's get out of here!"

They both broke across Binney Street for the garage. Some twenty cats were in pursuit. The garage was on seven levels and a block long. In their disorientation, neither Hale nor Ashton could remember what level they had parked on.

A stairwell with double doors allowed them to reduce their pursuers to four cats. Most of the other felines sat yowling, frustrated by the doors. However, the cleverest of the cats raced around the corner to the automobile entrance ramps and quickly re-joined the pursuit.

The two men fled from floor to floor, running the length of each deck, Hale clicking his key fob in hope of hearing a 'beep' from his car. In pausing momentarily to listen for what he thought was an answering call from his car, a pursuing cat leapt and sank its claws into Hale's back.

"Sam, get this thing off of me!"

Ashton, kicking at two cats attempting to climb his legs, was in no position to help. He continued to run, though his pace slowed with each step. He was a man not used to physical exertion of any kind.

Al Luchetti, the leader of the men sent up from New York, could at first not understand why three cats had converged on him, yowled loudly, and began scratching the pant legs of his custom Cifonelli suit. He leaned over and swatted away two of the cats, who promptly regained their balance and lunged for him.

The third cat, using a rear approach, sunk its claws deeply into Luchetti's leg and tore at the suit fabric with his teeth. Luchetti reached around and grabbed the cat by the scruff of its neck and flung it some ten feet into the plaza.

Luchetti's act drew the attention of several observers, one of whom yelled out, 'That's cruelty to animals!" That person's admonition drew the attention of a dozen others, who looked around to see who was being cruel.

A fourth and fifth cat had now joined the fray, and Luchetti angrily swatted at each one.

There was now a chorus of people, male and female, shouting, "They're just being friendly!" and "Leave them alone!" and "Stop it! They're just helpless cats!" and "Stop hurting those animals!"

People also began taking out their phones to video the event.

Luchetti had one enormously powerful weapon at his disposal: a Glock 26. Seeing the crowd around him – now some twenty people – he knew he dared not fire it. But with blood running down his legs and one pants leg torn at the knee, he needed… something. In frustration and pain, he took out the gun and began using its barrel to hit the cats in the head.

Two fell limp at his feet and someone screamed, either at the sight of the gun or of the limp bodies at his feet.

Luchetti could recognize a hopeless situation when he saw one. He clubbed two more cats and began running across the plaza, two cats in hot pursuit.

His three companions had fared no better in the cat onslaught. One was on the ground, a half-dozen cats on him with tails high in the air. As he ran, Luchetti yelled their names and screamed, "Get to the garage!"

At the first scream, a private security guard named Lucille and employed by the complex began running toward the sound. As she ran, she also used her shoulder mic to alert other security personnel assigned to the multiple plazas around the complex. Fifteen seconds later, the security guard was at the perimeter of people shouting at a man clubbing cats…

"Gun!" she shouted into her shoulder mic, then added, "Male, dark suit, white shirt, age approximately forty…" She followed with more details, chasing after the man as he now broke from the plaza for the tunnel leading to the garage. The man held his gun in the air as he ran, and so the guard kept shouting "gun" and giving her position.

At the complex's central security monitoring center, two things happened in rapid succession. At Lucille's first shout for assistance, her exact location was ascertained and video cameras began tracking her. When she shouted 'gun', a red button was pushed alerting Cambridge Police two blocks away on Sixth Street.

When Luchetti began running, his gun clearly visible, cameras tracked his every step and recorded his movements for posterity. The presence of cats behind him were of no importance: here was a man with a gun in a densely populated office complex. As he approached the West entrance of Building 1400, automatic locks shut the entrances to the building, preventing him from entering any offices.

When he emerged on Binney Street, now accompanied by two other men who were likely accomplices, a second contact was made to Cambridge Police, notifying them that a man with a gun was now on a public street. One Kendall Square security was informed that uniformed officers were already on their way.

As Luchetti and the two men ran into the parking garage stairwell, a call went to the garage's ticketing office ordering everyone to a) take cover for their personal safety and b) secure the garage exits to prevent any auto from leaving the structure.

In the meantime, a second report came of a man, also in a suit, lying prone and bleeding near a building entrance. Security officials assumed the man was a victim of the gunman now fleeing. The same report said the man was covered with cats. An ambulance call was made.

Within seconds, multiple police sirens could be heard on Binney Street as Cambridge Police converged on the scene.

One Kendall Square security officials, now using cameras located throughout the garage, found there were a total of five men fleeing as well as an unknown number of cats. The three men converged on one car, a black Lexus SUV with New York plates. The other two men appeared unable to find their vehicle or vehicles, but were acting suspiciously.

Al Luchetti threw open the car door and jumped inside, swatting away the last cat. He screamed for the others to join him and started the car, backing out of the space with a lurch. His two companions were bloody; their suits torn and ragged. One cat managed to make it inside the SUV but was thrown out the window by Luchetti.

There was little traffic in and out of the garage at midday, and only two cars in front of him at the pay station. Neither was moving and Luchetti blew the auto's horn to show his impatience. It was then that he noticed that no one was in the kiosk. He moved around the stationary cars and into the monthly pay lane. It, too was unattended and he sped forward, turning right to make for the street.

Two Cambridge Police cars blocked the exit. Four officers, guns drawn and pointed, stood waiting for them.

From the vantage point of her bench, Allie had been able to observe almost all of the events as they unfolded on the plaza. Now, she moved as part of a crowd onto Binney Street and watched as police cars took their positions. A black Lexus came screaming around the corner, then screeched to a stop.

I did all this with a third of an ounce of liquid, she thought. *This stuff is incredible.*

She decided it was time to start what Penny had described as

'Phase Two'. She took her iPad out of her backpack and began typing instructions.

* * * * *

Jason Curran was baffled. For the past two hours – and conscious that he did not know if he could bill his time to the Gerald and Abigail Rice Foundation – he had tried to make sense of the mountain of Pilgrim State Investments data by lining up various data-bearing folders in a logical progression.

Organization of the flow of incoming funds was a model of efficiency. For each account he could see every deposit over the life of the account as well as the source of that deposit. When it was a check, an image of both sides of the check was captured. When hundred-dollar bills were deposited, their serial numbers were scanned. Jason supposed that much of this caution was a product of laws enacted after 9/11 to ensure that terrorists could not easily move funds.

In the case of a financial advisor that catered to clients dealing in illegal activities, he noticed, it was also a nifty source of material for blackmailing a customer, though using it would bring Pilgrim State under the same microscope as the crooked businessman or politician. He would save that avenue of thought to ponder at a later time.

But it was the investment strategy and accounting that he could not fathom. Penny had told him the head of the firm picked a few opportunities and 'went big'. He had, according to Penny, bet big against the Venezuelan Bolivar. Searching the files and folders for 'Bolivar', the firm's trading sheet showed a transaction of $50 million selling short on one day, and closing out that bet the following day. The amount of the gain was $30 million. The gain was preposterous. On their worst day, currencies might move a fraction of a percent. The Bolivar supposedly imploded by sixty percent. Two days later, the firm placed another trade, also for $50 million, and the Venezuelan currency promptly fell by half, netting the firm another $25 million.

Searching the data further, when Pilgrim State traded stocks, the firm managed to buy a stock on the day before it rose or fell a sizeable percentage, and then sell it at the perfect time on the following day. These were all stocks with which Pilgrim State had no previous experience owning. In fact, according to the firm's own records, no stock was ever held for more than a day, and every stock it traded made huge moves up or down in that day.

No financial firm was that lucky.

Funds not being invested sat in a massive money market account earning negligible interest. Periodic modest disbursements were made to account holders and the ledgers showed funds being deducted. But there were also large, multi-million-dollar withdrawals that indicated only 'New York Capital Center' as its destination. That money never flowed back in.

The only way it all made sense was if Pilgrim State Investments was making everything up.

But that was impossible. Ponzi schemes were impossible to sustain these days. In the wake of Bernie Madoff, entire government organizations had been created to prevent a recurrence.

But what if?

He went back to Brian LaPointe's account. Each of his statements were there together with a record of trades, all in currency futures related to Venezuela and his share of those unbelievably lucky stock trades. LaPointe's account had been credited with more than three million dollars in gains in the previous year – all of it noted as being sheltered from U.S. taxes by something called a Cook Island Trust.

Except for the warning language contained in monthly account statements, there was no evidence that this 'Cook Island Trust' existed. The term existed in no trading or transfer documents. Pilgrim State invented it in order to prevent people from withdrawing their money except in dribs and drabs.

How much money did Pilgrim State actually have? The 'paper' balance sheet indicated there was $1.2 billion in assets against minimal liabilities. The assets were duly categorized into appropriate sounding compartments. But the assets seemed to tie to nothing else. All he could find was about $240 million in the money market account. Deposits regularly flowed into the money market account as new funds came in. But funds went out just as quickly. When those mysterious 'New York Capital Center' disbursements were taken into account, the pool of available funds was shrinking.

He tried a quick calculation to determine how much investor money had disappeared. *Let's say that half of that $1.2 billion represent gains and half of it represents money deposited from accounts. Pilgrim State has turned $650 million into $240 million. Whoever controls Pilgrim State has siphoned off more than $400 million...*

We are definitely in Bernie Madoff territory.

Which would explain why that Hale guy worked so hard at turning down Penny's account. He works awfully hard at telling you he doesn't want your money and can't take your money under any circumstances. He tells you your current advisor is doing a fine job and you should stay right where you are. He turns you down so well and so smoothly that he makes you want to give him your money.

And that was just Penny Walden, walking through the door, cold. Imagine what he can do when he has time to prepare for a visit? Imagine if someone has heard about what great returns he has been getting for them, and how he gets those returns year after year.

Madoff had it down to a science. He had people working for him who would brag about the fact that they were earning these fabulous returns. When someone was champing at the bit, these cohorts would say they could get you a meeting with Madoff. No promises; it would be just a courtesy. And Madoff would invariably do just what Hale did to Penny – tell her he was closed to new customers. Only at the end of a long meeting would Madoff relent and say he 'might be able to do something'. He kept that up for at least ten years and probably more than twenty."

A quick computer search showed that Madoff took in an estimated $18 billion over as long as twenty years. His clients thought they had $65 billion. When it all imploded, the lawsuits began flying and dragged on for years. In the end, maybe the investors got back about half of what they had put in. Anyone who had withdrawn all their money, including fictitious gains, got sued.

There had been other Ponzi schemes since Madoff. Some unraveled after garnering just a few million dollars. The largest Curran found had collected $200 million from unsuspecting investors. So, when Pilgrim State went bust, it would go down as something big. Not Madoff-size, but definitely newsworthy all the same. And, given that most if not all of Pilgrim State's clients were depositing stolen money, bribes, or kickbacks; the headlines would go on for months.

Curran knew he had to take this information to his boss. He tagged a few screen shots for illustration, picked up his computer, and made the short walk down the hall to Raymond Nittolo's office.

He noted the time: exactly 2:30 p.m.

* * * * *

At 3:01 p.m., a message blinked on a desktop computer. The computer was in a small office on the third floor of a nondescript building on Main Street in Hempstead, Long Island.

Marilyn Palumbo looked at the message. *About time, you morons,* she thought.

She tapped the message. It verified what she knew, that $10 million had just been transferred from Chestnut Hill. Marilyn lit a cigarette, waited exactly one minute, and called up an account on a window of her computer. She looked at deposits, expecting to see the funds on account at the Hempstead bank.

Nothing.

She hit the 'refresh' key. Still nothing. The transfers always took exactly a minute.

She banged the side of the monitor and again hit the 'refresh' key.

Still nothing. And it had been two minutes.

Marilyn called up the original message. Ten million dollars. Correct. Transferred to routing number…

"What the hell?" she said aloud.

She grabbed her phone and hit the speed dial for Chestnut Hill. The phone rang. No answer.

At 3:04, a second message blinked on her computer. This time, Marilyn immediately opened the link. Another $10 million had just been transferred. To the same, incorrect routing number.

Marilyn stubbed out her cigarette, opened her desk drawer and pulled out a sheet of paper. She ran her nicotine-stained finger down the list and found David Hale's cell phone number. She punched it in.

Four rings later, she found herself listening to Hale's voicemail recording.

"This is Marilyn," she said. "Where the hell are you? You've sent $20 million to the wrong account…"

A third message blinked. This time Marilyn opened it within seconds. It was a third, $10 million transaction. All headed for that same damned incorrect routing number.

She found Sam Ashton's cell phone number and punched it, muttering obscenities all the while. After four rings it, too, went to voice mail. She left the same message.

She found the third partner's cell phone number. Winston Bigelow. She stabbed the numbers. This time, after three rings, she heard an answer.

"Bigelow here."

"What the hell is going on there?" Marilyn fairly screamed. "No one's answering their damned phone and money is flying out of your account…"

Her tirade was interrupted by the 'ding' of another message. She stabbed at the keyboard. Another $10 million.

"What are you talking about?" Bigelow asked, his voice perplexed.

"Look at your damned system!" Marilyn yelled. "You just sent another ten million bucks out the door to God knows where…"

"Marilyn, I'm not in the office," Bigelow said. "David has everything under control…"

"It's not under control!" Marilyn screamed. "Get to the office and stop this!"

There was a silence on the other end of the line.

"Well?" Marilyn screamed.

"Marilyn, I'm in Morocco," Bigelow said. "I'm on vacation…"

Marilyn slammed down the phone.

Howard Kelly's office was one floor up. Marilyn took the stairs to save the minutes the elevator might consume. In the process, unaccustomed to exercise of any kind, she arrived at his office door looking like she might collapse at any second.

Kelly was on the phone but saw the look of distress on Marilyn's face. "What's wrong?" he asked.

Puffing, Marilyn said, "Someone is wiring money out of Chestnut Hill at the rate of about ten million every minute or so. No one answers at the office. Hale doesn't answer his cell. Ashton doesn't answer his cell. The only person who picks up the phone is Bigelow, and he's in Morocco or Majorca, or somewhere."

"Can't you stop the transfers?" Kelly asked.

Marilyn shook her head. "That's under their control. All I do is get notifications and check to see that we got the deposits…"

"I have four guys up there checking on a possible computer hack. One of them is Al Luchetti. He'll know what's going on."

Kelly pulled out a cell phone from his desk, scrolled through a list of numbers, and tapped the screen.

After five rings, his call went to voice mail.

"What is going on here?" Kelly said, staring into the screen of his phone.

* * * * *

In the property room of the Cambridge Police Department, no one paid the least bit of attention to the ringing of cell phones. The phones, along with other personal items, had been placed in plastic bags and sealed with an inventory of the contents and the name of its owner.

One floor up, Detective Nancy Donaldson tried to make sense of the paperwork in front of her. In thirty-two years with the Cambridge Police and twenty of those years as a Detective, Donaldson thought she had seen everything there was to see in law enforcement. Now, she knew she had one with its own, special folder.

Donaldson was a fair-skinned woman whose freckles were still a dominant feature of her face. She had allowed her hair to go silver and she kept it in a neat bob. Any perp who thought he could easily outrace an 'old lady' quickly and surprisingly found himself face down being handcuffed. She favored slacks and shirts, the more colorful, the better.

As near as Donaldson could tell after speaking with the security office at One Kendall Square, six men had been engaged in some kind of a stakeout at two buildings in the complex. Armed with a photo and a name, they had visited several companies in those buildings looking for a woman named Walden. Having failed to find her, they had taken up positions at the building entrances, presumably to wait for the woman to arrive.

At 12:37 p.m., the men were approached and then attacked by a band of feral cats; possibly as many as fifty. The men had fought them off and one man, Alphonse Luchetti, had pulled a rather lethal, unlicensed, and unnumbered handgun and used it to beat a number of cats. Video then showed Luchetti running through the plaza, his gun in the air, apparently marshalling his crew. Five men, including the gun-wielding Luchetti, raced into the garage. A sixth man, initially thought to have been assaulted by Luchetti but later determined to be one of his confederates, was injured by the feral cats and treated by paramedics.

Three of the men, all with New York driver's licenses, attempted to flee in one car. When they found the parking structure exit blocked by police cars, the driver – Luchetti – attempted to evade the blockade by driving through some trees and shrubs. They promptly got stuck between trees. The men surrendered without a fight.

Two of the men, one from Weston and the other from Newton according to their driver's licenses, followed Luchetti but stopped when they saw the police cars. They, too, surrendered without a fight.

All six men's clothes were in tatters. All had bleeding scratches. All except the unconscious man refused treatment. In fact, they had refused to cooperate in any way, saying they would speak only when their attorney arrived. An hour and a half after being apprehended, they were now in two holding cells; the four New Yorkers in one cell, the two Massachusetts men in the other. They spoke to one another when no one was within hearing range; when approached, they fell silent.

Detective Donaldson was left with the problem of trying to figure out exactly what the hell had happened.

Technically, five of the men had broken no law. Intuitively, however, all six men were engaged in a criminal conspiracy of some kind. It likely involved finding and abducting this Walden woman. 'Likely', unfortunately, had no weight in court. They would face no charges unless they again took up positions by those entrances.

Luchetti was the lone, easy catch. He had no license to carry the gun and the gun's serial numbers had been obliterated by acid. He had displayed the gun and menaced a crowd of people, to say nothing of whipping cats. In Massachusetts, and especially in Cambridge, he was toast.

Detective Donaldson's thoughts were interrupted by a Desk Sergeant bearing a printout. Donaldson read the two-pages and sighed.

She had just gotten herself mixed into an organized crime case. The four New York men were all members of what was left of the Capizzi crime family. They all had lengthy records, though no charges were currently pending. Luchetti and one other of the group was muscle. The other two were deemed data criminals with convictions for computer and wire fraud.

Donaldson motioned for the Desk Sergeant. "Call the FBI," she whispered and handed the printout back to the man. "Tell them what we've got and tell them to get here fast."

That left the other two; the local guys. Their business cards said they were the heads of a financial entity called Pilgrim State Investments. That they were part of whatever the organized crime guys were up to was without question. They had each gone into two companies flashing the Walden woman's photo. There was security footage of them conversing with Luchetti.

They looked soft. One was on the plump side. Neither had a callous on his hands.

She motioned for the holding cell officer. "Bring Hale upstairs," she whispered.

Five minutes later she was face-to-face across a table in an interview room with David Hale, the Chairman and President of Pilgrim State Investments, according to his business card.

"Mr. Hale," Donaldson said, "I'm sorry to inform you that your world is about to come crashing down around you."

The statement had no effect. The man sat impassively.

"You and your Mafia buddies…"

"They're not my 'buddies'," Hale said calmly. "We weren't together. I respectfully request to go back to that dungeon of yours downstairs. My lawyer should be here any minute. He will explain everything and I will expect an apology from the Cambridge Police."

"Well," Donaldson said, "that's one side of the story. Hedge fund CEO from Weston just happens to be enjoying lunch in Cambridge when, as he and his partner are leaving the garage, there's a bunch of Cambridge Police blocking the exit and pointing their guns. I can see that."

"Unfortunately, you went into two companies, flashed a photo of someone named Penelope Walden, and asked if she worked there. So did your companion. And so did those other four guys. Please don't expect a jury to believe that it was a coincidence. There's also security footage of the head of that little Mafia clique coming around and talking to you while you kept watch over one of the building entrances. You spoke back to him in what looked like an exceedingly serious manner. Your attorney can try to persuade a jury that he was just asking what time a film came on at the cinema down the street, but I think a reasonable person would…"

"Please take me back downstairs. Now," Hale said.

The man clearly does not like what I'm saying, Donaldson thought. *I have a suspicion he hasn't thought this through. Well, let's turn up the heat.*

"You know, Mr. Hale," Donaldson said, "the most remarkable part of this conversation is that you never once disagreed with me, or even expressed surprise, that those other four guys are Mafia, or at least what passes for the Mafia these days. The fact that you were knowingly consorting with them, and even helping them out with their little abduction scheme, is going to cause the Organized Crime folks to take a microscopically close look at your business. You're going to have accountants going over every transaction for every customer going back to the Reagan administration. You are going to be one really busy guy.

"You know what I would do?" Donaldson continued. "I

would cut a deal the minute they offer you one. Because you don't want to be on the same side as those Mafia guys. And if you think that the FBI doesn't have your best interests at heart, you haven't seen anything until you've had a bunch of goombahs thinking that you'd be better off dead."

For the first time, Hale's face showed visible emotion. Donaldson first noticed it just as she spoke of OCCU looking into his customers.

"I want to go back to my cell," Hale said. The defiance was gone.

"Just one question," Donaldson said. "And this is strictly off the record. What in the hell was going on with those cats? What did you do to piss them off?"

Hale shook his head. After perhaps ten seconds he said, "I have absolutely no idea."

* * * * *

Helga noticed the multiple security cameras around the office building on Boylston Street. She would have preferred to avert her face but that would have given anyone watching – now or later – a reason to suspect her.

And so she strode up to the building and opened the doors. Helga read the directory by the elevator and saw two tenants on the second floor: Pilgrim State Investments and an apartment rental service. She took the elevator, ignored the door to Pilgrim and walked into the rental office.

"Can I help you?" a receptionist asked.

"Oh, my son is graduating and I'm scouting some apartments for him. Do you have any brochures?"

"Brochures," the receptionist said to herself. "We don't really have any brochures."

"Lists of properties for rent, then," Helga said.

"Would you like to speak with a rental counselor…" the receptionist started to say.

"Oh, this is fine," Helga said, picking up an 'apartment finder' magazine from the table in the reception area. "I'll let him start with this." She smiled broadly.

"Sure," the receptionist said, mystified.

Helga left the office. From her purse she extracted a small bottle and allowed a few drops to dribble onto the carpet. A few more drops went into the elevator. More drops landed on the sidewalk and in the shrubbery along the building's foundation.

This was her last stop. Armed with the employee information Allie had downloaded from the Pilgrim State server, she had already sprinkled drops of the 'demon spawn' pheromone at the homes of ten employees. Those who lived in apartment complexes were spared, and David Hale's home had a gate across the driveway almost 300 feet from the house. She sprinkled some in the rhododendron but suspected it would do little good.

She looked at her phone. The time was 3:35. She could just beat the heading-home traffic back to Cambridge.

*   *   *   *   *

Marilyn Palumbo and Howard Kelly watched helplessly as the last transaction confirmation blinked at them.

Ten minutes earlier, Kelly had called Bank of America and tried to explain that they were transferring huge sums of money to the wrong bank.

"Are you the authorized person on this account?" asked someone in a call center that could have been anywhere in the world.

"I'm the boss of the 'authorized person'," Kelly said, trying to control his temper.

"Then I'll need that person's PIN," the call center person said.

"I can't get hold of that person," Kelly said, gritting his teeth. "That's why I'm calling you so that I can reverse these transactions."

"Unless you have the PIN, I can't help you," the call center person said. "I suggest you contact the receiving institution and have them reverse the transaction."

"I don't know who the 'receiving institution' is," Kelly said, gripping his telephone handset until his knuckles were white.

"That information will be on the nine-digit ABA routing number," the call center person said. "Thank you for your call. If you wish to complete a brief customer satisfaction survey, please stay on the line. The survey takes…"

Kelly didn't wait to find out how long it would take to complete the survey. "The routing number!" he said to Marilyn.

Marilyn opened two messages just to make certain the numbers were the same. "000-000-505," she said, and added, "What kind of routing number is that?"

"It doesn't matter," Kelly said. "When we find out what bank it is, we get someone on the inside to tell us whose account it is. Then we go pay that person a visit. They'll give it back. And then they'll pay for their little game with their lives. You must have some way to look up those numbers…"

"The American Bankers Association website," Marilyn said. Her fingers flew over her keyboard. A website opened. She typed in the number. She gulped.

"So what is it?" Kelly said. "I didn't bring down my reading glasses."

"It's the U.S. Government Department of the Treasury," Marilyn said. "Someone transferred $240 million to the Treasury Department."

"I am going to strangle David Hale with my bare hands," Kelly said.

Chapter Sixteen

Brian took a deep breath of the late June air, redolent with the sweet scent of new mown grass and roses. It was a picture perfect day, made even better because of Emily's apologetic call. *I need a huge favor*, she had said. *I will be so beholden to you if you can do this for me. I am so sorry I thought only of myself and stayed in town rather than come home to be with you...*

I have her wrapped around my little finger, he thought, *and it's time to slip that wedding band on her finger. What's the shortest engagement we can manage? Six months? How about a Christmas wedding?*

The admissions gate had called two minutes earlier to say two young women had an appointment to see him. *Young women? Emily had said they were graduate students*, he thought. *That would make them about twenty-two or twenty-three. What a great age. Would either of them be up for something on the really advanced curriculum? No, that could get back to Emily. Play it straight.*

A silver car – some kind of inexpensive Japanese crossover SUV – pulled up the stone driveway and into the staff parking area. The driver's door opened and out stepped an African-American woman, tall and with a great build. Definitely early twenties and with a terrific smile. The passenger side door opened and a knockout of a long-haired redhead emerged. She was shorter and wore a pantsuit, so he assumed she must be the interviewer. She, too, flashed a smile with dazzling white teeth. After exchanging a few words, the black woman opened the back end of the car and removed two cases, likely the camera equipment.

The redhead, carrying a small briefcase, began walking toward Brian, and so he advanced to meet her half way. She offered her hand, which Brian took and noted its warmth and softness.

"Zoe Matthews," she said. "I can't thank you enough for

agreeing to see me on such short notice."

"Not a bother," Brian said, flashing his best smile. "The rest of my afternoon is yours."

The African-American woman, wheeling the two cases, caught up to them.

"Let me introduce Tyler Malone," Zoe said. "She doesn't say a lot, but when she does, you need to pay attention." Another broad smile.

"My pleasure," Brian said. "What's your plan?"

Zoe responded. "Twenty minutes or so out here in the garden with you telling us the story of New England Green. Then, I'd like to interview you in your office; get your thoughts on where the organization is going. Its values. That sort of thing. Afterward, we'll get some 'B' roll of the gardens without you. I promise we won't take more than an hour of your time. We'll be out of here before four."

"I was told this is for your Master's project," Brian said. "University of Missouri. Is that right?"

"Well, yes," Zoe said. "But we're also trying to build our reel – excuse me – show TV stations that we have practical experience."

"Well, let me help you all I can," Brian said. "Are you staying in the area long?"

* * * * *

From the first time Brian laid eyes on her, Zoe felt his eyes had never left her, and had mostly focused on trying to see what she looked like under her suit. Emily had suggested she flirt, and so Zoe removed her suit jacket, revealing a white tank top. Brian's eyes went straight to her breasts. Tyler, on cue, said the jacket needed to stay on for filming.

"I have to do what she commands," Zoe said, giving her best Miss America smile. She put the jacket back on. Mission accomplished.

"Let's start in the CSA," Brian said, disappointment in his

voice.

For twenty minutes, Brian walked the two women through four gardens, speaking to Zoe as Tyler filmed from different perspectives, explaining how New England Green had come into being and how its mission had evolved. A practiced interview subject, he relied on a set of stock anecdotes. Zoe had to admire his talent: he had told these stories hundreds of times to hundreds of reporters, yet he made them sound spontaneous.

At the twenty minute mark, Tyler said, "We need to keep to the schedule."

Brian laughed. "Spoken like a great producer. Is she always a taskmaster?"

Zoe, too, laughed. "She can be a little uptight. We've been working together for a few years now."

"You never did say if you're going to be in the area for a while," Brian pressed as they walked toward Beckwith House.

"We're at my grandmother's place in Dennis Port," Zoe said, repeating the words Emily had suggested. "Of course, my grandmother left yesterday to visit my aunt in San Francisco and won't be back until later next week. So, I'm trying to line up interview subjects for next week. And Tyler has friends in Springfield she's anxious to spend time with. So, everything is in flux."

Translation: I've got an empty house and nothing on my plate for the next several days.

"I could make some calls," Brian said, casually. "What kind of interview subjects are you looking for?"

"Let me think about it," Zoe said. She cocked her head to one side and again gave that Miss America smile.

* * * * *

It's too bad we're supposed to be in Maine this weekend, Brian thought. *Then again, maybe Emily's plans changed. This girl is coming on pretty strong. Wait: she got here through Emily. How strong is that connection?*

"I got the request to meet with you from the head of a foundation in Boston," Brian said. "What sort of magic did you work to make that happen?"

"Oh, that's Grandmom," Zoe said. "She's an old friend of the woman who runs it. Grandmom initially suggested her, but I told Grandmom foundations aren't sexy enough for interviews." Zoe swept her hands across the gardens around them, but just managed to include Brian in her sweep. "*This* is sexy."

"Zoe," Tyler said, an impatient look on her face. She tapped her wrist.

"Ms. Malone seems intent on keeping you on a tight leash," Brian said, grinning.

"She can be strict," Zoe replied. "I guess I respond well to strict. Let's get started inside."

Oh, I can deliver 'strict', Brian thought. *I think I'd better block off next Monday and Tuesday.*

In Brian's office, Tyler asked for a minute to get an establishing video of the back wall of the office. Zoe explained, "It's just the one camera, so we're going to green-screen the two-shot. That way, I don't have to waste your time repeating questions. I suspect you've been through all this before."

Brian nodded his understanding. And, yes, he had been through this many times. This was going to be a slam dunk, but with a marvelous chaser. He decided he should ask at the end of the interview if he could drop out on Monday to Dennis Port to look at the rough video. He could offer to bring out some vintage footage of some of the properties to add depth to the piece.

"That's all I need," Tyler said. "I'm ready when you are."

Everyone took their places, Brian behind his desk, his wall of photos and honors behind him. Zoe sat in a straight-back chair opposite the desk. Brian thought briefly about removing the photo of Emily, but it would be obvious and, besides, only the back of the frame was in Zoe's field of view.

"You've been Executive Director of New England Green since you were in your early twenties," Zoe began. "Weren't you overwhelmed by the job?"

"Not at all," Brian replied. "I had come to New England Green as Chief Horticulturalist, and I couldn't help but see the inherent problems from the inside. The organization was faithfully following a plan that had been superseded by both economic reality and a changing population…" He gave a crisp, forty-five second response, lifted from a speech he had given just a month earlier. He made certain to use his hands to punctuate his most memorable lines, and to smile throughout.

"You also make no secret of your early years," Zoe said, inviting Brian to expand on the topic.

The girl has done her homework, Brian thought. He nodded and said, "I grew up on a failing truck farm outside of Athol, Massachusetts. It burned into me the lesson that, if you don't adapt to the times, you'll fail." He ended with a look of wistfulness on his face.

"And your Board of Trustees gave you their full vote of confidence to make those changes," Zoe said.

Great set-up, Zoe, he thought. "I encouraged them to find holes in my analysis," Brian replied. "They couldn't. *That* was when they gave me that vote of confidence." Back to the smile.

"You also had the right degrees," Zoe said, pointing at the wall behind Brian. "The Stockbridge School and Leeds, one of Europe's most prestigious universities. The Trustees wouldn't have entrusted such a mission to one of their gardeners."

Another great set-up. Thank you. "Yet, when you get down to basics, I *was* one of their gardeners," Brian retorted. "It took a gardener to appreciate the unused resources. It took those other degrees to know how to formulate a plan." He added an especially broad smile. "And to give those Trustees the confidence that the man they had put in charge could carry it out."

He saw Zoe's smile of appreciation for a virtuoso performance.

"Let's talk about the future," Zoe said. "Where do you see New England Green in five years – ten years?"

Brian gave his memorized two-minute 'elevator pitch' on the near-term future of the organization. He used it all the time to charm dowagers into making bequests. Now, his eyes boring into Zoe's, he used it to woo this striking woman into bed. Her rapt attention made it seem almost embarrassingly easy.

"You added to New England Green's portfolio of historic and sensitive sites, but you've also asked for endowments to maintain those properties," Zoe said. "You've boosted the organization's endowment to about $250 million."

"Yes," Brian said. "When I became Executive Director, the endowment was under five million dollars. That endowment protects our portfolio for all time."

"And you also spend part of that endowment ensuring that each property has no underlying issue that might become a serious problem."

"An exceptionally good point," Brian said, nodding agreement. "Just as you wouldn't buy a house with termites, so you want to make certain that every parcel of land is free of issues. That's our insurance policy."

"So you have lawyers, surveyors, engineers…" Zoe said.

"And even termite inspectors," said Brian. "Every property gets a clean bill of health. We make certain the boundaries are accurate, that there are no claims or encumbrances on it, and that it isn't some former tannery site someone wants us to remediate."

Zoe rewarded his answer with a huge smile. *If it weren't for that camera rolling, I could take you on this desk right now,* Brian thought.

"You've also repeatedly and publicly stressed a strict code of ethics," Zoe said. "Why is that especially important in an organization like this?"

Brian nodded, recalling the right speech. "New England Green is a public trust. We own some of the most historic homes and ecologically sensitive land in the region. We are entrusted with beaches and forests, watersheds and mountains. There can never be any question but that we are here to protect history and nature." *Did I get those quotes right? They sounded right*, he thought.

"But you take the code beyond just protecting land. It also permeates your workplace. Tell me about that," Zoe said, smiling beatifically and tilting her head, the better to make her hair flow over her shoulder.

It does? Brian thought. *I had no idea, but it sounds great.* "Everyone who comes to work for New England Green does so because they feel passionately about history and the environment. Many of our best people draw no salary. They're here because they want to give back after a long career, or because they want to be part of the future."

Brian continued. "We owe those people special care. We owe them respect. We owe them courtesy. If we don't listen to them and incorporate their thoughts into our planning, they'll go elsewhere." Brian realized he was winging it, but it sounded great. "It has to be more than just a 'thank-you' for laboring over a project. It has to be a recognition of the dignity to which they're entitled."

Zoe's face took on an academic look. "But what if you caught an employee stealing... or lying?"

"It has never happened," Brian replied, slowly shaking his head. "We screen every employee – paid or not – to look for those signs, and we politely turn away those who don't pass muster. I suppose if we did catch someone, we'd feel...extremely let down. Because, in violating *our* trust, they would have violated New England Green's public trust." *Good answer*, Brian thought.

"Five minutes," Tyler said. "Wrap it up."

Zoe nodded. "I have a few follow-up questions, but is there anything I didn't ask you'd like to add?"

Brian nodded. "I see New England Green as a template for other regions. We have a longer history here than, say, Florida or Arizona. But the development pressures in those areas are tremendous, and natural resources are finite. States can't afford to acquire every endangered landmark or wetland. We've perfected a process that makes it a public-private partnership. We invite anyone watching this to consider how New England Green can be adapted to their state or region."

"Perfect," Zoe said, nodding her head. "OK, just a few follow-ups."

"Fire away," Brian said, grinning. "This is fun."

"Ah, on education. You said your degrees gave your Trustees the confidence in you. How did you earn a PhD so quickly?"

Brian laughed. "You've never been to northern England. There's nothing else to do there except study." He added, "It also helps to be a fast typist."

"What if I said Leeds doesn't remember giving you a degree?" Zoe said this with a smile.

Brian blinked. The woman was smiling, but the look on her face was deadly serious. "I'd say that there was… some kind of clerical error. I remember being there. I remember getting the degree."

Zoe shrugged. "OK." She read down her notes. "You also spoke of employing engineers, surveyors, and attorneys to evaluate lands. How do you choose those firms?"

That's two inside fast balls in a row, young lady, Brian thought. *You're hot, but you're not that hot.* He shrugged. "I'm not even certain who chooses them. I just know they're extremely competent. They do an excellent job. They must have come highly recommended."

Zoe read from a list. "Dracut Engineering Services. Ellsworthy & Coe, Attorneys at Law. Fishman Surveying. Those are some of the firms you use?"

"I really don't know," Brian said, beginning to sound irritated.

"You just sign the checks," Zoe said.

"I'm not even certain who signs those checks," Brian said. "There are three or four people who have signing authority."

From the briefcase open at her feet, Zoe took three sheets of paper.

"These are three checks, each made payable to one of the firms I just mentioned. They were issued in March of this year and bear your signature."

Brian did not look at the checks. He was getting angry.

"I have no idea where this is going." Brian said, struggling to keep his face and his voice neutral.

"The checks total more than forty thousand dollars," Zoe said. "And, if you look on the reverse side of the checks, each one has been endorsed back to you, countersigned by you, and deposited into your account at Pilgrim State Investments."

"This interview is over," Brian said angrily.

"The three firms, and three other firms just like them, don't exist," Zoe said, her voice calm and her eyes on Brian. "Over the past eighteen years, New England Green has written, and you have signed, checks totaling ten million dollars to non-existent firms that have been deposited into your personal account."

"Who the hell are you?" Brian asked, his voice rising.

Zoe reached into her briefcase. "Here is your most recent account statement from Pilgrim State. You have a balance of $21 million, all of it the product of embezzling funds from New England Green. You deposited your first check less than a year after becoming Executive Director."

"Who put you up to these lies?" Brian said, his voice now a roar. "Get out of my office."

Zoe placed more paper on Brian's desk. "Here is the complete paper trail of your embezzlement scheme. More than six hundred checks over eighteen years. All signed by you. All endorsed over to you. All payable to firms that don't exist."

"I said get out of my office!" Brian screamed.

"Oh," Zoe said, making no effort to get out of her chair. She reached into her briefcase again and pulled out a single sheet of paper with a gold seal. "This is an affidavit from Leeds Beckett University stating that the doctoral degree on your wall is a forgery. That you never attended the college at any time."

Brian's face was bright red. Until now, his attention had been focused on Zoe. Now, he saw Tyler. "Turn that damned thing off! And I want that disk or whatever it is…"

In one swift motion, Tyler and the camera were out the door.

"Who put you up to this?" Brian's voice was now a rasp, his breath ragged,

"I have one more thing for you, Mr. LaPointe," Zoe said coolly. She withdrew an envelope from her briefcase, closed it, and rose from her chair.

"This is from Emily. It's the keys to an apartment. The address is in there. All of your clothes and other personal effects have been removed from Crow Point, and a security guard and town policeman will keep you from entering the house. There is also a list of names and dates in there. She said you would understand."

"So she's behind this," Brian said.

Zoe walked out of the office, listening for footsteps behind her.

Brian stared at the papers on his desk and picked up sheets at random. All copies, except for the Leeds affidavit, and he suspected Emily had more than one of those. That was the kind of person she was.

Why had she done this? Why would she end such a perfect relationship? He saw the envelope that bitch Zoe had given him at the end. He tore open the seal and a set of keys fell on the desk. A small sheet of paper gave an address; 155 George Washington Blvd. in Hull. *Oh, God, one of those ugly buildings at Nantasket Beach.*

Then he saw the second, typewritten sheet of sheet of paper. *'Ellen Cameron 2013'. 'Chloe Dupuy 2016', 'Justine Hamilton 2009'…*

Dear God, my trophy box. Emily went through my desk and found my trophies. That's what this is about. Emily is jealous.

She would calm down. He could come up with an explanation. Given time...

But where had she gotten the rest of this stuff? This was his personal account. She couldn't possibly know anything about it.

He pulled out his phone, scrolled to the 'favorites' tab for Pilgrim State Investments and tapped it. The site came up and he entered the password for his account. The top of the page had the same, reassuring number. He breathed a sigh of relief. At least no one had touched his money.

But someone has accessed their records, he thought. *I've got to warn David Hale.* He scrolled through numbers and tapped the Chestnut Hill office. It rang ten times. He ended the call. He also had Hale's cell number. He scrolled until he found that number. It rang four times and went to voicemail.

This is no day to be out playing golf, David, he thought. *Damned financial guys with their soft jobs.*

* * * * *

A much more productive use of Brian's time would have been to call the visitor gate and have it closed and locked. It took fully three minutes for Zoe and Tyler to reach their car, load it, and get safely off Beckwith Estate. All the while, they invented emergencies that would get them through the exit in the event it had been locked.

But instead, an elderly man only motioned that they should slow down as they reached the end of the road. They turned right, and began screaming with glee.

Chapter Seventeen

Jason Curran and Raymond Nittolo stared at one another across Nittolo's desk.

"I believe you," Nittolo said, "but this has to be a partners' decision."

"We're officers of the court," Curran countered, controlling the anger he felt. "There is a 'time is of the essence' factor here. We can't delay this because we're trying to decide how to milk it for publicity."

"There's no 'court' in session, Jason," Nittolo shot back acerbically. "There's no case we're involved in. This isn't going anywhere this afternoon. I haven't heard from Emily since I left her town house this morning. She has calmed down. She's off that ledge. In this case, silence is good news."

"And besides," Nittolo continued, "we don't know the significance of at least fifty of those names. How do we know one of them isn't VP of sales for one of our clients? Don't you think we owe a client billing five million a year a 'heads up' that one of its senior executives is pocketing kickbacks from someone in China?"

"We can also talk ourselves into doing nothing," Curran replied. "And, as for those fifty names, given that we have home addresses for everyone, a first-year associate can assemble a complete dossier in half an hour."

Curran rose from his chair to his full, six-foot-three-inch frame. "This is a Ponzi scheme and it's huge," he said. "You acknowledge it. We have no way of knowing who else has one of these hard drives and whether they're couriering it over to the FBI while we dawdle. When this breaks, the first person to raise his hand is going to get the credit. Everyone else is going to be asked, 'what did you know, when did you know it, and why didn't you say anything?' I'd hate to be one of those people trying to explain why they sat on the biggest financial crime of the year, especially if I were an attorney."

Nittolo looked up at his senior associate and took a deep breath. "Give the list to my PA and tell her to flesh out those unfamiliar names. I'm going to canvass the senior partners."

* * * * *

With Helga driving around spraying the 'Demon Spawn' pheromone all over Boston's suburbs, and the plaza and parking garage back to normal after the departure of the police, Allie decided it was time to go home. She took an Uber to Coolidge Hill only to find the house empty.

She checked her computers for evidence of trip wires having been touched. Everything was as it should be. At the coffee shop in Amsterdam, a computer had attempted twenty-four times to order tickets for a sold-out Amber Arcades concert in Rotterdam. Allie let that figure sink in: she had successfully wired $240 million out of Pilgrim State.

So, where was Penny? She wasn't supposed to leave the house.

She was about to call her mother when she spotted the note. *With Emily and two interesting women you'll meet later. Things are moving fast. P.*

* * * * *

Howard Kelly knew he had to make the call. Once discovered, the penalty for not doing so would be administered swiftly and ruthlessly. But he also knew that unless he was uncommonly persuasive, that same fate might well await him before the night was over.

So, Cosimo, I've got a problem and I'm looking for some ideas of how to solve it. A couple of days ago my guy at Pilgrim State had a walk-in from a lady named Fasanella. He sent me her license plate but I didn't get around to running it until late the next day and, by then, he had plugged a thumb drive into the cheap servers I authorized so I could save a few thousand bucks. Guess *what? The license plate didn't match the name he was given and the thumb drive had a virus on it. Yesterday afternoon, I sent four guys up to Boston to get some answers. I haven't heard from them since. Then – and you'll never believe this – this afternoon, someone drained $240 million out of your biggest cash cow and sent it directly to Uncle Sam's bank account. If I had to guess, I'd say it was done by the FBI. Cosimo, I keep calling Pilgrim State and my guys but they just don't answer their phones. What do you think I should do?*

He could finesse the information a hundred ways, but ultimately it came down to his having screwed up. He didn't jump on the license plate when he first got the image, he had pocketed five thousand on the servers, and he hadn't kept on either Al Luchetti or David Hale for updates.

There was really only one solution: run. He had half a million dollars in gold coins plus a Bitcoin account with another four million on deposit just for such a circumstance. The gold coins were at his home in his basement. He did the quick math: a half a million dollars of gold weighed twenty-eight pounds.

OK, there was Christy and the two kids. If he left them behind they would be used as bait to bring him home and then they would die. So, each member of the Kelly party needed to carry an average of seven pounds of gold in their carry-on luggage.

Where to? He had three passports, but Christy and the kids had just one each. The logical answer was the U.K. It was four o'clock and between six and eleven there were more than a dozen flights to Heathrow out of JFK. Once past customs, he and his family could get lost in London's eight and a half million people. He could plan his next steps from there, secure that he was leaving no paper or money trail to follow.

He called his home. Christy answered.

"Sweetheart, do you remember us talking about going to see a movie? Well, get everyone together. I'll be home in half an hour…"

Kelly, unfortunately, had been downstairs in Marilyn

Palumbo's office watching Pilgrim State's assets disappear in ten-million-dollar increments when the calls came in from Luchetti and Hale begging for the Capizzi family's Boston attorney to come to their rescue. Their pleas would remain on voice mail until retrieved several days later.

By then, of course, it no longer mattered.

* * * * *

The first 911 calls began as early as 2:25 p.m. By three o'clock, they could no longer be ignored. Police Departments in Brookline, Newton, and Dedham all had multiple calls about herds of cats.

The cats seemed to be assembling in front of eight or nine houses. There appeared to be no instigation, but the felines yowled and scratched at shrubbery and fences at those homes with such accoutrements, and front porches and doors where homes opened directly onto streets.

At each home, a patrol car responded to the appropriate address and, in each case, a perplexed policeman or two relayed a scene of frenzied behavior as cats behaved aggressively toward any human who tried to interfere with their scratching.

Homeowners three and four blocks away reported that their indoor-only pets were throwing themselves against doors and windows in an effort to escape.

In most cities, there are hobbyists, mainly retirees or homebound individuals, who listen in on multiple police scanners and report interesting tidbits to newspapers and radio stations. The first one in the Boston area to do so was a 77-year-old retired firefighter in Dedham who monitored his own and neighboring towns. The man had the presence of mind to use his phone to record some of the chatter.

He called WBZ, Boston's lone all-news radio station and played some of the anxious police calls. The station assigned reporter Carrie Mendoza to drive to a house on Brook Street in nearby Brookline where the homeowner told police there were 'hundreds' of cats outside her front door.

As soon as Carrie arrived, she took one look at the scene – an otherwise serene four-story frame house on a side street of the normally placid town – and requested the radio station's sister television station send out a camera crew. Carrie noted the cats had not surrounded the house but, rather, were focused on the front stoop and shrubbery. Risking hissing and clawing, she made her way down the narrow passageway between the house and its neighbor and banged on the back door.

The door was opened by a frantic woman who appeared to be anxious to tell her story. She said her name was Doris Foley and she was a part-time bookkeeper.

"One minute, I was having a peaceful afternoon reading Stephen King," Foley told Carrie. "The next minute, there were four cats scratching at the door. I looked out, saw them, and went to get some kibble. By the time I got back there were a dozen. They were all scratching and meowing like someone was stepping on their tails. Fifteen minutes later there were fifty or sixty. It was something Stephen King would write, but it was happening outside my front door. That's when I called the police."

Carrie filed her on-air report, complete with the sound of wailing cats in the background, from her car, where she said that at present the feline population appeared to be more than a hundred. She described their covering every square inch of the stoop and small planting of daylilies fronting the street.

It was not referenced in her story, but the one odd part of the interview from Carrie's perspective was that Mrs. Foley – who freely volunteered she was widowed and was prepared to share every intimacy about her two grown sons – grew strangely silent about her work.

"I'm not supposed to talk about what I do," Mrs. Foley said. "They swear me to secrecy. That's all I can say."

Had Doris Foley not been so otherwise chatty and cogent,

Carrie would have suspected she was speaking with someone who suffered from a bipolar disorder. But the living room where they spoke was a model of cleanliness and a shrine to a departed spouse and smiling boys grown to men.

"Can't you say anything about where you're a bookkeeper?" Carrie asked.

"No," Mrs. Foley said, her eyes darting from left to right. "Mr. Hale says we can never talk about what we do."

Carrie wrote down '*Hale*' in her notebook a few minutes after she heard the name.

As she drove back to the station, Carrie called and spoke with the news director. "Is anyone going out to any of these other homes with cats?" she asked.

"There's a TV crew at a house in Newton right now," the news director said.

"Call them and get them to ask the homeowner if he or she is an accountant or bookkeeper," Carrie said. "I just had the weirdest experience…"

"Well, there's now a report of cats swarming over a small office building across from the theater in Chestnut Hill. Can you talk to someone there?"

* * * * *

'Chestnut Hill' is not an independent city or municipality in Massachusetts. Rather, it is an amorphous, wealthy neighborhood that straddles the towns of Newton and Brookline. The only way to know which town you are in is to have an accident on Route 9 and see which town responds. The office building in question had a fire truck and police car from Brookline.

Carried showed her press identification and asked the fireman who had called in the report.

"Three businesses called it in more or less simultaneously," the fireman said. "We got calls from both floors."

Unlike the affected homes, where police responded,

investigated, and more or less told the homeowners to stay inside until the felines lost interest, here the cats were being rounded up with the help of the town's animal shelter.

Carrie made her way into the building and looked at the directory. The first floor was home to a pediatrics practice and a temporary help agency. The second floor housed a realtor specializing in apartment rentals and something called Pilgrim State Investments.

The elevator door opened and a policeman stepped out; a squirming, agitated cat under either arm.

"Be careful," the policeman said. "There are still half a dozen up there. It's crazy."

No one responded to either her ringing the bell for Pilgrim State Investments or knocking on its door.

She went next door to 'Your New Apartment', where a frazzled receptionist said she had no interest in speaking with a reporter about cats. She added that, if she never saw another cat as long as she lived, she would not miss them in the slightest.

"I'm interested in your neighbor across the hall," Carrie said. "Pilgrim State Investments."

"What about them?" the receptionist said.

"Is there someone named 'Hale' working there?" Carrie asked.

"I have no idea," replied the receptionist. "There's usually just one or two people there. Hardly anyone ever goes in or out. Except at the end of the month. Then there's ten or fifteen people who all show up. It must be a great business to be in. I'd like those hours."

Carrie left the apartment rental service, went downstairs, and spoke with enough police, fire fighters, animal rescue, and temporary help recruiters to file a lengthy story.

But driving back to the studio, Carrie could not help but wonder if the cats' presence at those homes and at an office building were linked in some way to a man named Hale and an outfit called Pilgrim State Investments where hardly anyone ever went in or out.

* * * * *

Emily was not certain what kind of mobile quarters Zoe and Tyler would need. She settled on a 26-foot Coachmen RV, rented from a delighted salesman at an RV dealer off Route 3, who had just received a week's payment for a rental that would be used for just a few hours. The RV was waiting a quarter mile from the entrance to Beckwith Estate.

When Zoe and Tyler arrived at a few minutes before four o'clock, Emily and Penny were waiting inside, Emily's personal driver was at the wheel. Penny took the keys to Tyler's Subaru and said she would follow them.

"Consider this your mobile editing studio," Emily told Zoe and Tyler. "I didn't know what you'd need, so I just took what I could find right away."

Zoe looked around the inside of the RV and wondered at the ability to walk into an RV dealership, say 'that one', and have someone gas it up and hand you the keys. The dining table was set up so she and Tyler could work side by side. There was electricity. Apart from the lack of a high-speed Wi-Fi connection, it was everything she could have asked for.

"I've been on the phone more or less constantly for the last hour," Emily continued. "The 'Brian' story is relatively easy to understand, explain and verify. Two stations have their news studios in Boston; the others are out in the western suburbs. What they know is that the two of you are independent producers and that you got the one and only interview Brian will ever give on the subject. They also know the other station has the same footage. We're going to drop off copies of whatever you can put together in the next forty-five minutes."

Emily paused. "They asked where you got the material. I told them I gave you the Leeds affidavit, which is true and easily verified. They also wanted to know where the financial records came from. You have forty-five minutes to come up with an answer."

Zoe nodded. "I was giving that thought earlier. I don't want to get Penny in trouble. I think the answer is 'ethical hackers'. I used to be in touch with a couple of them back at Rolla. They won't reveal themselves and, for anyone who looks, it throws them off the scent. I can handle that question."

Emily looked relieved. "Understanding the cast of clients at Pilgrim State Investments is more than a television station can handle. We're going to make a stop at the *Globe* on the way into town. You get full credit as the source, so start thinking up quotes. Right now, I'd start editing."

Emily stopped abruptly. "I never asked. Did you get what you went in for?"

Zoe grinned. "It was perfect."

* * * * *

Jason Curran looked over the list of names and the information Nittolo's PA had pulled together on each one. It included a doctor accused of Medicaid fraud who was cleared when investigators, after poring over his finances for six months, could find no evidence of personal gain. The good doctor had an account at Pilgrim in the amount of $8 million. The wife of a Waltham attorney who frequently defended drug dealers had salted away $3 million, all deposited as cash.

But the research also showed that, as Nittolo predicted, two of the names were executives at client companies. Both had made large, continuing cash deposits; and employees with stock options did not take their gains in hundred-dollar bills. Nittolo said Steele & Hanley owed it to its clients to give them fair warning. Further, of the four managing partners with whom he had spoken, all wanted a meeting to review the material before determining how – and even whether – to disclose it.

In short, nothing would happen today, or over the weekend. And it was entirely possible that Steele & Hanley would convince itself that there was a greater chance that having the firm's name associated with the data would bring bad publicity rather than good; and, thus, the information should be left for someone else to disclose.

But he owed it to Penny to tell her that this was more than a 'bank for crooks'. The Ponzi scheme aspect meant there was little chance of recovery of any money for New England Green.

He called Pheromonix and was told there was no such employee named Penny or Penelope Walden.

"She's in research," Jason said. "She's a scientist."

"I can put you through to Helga Johanssen's voice mail if you like," the operator offered.

"No thanks," Jason said and hung up.

He had also copied down Penny's cell number. He tried that and she answered. From the background noise, she sounded as though she was in a car.

"I hope you're sitting down," he said.

"I'm on the Southeast Expressway," Penny said. "It's kind of hard not to be sitting down. I ought to tell you a lot has been going on since we met."

"I went through the data on that drive you gave me," he said. "Do you ever remember hearing about a guy named Bernie Madoff?"

"Sure," Penny said. "Ponzi scheme, right?"

"Exactly," Jason said. "It's not as big as the one Madoff put together, but Pilgrim State Investment is a Ponzi scheme. It never made any investments. Just pulled in all that money…"

Penny interrupted him. "Jason, give me a second while I add Emily to this call. She and two other people need to hear what you have to say."

"What's going on?" Jason asked.

"Well," Penny replied. "I'm following an RV up the Southeast Expressway into Boston. Inside the RV is Emily and, with her are two journalists who just confronted Brian LaPointe on camera. We're making a stop at the *Globe* and then we're headed to a couple of TV stations. Like I said, a lot has been going on."

Thirty seconds later, Jason was telling everything he knew to three women, two of whom he had never met but who kept asking him to slow down so that they could get it all into their story.

* * * * *

Brian left Beckwith Estate within ten minutes after the conclusion of the disastrous interview. He did call the entrance gate and ask that it be locked to prevent two women in a small SUV from leaving. He was told his call was three minutes too late.

Brian drove directly to Emily's house at Crow Point. As her note warned, there was a Hingham Police Department car in the driveway and a man not in a uniform standing by the front door.

Brian parked on the street and began walking up the lawn. As he did, a door opened on the police car and a uniformed officer got out. Brian affixed a smile to his face and gave both men a wave. He got within ten feet of the front portico and said, "Hi, is Emily at home?"

The policeman, holding what looked like a photograph in his right hand, asked, "And you are?"

"A friend," Brian said, still smiling. "I just want to say 'hi' and see if she's all right. The police cruiser makes it look rather ominous."

"Your name, please," the officer said, clarifying his earlier question.

Brian could tell that that both men had photos and were glancing between his face and what they held in their hands. Maybe it wasn't a good likeness.

"Ken Cross," Brian said. "I live over on Cushing."

"We'll have to ask you to leave, Mr. LaPointe," the police

officer said.

"I just need to pick up a few things," Brian protested. "I live here."

The second man, presumably a security guard, took a step toward Brian.

"Please leave now, Mr. LaPointe," the police officer said. "If you don't, you will be arrested for illegal trespass."

"But everything I own is inside that house!" Brian said in exasperation.

"My understanding is that nothing of yours is inside this house," the police officer said in an even, modulated tone. "If you do not get off the property now, I will arrest you. This is your final warning."

Brian began backing away.

"If you return to this property at any time, you will be detained and arrested," the officer said. "You have been warned in the presence of a third party."

Brian returned to his car, shaken by the encounter. *She's really thrown me out*, he thought. *Just because of some souvenir panties in a desk drawer. But why go to all the trouble of bringing in that reporter? Fine. She embarrassed me. But she wouldn't actually use that stuff. Where did she get it? And why isn't David Hale answering my calls?*

* * * * *

At 4:29 p.m., Emily, Zoe, and Tyler stepped out of an RV at the Morrissey Boulevard entrance to *The Boston Globe*. Two reporters from the Globe, one from boston.com, and an editor met them at the glassed-arch entryway.

Penny remained behind in the Subaru, saying she had a few calls to make. She had, in fact, only one.

"Allie? It's Penny. Time to unleash the furies."

* * * * *

In Washington D.C. at exactly five o'clock, a U.S. Treasury Department clerk, as her last official act of the day, checked her computer monitor for the daily incoming receipts. Late June was the peak for quarterly withholding deposits and the target receipts for the day was a shade over $63 billion. The clerk copied the number into a spreadsheet and emailed it to half a dozen officials. Happily, the receipts were three-tenths of a percent above expectation. She sent the email, closed her computer, and left for home.

* * * * *

By 5:15, David Hale knew something wasn't right, though he could not put his finger on it. He had a personal attorney who, though more familiar with contracts and Letters of Agreement, had sufficient experience getting DUIs released from lockups in various communities to know how to navigate a police station.

Al Luchetti had told everyone – with a menacing look on his face – that there would be just one attorney representing everyone. When Luchetti's first call to Howard Kelly went un-returned after an hour, it seemed odd but not a cause for great concern. The next step was to call Cosimo. Except that you did not call Cosimo: you called a seemingly neutral third party who relayed the message. An appropriate attorney would call Cambridge Police headquarters and say he or she was on their way.

In theory, that call should have come an hour ago.

Also, in theory, Hale should not even be here. His sole 'crime' was to be in the car behind Luchetti's. The nonsense from that Detective – Donaldson? – did not stand up to scrutiny. There were a hundred plausible and quite innocent explanations why he and Luchetti would have spoken, and all were before Luchetti displayed a weapon. Hale knew he was an upstanding member of the area business community. He had no arrest record.

Hale was about to tell Luchetti that he was going to arrange for his own release when Detective Donaldson appeared in front of the two holding cells.

"I have some friends I'd like to introduce you to," she said to the six men. There was the sound of footsteps echoing behind her on the concrete floor.

A moment later, three men in suits and ties and carrying briefcases were alongside Donaldson. All three were smiling as though they had just heard the same extraordinarily funny joke.

"Allow me to introduce the Organized Crime Task Force of the FBI Boston Field Office," she said, joining in the smile.

"Where's our attorney?" Luchetti said, anger in his voice.

Donaldson shook her head. "We haven't received a call." She added, "And, by law, if we had been notified, we would be obliged to notify you. But whoever you called doesn't seem to be especially anxious to come to your rescue. I'd take that to mean that either this isn't a priority, or else they've got more important fires to put out."

Now, Hale knew exactly what was wrong. Or, so he feared.

* * * * *

It was 5:30 and Brian had no intention of going to some dump of an apartment on Nantasket Beach. He instead wheeled his Porsche into the Cohasset Harbor Resort and gave the valet his keys. He would get a suite, have a soothing dinner at a table on the water at Atlantica, and plot his next move.

He was greeted by name by the concierge. After all, he and Emily had dined here dozens of times and he was a generous tipper. He smiled and waved as he walked toward the reception desk.

"Welcome back, Mr. LaPointe," the desk clerk said. Her tag read, 'Sandy'.

"Hello, Sandy," Brian said. "I know it is last minute, but could I get a suite for tonight?"

Sandy tapped a key. "Just for the one night, though," she said. "We'll be full for Saturday and Sunday."

"That's fine," he replied. By tomorrow, all this would be straightened out. He would probably be on his way to Maine.

"I'll just need an imprint of your credit card," Sandy said.

Brian took out his American Express Black card and handed it across the desk. Sandy tapped in a series of keys and reached out to hand it back to him. She pulled back the card and a worried look appeared on her face.

"Your card was declined," she said. "I have no idea why. I'm so sorry. Can you use another?"

"Well," Brian said, "I'll call them and find out later. He extracted his standby Visa card. He seldom used it because of the superior perks provided by the Amex Black.

Sandy took that card and tapped in the number. She shook her head with an apologetic smile. "Same thing."

Brian sighed. "OK, last time around." He tried never to use the corporate American Express card because the miles and cash back accumulated to New England Green rather than to his own account. In fact, he couldn't remember the last time he had used it.

She looked at the card. "I'm afraid it's expired. Can you pay cash?"

Brian looked in his wallet. He had about fifty dollars. "Can I have this direct billed?" he asked.

"The General Manager left a little early today," Sandy said. "Can you call your credit card company and straighten out why they put a hold on your card? There are also two ATM's just down the street in the village."

Brian had a sense that the answer Sandy was too polite to give was that, if three credit cards were found to be invalid, the Inn's policy was to never, ever take on faith that someone trying to register would magically pay a bill presented by mail.

To avoid prying ears, he went out to the parking lot to call American Express. One of the Black Card benefits was that you deal with a small number of 'personal representatives'. Satisfyingly, his call was answered on the first ring. Brian explained his problem.

"I can tell you why," the representative explained. "We've had half a dozen fraudulent attempts to use your card in the past two hours. Two were attempts to charge more ten thousand dollars in jewelry. One was an attempt to charge first-class airfare to Tokyo."

"That's impossible," Brian said. "The card is in my possession. I'm looking at it right now."

"Sir, your card has been severely compromised. The people trying to use it even have the answers to your personal verification questions. But I can have another one in your hands tomorrow before noon."

"I'd rather you authorize my stay this evening at the Cohasset Harbor Resort," he said.

"Shall I send that to the Merrill Street address in Hingham?"

Brian started to say 'yes', then realized that wouldn't be possible. "May I have it sent to my office? New England Green?"

"I can do that, sir. I will have to verify your employment."

"Do that," he said, and closed the call.

His call to Visa was even more unsatisfactory because it took several minutes to reach a human representative. Once again, someone was using his card to make outlandish purchases. This time, he learned that a new card would arrive via first class mail – to Merrill Street. Well, he could intercept the card if he hadn't patched things up with Emily.

It was a warm, pleasant late afternoon – the sun would not set until nearly 8:30 – and he took the short walk into Cohasset Village where he found a Hingham Savings Bank branch. His money market account was with Fidelity and he pushed that card into the ATM slot and typed in his PIN.

A screen message said, '*Please see manager*'.

It was nearly six o'clock and the inside of the bank was dark.

He retrieved the card and walked to another bank, which displayed the same message. It had happened before and was annoying. This was the wrong time for bank computers to not be talking to one another.

So, here I am, he thought. *I have fifty dollars in cash and no way of getting cash until tomorrow morning. Emily has pulled every string she can to teach me a lesson. Fine, I'll go to that dump of an apartment tonight. Tomorrow, I'll rent something much nicer.* He began the walk back to the Inn.

Then he had a much brighter thought. *Amber. Why don't I stay the night with her?*

He tapped his phone to open his contacts and saw his Twitter icon with a bright yellow exclamation point. Curious, he tapped the icon. '*Your latest tweets have been seen by 3,197 followers and re-tweeted 121 times'.*

What tweets? Brian thought. He really didn't understand Twitter and would no more 'follow' some idiotic, pea-brained celebrity than he would watch… bowling. While nominally in his name, the Twitter account was the brainchild of New England Green's PR firm. They ginned up tweets three or four times a week about events at various properties. Those messages were usually seen by a few hundred hard-core followers. This one was obviously doing much better. He needed a distraction and tapped the screen to see what they had come up with.

'Big news on New England Green at 6 p.m. on Chs 4 & 7. Be sure to watch! Tell your friends! Brian.'

The idiots, he thought. But then he stopped. *I didn't tell the PR people Zoe was coming. If it was my stupid secretary, I'll fire her. But how could she know which stations? And how could two graduate students get this on the air so quickly? Unless…*

His phone showed it was 5:58. He started to break into a run for the Inn, but could not remember ever seeing a television in any common area or the bar. He looked up Main Street and remembered there was an Irish pub just around the corner. Mr. Dooley or something like that. He reversed course and found the pub. There was a television over the bar tuned to ESPN.

"Could you tune that to Channel 7?" Brian asked.

The bartender shrugged, picked up a remote and tapped a key. There was an ad for a chain of furniture stores. Then a desk of smiling anchors talking.

"Can you turn it up just a bit?" Brian asked.

"Can I get you something to drink?" the bartender asked, holding the remote but not making a move to increase the volume.

"Beer," Brian said. "Anything you have." He detested beer in any form.

The bartender turned up the volume so that it was just audible if Brian sat immediately below the screen.

The male anchor was saying, "…breaking news this evening that the head of one of the region's most cherished institutions may have stolen as much as ten million dollars from New England Green. We've obtained this exclusive footage of an interview conducted just hours ago with Brian LaPointe, who has headed New England Green for nearly two decades."

The screen switched to his office. He was speaking and gesturing with great animation about something, though no words were heard. Instead, the voice of a girl – Zoe? – was heard off-camera. "Brian LaPointe says he helped rescue New England Green from obscurity."

Now his voice could be heard. "I had come to New England Green as Chief Horticulturalist, and I couldn't help but see the inherent problems from the inside. The organization was faithfully following a plan that had been superseded by both economic reality and a changing population. A grand old institution was dying. I helped give it a new life and a new mission…"

I sound pompous, Brian thought. *She took it out of context.*

Zoe's voice was again heard while Brian gestured silently. "Part of that mission was to begin requiring properties being donated to the organization to provide an endowment, a practice common across many institutions with similar purposes."

Now, Zoe was on camera with him. "You added to New

England Green's portfolio of historic and sensitive sites, but you've also asked for endowments to maintain those properties," she stated. "You've boosted the organization's endowment to about $250 million."

"Yes," he heard himself say. "When I became Executive Director, the endowment was under five million dollars. That endowment protects our portfolio for all time."

"And you also spend part of that endowment ensuring that each property has no underlying issue that might become a serious problem," Zoe said.

He saw himself nodding agreement. "An exceptionally good point. Just as you wouldn't buy a house with termites, so you want to make certain that every parcel of land is free of issues. That's our insurance policy."

"So you have lawyers, surveyors, engineers…" Zoe said.

"And even termite inspectors," he heard himself say. "Every property gets a clean bill of health. We make certain the boundaries are accurate, that there are no claims or encumbrances on it, and that it isn't some former tannery site someone wants us to remediate."

Back to Zoe's voice-over. "But almost from the beginning, Brian LaPointe chose a curious group of specialists to review those properties."

A return to the interview. "You also spoke of employing engineers, surveyors, and attorneys to evaluate lands. How do you choose those firms?" Zoe asked.

Brian saw himself shrug. "I'm not even certain who chooses them. I just know they're extremely competent. They do an excellent job. They must have come highly recommended."

Jesus Christ, I walked into it. I could have changed the subject…

Zoe read from a list. "Dracut Engineering Services. Ellsworthy & Coe, Attorneys at Law. Fishman Surveying. Those are some of the firms you use?"

"I really don't know." Brian heard the irritation begin to creep into his voice.

"You just sign the checks," Zoe said.

He heard himself say, "I'm not even certain who signs those checks.   There are three or four people who have signing authority."

Did I really say that? Brian thought. *God, it's drilled into everyone that I'm the only person in the organization authorized to sign…*

He watched as Zoe produced three sheets of paper. "These are three checks, each made payable to one of the firms I just mentioned. They were issued in March of this year and bear your signature."

"I have no idea where this is going," he heard himself say. *And I didn't know*, he thought. *I was wondering how in the hell she got copies of those checks.*

Brian watched himself on camera studiously avoid looking at the checks even as he visibly struggled to keep his face and his voice neutral.

"The checks total more than forty thousand dollars," Zoe said. "And, if you look on the reverse side of the checks, each one has been endorsed back to you, countersigned by you, and deposited into your account at Pilgrim State Investments."

"This interview is over." He heard the anger in his voice and saw it on his face.

That's where I lost it, Brian thought.

"The three firms, and three other firms just like them, don't exist," Zoe said, her voice calm and her eyes on him. "Over the past eighteen years, New England Green has written, and you have signed, checks totaling *ten million dollars* to non-existent firms that have been deposited into your personal account." She really thumped the total he had diverted.

From the pub counter, Brian looked up at the screen, unable to watch but also unable to take his eyes off of what was happening.

Back on the screen he saw and heard himself say, "Who the hell are you?" his voice rising.

He saw her reach into her briefcase. "Here is your most recent account statement from Pilgrim State. You have a balance of $21 million, all of it the product of embezzling funds from New England Green. You deposited your first check less than a year after becoming Executive Director."

"Who put you up to these lies?" he said, his voice now a roar. "Get out of my office!"

He watched as Zoe placed more paper on his desk. "Here is the complete paper trail of your embezzlement scheme. More than six hundred checks over eighteen years. All signed by you. All endorsed over to you. All payable to firms that don't exist."

"I said get out of my office!" He remembered the visceral reaction as it became clear this was a setup. This wasn't about helping a graduate student build her 'reel'. This was about destroying his reputation for no good reason.

Now Zoe was standing out in the gardens they had toured. "The information on Brian LaPointe's finances, including copies of these cancelled checks…" Zoe held up the checks for emphasis. "…came from what is called an 'ethical hacking' organization that looks for illegal behavior from public officials. I asked Mr. LaPointe about the identical behavior he himself engaged in."

She's using little snippets of the interview. Brian realized. *She wanted to get me on camera sounding righteous.*

"New England Green is a public trust," he heard himself say, and that video operator – who was in on the whole thing – had moved the camera around so he was looking directly into it. "We own some of the most historic homes and ecologically sensitive land in the region. We are entrusted with beaches and forests, watersheds and mountains. There can never be any question but that we are here to protect history and nature."

So that I sound like a hypocrite, Brian thought.

Zoe was again in the garden. "I asked Mr. LaPointe how he would feel if he caught someone else doing what he stands accused of."

He watched himself say, "I suppose if we did catch someone, we'd feel... extremely let down. Because, in violating *our* trust, they would have violated New England Green's public trust."

She set me up! What else was I going to say!

Zoe was back in the garden. "And to add to what Brian LaPointe will have to explain to his Board of Trustees and the public he claims to serve, there's also a problem with his educational credentials. I asked Mr. LaPointe about the importance of those credentials, and especially the Doctorate in Horticulture he claims to have."

Now they were back in his office. "You also make no secret of your early years," Zoe said.

"I grew up on a failing truck farm outside of Athol, Massachusetts. It burned into me the lesson that, if you don't adapt to the times, you'll fail."

So, now it sounds like I stole because I grew up poor.

"And your Board of Trustees gave you their full vote of confidence to make those changes," Zoe said.

"I encouraged them to find holes in my analysis," he heard himself reply. "They couldn't. *That* was when they gave me that vote of confidence." Back to the smile.

"You also had the right degrees," Zoe said, pointing at the wall behind Brian. "The Stockbridge School and Leeds, one of Europe's most prestigious universities. The Trustees wouldn't have entrusted such a mission to one of their gardeners."

Now, the camera zoomed in on the Leeds certificate while he continued to speak. "Yet, when you get down to basics, I *was* one of their gardeners. It took a gardener to appreciate the unused resources. It took those other degrees to know how to formulate a plan. And to give those Trustees the confidence that the man they had put in charge could carry it out."

So I stole because I was poor, and I fabricated a degree because it was the path to being able to perpetrate a fraud. Nice going, Zoe.

Zoe was back in the garden, now holding a sheet of paper with a gold seal. "This is an affidavit signed by Sir Charles Pickney, the head of the Horticultural College at Leeds Beckett University. It says that Brian LaPointe never attended the University, then called 'Leeds Polytechnic' at any time. The last sentence states that while 'the framed diploma purporting to be a Doctoral Degree in Horticulture from Leeds Polytechnic and issued to Brian James LaPointe matches the style used by Leeds Polytechnic during the period that includes the clearly visible date on said diploma, we can state unequivocally that the diploma was not issued by this Institution.' This is Zoe Matthews reporting for Channel 7 News Boston."

The scene switched back to the anchors, who now all frowned.

"Sounds like someone has a problem at their next Board meeting," a frowning woman anchor said.

Her male counterpart shook his head. "I don't think this will wait until the next meeting."

The anchors all laughed and went back to their smiles. "Coming up next, herds of cats leave Brookline, Newton and Dedham residents prisoners in their homes… "

Brian stared at the screen, his mouth open. He could not believe this. It could not be happening.

He did not notice that the bartender had also been watching.

"That guy being interviewed looked like you," the bartender said. "He was even dressed like you. Was that you?"

Numbly, Brian got up from the bar stool and began walking out the door.

"Hey!" the bartender said. "You didn't pay for the beer!"

Brian ignored the bartender. He walked back toward the Inn. He would need his car. Going to Amber's apartment was out of the question. All that was left was the apartment Emily had rented for him.

He looked down at his phone, which was buzzing. The Caller ID was one of New England Green's Trustees. He ignored the call.

The Twitter icon was again glowing. He tapped the screen. *'Your latest tweets have been seen by 16,822 followers and re-tweeted 3,116 times'.*

As he walked, Brian opened his email. At the top of 47 messages was this, from Facebook: *'You have replies to your Facebook post'.*

What Facebook post? He thought. He found the icon for Facebook, which he used only when issuing congratulations for something fabulous done by New England Green. He found this:

'For those of you who have now seen or heard about the news reports regarding my conduct at New England Green, I am deeply ashamed of what I have done. The story was accurate. No words can express my regret and I take full responsibility for my actions. I will accept whatever punishment fate hands me. You deserved much better from me. Brian LaPointe.'

He read and re-read the post, noting that the number of 'shares' was past five hundred.

Below that email was another one. *'You have replies to your LinkedIn status update.'*

With trembling fingers, he tapped the screen to see what 'he' had posted to his network of eight hundred professionals around the country.

'To my LinkedIn community: This afternoon I was presented on camera with evidence of a long-running scheme in which I used my position to divert millions of dollars from the endowment of the organization I head, New England Green, to my own account. I can offer no explanation for my actions…'

He closed the window without reading the rest of his 'confession'. Now, he was angry. *This is Emily's doing. She's gone too far. She's using her money to buy hackers and camera crews. Well, I've got my own money. Tomorrow morning, I'm going to take a couple of million to get back my reputation, and then I'm going to take a few million more and start smearing your name…*

Brian retrieved his car, giving the valet ten dollars of the fifty in his wallet as a tip. He set his GPS for the address attached to the keys Zoe had given to him in the envelope. It was just fifteen minutes to the apartment and not yet seven o'clock. He had a lot to do; dozens and maybe hundreds of calls to make to rally friends to his side.

He had nearly four and a half million dollars in his Fidelity account. Living with Emily had allowed him to accumulate an unexpected bonanza of cash that would otherwise be spent toward housing. He would start tapping that account tomorrow. His first priority would be to hire a crack crisis management team. Yes, a good night's sleep would clear his head; give him a chance to plan. He needed to work on what he would say to the Trustees. He could talk his way out of this, he was certain.

He pulled into the building's parking lot. To his surprise, outside the entrance was a crowd of men and women. There were lights and cameras. They seemed to know it was him, probably by his car.

His anger boiled over. *Only Emily knows about this apartment. Emily gave out his address and a description of his car.*

Brian stopped his Porsche and the crowd surrounded him. Microphones were put in his face. Five, six, seven questions were shouted at him simultaneously.

He opened the door of his car, got out, and stood beside it.

"I wish to make a statement," he said. "This afternoon, as a favor to a friend, I agreed to be interviewed by a woman representing herself as a journalism graduate student. Obviously, neither she nor her camera operator was who they said they were. At the end of a forty-five minute interview, I was presented with several 'set-up' questions that I found odd but which I answered. I was then presented – more like attacked – with a stack of material purporting to be financial statements."

"Before going further, I want to acknowledge one aspect of the interview which was accurate. Twenty years ago, when I first applied to New England Green, I was aware that the organization expected all of its salaried employees to have advanced degrees. Though I had an undergraduate degree in, and a lifelong love of and experience in horticulture, I did not have that advanced degree. And so I invented one."

"Since becoming Executive Director I have declined every opportunity to play upon that degree or the title that comes with it. No New England Green literature references it. It is a two-decade-old transgression that I have had to live with, but have had no way of deleting from the record. Tonight I apologize for that twenty-year-old fabrication. I believe I have served New England Green well and devoted my life to its mission. If the Trustees choose to remove me from office for something I did so long ago, I will abide by their decision."

"The rest of the allegations made by the reporter were fabrications. I do not know why the individual who sent them chose to do so; I probably never will know. But a thorough investigation will show that they are without merit. The stations that aired the material will have to answer for their haste to air unsubstantiated allegations at a later time."

"Finally, many of you have seen Twitter feeds or Facebook and LinkedIn posts supposedly sent by me in the past few hours. I had no hand in them and was unaware of them until a few minutes ago. The same individual who sent interviewers with malicious material also successfully hacked my social media accounts. I unfortunately lack the average twelve-year-old's ability to…"

Brian had a sudden insight, but he could not stop speaking.

"I'm sorry, the average twelve-year-old's ability to delete

malicious social media material. That is all I have to say for tonight. I hope that as you report this, you will keep in mind my strong denial of the allegations relating to financial mis-dealings."

A dozen questions were shouted. Brian smiled, waved, and walked through the apartment building door. The reporters had the courtesy to not follow. He would have to remember to move his car when they had left.

The apartment was on the fourth floor and was a one-bedroom unit furnished with things he would never have owned. The view was of the parking lot and there were water stains on the living room and bathroom ceilings. But it would do for tonight, or for a few days.

His belongings were in moving boxes and bore labels such as 'shirts' and 'personal effects'. Somewhere in the latter carton was a rosewood box that had likely triggered all of this. He made no effort to unpack; he would not be here long enough to need to.

Right now, he needed to deal with the epiphany he experienced while giving that statement. Someone had gained access to his Pilgrim State account. Someone who knew to look for it and had the computer skills to hack it. That someone also had access to his credit card information and social media accounts and had used them to try to bring him to his knees.

Yes, Emily was in on this. Only *she* would care about a diploma and have the money to hire reporters and camera crews, and have the clout to get on two television stations.

But someone else was working with Emily. Someone who hated him enough to want to do him irreparable harm. Four years ago she was already preternaturally gifted in math and computer science. By now, that person certainly had the skills to carry out a scheme such as this.

That person was his daughter, Allie. Now, he knew his reaching out to her after he left was a mistake. His attempt at a reconciliation; to be a father to her, had been met with ferocious hostility. He knew Allie often poked around his desk. She had apparently retained an excellent memory of what she saw.

So, he had two enemies, not one. Somehow, they had joined forces.

He was, of course, playing for time. His bravura statement in front of the apartment building might keep the press at bay for two or three days, but he had to completely rebut the story. That meant erasing any trace of his account with Pilgrim State, and David Hale had to cooperate on that.

There was also the pesky matter of those checks and the names the 'reporter' had used. He could make all financial records related to the checks disappear from the files at Beckwith Estate; that was easy. And, without the New England Green records, the copies of checks could be dismissed as forgeries. But that left the question of who had done the work. Someone needed to step forward. Who did he know that he could trust?

He began making notes. It was going to be a long night.

Chapter Eighteen

At 6:30, David Hale and Sam Ashton were brought from their holding cell to an interview room. A laptop with a large screen was on a table. Around it were three chairs.

Detective Nancy Donaldson was sharing a laugh with two of the FBI agents.

"Gentlemen," Donaldson said. "Please have a seat. We have something that might amuse you as much as it amused us."

"We will not speak to you until we have conferred with our attorney," Hale said.

Donaldson waved aside Hale's words. "You don't have to say a word," she said. "We just want you to watch something incredibly funny that was on the news a few minutes ago." She then pointed to a pair of cameras high on the wall. "And, just as a reminder, to protect your civil liberties, these proceedings are being recorded for posterity."

She took a seat in the remaining chair and tapped the keyboard. Three well-coiffed and immaculately dressed anchors were seated behind a stylish, anchor-worthy desk. One of the male anchors said, "We have breaking news this evening…"

Hale watched as Brian LaPointe was trapped by his own greed. The man was an idiot, agreeing to an interview like that.

Several minutes into the interview and realizing he had been cornered, he watched as LaPointe shouted, "Who the hell are you?"

Donaldson tapped the computer and it froze with LaPointe's contorted face filling the screen. "Fascinating, isn't it?" she said. "But what comes next is the real grabber."

Donaldson tapped the keyboard again and the reporter placed several sheets of paper on the desk between interview subject and interviewer. The reporter said, "Here is your most recent account statement from Pilgrim State. You have a balance of $21 million, all of it the product of embezzling funds from New England Green. You deposited your first check less than a year after becoming Executive Director."

"Who put you up to these lies?" LaPointe said, his voice now a roar. "Get out of my office."

The reporter placed more paper on Brian's desk. "Here is the complete paper trail of your embezzlement scheme. More than six hundred checks over eighteen years. All signed by you. All endorsed over to you. All payable to firms that don't exist."

"I said get out of my office!"

Donaldson tapped the keyboard and, once again, LaPointe's face was caught in mid-scream.

Now, from her coat pocket, Donaldson placed two business cards on the interview table. "These were in your wallets. You two are the co-chairmen of exactly the same financial institution the reporter just mentioned. What wonderful publicity for you."

Donaldson tapped the computer. The reporter, now standing in a garden, said, "The information on Brian LaPointe's finances, including copies of these cancelled checks…" Zoe held up the checks for emphasis. "…came from what is called an 'ethical hacking' organization that looks for illegal behavior from public officials…"

She tapped the screen, freezing the image on a clutch of check printouts.

"Somebody hacked your computers, gentlemen. Now, my friends from the FBI are going to explain to you, in considerable detail, about the penalties for money laundering. That's not my area of interest. But I think I now know why the six of you were hanging around One Kendall Square this afternoon. It neatly explains why there were two Mob goons, two Mob-connected computer experts, and the two of you. You believed you knew the location of that ethical hacker, Ms. Walden, and you intended to, at minimum, abduct her."

Donaldson shifted in her chair. "Now, here's the fun part. The next segment of this newscast talks about hundreds of feral cats camped out on the doorsteps of half a dozen homes. This afternoon, the six of you were attacked by cats. Which got both me and my friends from the FBI thinking whether there might be a connection. Oh, and that little office building of yours in Chestnut Hill was also overrun with cats."

Donaldson continued. "So, tonight, the FBI has agents interviewing each of those homeowners. I tried to make a bet with these guys that every one of those homes is occupied by one of your employees, but I couldn't give them long enough odds. That's what we were laughing about when you came in. Their theory is that Pilgrim State Investments is a Mob front and that you specialize in clients like Mr. LaPointe who have a lot of money to hide."

"I've got a relatively small crime to solve: an unregistered handgun in the possession of and being displayed by a convicted felon. I'm pretty sure I also have an attempted abduction. My FBI friends have much bigger game on their minds. They are interviewing, and presumably scaring the bejesus out of, your employees. One of them, probably an accountant or a secretary, is going to offer to tell everything he or she knows in return for a suspended sentence. The two of you are slightly bigger fish, running the First National Bank of White Collar Criminals and all that."

"The way I see it, there are two clocks ticking," Donaldson said. "The first one stops when one of your employees offers to spill the beans because losing a job is a no-brainer compared to going to jail for a couple of years on a RICO charge. When that happens, any offer of assistance you make no longer is going to be of much interest. The second clock is a little more complicated. We've been talking among ourselves and wondering why it is that no one from the Capizzi family has stepped up to get the six of you out on bail. My friends suspect that either something has gone badly wrong down in New York, or else Cosimo Scordia knows exactly where you are and is planning a little 'going away' party for you and needs to get the arrangements in place for the festivities. That one's way out of my pay grade."

Donaldson rose from her chair. "So, here's what happens. One of you is going to stay in this room with FBI agent number one. Maybe the two of you can watch the segment on the crazy cats, which is pretty funny. There are even a couple of interviews with homeowners, so you can see who the likely snitch is going to be. The other of you is going down the hall with FBI agent number two."

"As for me, I'm going out for Italian. If your attorney shows up and wants to post bail, I'll try to come back by and wish you good luck with that second clock."

* * * * *

From his home in Wellesley Hills, Raymond Nittolo tried yet again to get Emily Taylor Rice to pick up her cell phone. For the fifth time, he went to voice mail. And, for the fifth time, he said, "Emily, it's critical that you call me as soon as possible."

What she had pulled off was nothing short of a miracle. The information was now out there about Brian LaPointe, and Emily's name was never mentioned. She had given just enough information to the reporters to allow them to hang her ex-boyfriend.

The cable channels and talk radio had covered LaPointe's strong denial. It was ludicrous, of course. A holding action at best. Tomorrow, or in two days at most, the whole story would be out.

It was a relief that Pilgrim State's name was mentioned only once, that only LaPointe's accounts were disclosed, and apparently no one had yet figured out the investment firm's true *modus operandi*. Steele & Hanley's partners would assemble for lunch on Monday, discuss the matter thoroughly, and determine if and when the firm should disclose what it knew. Privately, Nittolo believed the publicity would conservatively add ten million a year in fees from new clients. Steele & Hanley would become known as the law firm willing to quickly analyze information and selflessly act in the public interest.

* * * * *

In a palatial, 1930's-era waterfront home in Glen Cove, Long Island, Cosimo Scordia, the heir to what was left of the once-vaunted Capizzi crime family, listened carefully to the words from an underling regarding a tale of unimaginable carelessness and incompetence.

"Our four guys figured it might be some girl who called on Hale to see about opening an account. But she gave Hale one of those little keychain things. The computer couldn't tell the keychain thing had a virus on it and someone copied all the information in the computers. Our guys traced it as far as a couple of office buildings in Boston. Hale and Ashton had a picture of the girl, and they all started showing it to companies in those buildings. Then, something happened with some cats. Luchetti pulled his gun and the next thing they knew, everyone was under arrest."

A crystal tumbler full of Scotch flew across the room and crashed into a carved stone column.

"Then, this afternoon, Marilyn Palumbo is looking for Boston to transfer up a slug of money. All of a sudden she sees ten million come across the computer, but it doesn't go to our bank. Then it's another ten. Marilyn flagged it as soon as she saw the first one. She got Kelly. The she started calling Boston. No one was in the office because they were in holding cells. The only guy she got was on vacation someplace in Africa. Kelly called the bank making the transfers. He couldn't stop it because he didn't have the password. Only Hale and Ashton had the password, and both of them were in jail."

Another crystal tumbler, this one empty, joined its companion against the stone column.

"So, Marilyn checks to see where all this money went to. Somebody sent it to the Feds. Two hundred and forty mil."

Cosimo kicked over the drinks cart. Bottles of rare Scotch smashed against the floor.

"Then, two things happen. First, Kelly goes home early, except he ain't home and his family is gone. The house is empty. Then, on the news up in Boston, some girl TV reporter corners one of Hale's customers and shows him that he was stealing money from some do-good outfit he ran. The girl mentions Pilgrim State and says some hackers gave her the stuff."

"Where do we think Kelly went?" Cosimo asked.

"If he's got his family with him, he's probably on the run," the man said. "He probably hopped a plane. A car would be too easy to follow."

"And Hale and this other guy and our crew?" Cosimo asked.

"Still being held. Our guy up there has been told not to do anything until you know everything"

"Did you pay any attention to what you said?" Cosimo asked. "Three names kinda stand out. Kelly, Hale, and Ash-whatever. Hale and his buddy manage to let some hacker walk in the door and hand him this bug thing. He never suspects a thing. Kelly doesn't even bother to write down Hale's passwords somewhere so, when these hackers start sending money to the Feds, all he does is stare at the screen. The three non-Italians – plus that guy in Africa – screw up and cost us most of our nut."

"Here's what you do," Cosimo said. "You find out what flights went out of Kennedy since, say, six o'clock. You get on the horn and call people. They got seven hours to put someone on the other end of any flight that sounds like a place a family could blend in once they got settled. Right now, a family of four traveling together stands out. You bring them back here unless it's easier to take care of them there. Are Hale and the other guy still in jail?"

"Yeah," the man said. "Luchetti put the scare into them. They wouldn't dare make bail on their own."

"Spring them," Cosimo said. "Then make Hale and the other guy disappear." Cosimo paused. "Marilyn Palumbo. She has all the stuff from Boston... what do you call it... backed up? She has all that stuff down here?"

The man nodded. "She gets it every week, she says."

Cosimo nodded. "It won't be much, but we can go after everyone on that list. Squeeze them for a couple of million each. They got a lot to hide."

The guy snapped his fingers. "One more detail. What about the lady hacker they were after?"

Cosimo smiled. "Tell Luchetti in addition to taking out Hale and his buddy, he has one more thing to take care of before he comes home. That lady cost me a quarter of a billion dollars. Tell Luchetti to make certain she knows why she's being killed. I want her to suffer."

* * * * *

At *The Boston Globe*, five reporters, three editors, two accountants dragooned from the newspaper's auditors, and the paper's Managing Editor pored over two long whiteboards in the main conference room. The boards had taped to them photos, printouts, and scrawled notes.

The room also held a long conference table on which was a table-length sheet of newsprint. That sheet was a timeline stretching back twenty-three years to the founding of Pilgrim State Investments.

Five hours earlier, two young women, neither of them with any credible post-collegiate journalistic experience – had walked in the front door carrying a deck-of-cards size hard drive and a Secure Digital memory card containing an interview of a respected senior executive of a venerable conservation organization. In the normal course of events, a reporter would have heard their story and taken possession of the two digital storage devices. Sometime that day, the reporter would have summarized the content of the conversation with his or her editor and a decision would be made whether this was a genuine confidential news tip or merely a troll.

But the appearance of these two women had been preceded by a phone call to the *Globe's* Editor from one of New England's largest philanthropists. You did not put Emily Taylor Rice on hold or suggest that you would get back to her tomorrow. You listened because this woman was known to be intelligent and thoughtful, sat on the Board of Directors of four of the country's largest corporations, and did not deal in will-of-the-wisp stories. And, in the case of the *Globe's* Editor, you listened because Emily Taylor Rice was a personal friend, and had opened the conversation saying, "I am in a van, traveling up Route 3, and I am bringing you your next Pulitzer Prize."

Once in the *Globe's* building, in ten crisp minutes, she had outlined a compelling story: that in one of Boston's wealthiest suburbs was a money management firm with the white-shoe name of Pilgrim State Investments. Over almost a quarter century, the firm had cultivated and attracted an exceedingly special kind of client: people with money to hide. Most of its clients were people who had stolen what they were investing. They were union officials, politicians, businessmen, and judges. One of them – and this was personally painful – was her former boyfriend, who had stolen $10 million from the conservation organization he headed.

But the story was deeper, she explained. There was a con within a swindle. Pilgrim State Investments was, itself, nothing but a Bernie-Madoff-worthy pyramid scheme controlled by a New York organized crime family. The stolen money deposited by thieves was never invested. Instead, it was systematically siphoned off. On paper, the firm managed $1.2 billion of assets. In reality there was about $240 million in a money market account.

The hard drive told the story, she said as she handed it to the *Globe* reporters. The two young reporters had obtained it from a group of ethical hackers who would never come forward to take credit for what they had done. Emily knew of its content only because the two women knew of her former relationship to Brian LaPointe and wanted both her help and to spare her embarrassment.

And finally, she explained, time was of the essence. The interview with LaPointe on the thumb drive was going to be given to two television stations. By six o'clock, Pilgrim State's name would be out there. Moreover, that afternoon Cambridge Police had arrested two of Pilgrim State's executives along with four members of the New York crime family. They believed they knew the identity of one of the hackers and were staking out the building in which they believed the hacker worked. It was only a matter of time – hours, probably – before the FBI took an interest.

"This is a story that has so many layers it will take weeks to sort out completely," Emily said. "But by this time tomorrow you can be certain the FBI will be applying pressure on you to suppress publication. You have a few hours head start."

Now, it was nearing nine o'clock. Of Pilgrim State's 131 clients, photos of 67 were on the whiteboards. They were all well-known figures in Massachusetts or Rhode Island holding positions of public trust. The history of deposits for each of them – almost always large sums of cash – was established. Some of the deposits had even been tied to events such as the awarding of public works contracts or a bench decision in a controversial trial. In the case of union officials, deposits several times the annual salary of the head of the union local were made each year.

The Managing Editor walked the length of the whiteboards. Emily Taylor Rice was correct on several points. It would take weeks to explore all of this in articles. And, the information in those articles would be explosive. The FBI would lean on the paper to hold what they knew in abeyance until the Government's case was established. They would use threats of legal action, knowing full well the newspaper industry was no longer the deep-pocketed fourth estate of twenty or thirty years ago.

And, were the contents of this drive genuine? On the face of it, no one knew. The hackers would never come forward. However influential Emily was, she could have no way of knowing whether this information was, in fact, authentic.

But the Managing Editor had several data points from which to draw. The first was the Brian LaPointe interview. She had watched that interview twice and, each time, she had clearly seen the 'tells' – first, the look of complete shock when the interviewer read the names of the phony firms (and reporters had verified that all three firms existed only as shell corporations) and, second, when LaPointe heard that the checks had been signed over to him and that he had deposited them in his account. An honest man would have looked… baffled. LaPointe got angry.

If the information on the hard drive concerning LaPointe was legitimate, it was difficult to imagine that detailed data on the 130 other accounts were inventions. LaPointe was a test case; the canary in the coal mine.

The second was the timing and amount of deposits into accounts. A Rhode Island criminal court judge inexplicably ruled that a critical piece of information was inadmissible in a murder trial. Two days before that decision, the judge deposited cash amounting to twice his annual salary. A year later, the same judge issued a 'not guilty' verdict in a bench trial of a major drug dealer. A week before that ruling, the judge had deposited $150,000 in cash into the Pilgrim State account.

One large cash deposit, however improbable, might be the result of selling a house or settling an immediate relative's estate. Two such deposits – followed by half a dozen more in successive years – could only be a product of bribes.

There was also a matter of 'cut-out' figures: wives and girlfriends of public figures with accounts totaling millions. The job of record of the live-in girlfriend of a Boston City Councilman was as manager of a daycare center, where she likely made about $40,000 a year. Yet this woman regularly made $50,000 cash deposits.

The Managing Editor reached her decision. She called together the reporters. "Start making your calls," she said. "Let's see how many of these crooks will deny for the record that they have accounts. Then start writing. Let's get this for the city edition."

* * * * *

At that same hour, David Hale heard his name called.

"Hale and Ashton," the voice said. "You've been bailed out."

Hale froze. Ashton looked at his partner, his face pale with fear. "If we're going to do this, we have to do it together," Hale whispered.

Ashton nodded.

Hale's wife was at their Martha's Vineyard house, opening it for the season; Ashton was divorced. The Capizzi crime family was a shadow of its one-time might, but its reach was still considerable and lethal. To the best of his recollection, Hale had never mentioned the house in West Tisbury to anyone in New York. Molly should be safe there for the time being.

"Before we go, we'd like to spit in the eyes of those two FBI agents," Hale told the guard who had come to take them upstairs.

Five minutes later, the two men were promising to tell the FBI agents everything they knew about the Capizzi crime family and the nature of Pilgrim State Investments' clients.

* * * * *

At 8:30 p.m., an impromptu party was in progress at the house on Coolidge Hill Road. Six women, none of whom had known more than one of the other attendees a week earlier, were celebrating as though old friends. A dozen cartons of takeout food from Middle Eastern, Asian, and Vegan restaurants were spread across the dining room trestle table. Several bottles of wine, including one of Champagne, were open with more waiting in the wings.

They had all watched the television interviews, including Brian's rebuttal, and had replayed them several times to savor the highlights. A call from the *Globe* a few minutes earlier had confirmed what they expected: that the paper would publish its scoop with the morning edition. Other revelations would follow on as fast a schedule as the team of reporters could tie together the trails of suspicious deposits with actions that might trigger payments.

"You know you're on the right track when the first person you call threatens to sue you for everything you're worth if you dare to publish their name; and that same person is on the phone every week looking for the paper to cover something they're doing," the Managing Editor said.

For Zoe and Tyler, there were tantalizing hints of career mobility. Both stations that screened their interview praised the professionalism of the segment's content, technical production, and the speed with which it was assembled.

"If you really wrote and put this together in an RV on the Southeast Expressway at rush hour, your talents are being wasted anywhere but here," one news director had told them.

For Allie, there was the dawning realization that *I did this*. Her father's sins had been exposed to the world. His defiance on camera once he recovered from Zoe's interview was a brave face. Tonight or tomorrow, he would discover he was also penniless. His stolen money and its unearned gains were with the U.S. Treasury. His personal money and stock portfolio now rested in the account of New England Green. The Government might fight to recover it, but New England Green should see at least a partial restitution of its stolen endowment.

The rest of what Allie had done was still too new to sink in. Bring down a Mafia bank? Expose crooked politicians? She hadn't set out to do any of that but, once she learned what Pilgrim State Investments was, she emptied out its entire account. Zoe had described her as an 'ethical hacker'. She liked the description. Maybe there were other bad guys out there.

For Helga, there was pride in her daughter and a sense that the closure she had not felt over the past four years was finally at hand. Along with the joy, she felt satisfaction; contentment. Brian was finally paying a price for his actions, and she had some role in his downfall. But Helga wished she had done more. This was mostly Penny's plan and Allie's execution.

Helga also realized she would not be able to stay in the Josiah Willard House, but it was also time to move on. With Allie headed for college in two months, she no longer needed such a house. A condominium would suffice; someplace where she would not feel so isolated. Tomorrow she would contact a Realtor and begin her search.

An intense conversation was also underway between Penny and Emily. "I need a serious reading list on plant pheromones – books, dissertations, articles," Emily told Penny. "I also need a realistic business plan for what it would take to set up and staff a lab to do what you want to do."

"You don't owe me anything," Penny said. "I got blackmailed into this; I didn't volunteer."

"This isn't altruistic." Emily countered. "If what you were working on at Duke can be commercialized, this could be the best investment the Gerald and Abigail Rice Foundation ever made."

For Emily, there was an enormous sense of relief and gratitude. Relief because, until a week ago – *seven days!* – she had been willingly walking into a kind of marital cattle chute. Brian was the best match she could make and, while he had sometimes annoyed her with his egotism, everyone described him as a 'great catch'. Then, in the space of a few days, she first discovered he was a charlatan, then a thief and, finally, a heel. She had been spared a disaster.

The gratitude was because the people with her this evening had spared her embarrassment. This afternoon she had re-read the message she planned to give the press along with the affidavit from Leeds. Raymond Nittolo could be a horse's ass at times, but he had been absolutely right about what she wrote. It would have been a disaster. Now, she was a peripheral player as far as anyone, except a select inside few, were aware. Officially, he was a 'former boyfriend'.

Penny, physically and emotionally exhausted, felt as though a week-long roller coaster ride was finally coming to an end. It was odd that after more than six years, in the space of these few days, three people had deduced her identity. One had intuited it from a résumé. One had laboriously put together a jigsaw puzzle of clues. And one had simply recognized her from high school.

Perhaps it was time to come out from the cold. She had promised Zoe an interview as a condition of her assistance, and Zoe had more than fulfilled her end of the bargain. Finding P.D. Walden would help launch Zoe's career, as if Zoe needed any help now. Penny would endure a few days or weeks of notoriety. Then it would be gone and forgotten.

In the midst of these overlapping conversations, Helga heard the distinctive ringing of her cell phone. She excused herself from a three-way talk with Taylor and Zoe and answered the call.

Chapter Nineteen

Detective Nancy Donaldson never made it to the Italian restaurant where she had planned to have dinner. Being the kind of person who abhors loose ends and unanswered questions, she elected to make a two-block detour to the security office of One Kendall Square and asked to see selected footage from several cameras.

One camera showed that the six men arrived together and then almost immediately split up. They went into buildings, emerging twenty or more minutes later. As several of them openly carried what appeared to be a frame from a security camera of the elusive 'Penny/Penelope Walden', Donaldson deduced they first tried, but were unsuccessful at, divining which company in a small part of the complex employed her. It was interesting that they made no attempt to canvass the entire complex; just this one corner. Why?

When their canvass proved unproductive, they took to waiting singly and in pairs at various building entrances. Once again, they kept looking at their photos to refresh their memory of Walden's appearance. They looked at each woman walking by. Luchetti, their leader, made the rounds to ensure they were doing their job. Again, why?

They were not particularly skilled at their task. Their clothing caused them to stand out and they seldom paid attention to anything other than what was going on in their immediate field of vision. Women who might have been Walden walked freely behind them and one even paused to read something on her phone.

Donaldson stopped the footage. There, standing behind one of the men – one of the computer experts – was a teenage girl with long hair. She was in shorts and a tee and had on a small backpack.

"Can I zoom in on this?" Donaldson asked the security tech

assisting her. The tech showed her how to toggle the digital video between wide and tight views.

"Can you help me follow this girl?" Donaldson asked. She was certain the girl appeared in other frames.

Sure enough, the girl with the backpack seemed to be making a circuit of the men. Always looking at her phone. Always with something in her right hand. She would casually and almost imperceptibly wave her hand when she was standing behind the men. She even managed to intercept Luchetti, who almost never stood still, in the middle of the plaza. And, once again, that right hand did a little circle, pointing at Luchetti.

She could swear she recognized the girl.

"Do you know this girl?" Donaldson asked the tech. The tech, in turn, gathered two security guards. They agreed they had all seen her around the facility starting in early June, mostly around the entrance to 1400 West. She might be a summer intern at one of the companies housed there, but her comings and goings were sufficiently erratic that it was unlikely she was a full-time employee.

I've seen you before, Donaldson thought, looking at a clear image of the girl.

"How do I get a screen shot?" she asked.

The tech tapped a button.

"I want to email this to my daughter," Donaldson said. "And, while you're at it, send it to my phone, too.

The tech asked for and got email addresses.

A few moments later Donaldson called her daughter, who had just started working a summer job as a counselor in a sports camp in the Berkshires.

"Hannah, I just sent you a photo. Why do I know this girl?"

Her daughter sounded mildly annoyed. "She was in my class at BB&N. You only met her a dozen times."

"What's her name?"

"Allie," her daughter said. "Allie LaPointe."

Donaldson was speechless for a moment.

"Mom?" her daughter asked.

"Is she Brian LaPointe's daughter?" Donaldson asked.

"I have *no* idea who Brian LaPointe is," her daughter replied. "I know her parents got divorced three or four years ago. She didn't talk a lot and hardly ever about herself; I'm a little surprised she showed up for graduation. She spent her mornings at BB&N and her afternoons at MIT."

"Why MIT?" Donaldson asked.

She heard an exasperated sound from the other end of the phone. The universal teenage female sign that means, *How did I get such stupid parents?*

"Allie was the school 'brain'," Hannah said. "I've only told you this a hundred times. She's a math and computer whiz. She has special tutors. She's, like, already finished two years of college."

"Do you know where she lives?"

There was a moment of silence. Then Hannah said, "I know she walked to school, so it couldn't have been far. So, why are you asking?"

Donaldson mumbled an apology and ended the call. It seemed like she was always apologizing to her daughter.

Thoughts flashed through her head. *A computer whiz…* She tried out a theory: *The Capizzi wiseguys were looking for a hacker. They only knew about one but there were two… Allie LaPointe was the other one, and she walked right up to them. So what was she doing with her hand? Stealing information from their phones? This girl is the key to finding Walden. Who is the Head of School at BB&N? Rebecca…*

Donaldson called the Cambridge Police Emergency Command Center. "I need emergency contact information for the Head of School at Buckingham Browne & Nichols. And I need to know if there is a 'LaPointe' family living within a mile of the school."

Another thought flashed through her mind: *GPS tracker.* Quickly gathering her purse and notebook, she told the tech that the surveillance footage she had reviewed needed to be preserved and a copy sent to her at the Detectives' Unit. She went directly to the basement Evidence Room.

"The six guys from the One Kendall Square arrest," Donaldson said. "I need to look at their evidence bags."

"You're not a minute too soon," she was told. "We just got the call. They've all made bail and are being processed out."

The clear plastic bags were spread out before her. Luchetti's held a wallet, car keys he would not be able to use because his Lexus was not drivable after his attempt to evade the barricade, and what was clearly an inexpensive burner cell phone. Donaldson pushed that bag aside, along with the two from the Chestnut Hill investment firm. The three did not contain what she was looking for.

The most tantalizing of the remaining bags held the belongings of one of the two computer techs. In addition to the usual personal effects, it had both an iPad and a high-end Samsung phone. What was even more interesting was that the phone was strapped and cabled to a cell-phone-sized power pack. Whatever applications that phone was running either consumed a great deal of power or else were of a nature that running out of power was not an option. She called over the evidence room clerk and pointed to the phone.

"If you were looking for a cellphone tracker, what would you think of this?" Donaldson asked.

"I'd say you're right on the money," the clerk said. "Fast chips and lots of reserve power."

Donaldson nodded. "This doesn't rise to probable cause, but it doesn't mean I can't warn someone. Can I get a download of the booking photo of Luchetti and whichever guy had this on him?"

Donaldson next checked with the Desk Sergeant, who told her, "The Bail Magistrate wasn't exactly wild about springing Luchetti, but, in the People's Republic, only cops are criminals. Luchetti is out on something like a hundred-K surety bond. Everyone else is

OR."

"Any idea of who was representing them?" Donaldson asked.

The Desk Sergeant grinned. "The Boston's underworld's favorite mouthpiece. A five-star rating on shyster.com from Whitey Bulger himself. Danny O'Leary, Esquire"

"Isn't he, like, a hundred and fifty years old?" Donaldson asked. "I thought he moved to Florida."

"I'd say the Capizzi Family is scraping the bottom of the barrel," the Desk Sergeant said. "But Danny always delivered for Whitey, so he'll do in a pinch."

"So, if Alfonse Luchetti needs a car or a gun, he has a one-stop shopping at his disposal," Donaldson said.

"Gift wrapped, loaded, and gassed up," the Desk Sergeant said.

Donaldson's phone chimed a text alert. It was contact information for Helga Johanssen, mother of Alexandra LaPointe with an address on Coolidge Hill Road. She tapped in the number, closed her eyes, and whispered a silent prayer.

* * * * *

Helga hesitantly answered her phone. Updates from the *Globe* had been coming into Emily's phone.

"Helga Johanssen? This is Nancy Donaldson. I'm a Detective with the Cambridge Police. Am I speaking with the Helga Johanssen who is the mother of Allie LaPointe?"

Helga acknowledged that, yes, the Detective had the right person. She wondered, *What do they know?*

"Your daughter and mine just graduated from BB&N. My Hannah was the captain of the varsity lacrosse team. Yours would have been president of the school's varsity math team if it had one. Allie apparently is doing some kind of internship at a company at One Kendall Square. Is that right?"

"I work there," Helga said. "She enjoys being around the lab. It's not an internship or anything like that, though."

On the other end of the call, Detective Donaldson thought,

Jackpot!

"Ms. Johanssen, I'm going to take a wild guess that you work with someone named Penelope or Penny Walden."

Helga held her breath. *Why is she saying this? What does she want?*

"Ms. Johanssen, this afternoon, we arrested six men who were looking for Ms. Walden. They didn't find her. But they're about to be released on bail here, and I'm willing to bet a month's pay the first thing they're going to do is immediately resume that search, this time using an extraordinarily sophisticated cell phone tracking application. I don't know how many of the men will be involved, but I'm sending you photos of the two that I'm certain will be part of it. They are both part of an organized crime family out of New York; the Capizzi organization. The younger guy is a computer expert and he has the cell phone tracker. The older guy is muscle and extremely dangerous."

"Why are you telling me this?" Helga asked.

"Because I'm reasonably certain you know where Ms. Walden is," Donaldson said. "She is in imminent danger. And I also believe your daughter may also be in danger. I'm sure you know about the story on tonight's news about your ex-husband. He is in a world of trouble because he has been stealing millions of dollars from New England Green, and he invested that money with a firm whose files got discovered by some 'ethical hackers'. What the story didn't say is that the firm was a front for the Capizzi organization."

Donaldson continued. "Here's what you need to remember: Mob families don't let bygones be bygones. I suspect they know that Ms. Walden was one of those 'ethical hackers'. They had her photo and, apparently, her license plate number. Cell phone numbers can be had for a price."

"Why is my daughter in danger?"

"Because they'll figure out that your daughter was the other hacker," Donaldson said. "Why did the hackers go after your ex-husband? Could there be a family connection? They'll look for those connections and they'll discover Allie. And, if they start thinking about who was around them just before that bizarre cat attack, they'll think about the teenage girl with long hair and backpack. Allie was quite casual about it, but they've had several hours to think about it. Given time, they'll put two and two together."

Once again, Helga could not breathe. She gripped the phone tightly, wondering how to respond.

Donaldson took the silence as an opening. "Do you know where Ms. Walden is?"

"She's with me," Helga replied. "She's at my house."

"And your daughter?"

"She's here as well. We're all together."

"Ms. Walden…" Donaldson started to say.

"Penny," Helga interjected. "Her name is Penny."

"Penny needs to turn her phone off," Donaldson said. "But some tracking apps can even spot the 'last known location' for a phone that has been turned off. So, turn it off, take it somewhere, turn it on and then back off, and then preferably smash it into pieces with a hammer. The GPS chip in it is a little homing beacon, and criminals always have the best tools of the trade. I'm also going to send a car out there to keep an eye on the house. Not a police cruiser – that will just tell Luchetti and his buddies that Penny is inside your house. This may be a good night to check into a hotel."

"I'll tell her," Helga said. "I understand the danger."

"I'll be back in touch when I know more," Donaldson said. "These guys will be on the street in the next ten minutes."

The call troubled Donaldson. Helga Johanssen had said all the right things, but Donaldson now realized she was dealing with a bunch of scientists and engineers. They didn't act like most people. She was going to have to outguess both a bunch of hoods who played by their own set of deadly rules; and some computer vigilantes who, having gotten lucky once, were convinced they were immortal and invincible. In Donaldson's view, getting lucky once made people cocky. And cocky people often ended up dead.

* * * * *

Brian's evening was not going as he expected. First, he could still not raise David Hale. Brian desperately needed Hale to hide the funds in his account under some alternate identity, and do so quickly. Hearing that damned reporter say Pilgrim State's name had been a shock. He had no idea how such things were done, but Hale collected a sizeable management fee each year and, in earning that fee, Hale damned well ought to know how to do something as simple as change the name on an account so that nosy investigators couldn't gain access.

Second, news of the television interview had apparently spread like wildfire among his friends and professional circle. Both stations categorized it on their websites as 'major local news' and those who had not seen it when it first aired were now viewing it online. Worse, his Facebook 'confession' had been reposted more than eight hundred times. The comments appended to it were scathing and he could not figure out how to notify Facebook that the post was a hoax. He cursed the day his PR staff had talked him into opening a Twitter and Facebook account; and then cursed them doubly for not showing him how to control his feeds. Naturally, they were not answering their office phones and he had no home numbers for them.

He had made almost sixty calls. Fewer than ten said they accepted his denial and offered solace; and even that solace sounded tepid. Twice that number suggested he hire a good lawyer and more than a few added that 'counseling' would be a good step. Most ominously, half of the calls he made went to voicemail or were answered by a family member who swore that the person he asked to speak with was 'out of town' or 'out for the evening'. None of his calls to his Trustees were returned.

Brian also realized he was almost out of cash. He had foolishly tipped the parking valet ten dollars and gone to a nearby pizzeria where he spent twenty more on a pizza and a salad. Just under twenty dollars remained in his wallet. True, tomorrow morning he should be able to drive to the nearest bank and withdraw a few thousand dollars, but it felt odd to, well, not have any ready cash on him.

In getting the pizza, he noted his Porsche was down to an eighth of a tank of gas. Refilling it, always done with a credit card, would use the rest of his cash. In fact, it would put only a few gallons in the tank because his engine required 94 octane gasoline.

The idea occurred to him that it would be a good idea to move some of the investments in his Fidelity portfolio into cash. Writing checks against his margin account to hire those PR firms would add needless expense to what was already going to be an expensive proposition. He had nearly a million dollars sitting in ultra-safe bond funds. He could tap that money without triggering short-term capital gains.

He opened his computer, pulled up Fidelity on his 'favorites' tab and entered his login information. His 'account overview' page was always a comforting 50,000-foot look at the finances of a well-to-do man. While the four-and-a-half million in Fidelity paled next to his Pilgrim State account, it was reassuring that these funds were entirely liquid. He could buy a car on a whim if he wanted and, after this was over, he just might trade in his eighteen-month-old 911 S Turbo on something a little faster and flashier.

The account overview page opened. Brian's fingers were poised to begin the bond fund sales. His mouth opened and his fingers froze.

'Account balance: $0.00. Credit available: $0.00.'

It could not be true. Brian opened his 'equities' tab. Everything had been sold. Blue chips, tech stocks, health care. Each of the holdings showed a sale of all shares, and an outbound transfer of all proceeds. Everything in his bond portfolio was gone. Exchange-traded funds were all a digital memory.

His own daughter must have done this. *You had no right!* he thought, fuming.

The horrible thought occurred to him: had she done the same thing with his Pilgrim State portfolio? His fingers flew over the keyboard as he logged into the firm's website for the second time that day.

He was relieved to see that his accounts were still in place. He made a request for an immediate transfer of $50,000, the maximum allowed. Then he paused. Transfer to where? Not to Fidelity, where it might disappear. He had no other checking account. Those were for peons. He would have to pick up cash from Hale.

Except that Hale wasn't answering his phone or returning calls. Could Allie have cleaned out that account as well? He needed to confront his daughter as soon as possible. He had to have answers. He needed to confront Allie tonight.

* * * * *

Helga tapped the phone to end the call. *What have I done?* she thought. *This was never Penny's battle, and now she is the one in danger.* She thought about her options. *I need a plan...*

Two minutes later, Helga took Allie aside. Quietly, she asked, "Do you know where Penny's purse is, and can you get her phone out of it without being noticed?"

Allie nodded.

"Do you still have the sprayer you used this afternoon?" Helga whispered.

Allie again nodded.

"Get the phone and the sprayer. Out in my car is the fifteen milliliters of the other pheromone you asked the lab techs to find and, in the trunk, a roll of duct tape. I want you to get both of those, too, and I'll meet you at Penny's car."

Allie nodded a third time.

To the other four women, Helga said, "My daughter has just announced that this party will not be complete without ribs. I've called in an order and Allie and I are going to pick it up." Then Helga paused. "Penny, my car is almost out of gas. May I use yours?"

* * * * *

Al Luchetti breathed the air of the warm June evening. It was 8:45 and the sun was just setting. His hours in the cell had given his legs time to stop hurting and his mind time to think. The cats couldn't have been a coincidence. Walden somehow made that happen. And, before she died, she would tell him what she did, and who else helped her.

And now, he knew exactly how to find her. While he was in the Cambridge holding cell, his little throwaway phone had received a text with a telephone number. With luck, they could have the job finished and be on the road by ten o'clock.

Rocco, the computer nerd, took out what he called his 'fat phone'. "Fully charged," he said. "Loaded for bear." Rocco input the number on Luchetti's screen. Seconds later, a bright red pin appeared on the Samsung phone's screen. "God, I love this thing," he said.

Danny O'Leary's black Escalade was ready to go. The two men climbed in. "Where to?" O'Leary asked.

Rocco looked at his screen. "Chester Street. Davis Square, wherever that is."

O'Leary tried tapping the address into his GPS without success. "Hell, everyone knows where Davis Square is," he said. "Less than twenty minutes, even with Friday evening traffic."

Luchetti opened the Escalade's glove box. Inside, wrapped in a cloth, was another Glock 26 and, along with it, a silencer. The Glock would be used only if he needed to finish off Walden quickly. In a second cloth were two stiletto knives; one more akin to an ice pick than a knife. These would be his preferred instrument with Walden. They would inflict the maximum pain while keeping her talking.

O'Leary glanced over from the driver's seat. "Cosimo told me exactly what you would need. I hope everything is to your satisfaction."

Luchetti just smiled and placed the gun and silencer in his pants pocket and the knives in his inside jacket breast pocket. Rocco might be 'loaded for bear'. He was loaded for murder.

* * * * *

Helga kept saying to herself, *Think! Think! What are you forgetting?* In theory, it all seemed so simple. Penny's phone was turned on and taped to the underside of the bar counter at a ribs joint called Redbones.

She had chosen the restaurant because it would be crowded and, because no reservations were accepted, there would likely be a Friday evening crowd both outside the restaurant and in its tiny foyer. She was not disappointed. At least twenty people were outside the red door, laughing and talking.

She had memorized the photos of the two men. She also had the information, now just five minutes old, that the two men had climbed into a shiny black Cadillac Escalade. They were being driven by a third man, identified to Donaldson as an elderly but uncommonly sharp lawyer with long ties to organized crime going back to the days of the Winter Hill Gang. They could be at Coolidge Hill as soon as fifteen minutes from now.

Detective Donaldson had ended her most recent call with a caution. "I can only help you if you're in Cambridge, and the route these guys took is not the one I'd take if I were headed toward your home. If you're ditching the phone in some other town, I can't help you. You're on your own."

Allie was in the small municipal parking lot behind the restaurant, doing her part. Now, she began to do hers.

* * * * *

Somerville's Davis Square is considered the 'poor cousin' to the other 'squares' along the MBTA Red Line. Kendall Square, of course, has MIT and Harvard Square has its eponymous University. Both are filled with cachet-laden restaurants and shops. Davis Square is fully half a mile from the southern edge of Tufts University and its heyday as a shopping mecca is half a century in the past.

What Davis Square has in abundance is restaurants and bars. The long block between Grove Street and College Avenue features more than a dozen reasonably-priced restaurants and half a dozen student bars. Each restaurant and bar has one or more dumpsters filled with the detritus of meals partly eaten. The adjacent streets are filled with closely-spaced houses, many broken up into apartments. Trash cans abound.

In short, Davis Square closely approximates heaven to the feral cat. And twilight begins the foraging time. After long naps to pass the afternoon, it is the time when humans are less of a nuisance.

But one female human was doing something particularly intriguing. She was walking from dumpster to dumpster, but leaving behind a scent as she did so; a continuous trail that seemed to come from a metal stick she held in her hand but trailed along the ground. The scent was wonderful, at least to the males. It was an aphrodisiac. The scent said, *I am in estrus. Come mate with me.*

Allie had learned of it while talking with the lab techs one day. It was a remnant of one of the earliest pheromone trials the laboratory had run. It had come from a one-year-old un-spayed female named Susie. When they coated the curtains and sofa with it, the male cats went berserk. Because it was the ninth molecule to be isolated, the techs automatically named it, 'Love Potion No. 9'.

* * * * *

The Escalade navigated Somerville's Highland Avenue and made the turn onto Elm. "Nothing like what it was in the old days," O'Leary said. "It was families back then. Now, it's just students and they're all drunk or high."

Luchetti ignored the patter. The old man was transportation and logistics. The sightseeing tour was background noise. He was looking for a place to do his work. The Escalade passed a long pedestrian passage between two buildings. It was filled with people. A Starbucks, a bar, another restaurant. All with foot traffic.

The Escalade turned right on Chester Street and slowed. An Indian restaurant, and then a low, single-story white building. A vertical red-and-white sign proclaimed, 'Redbones'. He looked down at the cell phone. The red pin filled the screen. She was in there.

But the sidewalk was filled with people waiting to get inside. This was not going to be a smash and grab. He needed to reconnoiter the restaurant. Figure the exits. He motioned the driver to go on.

The Escalade made the next right and, thankfully, half a block down was a parking lot.

"Here is good," Luchetti said.

The Escalade turned in, hunting for one of the few parking spaces.

"Stop!" yelled Luchetti. Smiling, he rolled down his window and pointed.

There, just ahead of them, was a tan Honda Civic. The North Carolina license plate read BHA-2907.

Turning to the back seat and Rocco, he said, "Let's get this over with. We do what we were paid to do." To O'Leary, Luchetti said, "We may have to finish the job somewhere a little less crowded. It can't be helped. You stay with the car. You have her photo. If she comes out here, you call me, you block her car if necessary, and you lean on the horn."

* * * * *

There were five 'Love Potion No. 9' pheromone-laced paths in all. They reached a block away from alleys and culverts, and they all lead unerringly toward the entrance to Redbones. But they stopped some fifty feet short of the crowd of people.

The male cats sniffed the heady aroma. Their fur puffed out, the better to present themselves as strong and virile. It would not be unfair to say that they strutted. Each was well aware that the other toms were undergoing the same transformation, but all male cats believe they are the ideal sire for every female on the planet.

First singly and then in lines, they began to follow the trail; their noses to the ground to better imagine their conquest.

* * * * *

O'Leary found the next-to-the-last vacant space in the lot and backed in to have a good view of the Honda and pedestrians coming into the parking lot. He did not like getting so close to a crime and, in a different era that had more civilized rules, he would have flatly told Luchetti to steal a car to kill the woman. But he was close to eighty now, and the world had changed. The Young Turk lawyers had no problem with getting their hands bloody if it helped ingratiate them to their principal sources of income. In the light of it all, merely transporting a screaming woman a few miles was not so bad, especially if there wasn't yet any bloodshed. He even knew of a good spot. Provided some idiot hadn't built a Target store on it in the past year.

O'Leary's attention was interrupted by a 'thump' on his car. He looked in the rear view mirror to see a teenage girl leaning over, shining a flashlight under the car.

He rolled down his window. "What the hell are you doing around my car? Get out of here!"

Instead of running away, the girl gave him a plaintive look. "I lost my wallet," she said. "We were parked here just ten minutes ago."

"Well, what do you expect me to do about it?" O'Leary said.

The girl came up to his window and was inches from his face, her pleading look was augmented by tears. "My parents will kill me if I go home without it. Would you please move your car out of the space for a second? I'm sure it's underneath."

The lawyer considered the request. His own grandchildren would have nothing to do with him. This one lived in fear of her parents, which was good. And, besides, she was being polite. On the whole, doing this one good deed might make up for cutting his grandchildren out of his considerable will.

O'Leary moved the car forward. The girl shouted, "I found it! I found it!"

She ran around to his window and showed him her prize. "Can I give you a kiss on the cheek by way of thanks?"

Why not? O'Leary thought. He turned his head to accept a kiss on the cheek. In doing so, he never noticed the vial of liquid that trickled down the back of the driver's seat, any more than he noticed the spray of liquid around the outside of his shiny black car.

The girl waved and ran away.

* * * * *

Luchetti pushed his way through the crowd of young people and went into the restaurant. A woman with a nose ring, black lipstick, and spiked jet-black hair stood behind a lectern. To the left was a bar; to his right, long tables crowded with people. The red pin pulsed. She was within twenty feet of him.

"It's about an hour's wait," the woman with the black lipstick said. "If it's just you, I can seat you at the bar in about half an hour."

"I'm looking for a friend," Luchetti said.

The woman shook her head. "There's not an open seat in the place. Downstairs is closed tonight. If you don't see her in this room, she must be outside waiting."

He didn't see her. Maybe she was in the head. He and Rocco would have to tag-team her. Reluctantly, he turned to go back outside. As he stepped outside, he jostled someone. Liquid was splashed down the back of his suit jacket and he felt it on his pants.

"Watch where you're going!"

He turned to see an angry older blonde woman. She was holding a drink cup, now empty. She was good looking. Well-built. A little overweight. On a different night…

"Good thing for you it was almost empty," the woman said, her anger turning to a smile. Luchetti thought he heard a little British tinge to her voice.

He shook his head. "My fault." He walked off to find Rocco, who was determining if there were other exits to the building.

* * * * *

The thought of money, or lack of it, had become all-consuming. His last half-dozen calls had ended dismally. His friends – or perhaps more accurately *former* friends – were evidently calling one another. If they hadn't seen the news clip, they had read the LinkedIn update, which apparently detailed his crimes and begged forgiveness. No one, *no one*, was prepared to advance him a few hundred dollars.

Where else do I have money? Brian thought. *Do I have cash in my desk in the office? Could I get cash out of New England Green's petty cash account?* He had been in old lady Wilkerson's office when someone needed money to buy lunch for volunteers. There was usually at least a hundred dollars in a box; sometimes considerably more. And he just might have slipped a few twenties into his desk drawer.

He could stand it no longer. Abandoning his call list, he left his apartment and jumped into his Porsche. It was twelve miles to Beckwith Estate and he covered the distance in under fifteen minutes though, because he gunned his engine from every traffic light and stop sign, he dropped his 'distance to empty' from 83 miles to 56.

The main gate was locked for the evening but his master key opened it. He raced up the driveway and parked in his reserved spot. Opening the side door nearest his car with his master key, he ran down the hallway to his office. He pulled open each drawer and found no cash. He tried his secretary's desk. It, too, was empty of cash. But he did find a compact LED flashlight.

Cursing, he walked hurriedly to the finance office, where doddering old-lady volunteers processed membership and program fee checks and credit card payments. Old Mrs. Wilkerson's desk was in the center of the office.

Not wishing to draw unwanted attention to what he was doing, Brian used the flashlight to navigate his way through the office. The cash box was not on her desk and her drawers were locked. His master key did not fit the lock, but the desk was an old, cast-off Steelcase model and the locks could probably be opened with a screwdriver.

He shined his flashlight around the office and there, in a jar holding surplus pens and pencils, was a small screwdriver of the kind used to tighten eyeglass frames. He took the screwdriver over to Mrs. Wilkerson's desk and began working the lock on the large, lower-right-hand drawer where the cash box most likely resided. It took several minutes, but the drawer opened.

Breathing a sigh of relief, he lifted out the cash box. It felt heavy. Maybe there was more than a hundred dollars in it. Maybe there was a thousand. It, too, was locked, and he began jimmying the keyhole with the screwdriver.

Just then, the lights in the room went on. Startled, Brian looked up to see his night watchman, an elderly man in a uniform. *I should greet him by name. Now, what the hell is his name?* Brian thought.

The guard walked over, a puzzled and wary look on his face.

"What are you doing in here, Mr. LaPointe?" the night watchman asked, his eyes on the flashlight, screwdriver and cash box.

Brian smiled, realizing as he did that his face was covered with sweat from the exertion and the tension. "Everything's fine," Brian said. "I just needed to check something. I'll be all right."

"You didn't turn off the alarm when you came in," the night watchman said. "The police are on their way."

"Well," Brian said, "just call them and tell them everything is fine. Let's save them a trip. Tell them the forgetful Executive Director neglected to turn off the silent alarm." In point of fact, Brian had no idea there even was an alarm, much less a silent one. And he had no idea of the code required to de-activate it.

The night watchman's face did not lose its puzzled look. Here was a man in what had been a dark office, a screwdriver in his hand, trying to open what was clearly a petty cash box. The night watchman's eyes kept going between LaPointe's sweaty face and the cash box in his arms.

"I saw that news show tonight, Mr. LaPointe," the night watchman said cautiously. "Why don't we just let the police sort this out?"

Brian could see the old man had no gun. He had only a radio and, presumably, a phone.

"Please call the police and tell them everything is all right," Brian asked, a note of pleading in his voice. "This is all a misunderstanding."

"That lady said you took millions from this place," the night watchman said. "That isn't right. Why don't we just wait here and see what the police think is best."

Seeing he was getting nowhere, Brian clutched the cash box to his chest and bolted out the door. His car was perhaps two hundred feet away and he could easily outrace a pathetic old man.

Brian covered the ground quickly and jumped in his car. He started the engine and tore up the driveway, spewing rock behind him. As he reached the main gate, he saw blue lights approaching from the right, maybe five hundred feet away. He turned left and floored the gas pedal.

* * * * *

The two men stood across a narrow street from the restaurant. Rocco confirmed the two emergency exits from the restaurant were both alarmed. There was no way Walden was going to get out of the restaurant other than through the main entrance.

"I'll stay here in case she comes out. You go inside and ask to have a look around," Luchetti commanded. "There's some lady vampire inside who didn't take a shine to me. Maybe you can work your magic on her. Maybe Walden was in the head."

Rocco nodded, crossed the street and made his way through the crowd. Luchetti saw the blonde lady had left. Maybe her table was ready.

It was then that he felt the rubbing against his legs. He looked down to see two cats.

Not this again, he thought.

He kicked at the cats, who refused to leave him alone. Suddenly, there were half a dozen cats. Huge cats. They purred loudly.

Then there was one on his back. Then two. He whirled around to shake them. One fell off, the other did not. Now a third and fourth one was climbing his pants leg. He would swear that like dogs, they were trying to hump his leg.

A cat made its way to his head. He swatted it away and the cat's claw opened a gouge in his forehead. Two more cats were on his shoulder. He had a gun in his pants pocket and a pair of knives in his jacket's breast pocket. He reached into his breast pocket for a knife and a cat promptly sunk its teeth into his wrist. He slashed at the cat with the knife.

He knew he was yelling, but it brought neither assistance from the crowd, which looked on as though in amusement, nor relief from the cats. Another was on his head and he again swatted at it with one hand while trying to knife it with the other. There was now blood in his eyes.

He could not just stand here. He had to run. Which way? His

vision was clouded and he was disoriented. There were cats coming at him from multiple directions. He chose the one with the fewest cats in his path.

He bumped into a parking meter and a bicycle but kept stumbling forward. The cats were biting him as they purred contentedly. He stepped off a sidewalk. Was this the way to the Escalade?

He heard the squeal of brakes and smelled exhaust.

It was only a motorcycle and the low-speed impact did nothing more than cause him to awkwardly fall down into the roadway. In a way it was almost a relief. The cats scattered, running for their lives.

It was only as Luchetti tried to stand up that he felt the sharp pain and the sticky warm liquid. He wiped his eyes in an attempt to clear his vision. It was the damned knives. The one he had been holding was now deep in his side, right about where he knew his kidney was located. The other knife – the stiletto that had remained in his breast pocket – was lodged in his chest. From the amount of blood spurting out of him, it had likely punctured an artery.

Now, a crowd was gathering. He looked up as if to ask for help, but had only time to think, *son of a bitch* before he lost consciousness.

* * * * *

Rocco heard shouts emanating from outside the entrance to the restaurant. He had been in Redbones less than two minutes. He pushed his way outside, saw several cats across the street where he and Luchetti had been standing, and felt a sense of déjà vu. Looking left, a crowd had gathered around a motorcycle stopped in the main street. A sickening feeling in his stomach told him whatever had happened involved Luchetti.

He turned right and raced around the corner to the parking lot. It was easy to spot the Escalade. Its lights were flashing and someone was slumped over the steering wheel.

He ran to the car, which was covered with cats. He threw open the passenger door and immediately regretted doing so. There were fifty cats inside. The old lawyer was unconscious. He had apparently activated the emergency flashers before he passed out.

The driver's side door was ajar. Rocco's guess was that O'Leary had tried to push cats out of the way of the Escalade, which only allowed them entry to the car itself. There must be something inside the car that was attracting the cats.

Rocco was trained in computers, not cat removal or emergency first aid. What he knew was that he had to get as far away from the area as quickly as possible, and the Escalade was the nearest tool available. He pulled O'Leary over into the passenger seat and ran around the car to the driver's side.

He started the engine, stopped the flashers, and drove forward, not caring if he ran over cats in the process. He rolled down all four windows. The area was a labyrinth of one-way streets but he didn't care. As he drove, he began ejecting cats as fast as he could grab them by the scruff of their necks.

He did not count, however, on cats occupying the floor in front of him, interfering with the gas and brake pedals. Nor did he imagine that a cat would climb across the ample dashboard and lunge for his face.

In all, Rocco travelled just three blocks, hitting five cars in the process. His escape path ended at Massachusetts Avenue, where, traveling the wrong way down a one-way street, he entered the intersection and smashed into a light pole.

Right behind him was Detective Nancy Donaldson. She activated the flashing blue light on her dashboard for the last two blocks where Somerville became Cambridge.

She walked up to the driver's side door and opened it. Four cats jumped out.

Donaldson looked at Rocco's bloody face and the limp body of the lawyer in the passenger seat. Without breaking into a smile she asked, "Do you have vaccination certificates for all these cats?"

* * * * *

Brian was intimately familiar with Scituate's winding back roads and he easily kept his speed over sixty. He knew all the shortcuts, including a few the police would not expect, that would get him five miles to the safety and anonymity of Route 3. In five minutes, this would all be behind him. He could stop for gas a few exits up the highway. Then he would drive to Cambridge and confront Allie. She had *stolen* his money. She was probably holding it in her own bank account, God only knew why. He would try reasoning with her but, if she wouldn't agree to turn the money over to him, he would… face that eventuality. He was *her father!* Didn't that count for *something?*

And, in the morning he would come up with a plausible explanation for why he had taken the cash box. *I am the damned Executive Director, after all*, he thought. Also, he would intercept his new American Express Black card. *All this stupidity will be in the rearview mirror. It is so ridiculous.*

Now he was on the state highway; just a mile to the Route 3 entrance ramp. Pushing his speed to 110, he blew through a red light after glancing in either direction. No one was behind him and he began to ease off the gas. A quick look down at the dashboard showed his distance to empty was down to 13 miles. Once he was on Route 3, he would need to conserve gas to get him to the next exit.

When he raised his eyes back to the windshield he saw the blue lights in front of him blocking the final intersection before the expressway. There wasn't a side road he could turn down; only businesses. He would have to execute a U-turn. He had never done one before but this was a sports car and supposedly the most responsive one on the market.

He braked and jerked the wheel violently. What happened next was that his Porsche obeyed the laws of physics. The vehicle's forward momentum slowed only fractionally, but now that momentum was working against wheels that were turned to an angle that was at odds to the vehicle's vector. The passenger-side front and rear tires acted as a brake, causing the driver's-side tires to rise up. Those tires lost contact with the road.

Brian felt the terror of being lifted when he ought to be pressed against the back of his seat. And, in that instant, he finally realized that he had been beaten – humiliated. His own daughter and his girlfriend had conspired against him. They hated him for who he was, what he had become, and what he had done to them. This was their moment of triumph. Knowing he cared most about money and power, they had used that knowledge in some kind of *jiu-jitsu* against him. Now, he was penniless and without control over something as basic as his own car.

With the center of gravity continually shifting as the driver-side tires rose ever higher in the air, the Porsche began to tumble sideways. In all, it flipped over three times before coming to a rest.

SATURDAY

Chapter Twenty

Brian LaPointe awakened to find himself in a hospital bed. Every part of his body ached. He dimly remembered the accident, the flashing red lights of the ambulance, and arriving at an emergency room. Everything else was a haze. He sensed his head was wrapped and lifted his right hand to feel the extent of the bandaging.

His right hand lifted eight inches and stopped. He tugged. Eight inches and no more.

What the hell?

Painfully, he turned his head to see his hand. A metal cuff encircled his hand; another was attached to the hospital bed rail. Between them was an eight-inch-long length of chain.

His left arm was encumbered by IV lines but, within easy reach, there was a button to summon assistance. He pressed the button for more than a minute.

As he waited, he took in his surroundings. He was in a curtained-off area of what appeared to be a larger room. There was light and movement beyond the fabric but little activity.

A nurse, or maybe a nurse's aide, appeared. Her smile was perfunctory.

"Where am I?" Brian asked.

"South Shore Hospital," the woman said.

"What time is it?"

She looked at her watch. "Just about noon." She looked at a monitor he could not see. "Your vital signs are back to near normal. I wasn't here when you came in, but I heard you were pretty banged up. Nothing life-threatening. A couple of broken ribs, a few head lacerations, and a lot of bruising."

Brian lifted his arm. "Is this necessary?"

The woman gave what Brian suspected was a stifled laugh. "You *are* under arrest. There's a bedside arraignment scheduled for two o'clock. We've been keeping the TV camera crews at bay, but the Scituate Police, the Mass State Police, and the FBI all want to interview you. You're quite the celebrity, Mr. LaPointe."

She turned to leave and took a step toward the curtain. Then she stopped at the table at the base of the bed on which rested his charts. She picked up an envelope and held it out for him to see.

"This was delivered about an hour ago," she said. "It's marked 'personal'. Do you want me to leave it where you can open it?"

Brian raised his two arms to show that, between the restraints on one arm and the IV's on the other, opening an envelope was beyond his capabilities at the moment. "Would you hold it where I can read it?"

She nodded, tore open one end of the envelope, and extracted a single sheet. She held it twelve inches from his face. He could not focus on the typewritten letters.

"Can you read it to me?" he asked.

The woman nodded. "It's addressed to you in care of South Shore Hospital and is dated today," she said. "It's just two paragraphs."

Dear Mr. LaPointe,

The Trustees of New England Green are in receipt of a certified affidavit from Leeds Beckett University and have had the affidavit's contents verified via a videoconference with its author. The Trustees have determined that, based on fraudulent representation of your academic credentials, you have voided the terms of your employment contract. You are herewith dismissed from your position.

The Trustees have also become aware through news reports that you may have engaged in criminal activity regarding the diversion of New England Green funds. We are cooperating fully with federal and state investigators to ascertain the extent of any such diversion and will seek restitution and will assist in criminal prosecution if warranted.'

"I'm sorry if I embarrassed you by reading it," the woman said.

"I also have a copy of this morning's *Globe* out at the nurse's station. I definitely don't think you want to see it. The front page is all about that Pilgrim State outfit. Apparently, you were one of at least fifty people who… well, gave them money that didn't belong to you. And it all turned out to be a scam."

Brian squeezed his eyelids, trying to focus on the woman. "What do you mean, 'a scam'?"

The woman looked surprised. "You didn't know? The whole thing was one of those Ponzi schemes being run by some mobster down in New York. None of the money was ever invested. All the cheaters got cheated."

The woman turned and left, closing the curtain behind her. Brian was certain she was suppressing a smile.

He stared at the spot where the woman had stood. Everything was gone. Just twenty-four hours earlier he had been on top of the world. He was wealthy; he had the love of a rich, beautiful woman, and he was famous and admired. Now, he was destitute, under arrest, and about to be charged with God-only-knows-what crimes. He had no car, no means of making bail, and no way to pay for his defense.

Why me? he wondered.

And then, in a flash of memory, he saw an evening, four years earlier. It was the night after the fateful dinner with Emily, when he told Helga and Allie that he felt he was living a lie, he needed his freedom, and he was leaving. Helga had shown no emotion and said only that she needed to monitor an experiment.

Allie, though, had stared at him with a burning hatred in her eyes. As he packed a bag he remembered her coming into his bedroom and saying softly, *I don't know how or when, but I'll make you pay for this.*

A Few Weeks Later

Detective Nancy Donaldson sat at the antique trestle table in the kitchen of Helga Johanssen. Or, at least her current home. Around the kitchen, packing boxes were filled with kitchen items. Most boxes were marked 'Goodwill'; perhaps a third bore the inscription, 'condo'.

Donaldson's notebook was open, a pen was in her hand, and a file folder lay to one side. Across from her sat Helga, her daughter Allie, and Penny Walden.

"I need to close out this file," Donaldson began. "If I can't deliver a neat package to my Captain, he'll send out some over-eager kid trying to make his chops. The kid will go after this case like a three-month-old puppy, and keep digging until everything is a mess. None of us want that."

Donaldson looked at the three women's faces to make certain they understood. She opened the file folder and brought out numerous sheets of paper.

"I have what ought to be a simple case," Donaldson continued, and turned her gaze on Penny. "Four Mafia types and two white-collar criminals were looking for you. They all worked for this guy."

Donaldson passed a sheet of paper across the table. It was a Xerox of a clipping from *The New York Post*. The headline read, 'Mafia Boss Found Drowned Off Long Island Estate'.

"Cosimo Scordia isn't going to be answering any questions, and his former lieutenants seem to be in hiding," Donaldson said. "All I have are two songbirds telling the FBI everything they've learned since kindergarten, including the interesting tidbit that you paid a visit to their office in Chestnut Hill three days before everything hit the fan."

"I'm new to town and I was looking for a financial advisor," Penny said.

Donaldson nodded. "Hold that thought for a moment, Ms. Walden." She turned her attention to Allie and picked up another sheet of paper. "The same afternoon that everything was going on at One Kendall Square, two young journalists were interviewing your father, and confronted him with what looked like reams of information gleaned from the computers of Pilgrim State Investments. According to this broadcast transcript, the on-camera lady – whom I note now seems to be Channel 4's new star reporter – made the statement that the information had been obtained from what she called 'ethical hackers'. It seems odd that, with all the dirtbag politicos and judges the *Globe* has identified from that mother lode of data, Ms. Matthews and Ms. Malone would choose as their first exposé to drive all the way out to Scituate just to nail your father. A reasonable person might conclude that you, Ms. LaPointe, were one of those ethical hackers, and that you were aided and abetted by Ms. Walden."

Donaldson pulled out another sheet of paper. "But a review of Ms. Walden's academic record at Duke shows no special proclivity toward computer technology. She does know all about pheromones, however, which we'll get to in a moment." Donaldson pushed two sheets of paper across the table to Penny.

"In my research, Google produced an oddball result that I first started to throw out, but then read more carefully," Donaldson said. "This is an article from *The Bergen Record*, which serves the posh suburbs of New Jersey. It says that one Patricia D. Walden, a researcher at a pharmaceutical company in one of those leafy environs, has filed a $5 million invasion of privacy suit against an outfit called 'Entertainment Now! Enterprises', which has one of those TV shows I wouldn't watch even if I had time. It seems the clown at the show thought they had found a mysterious, reclusive writer named 'P.D. Walden'. They more or less ambushed Ms.

Walden as she was walking out to her car after work."

Donaldson continued. "I asked my daughter if she knew this 'P.D. Walden' character, and I could hear her eyes rolling all the way from Stockbridge. I am such a fossil. She says 'P.D. Walden' wrote the greatest book in the world on the subject of – wait for it – revenge, called *The Professor with the Wandering Hands*. Now, this Patricia D. Walden turned out to be the wrong person, but I wonder if they were really looking for Penelope Danforth Walden?"

Donaldson turned over another sheet of paper. "And in one of the most amazing coincidences of all time, WBZ's press release about the hiring of Ms. Matthews and Ms. Malone says that Zoe Matthews was previously associated with – drum roll here – Entertainment Now! Enterprises."

"Which brings us to the cats," Donaldson said, turning to Helga. "You, Ms. Johanssen, turn out to be one of the world's authorities on pheromones, with a string of papers from MIT that go back almost two decades. Then, you got hired by this company called Pheromonix." Donaldson turned over yet another sheet of paper. "The Boston Business Journal says Pheromonix is going to 'product-ize pheromone research and is a start up with blue-chip funding.' And, for the past several months, a stream of ladies have been going in and out of your offices carrying… cats. You take swabs from them, you have cats investigate furniture. You are widely known as the easiest fifty bucks in Cambridge."

"When those six guys got too close to finding Ms. Walden, Ms. LaPointe rode to the rescue by hosing down the men with a whiff of the essence of cat," Donaldson said. "I have some fascinating surveillance footage archived of Ms. LaPointe passing among the bad guys, waving her right hand in a most interesting way. The next thing anyone knows, the cats have descended. Then, later that evening, my one perfect perp, the late Alphonse Luchetti, goes chasing after Ms. Walden's phone with murderous intent, only to cut his carotid artery with his own knife. The Somerville Police quickly ruled it an accidental death of someone the world will not miss. But their report also says Mr. Luchetti was also beset by cats in the minutes before his encounter with a motorcycle. Alas, there is no film to show you."

"So, I have this theory," Donaldson said, leaning back in her chair. "You, Ms. Johanssen, either deliberately or inadvertently hired the author of a unique tale of revenge, and either you or your daughter co-opted Ms. Walden into a plot to get even with your ex-husband. The plot involved some cyber theft which turned out to be a lot more complicated than anyone could have expected."

Donaldson continued. "When Alphonse and his boys came after you looking for their missing data, Ms. LaPointe was ready with the deterrent to end all deterrents. How Ms. Walden co-opted the reporter and her video person is anyone's guess, but she did, and Mr. LaPointe's many transgressions were revealed in a way that will keep him a star on YouTube for at least a year. What happened in Davis Square is none of my concern, although I made a very interesting collar of a computer geek who is so far out of his depth in the criminal world he can't even see the top of the well. He, too, is singing to the Feds."

"If your story was true," Helga asked, "did any of us do anything illegal?"

Donaldson tapped her pen again the pad. "The amazing thing is, no; at least not as far as the City of Cambridge is concerned. When I write this up, I think I'll go easy on the computer stuff, just to be certain. My Captain has trouble opening email attachments. I don't want to overtax his limited computer knowledge."

"So, we're good?" Allie asked.

"In my mind, you're not good, you're great," Donaldson replied and closed her notebook.

Acknowledgements

Every work of fiction begins with an 'aha' moment. Something – an overheard conversation, an event witnessed, or a memory recalled – lands in an author's lap. There is a realization that this 'thing' can be the seed that will grow into 90,000 words of prose. The 'aha' moment for *A Whiff of Revenge* was the landing in my lap – literally – of Hope Jahren's lucid and thoroughly enjoyable memoir, *Lab Girl*.

Ms. Jahren, a geochemist, intersperses the story of her becoming a scientist with a series of riveting mini-essays. One of those essays was on the role of pheromones in the plant and animal kingdom. I was off and running.

Many readers comment on the amount of 'useful' knowledge I wedge into my stories. Several have told me *How to Murder Your Contractor* has served as a handbook for establishing a working relationship with contractors. (Others say they just leave the book in plain sight when someone comes to do work on their home.) In addition to print and online research, I call on specialists to lend a hand getting details right. *For A Whiff of Revenge*, I owe special thanks to Emily G. Wood, who gleefully dove into the mire of determining how a Ponzi scheme might escape detection in a post-Bernie-Madoff world. I also found Abigail Tucker's *The Lion in the Living Room* a useful primer on cat behavior. While almost all of the locales mentioned in this book exist, including the massive One Kendall Square complex, Pheromonix is a figment of my imagination. On the other hand, the notion that there may be a molecule that will tell your tabby to go claw elsewhere is quite within the reach of pheromone science. If someone isn't already conducting such research, they ought to.

At the head of my thank-you list for making this book possible is my wife, Betty, without whose constant encouragement I would have long since taken up golf. There is also a group of 'first readers' who humble me with their eagle-eyed attention to my poor grasp of punctuation and spelling, and who also subject my plots to tests of plausibility. That group includes Jan Martin, Faith Clunie, Connie Stolow, and Linda Jean Smith. Your assistance shows on every page.

Finally, what started four years ago as a trickle of requests from libraries and garden clubs to speak about gardening and my books has mushroomed into something I could never have imagined. My three talks, 'Gardening Is Murder', 'Gardening Is a Mystery', and 'Strong Independent Women', now take me all over New England (and with a growing number of availability queries from other regions). Those talks allow me to meet and interact with readers, and all I can say is, 'please keep the requests coming'. I continue to look forward to every presentation.

Other books by Neal Sanders
All titles are available in print and Kindle formats

Murder Imperfect. A Wellesley Hills housewife plots to kill her philandering husband before the SEC can arrest him for securities fraud. She succeeds, but the police suspect foul play, the SEC wants to know where she's hiding millions of dollars, and her husband's pregnant mistress wants half of his estate.

The Accidental Spy. In 1967, a Pan American stewardess' attempt to deliver a misdirected bag to its owner results in a cross-country chase to outrun multiple intelligence services that want the bag's contents: plans for what may be the first microprocessor. She will be aided by a handsome Mossad agent.

Deal Killer. A young investment banker is perceived by a corporate executive as the lone impediment to his stealing millions of dollars as a failing company is acquired by its larger rival. When her car is run off the road, the banker understands she must determine which executive is the potential murderer.

How to Murder Your Contractor. An exceptionally resourceful suburban Boston housewife and her husband want to build their retirement dream home. What stands in their way is the world's worst contractor who sees the couple as his ticket to riches. Aided by friends with unusual areas of expertise, a battle of wits ensues between the couple and the contractor. *Also available in audio through iTunes or Audible.*

The Garden Club Gang. Four 'women of a certain age' devise and carry out the perfect crime: robbing a large New England fair. Complications ensue when they discover they've stolen far more money than they should have, and some very bad people want their money back.

Deadly Deeds. To atone for robbing a fair, the four ladies of *The Garden Club Gang* help an insurance investigator bring down an unscrupulous car dealer and investigate the death of an elderly friend in an upscale nursing home. Neither good deed goes unpunished.

A Murder at the Flower Show. When the head of a major Boston cultural institution is found dead, his identity unravels; leading to a search not just for his killer, but for priceless artifacts he has stolen. A young Chinese-American Detective and her about-to-retire partner are in a race against time to find his killer.

Murder in Negative Space. A prominent but universally disliked Russian floral designer is murdered at an international floral design conference in Boston. A young Chinese-American detective and a garden club president must sort out the multiple motives.

A Murder in the Garden Club. A suburban Boston garden club president discovers the body of a close friend. The town's Detective thinks it is an accident. It will be up to the club president to prove otherwise.

Murder for a Worthy Cause. The body of a suburban Boston town selectman is found dead at the site of a home being built by a popular TV show. Was the selectman murdered because he was in the wrong place at the wrong time, or was he involved in something criminal?

Made in the USA
Middletown, DE
09 April 2023

28263243R10182